PRETTY
LITTLE
THINGS

JILLIANE HOFFMAN

PRETTY LITTLE THINGS

Vanguard Press
A Member of the Perseus Books Group

Published by Vanguard Press
A Member of the Perseus Books Group

Designed by Trish Wilkinson
Set in 11.5 point Minion Pro

Library of Congress Cataloging-in-Publication Data

Hoffman, Jilliane, 1967–
    Pretty little things / Jilliane P. Hoffman.
        p.   cm.
    ISBN 978-1-59315-607-7 (alk. paper)
    1. Online sexual predators—Fiction. I. Title.
PS3608.O478P74 2010
813'.6—dc22   2010019479

Vanguard Press books are available at special discounts for bulk purchases in the U.S. by corporations, institutions, and other organizations. For more information, please contact the Special Markets Department at the Perseus Books Group, 2300 Chestnut Street, Suite 200, Philadelphia, PA 19103, or call (800) 810-4145, ext. 5000, or e-mail special.markets @perseusbooks.com.

10 9 8 7 6 5 4 3 2 1

PROLOGUE

A small, portly man in a white suit, deep purple shirt, and patent slip-ons ran around the stage with a microphone in hand, reaching out to touch any one of the hundreds of sweaty palms that waved back and forth before him in the Unity Tree of Everlasting Evangelical Life church auditorium. He slicked back a thick band of gelled gray hair that had broken form and swooped down across his forehead and over his eyes. The amazing camera work practically let you count the fine lines in the preacher's full face, the beads of perspiration rolling off his red cheeks and down through layers of neck fat.

"Now when Moses went to meet the Israelites after their victory over the Midianites," the preacher boomed as he worked the stage from one end to the other, "he had all the princes and the priest, Eleazar, with him. And he sees what? What does he see that the Bible tells us made Moses so incredibly angry? He sees *women*!" The crowd, which looked to be made up of mostly females, booed loudly.

Seated in front of the living room TV in his worn, comfortable La-Z-Boy, the man nodded along with the church audience, watching the drama unfold on his television screen as though he had not already seen this video a hundred times before.

"The Israelites have saved the *women*!" the preacher boomed. "And Moses, well, he says, 'So you've spared all the women? *Why?* Why, when they're the very ones who have caused a plague to strike the Lord's people! Why did you spare them?'"

Somewhere in the church audience, a female yelled, "Because they were men!"

The preacher laughed. "Yes! Because they were men. And because they were men, they were weak to the ways of women! To the smell of a woman and the taste of a woman and the feel of a woman!"

The man wiped his sweaty palm on the recliner's worn armrest, nodding enthusiastically at the preacher's words.

"They were *weak*!" the preacher continued. "And so these weak men spared these vile women who had wreaked havoc on their tribe. But Moses is not just upset, ladies and gentlemen. He doesn't just say, 'That was a stupid thing to do!' and leave it at that. No. Moses knows what will happen now that these vile women have been saved. Their delicious scent and their warm skin and their soft curves will soon sway their captors. Wickedness takes on many forms, folks. Many forms."

The preacher summoned a young woman in the church audience then by pointing at her. She couldn't have been more than seventeen or eighteen. "Come on, child, come on up here." Encouraged by her parents and the enthusiastic crowd, the girl hesitantly climbed on stage. "Look at how beautiful she is," the preacher said, walking around the slight figure with his arms outstretched, as if she were an animal on a pedestal in the circus and he was the ringmaster introducing her to them. He sniffed exaggeratedly at her and smiled. "She smells good. She sure looks good. She doesn't seem evil. What man would not be tempted?" He turned back to the crowd. "Like many of us in our everyday lives, Moses must make a difficult decision. A terrible deci-sion. One that many will find objectionable, but yet Moses—well, Moses knows it is necessary. A difficult choice, but a necessary one."

A pregnant hush fell over the crowd. "What does he tell them?" the preacher asked his flock, staring as he did right into the eye of the camera, speaking to the thousands of lost sheep all across the country who waited on his every word. "What? He tells them—and this is right out of the Holy Bible, folks—he tells them, 'Slay, therefore, every male child and every woman who has had intercourse with a man. But you may spare and keep for yourselves all girls who had no intercourse with a man.' What does that mean, folks? 'Only the young girls who are virgins may live,' Moses says. 'Only the *virgins* can live amongst your people. Only the *virgins*, those who are pure in thought and deed, can be saved.' Why? Because they are pure. They have not been corrupted." He looked back at the young girl on stage and bellowed, "Tell us, young lady, are you a virgin? Are you pure in thought and deed? God is watching you! Remember that! We are watching you! Are you pure in both thought and deed?"

The girl nodded as tears ran down her cheeks. She smiled at the preacher and then out at her parents. "Yes," she answered. "I am pure."

The crowd went wild.

The man wiped his palm again on the easy chair. The preacher certainly was mesmerizing. He had the crowd eating out of his hand. Had the young virgin not been so pure, he would have had no problem rousing the masses to stone her, if that was what he so wished.

It was inspiring.

The man pressed rewind on his remote, and while the tape noisily chortled in the VCR, he unfolded the brown canvas bag on his lap. He ran his fingers over the soft brush tips inside, finally selecting a flat bristle and his dull painting knife. He picked up his artist's palette from the side table and slowly mixed his carefully selected paints. The heavy scent of the oils was intoxicating. The tape started again from the beginning. As the preacher took to his stage, the people hailed him as though he were a general coming back from war. As if he were the Messiah himself.

The man listened to the sermon one last time as he worked the final touches on his latest piece, finding the raw energy of the preacher's words to be as soothing and stimulating as a surgeon might find listening to classical music in the OR.

"Like many of us in our everyday lives, Moses must make a difficult decision. A terrible decision. One that many will find objectionable, but yet Moses—well, Moses knows it is necessary. A difficult choice, but a necessary one. What does he tell them? What?"

When he was done, the man turned from his work and put his brush into the turpentine mixture to soak. Next to the TV was his computer. He got up from the La-Z-Boy and moved to the swivel desk chair. His hands were shaking just a little as he rubbed a stubbly five o'clock shadow with fingers that were still wet with paint. On the screen before him, the pretty girl sat on her pink bed in her pink bedroom, surrounded by movie stars, pirates, and vampires, chatting on the phone while she tried to paint her toenails.

"He tells them, 'Slay, therefore, every male child and every woman who has had intercourse with a man.'"

The man licked his lips and swallowed hard. For just a second he felt ashamed, wondering why it was he thought the things he thought. But it was too late to get a conscience. Neither his thoughts nor his deeds were pure. His soul was already damned.

"'But you may spare and keep for yourselves all girls who had no intercourse with a man.'"

He typed something on the computer and hit "send," then watched as the pretty girl hopped off the bed and hurried with a smile across the room to her computer.

It was a simple question, but it had certainly gotten her attention, hadn't it?

It always did.

r u online?

1

Lainey Emerson nibbled on the ragged nub of Krazy Glue and broken press-on nail that was still stuck to her thumb and stared hard at the computer. With her free hand on the mouse, she guided the arrow across the screen. Her palms were melting, and her heart was beating so hard and so fast it felt as if it was gonna push right out of her chest. The thousands of butterflies trapped in the pit of her stomach furiously fluttered their wings as the arrow approached the "send" box. All she had to do was hit the button. Just hit the button and send the stupid two-sentence email that'd literally taken her— she looked at the clock in the bottom right corner of the screen and grimaced—*hours* to word just right. And still she hesitated, rolling the mouse back and forth with sweaty fingers.

You should never put anything in writing or in pictures that you wouldn't want to see or read on the front page of the New York Times, *Elaine.*

The ominous words sounded so loud and so clear in her head, Lainey could swear she smelled the stink of cigarettes on her mom's breath as she preached them. She pushed back from her desk, shook the dire "Don't learn things the hard way like me!" Parental Advisory Warning out of her brain, and looked around her now almost-dark bedroom. Long shadows blacked out the faces on the dozen or so movie posters that covered her walls. Outside, all that remained of the late afternoon sun as it sunk into the Everglades were a couple of faint orange ribbons.

5:42? Was it really that late? She suddenly heard the quiet and realized the boisterous shouts from the roller-hockey game that'd been playing in the street all afternoon had stopped—the players and cheerleaders all long gone, home to dinner and homework. Two things Lainey hadn't even started yet. And Bradley? She hadn't heard from her little brother in a while, either. A long while, now that she thought about it. She chewed the inside of her lip. Usually a good thing, but *so* not a good thing now that her mom was gonna be home soon . . .

The front door opened and Lainey prayed it wasn't her mother. It closed with a slam. Thirty seconds later gunfire erupted in the living room as Brad resumed blowing away cops on *Grand Theft Auto*, the dumb video game that he had to play at full blast just to annoy her. Anger quickly displaced relief and she regretted wasting a good prayer on her brother's obnoxious well-being. At least he was home and she hadn't lost him. She raised the volume on her Good Charlotte CD to drown out the screams and machine-gun fire and turned her attention back to the computer. She so needed to stay in the moment or she'd never be able to do this.

The picture on the screen glowed in the dark room, waiting impatiently to be shot off into cyberspace. A pretty girl she barely recognized, with sleek dark hair and smoky eyes, smiled provocatively back at her. A pretty girl Lainey still sheepishly thought looked nothing like her. Tight jeans and a midriff-baring T-shirt showed off a slim but curvy shape. Full, glossy red lips matched equally glossy, long red fingernails, which were posed confidently on her hips, like an *America's Next Top Model* contestant—her friend Molly's idea. Normally Lainey didn't like how she looked in any picture, but, then again, normally she didn't look anything like she did in *this* picture. Normally her waist-length unruly chestnut hair was pulled back in a low ponytail or put up in a clip, her boring brown eyes hidden behind wire-rimmed glasses. Normally she didn't wear any makeup or jewelry or high heels or long red fingernails. Not because she didn't want to, but because she wasn't allowed.

But besides looking a little older than she was—and a little, well, *sexy*—Lainey rationalized that the picture wasn't *that* bad that she wouldn't want to see it in the newspaper. Some MySpace photos were a hell of a lot worse than this. It wasn't like she was naked or doing porn or anything. The most you could see besides her stomach and the fake belly-button ring was the pink outline of the padded bra she'd stolen from her older sister, Liza, under the white T-shirt that she'd also stolen from Liza. Maybe the jeans were kinda low and the shirt kinda tight, but . . .

Lainey shook the creeping, noisy doubts out of her head. She'd already taken the picture. She'd already broken the rule. And the truth was, she looked pretty hot, if she did say so herself. The real worry at this point was, what would Zach think when he saw it?

Zach. ElCapitan. Just the thought of him made Lainey's hands sweat. She looked at the picture taped to the side of the computer screen. Blond hair, bright blue eyes, the quirkiest, sweetest smile, and just the cutest shadow of face gruff. And muscles . . . wow! She could see them even through his Hollister T-shirt. Nobody she knew in seventh grade had even the hope of either a muscle or a hair on their scrawny bodies. Since she'd met Zach a few weeks ago in a Yahoo chat room for the new *Zombieland* movie, Lainey had been forming a mental picture of what he might look like. This fabulous, funny guy who liked the same movies—even the really bad ones—listened to the same music, hated the same subjects, distrusted the same type of plastic people she did, had the same problems with his own parents. It would be too much to ask for him to be anything more than a geek with bad acne and even worse hair and an uncle who'd pulled strings to get him on the varsity football team. But then last Friday Zach had finally sent her a picture, and the very first thing she'd thought was, "Oh my God, this guy could model for Abercrombie & Fitch!" He was that amazingly good-looking. And what was even more amazing was that this totally cool, captain of the football team with model looks liked her. That's when she knew reciprocating with a snapshot of her own boring self just wasn't gonna happen, especially since that self was still three years away from the sixteen she'd told him she was. A small fib that would definitely matter to a senior in high school being scouted by colleges. She knew he'd never be into that, and their friendship—or whatever it was that was happening between them—would be over before she could hit the reply button to his Dear Jane email. If he even bothered to send her one.

She nibbled off the last chunk of nail and spat it in the garbage. The entire fake set had taken her and her best friend, Molly, hours to put on last Saturday for the "photo shoot," and only a few short seconds to rip off this morning in gym class. The nails were her favorite. Long and pointy and oh-so red. More than the shoes or makeup or wearing Liza's clothes, it was those nails that had made her feel so . . . glamorous. So grown-up. She loved tinking them on glasses and rolling them impatiently on tables. It'd taken her the whole weekend to figure out just how to pick up a piece of paper! And now, like Cinderella's ball gown and crystal coach, they were just a memory. At least Cindy got to keep a glass slipper as a memento of her time as a princess. All Lainey got was a chunk of chewed acrylic.

And, of course, a picture.

She stared at herself on the screen. That was it. If she thought about it any more she'd never do it. She closed her eyes, said a prayer, and clicked the mouse. A little envelope zipped across the monitor.

Your message is on its way!

The cell phone in her back pocket buzzed and Gwen Stefani belted out "The Sweet Escape." Molly. She blew out a long held breath. "Hey, M!"

"Did you send it?" an excited voice asked.

Lainey sighed and flopped back on her bed. "Finally, yeah."

"And?"

"I haven't heard back yet. I just sent it, like, two seconds ago."

Molly Brosnan had been Lainey's best friend since way back in kindergarten, and everyone—teachers, coaches, friends, parents—everyone always said, if the two of them looked even a little bit alike, they'd be identical twins. That's how close they were. Or used to be, anyway. It was no coincidence Molly had called at almost the precise moment Lainey had clicked "send." Things like that happened all the time—Molly thinking what she was thinking and vice versa.

That's what made this year suck so much. No matter what her mom said, different schools meant different lives. She picked the fuzz off her alien-green shag pillow. "I'm so nervous, M."

"What took you so long to send it?"

"I'm a chicken."

"You have to call me the second you hear from him, Lainey."

"I will, I will. What do you think he's gonna think?"

"I already told you. You look hot. I mean it. He's gonna love it."

"You don't think I look fat?"

"Please!"

"Stupid?"

"I wish I looked that dumb."

Lainey sat up and stared at the computer across the room. "If I don't hear back from him soon, M, I'm gonna freak! This waiting sucks."

The bedroom doorknob suddenly began to violently jangle back and forth. "Lainey!"

"Get lost, Brad! I mean it," Lainey yelled. "Get out of my room!"

"You're not allowed to close the door! Or lock it! Mom says!"

"G'head and tell Mom, you tattle-tale! Lotta good it's gonna do you, 'cause she's NOT HERE! And I can't wait till I tell her about you playing that video game you're not supposed to play till after you've done your homework!" she added as she fell back down hard on the bed.

"Is that The Brat?" Molly asked. "What's he doing in your room?"

"He's not. He's just outside the door. I can hear him breathing heavy through the crack. I wish I had some bug spray." Lainey squeezed her eyes shut. "I hate him sometimes, M. I swear it." Molly had a little brother, too, but hers was nice. Most of the time.

"What'd he do now?"

"He went through my books again. He drew mustaches on all of my *Seventeen* magazines and ruined them. Totally ruined them. He's such an asshole."

"Did you tell your mom?"

"Like that'll do any good. She probably gave him the magazines and the marker 'cause the poor baby was bored." She sat up and reached for the bottle of nail polish on the cardboard box that was supposed to be a nightstand. She shook it and started to paint her toes.

"You should tell her," Molly sniffed. "He shouldn't be able to go into your stuff."

"She's not home. She's still at work."

"What about Todd?"

Todd was her stepdad and an entirely different story. If her mom babied Bradley, Todd definitely played favorites, which made sense, since Bradley was, after all, his kid and she wasn't and that was life. "He's not home yet, either, thank God. I'm babysitting." Lainey looked over at the door with a frown. "Not that he listens to me."

"Babysitting? Oooh. That means you're in charge. My mom told Sean that corporal punishment is legal in Florida, which means she can use her hairbrush on his ass and you can beat Bradley's with a belt." They both laughed.

"If the prince gets a single bruise on his milky-white butt cheeks, I'll be grounded till high school. Nice idea, but I'm just gonna IG-NORE HIM while he breathes under my FREAKIN' DOOR like a FREAKIN' WEIRDO!!!"

The computer melodically blurped. An incoming IM.

Lainey looked over at the computer, her heart suddenly racing once again. She knew right away who it was.

ElCapitan says: r u online?

"Oh my God, M!" she whispered into the phone. "He just IM'd me. What do I do?"

Molly laughed. "Tell him hello!"

"Yeah, but that means he must've got the email."

"No, it doesn't. Maybe he's IMing you from his phone. You don't know he's seen the picture."

Lainey stood up and paced the room. "He wants to know if I'm here."

"Just say hi, you dork. Do it. Do it now."

"OK, OK . . . " Hitting letters on the computer had never taken so much darn energy before. It felt like someone had poured lead into the tips of her shaking fingers.

LainBrain says: hi

Deep breath. Stay calm. "OK, M. I did it."

The computer blurped again.

ElCapitan says: just got home. practice ended late. coach still pissed over last weeks game

"What? What'd he say?" Molly whined. "Tell me!"

"Nothing. He said he just got home from football practice. Maybe you're right. Maybe he didn't get it?" She paused for a second. "Or maybe he got it and he hates it! M!"

ElCapitan says: got ur mess

Lainey held her breath.

"What'd he say? Lainey!"

ElCapitan says: nice pic ☺

Lainey let the air out all at once, as if someone had popped her screaming lungs with a pin. "He said nice pic, M! You think that's good?" Even asking the question, she couldn't help but grin.

"You're a moron. I told you you looked hot. You better not let your mom see that picture. She'll freakin' flip. Speaking of flipping moms, mine's downstairs having a breakdown. I gotta go eat. Say hi to Bradley Brat for me." She laughed. "*Not.*"

"I'll call you later." Lainey hung up the phone and stared at the words on the screen. She'd never felt this good before in her whole entire life. She wanted to scream. Then, another sentence appeared with a blurp.

ElCapitan says: even better than i pictured, and i have a great imagination . . .

ElCapitan says: want 2 c even more of u

Lainey felt her cheeks light up as she looked around the bedroom. There was, of course, no one there but her, but she still felt strangely embarrassed. What should she say to that? What would Liza say? Did he mean that the way she thought he meant that?

The door to the garage opened with a loud creak. "Brad? Elaine? Hello? Where is everyone? Why is this video game on?" The sound of her mom's irritated voice echoed through the house, along with the click-clacking of her high heels on the ceramic tiles. She heard Bradley run down the hall and into his room. Coward. Lainey mouthed the next words out of her mother's mouth.

"Elaine!"

"I'm in my room!"

"Get off that computer. Did you even start dinner?"

And it was back from the ball once again. Back to reality.

LainBrain says: GTG. P911

IM quick-speak for "Got to go—a parent is coming."

ElCapitan says: who?

LainBrain says: mom

ElCapitan says: damn! and we were just about 2 get on my favorite subject . . .

The funny, uncomfortable feeling was back, and she pushed it aside. Why was she always such a baby? She had to get over that.

ElCapitan says: thought she worked late mondays

ElCapitan says: or is that fridays?

LainBrain says: fridays and every other monday. sorry about coach ☹

"Elaine! Did you hear me? Off that friggin' computer *now*!"

LainBrain says: ☹ LTL. shes pissed.

LTL meant "let's talk later." Lainey opened up her social studies book to make it look like she'd been studying and crumpled a few pieces of notebook paper for effect, just in case her mom headed this way. Now it was time to boil hot dogs and listen to twenty minutes of shit as to why it was irresponsible of her to allow the aspiring psycho in residence to gun down cops and steal cars for two hours on the video game that his own dad had given him for Christmas. "Practice for the real world," Lainey wanted to say when the interrogation finally got started. "Let's face it, Mom, Brad's career options are gonna be limited." But that remark would probably get her smacked.

Just as she opened the door, the computer blurped again. She ran back over to the desk and stared at the words on the screen. She blushed, wrapping her arms absently around her chest.

ElCapitan says: FYI. pinks definitely your color ☺

2

"I don't know if all of you have Halloween on the brain, but these test grades were not what I wanted to see," Mrs. McKenzie said, her voice withered with both age and perpetual disappointment, as she walked down the aisles of the classroom handing out papers. When she got to Lainey's desk, she paused. Not a good sign. "Ms. Emerson, I expected more from you," she sniped without even attempting to lower her voice. Then she dropped the paper as if it was covered in dog poop and she couldn't stand to touch it anymore. A big red D+ landed faceup on the desk.

Another D. *Damn* . . . Lainey could feel her cheeks flame up. She couldn't remember any of the A's she used to get ever being so large. Or so red. She quickly shoved the test into her book bag, avoiding eye contact with any of the twenty-three gawking, smirking strangers around her.

"Report cards are going out next week, people," Mrs. McKenzie warned with a shake of her poofy, margarine-colored head as the bell rang and a mass of bodies rushed past her into the hall. "I know there are a couple of you who aren't going to be happy to see the mailman!"

It was a safe bet that she was one of those people, Lainey thought, feeling the acid churn like cement in her stomach as she slowly made her way through the noisy crowd to the lunchroom. Her mom had no clue how to pull grades up on Pinnacle or Virtual Counselor, but she had a pretty good idea when report cards were sent out. And she was sure to birth a cow when she opened that envelope—algebra probably wasn't the only class Lainey was getting a D in. *Serves her right*, Lainey thought bitterly; she'd never wanted to switch schools anyway. All her friends were still at Ramblewood Middle, while she was completely lost here at stupid Sawgrass with absolutely no one. No one. Zero. Zilch. No one to study with. No one to walk home with. No one to eat lunch with, she thought miserably as she made her way past the tables of cheerleaders and dorks and jocks to an empty seat in the back of the cafeteria. She still didn't see why they'd had to move, either. The old house was fine and it was—what?—a mile away from the "new" one, which was a lot smaller and didn't even have a pool. But, as usual, no one bothered to ask for her input on anything before turning her life upside down. The only future she'd heard her mom and Todd worry about was Bradley's. She and Liza weren't even a thought. Not that Liza gave a shit. The girl was never home anyway, and seeing as she didn't have to change high schools and all her friends drove, not getting to see them was never a worry. Plus Liza was almost seventeen—just a couple years from getting out on her own. Lainey, though, was just plain stuck.

"Hey," a voice said softly behind her as she unpacked a flattened peanut butter and jelly sandwich from her book bag. It was bad enough she had to brown-bag it, but her sandwich was downright embarrassing. It looked like a bled-through Band Aid. A girl she vaguely recognized stood over her, lunch tray in hand. "You're in algebra with McKenzie, right?" the girl asked.

Great. The whole stupid school knew she was flunking algebra. "That's me. Hope I'm not too famous," Lainey replied with a short, nervous laugh that sounded a lot like a whoop.

"I got a shitty grade, too," the girl replied casually. She looked around the table. "You alone?"

Lainey shrugged. Was it that obvious? God, she felt like such a loser. "Yeah," she replied, shifting in her seat. "Just me."

"Can I sit? I just switched to this lunch period and don't know anyone yet."

Lainey moved the stack of books she'd placed in front of her to make it look like she was busy doing work. "Sure."

"I'm Carrie," the girl said, popping a straw into her juice box. "You new?"

"Yeah. I was at Ramblewood, but we moved and now I'm zoned here, I guess."

"Your name's Elaine, right?"

"My friends call me Lainey."

"I'm new, too. My dad got transferred in August. I moved here from Columbus, Ohio."

"Wow . . . Ohio. Do you like Florida?"

Carrie shrugged. "I never had a pool before, so it's cool. My friends back home are, like, so jealous. They all say they're gonna come visit when it gets cold up north. They wanna go swimming in January. That'll be fun."

Lainey felt a pang. It's not as easy as it sounds, she wanted to tell Carrie. Her own friends lived less than a mile away and she practically never saw them anymore. "My best friend still goes to Ramblewood," she said softly as she nibbled on her sandwich. "All my friends still go to Ramblewood."

"Ramblewood, is that a good school?"

Last year Lainey probably would've said, "It sucks," because all schools do. But she finished a sip of disgusting warm milk before replying, "It's a great school. The best."

They chatted about bad teachers and too much homework and riding the bus. She wasn't Molly, but it was someone to talk to. "I like your backpack," Carrie said as she packed up her lunch, nodding at Lainey's book bag. "I must've seen *Twilight*, like, fifty times. Taylor Lautner is so hot."

Lainey smiled. "I like Rob Pattinson. Can you tell?" On the cover flap of her black-and-white shoulder book bag was a picture of Edward Cullen, the teenage vampire played by Robert Pattinson in Lainey's all-time favorite movie. *What if I'm not the hero?* was silk-screened across the front. Her mom refused to buy fancy backpacks or lunch boxes, because, she said, "those celebrities already have enough damn money," so

Lainey had saved up all her birthday cash and bought it herself. She'd gotten the very last one at Target the day before school started. She'd worried at first that maybe it was too young for middle school, but her friend Melissa had one and Molly wanted one and Liza hadn't made fun of it when she saw it, which was definitely a good sign.

"I want to see *New Moon* the day it comes out, like, the very first show. That would be so cool. Hey, maybe we can go together!" Carrie offered.

"Sure," Lainey replied with a smile. "That'd be fun. November 19th. I'm so there."

"Do you think your mom would let you maybe go to the midnight show?"

Lainey shrugged. "I'm not sure . . ."

"Mine can be like that, too," Carrie said with a roll of her eyes. "She treats me like such a baby sometimes. It's just a freaking movie."

"I got *Twilight* on DVD for my birthday. I've watched it, like, a hundred times already. I really love the part when Bella asks Edward how old he is and he says, 'Seventeen.' And then she asks him, 'How long have you been seventeen?'"

Carrie nodded. "And he just answers, 'Awhile.' And the way he looks at her when he takes her up in the tree." She bit her lip and sighed. "Those eyes . . ." Then she pointed at the science notebook in Lainey's hand. "Hey! Who's that?" Carrie asked suddenly.

Taped across the cover of the notebook was the picture of Zach from her computer monitor. Lainey tucked a piece of hair behind her ear. "Oh, that's my boyfriend," she replied quickly, as the blood 911'd to her cheeks, lighting them up, she was sure, like a Christmas tree. She swallowed the large lump that was now blocking her airway.

Time stopped. Lainey could hear her heartbeat whooshing in her burning ears.

"Oh," Carrie finally said, with a slow but unsure smile. "He's cute!"

Thankfully the bell rang before Carrie could fire off another question. Lainey quickly shoved the notebook in her bag, slung it over her shoulder, and waved goodbye, disappearing into the stampede headed out of the cafeteria.

Boyfriend? Jeesh . . . where did *that* come from? The word had just totally slipped out of her mouth. She hadn't planned on saying it. She'd never thought about saying it. She'd never even pretended it was true in the privacy of her own room when no one was looking, like she had on occasion with movie stars. She felt really embarrassed— like she'd been caught doing something she shouldn't—but oddly enough, really happy. Like she'd finally been let in on the biggest secret in the world.

She had a boyfriend.

There it was again. After all, when you thought about it, that's what Zach sort of was, wasn't he? She bit back a smile as she made her way through the crowd. She suddenly didn't feel as alone as she had all morning. Or like such a loser. *Because she had a boyfriend.*

The more she thought about it, the more comfortable the word sounded in her head. Lainey had never had a boyfriend before. Unlike Molly and Melissa, she'd never been asked. But Zach was more of a boyfriend to her than Peter Edwards had ever been to Molly. All they did when they were "going out" last year was talk in the hall in between classes and a couple of times on the cell phone for—what?—a few minutes? True, Molly'd kissed him—but that was only 'cause Peter had jammed his tongue in her mouth as his friends were walking down the hall, just so they could see him making out with her. Molly had almost bit it off, she was so surprised and so completely grossed out. She said it was like getting frenched by Stubbs, her uncle's bulldog. Lainey had laughed, but she'd felt so jealous of Molly when she'd said that. Not because she liked weird Peter Edwards or wanted to get tongued by him or anything, but because, well, because Molly had. And Lainey was still stuck on the other side of the fence, as usual, looking in. Waiting for her boobs to show up. Waiting for her period. Waiting to have a boyfriend. Waiting to catch up, it seemed, with what everyone else was already doing. But now, today, this past weekend, these past couple of weeks—things were different. Unlike Molly and Peter, Lainey talked to Zach every night. And even though she hadn't met him in person yet or heard his voice, they'd sent each other pictures. Plus, Lainey knew he liked her like that. Like a girlfriend. If she wasn't totally sure before, she definitely knew from his IMs yesterday. *He wanted to see more of her. He liked pink. He liked her picture. It was better than what he'd imagined.* Which meant that he was imagining what she looked like. He was *thinking* about her. And Molly could never, ever say that about Peter.

She followed the last of the hall stragglers past Ms. Finn, her language arts teacher, who stood in the doorway impatiently tapping her orthopedic shoes and checking her watch even though the bell hadn't rung yet. Ms. Finn didn't tolerate latecomers. The second the bell rang, the door to her class closed and short of either a fire, terrorist attack, or medical emergency—and that did not include having to pee—she wouldn't open it again till the bell rang at the end of the period. "LIT PACKET DUE TODAY" was scrawled across the blackboard.

It felt like someone had popped her new balloon. Lainey had completely forgotten about the *Wuthering Heights* assignment. That now all-too-familiar icky-loser feeling enveloped her once again. It didn't take a genius in algebra to average out her grades in English—one more D for the mailman to deliver. Her mom was gonna totally freak.

She slid into her seat and slunk down low to avoid Ms. Finn's steely, missile-guided eyes. Next up was probably a pop quiz. Oh joy. She rubbed her finger across Zach's smiling face on her notebook. *It's all gonna be OK*, she told herself. Everything was gonna be OK. Screw this stupid school and the nasty teachers who delighted in giving tests and extra homework. It was only a dumb grade in a dumb class about a dumb old book, right? In the grand scheme of life it all meant nothing. What was really important was staring her right in the face with his sweet smile, and she knew *he* didn't care if she got a D. Zach had already told her he was flunking Spanish. Everything was gonna be OK because she had a boyfriend now. Someone who cared about her. She smiled to herself as Ms. Finn slammed the door closed and the next fifty minutes of hell started up.

Everything was gonna be better in her life. Prince Charming had finally arrived.

And she couldn't wait to get back to her computer to talk to him.

3

Florida weather could be so freaky, Lainey thought as she watched the blob of black to the west slowly make its way over the Everglades and toward Coral Springs. Just twenty minutes ago there wasn't even a cloud in the sky. She hurried across the patch of brown grass that led to the duplex where Mrs. Ross, Bradley's after-school sitter, lived. The warm afternoon breeze had degenerated into cool gusts that made the palm trees rustle and bow. Thunder rumbled in the not-so-far-off distance. The storm was getting closer. She wondered what the weather in Columbus, Ohio, was like. If it ever rained on only one side of the street, or poured when the sun was shining. She wondered what it felt like to play in snow . . .

A zimmer frame with two tennis balls stuck on its front legs sat just outside the screen door on the cement step-up. Taped above the doorbell was a tiny piece of paper with the number 1106 scribbled in old-lady chicken scratch. Hopefully Bradley had his stuff ready to go, Lainey thought as she rang the bell and looked at her cell. If he didn't have practice, Zach was home by five. "Hi, Mrs. Ross," she said sweetly when the door opened. A cat ran out between the old woman's legs and scurried into the bushes.

"Sinbad, you get back here now!" Mrs. Ross scolded in her soft, shaky southern twang.

Bradley's elementary school got out an hour and a half before Lainey's middle school, so Mrs. Ross served as the afternoon pit stop until Lainey could come get him. Her mom used to let Bradley just go home alone, but one of the new neighbors threatened to call the Department of Children and Families and report her, so now she had Mrs. Ross watch him. In Lainey's opinion, Bradley would have been better off on his own. Mrs. Ross was nearing what looked to be a hundred and couldn't see, hear, or remember very well. And her house always smelled like pee and boiled eggs. "Hello there, Elaine," she said. "Come on in, now."

"Do you want me to get him for you, ma'am?" Lainey asked.

"Who?"

"Sinbad."

There was a pause.

"The cat," Lainey added.

Mrs. Ross looked around. Then the light snapped on. "Oh, no, no. Just let him be. He'll come on home, I suppose. That's where the food is."

Bradley popped out from behind the door that led to the living room. His face was pale. "A severe storm warning's been issued. They're saying tornados are possible."

Uh-oh. Her brother could watch *Texas Chainsaw Massacre* and *Saw IV* back to back, but ever since Hurricane Wilma had taken out his bedroom window a couple of years ago, five minutes with the Weather Channel sent Bradley into a complete tailspin. The weather alert must've broken into his cartoons.

"Maybe we should wait it out," he said, his eyes wide with fear. Mrs. Ross gummed her lip and looked back and forth at the two of them. Obviously she wasn't too worried about tornadoes. She wanted her TV back. *Oprah* beckoned.

"Don't freak. It's not even raining yet," Lainey replied calmly.

"I don't know . . . They say tornadoes sound like a train's coming."

"We have to go, Brad. Come on." She looked over at Mrs. Ross. "We can't stay here."

Mrs. Ross shrugged.

"Don't know . . . ," he muttered again.

"Look, we'll run home together before the rain starts. I'll race you."

Bradley looked past her. Another rumble of thunder sounded and his lip began to tremble.

Lainey sighed. The sight of her normally totally obnoxious brother melting into a pile of tears should have made her smile, but it did just the opposite. She actually felt bad for the kid. He looked terrified. "You can hold my hand, Brad," she said quietly, crouching down on her knees to look him in the eye. "It'll be OK. I promise. But we gotta go, like, now."

Just as they rounded the corner of 43rd Street onto 114th Terrace, hand in hand and at full speed, God turned on the faucet. And the thunder. A huge boom that sounded as if it was right above their heads set off three car alarms. By the time they made it inside the house three blocks later, they were both soaked right down to their underwear, which made a now completely freaked-out Bradley chuckle for a split second.

She stood right outside the door and waited while he changed into dry clothes, then she led him back into the family room, closed the blinds, and popped *Resident Evil* into his PlayStation. A video game meant no more weather alerts, and the screaming zombie victims took care of the thunder. She watched him from the kitchen until the rain band had passed over and it was clear Bradley was more concerned with a cannibal finding him in a closet than he was about a twister taking out the family abode. In twenty minutes the storm would be over, he'd be back to his old self, and she wouldn't feel bad anymore. There wasn't much time.

While he jumped on the couch in his Spider-Man jammies, killing zombies left and right, she quietly slipped out of the room and headed down the hall into her bedroom.

Then she locked the door behind her and turned on the computer.

4

Before the screen had even warmed up, the computer blurped. An IM. While she changed out of her wet clothes, she clicked on the flashing orange tab.

ElCapitan says: r u online?

It was like he knew she was there. Like he sensed her presence. That was so cool!

LainBrain says: hi! was just guna rite u

ElCapitan says: sup?

LainBrain says: tried to beat the rain & lost

LainBrain says: i love storms, but its nasty out

ElCapitan says: does that mean ur soaking wet?

LainBrain says: pretty much

ElCapitan says: ooohhh. i like

LainBrain says: drying my hair

ElCapitan says: what happ on math?

LainBrain says: don't ask

ElCapitan says: u wont be 1st to fail algebra

LainBrain says: didnt fail. D

ElCapitan says: (::[ ]::)

Lainey smiled.

LainBrain says: thanks 4 the pity

ElCapitan says: been there. HATED trig. got a C

LainBrain says: moms gonna scalp me. prob grounded 4 life

ElCapitan says: 2 bad. i like ur hair ☹

ElCapitan says: & ur pretty head

She blushed, absently stroking a damp piece of hair that had escaped her towel turban. He was so easy to talk to.

ElCapitan says: have to meet u

Lainey stared at the screen. She totally wasn't expecting that.

ElCapitan says: what about friday nite? wanna c Zombieland?

ElCapitan says: we can grab sum food 2

Oh my God. He was asking her out. Wait—*was this a date?* She looked around the room, as if hoping to see an audience there who could corroborate what she'd just read and interpret exactly what it meant. Where the heck was Molly when you needed her? Of course it was a date . . . Movies meant date. Food meant date. Movies and food definitely meant date. A *real* date. She had just been asked out! Then the complete joy that had her jumping up and down in her room, squealing like a piglet, stopped as quickly as it had come on, replaced by icy, realistic panic. What was she doing? There was no way her mom was gonna let her go. No freakin' way. Especially if she knew Zach was seventeen. She nibbled on a nail. Shit. She didn't want to tell him no. What if he didn't ask again?

ElCapitan says: hello?

LainBrain says: hmmm . . . I definitely want 2 see that

ElCapitan says: will ur mom b cool?

LainBrain says: dont know. specially after today

ElCapitan says: then dont tell her

Lainey stared at the computer as if it were alive, watching her carefully through its blinking cursor. Her stomach twisted with both unease and excitement.

ElCapitan says: what she dont know cant hurt her

She looked around the empty room. A strange tickle itched the back of her throat, as if something had gotten stuck halfway down and wasn't budging any more. That could work. She could tell her mom she was going to the movies with that new girl, Carrie. It's not like she'd ever check, anyway. Liza was the problem child, not her. And short of, "Did you have a good time?" she knew there'd be no questions asked. There never were.

LainBrain says: i cant b home 2 late though

ElCapitan says: ull b home by 10. i have practice @ 8

ElCapitan says: thats AM!!!

Lainey chewed on her lip. Her brain was a mush of thoughts. *What should she do?*

ElCapitan says: u still there?

LainBrain says: ummm . . . thinking

ElCapitan says: ill pick u up at school. weve played CS High b4. stay late and meet me @ 5:30 in the parking lot in back by the baseball field. ill b in a black BMW

LainBrain says: 5:30?

ElCapitan says: cant get the car till dad gets home. CS is a hoof

That's right. Zach lived in Jupiter, which, according to MapQuest, was, like, an hour away. *He's gonna drive an hour just to see me . . .* Lainey took a deep breath. Her heart was pounding. She'd never done anything wrong before. Besides the picture, she'd never gone against the rules. But her mom would just say no for the sake of saying no, and because she had these dumb, arbitrary rules about how old you had to be to do certain things. Twelve for makeup, thirteen for group dates, fifteen for car dates. A knee-jerk reaction to Liza's screwed-up adolescence. If she didn't go on Friday, when would she ever meet Zach? Never, that's when.

LainBrain says: k. sounds like fun

ElCapitan says: cool. keep it low. I don't want ur mom or step to trip. find a theater near u where its playin

LainBrain says: k

ElCapitan says: cant wait to finally meet u

LainBrain says: me 2

She leaned back in the chair. Her brain was spinning. She not only had to figure out how she was gonna get herself across town on Friday afternoon to Coral Springs High—which she'd never even been to before—she also had to figure out how that self was gonna look like the girl he thought she was when she got there. Then an icy thought gripped her, causing a race of goosebumps to ripple across the back of her neck.

What if it didn't work? What if he saw right through her and knew she was thirteen? What would he do then?

The computer blurped.

ElCapitan says: dont worry. ull b safe w/me

She smiled. It was as if he'd just read her mind. Again.

ElCapitan says: im no psycho ☺

5

When the last bell rang on Friday afternoon, Sawgrass Middle exploded like an overfilled cake pan in a hot oven. A thousand bodies simultaneously poured out every door, scrambling for a school bus or the car rider pickup line, hurrying to unlock bikes or meet up with friends for the walk home. Homework, tests, and projects were three long days off. For a half-hour, deafening chaos ruled the crowded schoolyard.

And then it was over.

Perched on her tippy toes atop the institutional-sized hand dryer in the girls' bathroom, Lainey watched out the tiny crank window as the last of the packed yellow buses pulled out of the roundabout, and the crazed chatter of fifty or so screaming voices slowly faded away. Crumpled pieces of paper and empty snack bags dotted the deserted schoolyard, rolling like tumbleweeds across the parking lot and football field. There were no after-school activities, club meets, or conferences on Fridays at Sawgrass—even the teachers left when the last bell sounded. By now, the halls were as lifeless as the parking lot.

Lainey exhaled the breath she'd seemingly been holding all day— all week, actually—and climbed down from the dryer, grabbing her book bag from the handicap stall, where she'd hidden out since the bell rang. With her bus long gone, she was now one step closer to going through with this. She checked her cell—it was 4:10. She had time, but not too much, considering she still had to put on makeup, get dressed, and catch the 5:10 bus up on Sample Road that would take her over to Coral Springs High. Then she had to find the base-ball field parking lot. Not too much time was good, she told herself, as her stomach started to flip-flop again. She didn't want any down-time to think about what she was doing or why she shouldn't be do-ing it, because she knew that she'd probably chicken out. That was one reason why she hadn't told a soul about meeting Zach tonight. Not even Molly. Because she didn't want anyone talking her out of it. The other was more of a personal safety net. If, God forbid, Zach *didn't* show up—if, say, he stood her up—well, then no one would ever have to know about *that* either and she wouldn't have to feel like such a total loser for the rest of her life every time she got with her friends. *"Remember Lainey's first date? Not!"*

She shook the voices out of her head. She'd come this far and she wasn't turning back. Just wait till she told everyone about her date with her football-player boyfriend. That he took her to the movies. And dinner! And he didn't just have a car—he had a BMW! Jeesh! She'd have to figure out a way to get him to take a picture of her with the car on her cell just so she could show everyone, she thought as she changed into Liza's prized jeans and a cute Abercrombie T-shirt. She'd wear her sneakers for the walk to the bus stop, then change into Liza's BCBG booties when she finally got to the high school. She dumped the plastic sandwich bag full of makeup that she'd pilfered from Liza's dresser into the sink next to hers. If her sister knew she'd raided both her closet and her drawers, she'd go postal, so everything had to be back in its proper place by midnight, which was when Liza got off work at the bowling alley. She picked through the pile of com-pacts and lipsticks, before settling on a brown and green eyeshadow palette. She hesitated for a moment, swirling a finger over the shim-mery powders. Besides Halloween and the occasional lip gloss, Lainey had never really put on makeup before. She hoped she could remember what stuff Molly had used on her face last weekend and in what order she'd used it. She didn't want to look like a clown.

A half-hour later she stepped out of the bathroom and smack into the janitor, almost landing face first in the oversized yellow mop bucket he was pushing. They both gasped. Then the janitor looked around frantically, like he'd recognized Lainey from an FBI wanted poster, yelling something that she didn't need to speak Spanish to understand.

Time to go. She walked as fast as she could without running for the main doors, praying that the rule of no one sticking around the school on Friday afternoons applied to those warm bodies in administration as well.

It was a good thing she'd worn her sneakers. By the time she made it to Sample, she was completely out of breath and had to run to catch the bus. She settled into a front seat, all the while avoiding the stare of the disheveled old man across from her who was slurping an orange and eyeing her carefully. She wiped her hands on her jeans and quietly asked the driver to let her know when her stop was, then watched out the window as the string of stores, banks, and restaurants slipped past in a blur. Places she'd eaten at or shopped at dozens of times, but today, she thought, trying to restrain the smile that threatened to commandeer her whole face, it was like she was seeing them all for the very first time.

6

From his parking spot in front of the two-story Allstate office building, he watched as the slight figure with the long chestnut hair stepped off the bus and looked around, like a tourist taking in New York's Empire State Building for the very first time might—with awe, wonder, and excitement.

No doubt. It was definitely her.

She was pretty, in her tight blue jeans and cute, funky T-shirt, a book bag slung clumsily over her shoulder. She had a really nice figure—not too curvy, not too straight. He didn't like the Kate Moss waif look, but he didn't like a voluptuous hourglass figure, either. Too many girls tried too hard to look like something they were not. First came the padded bras and shaping underwear, then the breast implants, liposuction, nose jobs, botox. What you saw was not necessarily what you got. It was nice to see someone as yet unaffected by the Barbie bullshit spouted in fashion magazines and paraded about on MTV. Someone whose beautiful body was still . . . *pure.* He watched anxiously as she stopped in front of the main double doors of the school and hesitated, looking around. He feared for a moment that she might try to go in. Although he didn't think anyone was still around, he didn't want to find out he was wrong. That would ruin everything. He felt his heart beat a bit faster. But after a few seconds, she turned and trotted through the deserted parking lot, heading over to the baseball field in the far back of the school to wait.

For him.

His mouth felt as though he'd swallowed a jar full of cotton balls and he rubbed his hands together to stop them from shaking. It was a bad habit—a *quirk* was what his mother called it. His hands would shake whenever he got too excited. His quirk always made meeting new people quite difficult. Especially pretty girls.

He looked down at the photo on his lap one last time. Then he slipped it into the glove compartment and started up the engine. The sun had just dipped under the horizon and night was officially here. All that was left of the day were a few smudges of purple and tangerine. It was a beautiful sunset. He looked at the clock. 5:29. Right on time.

So nice, he thought as he pulled out of the parking lot. *So very, very nice.*

He liked a girl who was punctual.

7

The bus pulled away from the curb, leaving Lainey behind in a noxious cloud of diesel fumes. Across the street, Coral Springs High loomed imposingly under the umbrella of an enormous ficus tree. She checked her cell. 5:23.

No time to think. No time to dawdle. No turning back.

The football field looked like it was over to the left, so she figured the baseball field was probably in the back of the school. She hurried across the street, cutting through the empty parking lot. She stopped for a moment at the main doors of the school and saw that they were already chained. It looked like no one stuck around here on Friday afternoons, either. Shadows sliced through the trees and across the broken asphalt. In a few minutes the sun would be down. Lainey loved the fall and Halloween and Thanksgiving, but she hated the shorter days. By the time December got here, you were down to—what?—an hour of daylight after school? She followed the chain-link fence to the back of the school, and there it was. The baseball field. No cars in this parking lot, either. No players on the field. It was as deserted as Sawgrass, which was good. Seeing other teenagers eye her like she was an impostor would drive her nerves completely over the edge.

She sat down on the curb and changed into Liza's boots, throwing her sneakers into her book bag. Damn! Time to panic. Why'd she bring her stupid *Twilight* bag? She'd meant to switch to Liza's old silver knapsack. She put a hand over Rob Pattinson's handsome face. This could ruin everything. She'd have to keep that covered up or out of sight somehow—if Zach saw it she'd be so embarrassed. He'd definitely know then that she wasn't sixteen. Maybe she should say her book bag broke this morning and she'd had to borrow her little sister's from last year? Another couple of lies, including a sibling she didn't have. A pang of guilt hit her. She'd told so many the last couple of days. It was getting real hard to keep track of them all . . .

She stood up and walked around the parking lot, trying to force her conscience onto another subject and adjust to Liza's heels. If the *Twilight* bag wasn't a dead giveaway she was a fraud, kissing the movie theater steps sure would do it. She popped a piece of gum in her mouth and put on another coat of berry-flavored lip gloss, shaking her hands out to stop them from sweating. The very real thought occurred to her then that Zach might try to kiss her tonight.

Her first kiss . . .

That was it. She flipped open her cell and speed-dialed Molly. Pacing the parking lot, she spun her book-bag strap around and around, until it was all twisted.

It went straight to voice mail.

"Hey, M, it's me," Lainey began excitedly. "You're probably at piano, but I wish you'd picked up! I have something so—you'll never freakin' guess where I am! Never!"

The car had pulled up behind her so quietly, the loose gravel on the asphalt had not even crunched. It was his voice she heard first.

"Lainey?"

She literally jumped in her sister's boots. There was no time to finish. No time left to think. The moment was finally right here, right now.

"I gotta go," she whispered quickly into the phone. "Look, don't call me back. I don't want the phone to ring. I'll call you in a couple of hours."

Then she licked her lips to make them shiny, snuck a deep breath, and spun around to meet the totally awesome guy she'd literally been dreaming about these past few weeks.

Cindy was finally going to meet her prince. Let the ball begin.

8

"Hey!" she said into the half-open car window, trying to noncha-lantly unspin the tangled book bag. It was almost dark and the win-dows were tinted black, like a limo. It was hard to see inside. "I didn't hear you drive up."

"S'up?" he replied softly. His face was obscured in part by the baseball cap on his head and dark sunglasses, but she caught the flash of his megawatt smile, and her knees shook just a little. His light blond hair spilled out from under the cap, barely touching his shoul-ders. Dressed in a tight long-sleeved black T-shirt and dark jeans, the rest of his body blended like a chameleon with the all-black interior. He waved a hand toward the door. "Hop in."

And so she did.

She slid into the passenger seat, which was buttery soft and smooth, but ice cold. The car smelled like new leather and old smoke. And Paco Rabanne, Todd's favorite cologne. She pushed that thought right out of her head. Her stepdad was the last person she wanted to be thinking about.

"Nice car," she said with a smile as she closed the door. She bent over and casually tried to rearrange the book bag at her feet so that Rob Pattinson was flipped facedown on the floor. She could shoot herself for forgetting to switch it out.

"Thanks," he replied.

The window slid back up, and he turned up the radio. Lainey recognized the song from the movie *Thirteen Going on Thirty*. It was Michael Jackson's "Thriller."

That's a weird song, she thought. Who the hell listens to Michael Jackson that wasn't, like, her parents' age? She would have expected maybe Linkin Park or The Fray, Zach's two favorite bands. Maybe he was playing it in the spirit of Halloween—as a buildup to the movie. *God*, she thought, *please, please don't let him be a geek*. Or a weirdo. "*Zombieland*'s playing at a couple of places," Lainey said. "The next showing is 6:10 at Magnolia, which is just up the road. Or we could go to the 7:15 at the mall." There were a couple of other theaters within driving distance, but those were the two she knew didn't care if a kindergartner walked by himself into an R movie, as long as he bought himself a ticket.

"OK."

You start to scream, but terror takes the sound before you make it . . .

Michael Jackson crooned and squealed on the radio. "You want to go to the 7:15? Then, um, make a left out of the parking lot. I can take you the way I always go, but I have to be on Atlantic Boulevard to get there." She giggled and looked around the dashboard. "I hope you have a navigation system on this thing. My friends always say I'm geographically challenged. I have a hard time finding my way back to my locker after lunch."

Embossed in metal on the steering wheel was a raised, scripted *L*. Lainey recognized it from Molly's dad's car. He had a Lexus.

'Cause this is thriller, Thriller Night! And no one's gonna save you from the beast about to strike . . .

She wanted to ask him why he wasn't driving the BMW, but that sounded shallow. And it was shallow. A Lexus was just as nice. Nicer, maybe. She fidgeted with the mood ring on her finger. She hoped making conversation wasn't gonna be this hard all night. Molly was the conversationalist, not her.

"Are you hungry?" she asked as they pulled out of the lot and made a right onto Rock Island. "We can go to the food court at the mall, if you want." *That would be perfect*, she thought. There was a really big chance that she'd see someone from Ramblewood there. Maybe even Melissa or Erica.

"Sounds good," he said softly.

The creepy-sounding old guy started to rap on the radio. Vincent Price, the horror movie king from, like, a thousand years ago.

Darkness falls across the land. The midnight hour is close at hand . . .

"I really liked your picture," Zach said, but he didn't look at her. She watched as a single drop of sweat trickled down the side of his neck, disappearing into his shirt.

His arm was on the armrest, his hand dangling casually off the edge. Rough fingers tapped the gear shift. Wiry black hairs sprouted from the flesh above his knuckles. Lainey's eyes slowly moved up his arm. Coarse black hairs stuck out of his cuff, like spindly spider legs.

She suddenly felt incredibly cold. Prickly goosebumps raced across her flesh. It was as if all the air had been sucked out of the car.

Zach was blond.

And though you fight to stay alive, your body starts to shiver . . .

He turned into an empty lot with a bunch of power station lines. Across the street was a park. Molly's mom had taken her and Molly there once before. It had a nature reserve running through it. The mall was in the other direction.

For no mere mortal can resist the evil of the thriller . . .

She reached for the door handle, but it wouldn't budge. The king of horror broke out into maniacal laughter. The song was over.

The cloth came across her face with lightning speed even as the car was still moving. The wicked taste burned her eyes and closed her throat. It was hard to breathe. Then he punched her hard in the head. She felt her face smash against the glass. She felt the warm blood trickle from her forehead, running past her eye and down her cheek. He shoved her head down hard under the dash. She felt her hands fall to the floor, her legs twitch and just stop working, as everything went to black.

The horror king just kept on laughing.

9

The hall clock started to chime. Debbie LaManna could hear it, even over the blare of the television. Even two rooms away. It chimed every quarter-hour, then struck in the number of hours at the top of every hour. It took five fucking minutes just to get through midnight. She cracked off a smoke ring. The ornate grandfather clock and a bank account with $3,714.22 in it was what her mother had left her nine years ago when she'd died of lung cancer, an oxygen tube strapped to her nose and a pack of Newports in hand. Of course the money was long gone, but damn it if that hideous Mack the Knife moon-face clock was still here—dragged along behind her from husband to husband, apartment to apartment, rental to rental. Toasting each lost hour of her life with a loud, distracting clang. One of these days she was gonna call the Salvation Army to come and haul it away.

Debbie counted as the dings hit eleven. Just to be sure, she looked at her watch. She was gonna kill Elaine. Really kill her. Who the hell did she think she was, staying out till eleven at night? She crushed out her cigarette. This was how it had all started with Liza. Breaking curfew, coming home stoned. Smelling like a fucking bottle of Bud. If that kid thought for one second that she was gonna get away with half the shit her older sister had pulled, she had a cold, hard reality check coming. What was that saying her own mother used to love?

Fool me once, shame on you, Debra. Fool me twice, shame on me. And Debbie was no fool. Not anymore. Elaine Louise was so gonna have her ass handed to her when she walked through that door. That was for certain. She swallowed a big chug of her Mich Ultra and tried to concentrate on the news.

"Is she home yet?" Bradley called out from his bedroom down the hall. His voice had the baiting tone of a kid who was happy that his sibling was gonna be in a shitload of trouble.

"Brad, if you don't close that damn door and go to sleep in the next five minutes, there is no laser tag tomorrow with Lyle. I can promise you that!"

The door closed with a thud and Debbie tried to focus once again on the news. Listening to everyone else's tragedies seemed to help for a little bit. A local fire. A bank robbery. Nine dead in an Iraq suicide bomb. Then her thoughts came around again. This time they landed on Todd, who was also not home yet. He was the real reason Debbie was so pissed off. Where the hell was he?

An after-work beer with the boys, honey. Just unwinding from a long, hard day of making money to feed your kids.

My ass, Debbie thought, bitterly. She knew he was probably drunk and fucking that new girl from the office in some sleazy Lauderhill motel or on a beach towel in the backseat of his car. The receptionist named Michelle that he swore up and down didn't work at his office, even though that's who'd answered the phone yesterday when Debbie had called to check.

Debbie rubbed her throbbing temples and lit another cigarette. She looked around the family room, littered with crap the kids hadn't cleaned up, including petrified cereal bowls left over from breakfast, video games, clothes, and stacks of crumpled school papers pulled out of book bags and thrown wherever. When Liza did feel like coming home, she loved to dump whatever she didn't want to wear or carry anywhere she felt like it. And then there was the other prince in the house, Bradley. Thanks to his dad's testosterone-fueled edict that housework was a woman's job, he didn't lift a finger to pick up his shit, either. After working another nine-hour shift, this is what Debbie got to come home to—a messy house, a rat-bastard husband, kids who drained every last bit of energy from her body. And of course, no respect. Now, after she'd just gotten through what she hoped was the worst with the oldest, Elaine was gonna try and give her patience a run for the money. She shook her head and slapped the newspaper off the couch. This was not how life was supposed to have turned out.

Rosey, the kids' golden retriever, walked in with a big bear stuffed in her mouth, and nuzzled her head on Debbie's lap. Rosey had a habit of stealing every loose sock and stuffed animal in the house. This time it was Elaine's ratty old teddy bear, Claude. She must have pulled it off Elaine's bed. Lainey never went to sleep without him. She was thirteen going on thirty, maybe, but she still needed her teddy to go to sleep. Debbie pushed back the bad thoughts that kept trying to force their way into her head. She fingered the numbers on the cordless beside her, wondering if maybe she should call the police. But then she remembered from her escapades with Liza what life was like once you got the cops involved. Once they were in your business, they never got out. Never. Instead, she tried Todd's cell again. "Where the fuck are you?" she barked when her husband told her to leave a message at the tone and he would get back to her as soon as he was able.

As soon as I've dismounted my invisible receptionist with the great boob job whose name is not Michelle, I'll be sure to call you back. Beeeeeep.

She probably was sleeping over at that new friend's house, Debbie told herself. What was her name? The one Lainey went to the movies with? Carly? Karen? That was probably it. Maybe she'd even told her she was gonna be sleeping over. It was so crazy this morning, trying to get them all out of the house and herself off to work, she probably just didn't remember Elaine telling her, was all. And the reason she's not answering her cell? That one's easy. Because she never fucking charges it, that's why. No surprise there.

Debbie pulled Claude from Rosey's mouth and wiped the dog spit off on the cuff of her robe. She finished off the last of her beer with a single swallow and cracked open another from the portable cooler next to the couch. Then she turned up the volume on the TV, absently rocking the mangy teddy in her arms just as Conan O'Brien started his monologue and the clock began to count down yet another half-hour of her life.

10

This is the way nightmares begin. Or perhaps, end.
—ROD SERLING, *THE TWILIGHT ZONE*

The rumble of a lawn mower going right past his bedroom window was what woke Florida Department of Law Enforcement (FDLE) Special Agent Supervisor Bobby Dees from the weird dream he'd finally slipped into. For a few seconds his exhausted brain scrambled to reconcile the sound with the strange golf game he'd been playing with his dead dad. A groundskeeper mowing distant swales on the eighteenth, perhaps? A low-flying jet? The rumble slowly faded off, a hush grew over the excited crowd, his dad lined up the putt . . .

Then his neighbor turned the John Deere back around.

It was no use. Bobby lifted a lid. The sun streaks that squeezed through the drawn blinds were tinged a soft pink. He looked over at the nightstand clock: 8:03 a.m. That was when he remembered it was Sunday.

He rolled over with a grunt and the new John Grisham he'd fallen asleep reading slipped off his chest, hitting the floor with a thump. His wife's side of the bed was warm, but empty. He heard the door to the bathroom shut softly with a click. The shower turned on a few seconds later. LuAnn's shift at the hospital didn't start till ten, but especially on weekends she liked to get in a little early, have a cup of coffee and read the paper in the cafeteria before taking on an ER still chock-full of Saturday-night drunks and car-crash victims.

Bobby pulled a pillow over his head and lay there with his eyes closed for a few minutes, reluctant to accept the fact that he was now awake. The last time he remembered looking over at the clock it had read 5:49 a.m. The rumble of the mower slowly faded away like the ending of a song on the radio, the crowd on the green quieted once again, and he started to drift back off . . .

Then his Nextel rang.

Ugh. He grabbed the cell off the nightstand and pulled it under the pillow with him. "Dees," he grumbled.

"Man, you sound like shit," replied the familiar voice on the other end with a chuckle. "What's up there, brother? Somebody piss in your cornflakes?"

"What's up? Why don't you tell me what's up at, ah, eight-fucking-o'clock on a Sunday morning, Zo?"

Lorenzo "Zo" Dias was the recently promoted assistant special agent in charge of the FDLE Regional Operations Center in Miami—aka: Bobby's boss. "Don't tell me you ain't up yet . . ."

"I sure as hell am now." Bobby sat up and rubbed his head. "There goes your overtime budget, Boss. I'm officially back on the clock."

"What if I wanted to see if you were up to hitting a few on the Blue Monster this morning?"

Bobby yawned. "Now I know I'm coming in. Your balls couldn't find a hole with a map, a flashlight, and a personal guide. When was the last time you played golf?"

Bobby and Zo had been good friends long before Zo had begun his lonely ascent up the FDLE chain of command. They'd met in the FDLE agent academy almost a decade ago—Zo had retired early from the Miami Beach Police Department to become a special agent; Bobby had decided he'd had enough of New York and the bullshit politics of the NYPD and had headed south for better weather and a slower change of pace, which was rather ironic, considering hurricanes had become almost as commonplace as thunderstorms in South Florida and his caseload in the Crimes Against Children squad was double what it was as a Robbery detective in Queens. But he and Zo had stayed close throughout the years and the titles, and even through all the crazy administrative bullshit of the past few months. Zo was one of very few guys Bobby had met in his career who had successfully managed becoming a good boss while remaining a good friend. Most people, he'd found, turned into assholes before the ink dried on their promotion paperwork, throwing colleagues under the bus just to show some stuffed shirt in Tallahassee that they could. Of course, Zo had only been an ASAC for six months . . .

Zo sighed. "You got me. I'd rather have my teeth cleaned than chase balls smaller than my own around a big green lawn. G'head and call me un-American. I'll see you in thirty."

"What's up?"

"We got a kid gone missing after school Friday," Zo replied, growing serious. "Thirteen-year-old Elaine Louise Emerson out in Coral Springs. Looks like a runaway, but we're dotting I's and crossing T's. Springs PD asked for assistance. You know the drill."

Unfortunately, that was true. Bobby did know the drill. Missing kid. Parents call in the locals. Locals call in FDLE. FDLE calls in him. First twenty-four hours is critical, which meant they were already way behind schedule. He rubbed his eyes. Bobby had gotten the same phone call too many times before. Nobody knew better than he that with missing kids, nothing was routine and rarely did things ever turn out "looking like" everyone had said they would. "Has anyone called the Clearinghouse?" he asked, referring to the Missing Endangered Persons Information Clearinghouse.

"Party's waiting on you. Mom just called it in late last night. Waited almost two days for the kid to get home from some sleepover. Says she figured her daughter was maybe staying over at a friend's house." Zo sighed with annoyance. "Don't ask me why she waited till midnight on day two to call the kid's friends and find out whose house she was fucking sleeping at. Unfortunately, brother, ya don't need a license to be a parent."

There was a brief, uncomfortable, silence.

"You know what I'm saying," Zo tried when Bobby didn't say anything.

"Where am I going?"

"Let's meet at the house. You can talk to the parents, get a feel. If you don't like what you hear, call it in. It's 11495 NW 41st Street. FYI, that's Section 45."

"Section 45" was code for "Shitsville." Coral Springs was a sprawling suburb stuck out in the middle of what was not so long ago considered nowhere. Kissing the Everglades twenty miles to the west of Fort Lauderdale and forty-five miles northwest of Miami, Coral Springs' dirt roads had all been paved over into four-lane highways and its bean farms replaced with gated communities, office parks, and, of course, a Starbucks on every corner. Voted one of the top places in the U.S. to live by *Money* magazine, like any growing city, Coral Springs also had its share of problem pockets and rough neighborhoods that town commissioners would rather see annexed to some other city's limits. "Section 45" was one of them.

"All right," Bobby said, reaching for the *People* magazine on Lu-Ann's nightstand and jotting down the address across John Travolta's forehead. "I'll be there in a half. What? You don't have anything better to do on a Sunday than hang with me? Does misery love company that much?"

"Trent asked me to go along, since the Springs chief called him in special. Like I said, they're saying runaway, they just want us to dot their I's and cross their T's for 'em. You know, they're not in need of any more bad publicity out there."

Trent was Trent Foxx, the new FDLE Miami Regional Director—aka the Really Big Boss. "All right," Bobby replied with a yawn. "It'll be like old times, Boss. I'll pick up the coffee."

"Make it three cups. Another FYI, Veso will be meeting us there, too."

Bobby pretended he didn't hear that last bit of news and hit the "end" button before he said something to Friend Zo that Boss Zo wasn't gonna like much. Frank Veso was just the latest in a string of green agents who had transferred down to Miami from some other bum-fuck part of the state to take a stab at his job. Not that he had anything against Veso personally—hell, he didn't even know the guy—but it was growing real old real fast having to teach the lines to all the understudies gunning for his position as special agent supervisor. It was no secret that the new regional director wanted "a change" in Crimes Against Children—namely SAS Bobby Dees out and an "as yet to be named" replacement in. But the reality was, no matter how good the raise or prestigious the title, in the end, no one really *wanted* Bobby's job, and Bobby, Zo, and the director all knew it. To date, all the wannabes who had headed south to try their hand at a new job description had hightailed it right back to the FDLE Regional Operations Center they'd transferred in from. Because while working Crimes Against Children might get your face on TV more than running down unscrupulous accountants, it was always for a really bad reason. Beaten kids. Exploited kids. Abused kids. Missing kids. Dead kids. For most cops, the carrot at the end of an investigation was knowing justice had been served—the bad guy caught and locked up tight behind bars, the case closed nice and neat. Car stolen/car returned. Defendant off streets/victim happy. But with child predators, often you opened your investigation with one victim and ended it with a few dozen. And even when you sent the scumbag to jail for a couple of decades and the case was closed out and put in a box on a shelf, you never really felt it was over. You could never be sure you got all the victims. And because kids generally made for crappy witnesses, and parents didn't want their babies to have to go through any more trauma, sometimes a cop never tasted the carrot at all—a slap on the wrist and long-term probation was the only justice being served on the courthouse menu. Working Crimes Against Children was like pulling off a Band-Aid and debriding what you thought was a scratch—only to find out under the scab was an infection that was a hell of a lot worse than anything you'd ever imagined. The layers of healthy flesh it had rotted away, unchecked, were horrifying. Only then did you begin to understand just how pervasive evil really was. Only then did you understand that for the smallest and most innocent of victims, the nightmare that would last a lifetime was only just beginning. And at the end of the day or the apprenticeship, few cops could handle that reality, no matter how much bigger the paycheck or how bright the limelight shone down on their careers.

Bobby got out of bed, opened the blinds, and looked out the window. Outside, his wooly-chested, red-faced neighbor, Chet, was dragging the mower back into the garage. In another driveway he spotted a purple jogging stroller and a determined new mom stretching her Achilles against a curb. The twin toddlers next door were probably popping fistfuls of Cheerios, their wide eyes glued to SpongeBob. If he stuck his head out the window, he could smell the bacon frying and the coffee brewing on this sunny Sunday morning. Inside his own home, the shower had turned off, and the silence was almost deafening.

Good morning, suburbia. Bobby watched with a bitter twinge of contempt as everyone's life went on as usual, as if nothing at all was wrong in the world. Rising gas prices, falling stock prices, and a war being fought 6,000 miles away by kids they didn't know anyway were just mildly worrisome headlines in the morning's paper. Then it was on to the sports page for last night's stats and the travel section for some fun ideas on next summer's vacation.

Snug in their lucky little cocoons, where really bad things only happened to somebody else. Or better yet, to really bad people who really deserved them. Unaware and completely unaffected by the cold fact that somebody else's child had just gone missing among them.

11

"I thought you were gonna try and sleep in," LuAnn said into the mirror, mouth open and mascara brush in hand, when he stepped into the bathroom.

"Try's the magic word. Who the hell can sleep through that?" Bobby grabbed the tube of Crest off the counter, watching as LuAnn went back to finishing her face. Her short robe clung to the curves of her damp body, glistening with freesia-scented lotion. Against the stark white cotton, her muscular legs looked even more tan than they normally did. The robe was slightly open in the front, tied loosely at the waist, exposing the pale curve of one of her breasts, her flat, toned stomach. At forty-one, his wife still had an incredible body. Just looking at her standing there, doing her makeup, stirred things in him, both emotionally and physically. LuAnn had always had that power over him, from the moment they'd met under the blinding fluorescents of Jamaica Hospital's trauma room. It was her face that had calmed him, her words that had made sense as he lay on that cold, steel table, bleeding out from the gunshot wound that had severed his brachial artery. Bobby hadn't remembered much when he'd woken up days later in a hospital room full of anxious buddies in NYPD blue jackets, still groggy from all the drugs and weakened by the infection that had routed his body, but he couldn't forget her—the dark blonde with the Midori green eyes and light, melodic southern drawl. He could still hear her whispers in his head, the bright lights of the trauma room backlighting her head like a halo.

Officer Dees . . .

Dees . . .

Bobby, come on, now.

Don't be going nowhere on me, Bobby . . .

Just stay right here . . . right here . . . with me . . . stay . . .

He knew her the instant she walked into his room the morning he was being discharged. She had an angelic face that perfectly suited her name, he'd thought. LuAnn Briggs, the tag on her uniform read. LuAnn—sweet, simple, soft, southern, delicate, bubbly, delicious. When she'd sat on the edge of his hospital bed and explained how she wasn't even supposed to have been working the night he was brought in, how it was only her second day in the ER, how she'd checked on him every night when he was in the coma, he knew his life would forever change. He proposed three months later. They were married that same year, ten days before Christmas. This December would mark nineteen years. He shook the distant memories out of his head and turned back to the sink.

"You should talk to Chet," LuAnn said, waving the mascara brush in his direction. "I have to get up, but you don't. It's not right on a Sunday, especially with your insomnia."

He squirted a gob of Crest onto the brush. "Helen told me he's OCD."

"That's no excuse."

Bobby nodded in the mirror, staring at his own reflection. He looked like shit. The silver hairs in his morning gruff looked like they were beginning to outnumber the brown ones. And the laugh lines that feathered out from his blue eyes had apparently decided to take up permanent residence—whether or not he had anything to laugh about. More than a few grays had taken up residence in the waves of his dark brown mop, too, which, he realized as he ran a hand through it, was in need of a trim. Long, shaggy, and overgrown only worked if you were a rock star, a defense attorney, homeless, or under twenty-five. Bobby was none of the above. What turned distinguished into disheveled? He was forty-two by—what?—a couple of months? Daily five-mile runs and twice-weekly trips to the gym kept the stress at bay and the pounds off his six-foot frame, but the mileage was definitely starting to show. It was only a matter of time. The fact that he just didn't sleep anymore wasn't helping. The past year alone had aged him ten.

LuAnn dropped the mascara into her makeup bag and leaned against the sink, pulling her robe closed and folding her arms across her chest. "Any reason you're all dressed up?"

Even on that rare Sunday Bobby did go to church, it was usually in jeans and a T-shirt. The pressed black slacks, white dress shirt, and gray silk tie slung around his neck were a clear indication something was up. No one had died and nobody was getting married—it wasn't too hard to figure out he was headed to a scene. He wiped his mouth on a hand towel, reached for the shaving cream, and turned on the hot water. Steam fogged the mirror. "I gotta go in," he said quietly.

"I thought you were taking some time off this week," she tried.

"I was. But I gotta go in."

She stared blankly at him in the mirror, her face blurring from the steam, waiting for the rest of the explanation that he knew she didn't want to hear.

He turned to face her. "There's a kid," he explained softly. "She didn't come home from school Friday."

LuAnn said nothing. She just kept staring straight at him. Through him. Like the lyrics go from a bad song, there once was a time when he could feel himself getting lost in those green eyes. Eyes that just made you want to kiss her when you looked at them long enough. Now they stared at him, cold and empty. Concealer barely hid the dark circles and the stress fractures that feathered out from the corners. They were standing only a couple of feet apart, but there might as well have been a mountain between them in that small bathroom.

"It looks like a runaway."

"Oh," she muttered with a blink and headed past him into the bedroom.

He shaved while she got dressed in silence. He stepped back into the bedroom just as she was tying her shoes on the bench by the foot of the bed. He finished buttoning his shirt and doing his tie, then slipped his badge around his neck and clipped the gun belt to his side. Out of respect, he waited until she went back into the bathroom and out of sight before he unlocked the gun safe, took out the Glock, and slid it into the holster. He knew it got her upset to see it. It always had, even when he'd gone back into uniform after his shoulder had healed. He was probably the only guy on the NYPD back then whose girl *wasn't* turned on by the fact that her boyfriend was a cop. It wasn't that LuAnn hated guns or was a gun-control nut, it was just that she hated to see *him* with a gun. She said it reminded her what he had to do all day, and why it was he needed a gun to do it.

He slipped on a sport jacket and walked back into the bathroom. She was standing in front of the mirror just staring at the image before her. As he came up behind her, she started to mechanically brush her wet hair. His hand found her shoulder and rubbed it gently. "Don't work too hard. See you tonight, Belle," he said into the mirror, then kissed her softly on the cheek.

Belle, for Belle of the Ball. His sweet Southern Belle. LuAnn just nodded and kept brushing. Her skin felt cold and slightly damp, like the inside of a window pane on a snowy day.

He walked out of the bathroom, grabbed his car keys and cell off the nightstand, and headed down the hall, past the framed family pictures that covered practically every inch of the honey-colored walls. The last door at the end was slightly ajar, a battered street sign affixed to it warning "Trespassers Will Be Prosecuted." Inside the bubble-gum-pink room, the morning sun warmed the dozens of teddy bears posed neatly atop a metallic silver comforter. A stack of laundered, folded clothes sat on the desk chair, still waiting to be hung up. He stopped to pull the door closed, his hand lingering on the cold door-knob for just a second. A million thoughts rushed him and he quickly pushed them back out of his head.

As he rounded the banister and hurried down the stairs, he licked his dry lips. They tasted salty. That's when he knew for sure she'd been crying.

12

No media trucks, no mob of flashing patrol cars, no flock of hovering copters.

That was the first thing Bobby noticed as he pulled his Grand Am in front of the tired white ranch. Atop a sagging roof, a faded blue tarp flapped in the breeze, a bike lay propped against a plastic carport. Down the block, a group of kids laughed and joked as they skateboarded into the air off homemade ramps. Obviously the failure of some teenager to come home after a weekend of partying was not on anyone's radar.

"Hey there, Dapper Dan," Zo called, tapping on the car's back window. He walked up to the driver's side and leaned in, a toothpick stuck in the corner of his mouth, his eyes hidden behind Ray-Bans. He wore khakis and a light blue dress shirt, the sleeves rolled up to the elbows, the collar open and tie loose, like he was about to work on a car or deliver a baby. It was obvious Zo felt more comfortable in flip-flops and shorts. He fingered the lapel of Bobby's sport jacket. "That real polyester?"

"Very funny. I'd lie and say it's Armani, but the joke would be lost on you. What's with the stick, Kojak?" Bobby asked, opening the door and stepping out.

Zo sighed. "I quit smoking."

"Yeah? Since when?"

"Yesterday."

"I thought you were trying to quit drinking."

"Nah. I gave up on that. Camilla said she'd rather have me drunk than dead of cancer. I've been told I'm a lot of fun at a party."

"I'll second that."

"I've eaten a whole fucking box since last night. Not a single butt, though." Zo spit the gnawed toothpick to the ground and popped another one into his mouth.

"What about those patches? They're supposed to work."

Zo pushed up the sleeve of his shirt. Three flesh-colored squares dotted a muscular bicep the size of Bobby's thigh. The silver hair on Zo's buzzed head might betray his forty-five years, but his body sure as hell didn't. He trained the new agents in tactical defense, headed up the Special Response Team—FDLE's version of SWAT—and was very much a physically commanding and intimidating presence both in the office and out in the field. When Zo said, "Jump!" most guys simply asked, "How high, sir?"

Bobby shook his head. "In other words, don't fuck with you today." He looked at the house. "OK. What am I walking into?"

"Just got here myself. Haven't been inside yet. Waiting on Veso. By the way, don't hang up on me again," Zo said with a frown and a wag of his finger as he pulled out a notepad from his pocket. He leaned back against the hood of Bobby's car. "Elaine Louise Emerson. DOB, 8/27/96. Brown hair, brown eyes, five feet tall, about ninety-five pounds. A seventh grader at Sawgrass Middle." He held up a color copy of what was obviously a school portrait of a young, lanky girl seated behind a desk, her hands folded in front of her, with long, frizzy hair the color of coffee ice cream. Light brown eyes were hidden behind glasses that were just a little too big for her face. She was smiling but didn't show her teeth, which probably meant either she hated them because they were crooked, or she had braces. She didn't necessarily look like a geek, but she was definitely in that awkward adolescent stage of not being a little girl anymore, and yet still years away from becoming a woman. "That was the fax that came in this morning," Zo finished, handing him the copy.

"August twenty-seven, huh?" Bobby said. "That's my birthday."

"And what a party we had. I think you stayed out till—what?—eleven?"

"Is this recent?" Bobby asked, ignoring the jab. "She looks young for thirteen."

"That's from fifth grade, I'm told."

"Elementary school? Two years is a world of difference at this age, ya know."

"Mom's looking for something more recent."

Bobby thought of LuAnn and the pictures she covered every wall in the house with. The library of photo albums that she kept in the family room. If you stacked them all together and flipped through them fast enough, it would probably run like a flip-book movie of their daughter, Katy's, whole life. There would be no missing pieces. No empty gap of memories for two years that she'd have to go searching for . . .

"I'm told she's inside and she's pretty pissed off," Zo added.

"At who?"

"The kid, the cops, the husband—you name it. You're up next," he warned. "Debra Marie LaManna, age thirty-six. She works at Ring-a-Ling Answering Service in Tamarac."

"Dad?"

"Stepdad, aka hubby number three. Todd Anthony LaManna, age forty-four. CarMax salesman of the month," Zo said, raising an eyebrow. "In fact, he's working right now."

"I'm guessing he's not too worried about little Elaine," Bobby said.

"I'm thinking that'd be a good guess."

"Real dad?"

"California somewhere. No one's heard from him in a couple of years. Mom's got three kids: Liza Emerson, age sixteen, Bradley LaManna, son of our used-car salesman, is eight, and Elaine, the one who's missing, is thirteen by, as you can attest, a couple of weeks. Latchkey kids."

"Anyone call the hospitals?"

"Done. Nothing."

Bobby looked over at the weathered and faded cardboard boxes stacked up along the side of the house. Moving boxes. "How long have they all been living here?"

"Both Mom and Step changed their DL address to this house in June. They're renting. Records place them before that in another rental in Ramblewood, a couple of miles from here."

"Any history?"

"Not with this kid. But cops have been out to both houses a few times. Once for a domestic and a few times for the sixteen-year-old. She's been in trouble for drinking, marijuana possession, truancy. The latest last month was a burglary. It was dropped to trespassing on school property."

"Ouch. A bad apple?"

"Spoils the whole friggin' barrel," Zo replied. "Sis has also hit the road before. Miami-Dade picked her up on an NCIC missing juvi report a few months ago down in Little Havana, hanging with some boys from the Latin Kings at two in the morning."

NCIC stood for the National Crime Information Center, a nationwide criminal information system for law enforcement. "That's not good company to be keeping," Bobby replied, kicking the curb. The lawn was overgrown by a couple of weeks. The edging longer than that. "Who's working it inside?"

"Springs GIU responded last night when Mom finally decided to call it in." GIU stood for the General Investigations Unit, an all-purpose detective squad. "Bill Dagher and Troy Bigley. You know 'em?"

Bobby shook his head. He knew most every cop in South Florida who worked Crimes Against Children or Special Victims. The fact that he hadn't heard those two names before probably said more than if he had.

"They peg the kid for a runaway. The Springs chief called Trent this morning for assistance to clear it. You know, after the shit storm that hit last year with that Jarvis girl, CYA is the name of the game in this town."

CYA as in Cover Your Ass. Bobby nodded. Normally only endangered missing kids (i.e., snatched) were investigated by FDLE, not
runaways. With thousands ofs kids hitting the pavement each year in
the state, there just wasn't enough manpower to go looking for every
kid who didn't want to be found. The locals usually handled their
own, calling in FDLE and the Clearinghouse for assistance on abductions, endangered runaways, and exceptional cases. But then came
the Jarvis debacle.

Makala Jarvis was fifteen when she was first reported missing to
the Coral Springs PD by her grandmother. Two days after cops took
the report, Mom called, claiming Makala had returned home. Without verification, the case was closed and Makala's name was removed
from NCIC as a missing juvenile, even though Grandma kept insist-
ing Makala hadn't really come back home. It was two years before a
school resource officer finally listened to the old woman and put
Makala's name back into NCIC. Within a month, the skeletal remains
of a young female found stuffed in a suitcase and floating in the St.
John's River eighteen months prior were finally identified. Makala
Jarvis had died from blunt-force trauma to the head. The subsequent
homicide investigation revealed that Makala had been scheduled to
testify against Momma's boyfriend in a domestic violence case just
two weeks before Grandma initially reported her missing. A convic-
tion would've violated boyfriend's parole and sent him back to
Florida State Prison for twenty years. Mom didn't want to lose her
meal ticket, and since cops don't go looking for people who aren't
missing, Makala's name wasn't even on the list of possible victims
back when her body was fished out of the water. She sat, unidentified,
in a black evidence bag on a shelf at the Medical Examiner's Office in
Duval County for almost two years.

The fallout from Jarvis was bad. The reporting Coral Springs detective was fired, virtually the whole General Investigations Unit was
reassigned to road patrol, and the department took a beating in the
press. And a new departmental policy was instituted: Cover Your
Ass. But for that new policy, most likely Bobby would never have

even heard the name Elaine Emerson. "Assistance to clear it" was code for "we already investigated, just sign off on the report already."

"Where was Stepdad on Friday?" Bobby asked.

"Out with the boys. Or girls. The Mrs. says he stumbled home around three. Stumbled was actually my word. Pulling from personal experience, I think most people are stumbling when they get home at three in the morning."

"Anybody interview him yet?"

"Not yet. He got home too late last night and left too early this morning. Given the shit he's had to put up with from stepdaughter numero uno, maybe he's expecting the same from this one, and thinks, 'Fuck that, I'm going to work and getting the hell out of Dodge.'"

"One rotten apple . . . ," Bobby said softly.

"Spoils the whole friggin' barrel." Zo flipped his notebook closed.

Bobby looked at the overgrown lawn, the overflowing garbage, the house in need of a paint job. Didn't look like Todd LaManna liked to come home much at all. "Your boy Veso's late, Boss," he said, glancing at his watch. "'Fraid he's gonna have to hear what he missed out on at briefing," he called out as he started up the cement walk. "The morning's getting away from us and I wanna find out where the hell this kid is."

13

"I think her name was Karen or Carla." Debra LaManna shifted on the mauve sectional and reached for another Marlboro, even though there was a crushed butt still smoldering in the ashtray on the cushion next to her. A thin haze of blue smoke hung in the modest but cluttered family room. "It was only a movie she was going to, for Christ's sake," she added with a roll of her eyes. "Sorry if I didn't think to get the kid's social security number she was going with."

Bobby studied the slight woman with the bony, freckled cheeks and mistrusting stare across from him. Her pin-straight, long brown hair was pulled off her face and into a low ponytail, which she draped over her shoulder and absently stroked like a cat's tail. She looked tired and stressed, but for a mom whose kid had been MIA going on two days, what she didn't look was sad. No red-rimmed eyes. No messed-up makeup from crying rivers of tears. No look of rabid panic or fear. Just plenty of anger, which radiated from her thin frame like a force field. The message was clear: Boy, was little Elaine gonna get it—if and when she finally decided to come home.

"Sometimes it's the one question that wasn't asked," Bobby replied, looking around the room. Bill Dagher, the Coral Springs detective, stood over by the kitchen, texting on his cell. As far as the locals were concerned, this investigation was over: The report had been taken and

Elaine Emerson's name entered into NCIC as a missing juvi. The kid didn't want to come home, plain and simple, and one look at the mom and the history on the sis gave them a pretty good idea why. It was up to a social worker with the Department of Children and Families to fix what had made her want to leave in the first place. "Did she tell you what class they were in?" Bobby asked. "Where the girl lived? A last name? Did she maybe mention a theater or the name of the movie they were going to?"

Debbie blew a plume of smoke in his face. "No, no, no, and no."

The more questions Debbie LaManna didn't know the answer to, the more she felt judged as a shitty mother, the more she clammed up. Not quite the distraught "I'll do anything I can to help you find her" reaction one might expect, but then again, if ten years heading up Crimes Against Children had taught Bobby anything, it was that there was no "right" way to behave when a kid disappears. He'd watched perfect moms sob perfectly on national television, begging for help in finding their babies, only to cuff the same coldhearted bitches a few hours later in an interrogation room. He'd also seen the polar opposite—the reserved, seemingly heartless mother who can't cry. The one whose indifference is viewed as most suspicious in the eyes of the public at large. The one who holds every emotion tightly in check because, Bobby knew, like a shattered vase gingerly held together with glue, if you removed just one piece, just one, then all the others would collapse and you'd never be able to put it back together again. So no reaction—or lack thereof—was ever "normal" in these investigations. But even if he wasn't necessarily reading "sinister" in Debra LaManna's overt hostility, it still wasn't a good feeling to dislike the parent of the kid you were looking for. In this instance, it just made it that much easier to see why the girl might've left in the first place.

"And none of Elaine's friends who you've contacted"—he looked down at his notepad to read back the names—"Molly Brosnan, Melissa and Erica Weber, Theresa M.—none of them know this girl Karen/Carly or how to get in touch with her?"

Debbie sighed loudly. "Like I said, it's a different school than last year. Melissa, Erica, Molly—those girls are Lainey's friends from the old house."

"Lainey? That's Elaine's nickname?" Zo piped in from his seat on a fold-up chair next to the couch where he'd been sitting quietly for most of the interview.

Debbie shrugged. "Her friends call her that."

"New house, new school, new friends. How'd Lainey feel about all that change?" Bobby asked.

Debbie rolled her eyes again. "Please. She wasn't happy about it. Is that what you wanna hear? That she was unhappy? OK. She was unhappy. Drama, drama, drama. It's all about the drama at this age. She had to leave her friends a few miles away and change schools, but we all have to make sacrifices. If that's the worst shit she has to face as a kid, then she's damn lucky."

"What about boyfriends?" Bobby asked.

"She doesn't have a boyfriend."

"You're sure? Is there a boy she likes, maybe?"

Debbie cut him off with a dismissive wave. "I'm very sure."

Behind where she sat on the couch, Bobby could see into the kitchen. Empty beer bottles dotted the countertop and spilled out of the top of the garbage can. He'd already spotted the portable cooler next to the couch. "Does Elaine do any drugs? Drink alcohol?"

She stared at him like he had three heads. "Look, if you just call some of the girls in her new school, you'll find her. Just do some police work and call the principal and have him give you a class list or something. I can even look it over and see if I recognize the name or something. You know, maybe I'll recognize it if I see it? I'm sure Elaine is at that girl's house, I'm sure she's not doing crack or drinking, and I'm sure I can deal with her once she's back home. I just need some help in getting those names, you know?"

Even with an older kid who'd run amok, the lady was still wearing a sturdy pair of parent blinders. She might not have come out and said it, but if Bobby had a buck for every time he heard a parent tell him, "My kid wouldn't do that," he'd be a millionaire. *My kid wouldn't have sex at fourteen. My kid wouldn't do meth. My kid wouldn't smoke. My kid wouldn't drive drunk. My kid wouldn't shoplift.* Statistics said 80 percent of teens have screwed up in at least one of the above categories, but not My Kid. Like the invisible ghost "Not Me" who wreaked havoc in the Family Circle comic strip, it was always Somebody Else who was a fuckup or a bad influence. There wasn't much more he was going to extract from the lady.

"Where's your husband?" Zo asked.

"Work."

"Where was he Friday night?" Bobby asked.

"Don't know, don't care," Debbie replied icily. "And I'm thinking that's none of you all's business, seeing that Elaine's the one who didn't come home."

Ouch. He'd definitely hit a nerve, but Debra LaManna wasn't giving up anything to the cops without a fight, including dirt on her cheating spouse. "We'll need to talk to him," Bobby replied, closing his notebook. Then he added, "I'm not gonna beat around the bush, Mrs. LaManna. I know you've had some problems with your older daughter, so let me ask you, is there a reason why Lainey might not want to come back home?"

Debbie's eyes flared like a cornered animal's. "You cops are something else! I don't know who the hell you think you are. Because my older daughter's a piece of shit means my younger one is, too? Means I'm a horrible mother and the kids just can't wait to get away from me?"

The grandfather clock started to chime the hours down the hall and no one said anything.

Debbie stroked the ponytail, eyes focused on her lap. She sucked in a sniffle. It was the closest thing to an emotion Bobby had seen besides pissed off. "Just find her. Please," she said finally in a small voice.

"That's what we're trying to do," Bobby replied softly. "Does Elaine have access to a computer?"

"In her room. Todd gave her his when we moved."

"What's her email address?"

"Damned if I know. I don't email her."

"Does she have a MySpace? Facebook? An AOL networking account?"

"What?" she asked. It was obvious Debbie didn't know what he was talking about. Most parents didn't. Obviously, no one had asked her that question yet. But then, Bobby suddenly caught a flicker of something other than confusion in her brown eyes. A flash of fear, perhaps, like the mother of a toddler who's wandered out of sight in the backyard suddenly remembers that her neighbor has an in-ground pool. *MySpace, Facebook, AOL.* A creepy mental picture had popped into Debra LaManna's head, perhaps from newspaper articles she'd read or *Dateline* segments she'd caught, expounding the dangers of the Internet for kids. "No, no," she said defiantly, catching herself, not letting her thoughts go there. "Elaine's allowed to use the computer for homework and some video games—that's it."

"Do you mind then if we take a look at the computer, as well as her room?" Bobby asked.

She shrugged again. The fear was dismissed as quickly as it had surfaced. The lone tear had dried up. *My kid wouldn't do that. My kid knows not to go in the pool when an adult's not around.* "G'head. It's a mess. She's a slob, you know."

"Thanks for your cooperation, Debbie," Bobby finished, rising.

"Third room on the left," she answered without looking up, as she crushed out another cigarette.

14

Thumbtacked posters of Robert Pattinson and Taylor Lautner from *Twilight* movie fame, a swashbuckling Johnny Depp from *Pirates of the Caribbean*, a coy Jesse McCartney, and most of the cast from the TV show *Heroes* covered light pink walls. The twin bed was not just unmade—it was everywhere, as if it had exploded when the alarm clock went off. Cardboard boxes filled with books, comics, trophies, and what looked like miscellaneous junk were pushed against the walls. Clothes spilled from other boxes. Obviously Elaine had not completely unpacked yet from her move. The drawers were not emptied, but Bobby knew it would be pointless to ask Mom what, if anything, was missing.

The computer sat on a cluttered desktop. Back when Bobby was in high school, the telephone and good old-fashioned note-passing were the communication methods of choice. Now it was all about email, texting, IMing, blogging. All you ever wanted to know about most teens could be found either in their cell phones or somewhere on the hard drive of their computer. And, more specifically, usually on a MySpace or Facebook page—social-networking sites that allowed subscribers, notoriously teens and young adults, the opportunity to have their own "space" on the World Wide Web. A place where they could post pictures, "blog" their thoughts, voice their worries, pontificate on

politics or global warming or yesterday's hangover, identify their hobbies, list their friends, and name their enemies. It was all there—down
to addresses, birthdays, telephone numbers, schools, places of work,
and where they'd be hanging out on Friday night. A treasure trove of
information—you just had to know where to look. Which was the
problem with most parents—they didn't have a clue. Technology had
stepped on the gas in the past fifteen years and left most of them way
behind, still fiddling with the "start" button on their Windows
Explorer.

He flipped on the computer and sifted through the pile of papers
on the desk as it warmed up: poems, math problems, science work-
sheets, a social studies test with a big D on it, doodle sheets filled
with red hearts. Finding a printout with Elaine's email address would
sure make life a lot easier than a search-and-guess game. Colored
pencil drawings of pandas and ferrets decorated the inside of the
desk's hutch. Pretty impressive, Bobby thought, for a kid who'd just
turned thirteen. If school continued to bottom out, all hope wasn't
lost—the girl had serious potential as an artist.

No email info in the stack. He opened the browser on her Internet
engine and pulled down the list of sites visited; www.myspace.com
popped up first. That meant it was the last site visited. That meant
she had an account. On the MySpace homepage he fiddled with
name combinations under the search button. He was pretty good at
what he did—after only a couple of tries he found what looked like
her under her nickname.

LAINEY
Headline: VAMPIRES AND FERRETS RULE!!!!
Orientation: Straight
Here For: Friends!
Gender: Female
Age: 16
Location: Coral Springs, Florida.
Profile Updated: October 22, 2009

The wrong age didn't faze him. To join MySpace you had to promise you were fourteen or older and enter a birthday accordingly. There
were no stats, but he'd be willing to guess that a good chunk of the
"teens" on MySpace were closer to eleven or twelve. He'd interviewed
kids as young as eight or nine who'd had MySpace or Facebook pages,
with profiles that claimed they were thirty-five. He clicked on Lainey's
profile. It wasn't set to private, which meant anybody surfing MySpace
could see it, member or not. Gwen Stefani's "The Sweet Escape" started
to play. Brilliantly colored butterflies served as wallpaper. Pictures of
young teenage girls, who he guessed were friends from Ramblewood,
decorated the site—laughing, kissing the camera, making goofy faces,
giving the finger, trying to look way too sexy for thirteen-year-olds.
Cigarettes dangled from the slight fingers of a couple of girls; others
toasted the camera with strange-looking drinks. A girl with long,
brown, coffee-colored hair was in a few of the group shots. A girl who
looked a lot more grown up than the lanky, awkward fifth grader in the
photo Bobby held in his hand. Each picture was captioned with inside
jokes:

Molly B. & the ferret bandits!
No one home . . . LAINBRAIN
Bite me, please!!!
E and M pre-concert jelly-jollies . . .
Was I just at the bathroom and then at the stairs?

He looked at his notepad: *Molly Brosnan, Erica and Melissa Weber, Theresa—Last Name Unknown.* He glanced around the room.
Vampire movie posters adorned the walls. Sketches of ferrets decorated the inside of her hutch. He definitely had the right site.

Tiny picture icons of Lainey's favorite movies, rock bands, and
books covered half of the first page. Blogs, angst, and general teenage
drama filled the next two. Akin to a lot of MySpace pages, her site
read like a diary, supplemented with postings and comments from
her fellow MySpace friends. Three pages told Bobby more about

Elaine Emerson than her mother could manage to communicate to police over the past eight hours.

"Whatcha got?" Zo asked, standing over his shoulder.

"She's got a MySpace. Last time she logged in was Thursday, the day before she went to the movies with the unknown friend. Hates school. Can't stand bro, stepdad's an asshole, mom's a bitch, and sis is pretty cool. Loves animals and her BFFs. Typical shit. Wishes she could, quote, 'just get the hell away from here.' Endquote."

"Sounds like that's just what she did," Zo muttered. "So much for, '*my* daughter wouldn't do that.' Damn, you're quick. Are we out of here, then?"

"Not yet. She's got eighty-four names on her friend space, but only six in her top," Bobby said, hitting the print button. MySpace was a membership-only social networking site, which meant that to communicate with somebody on MySpace you had to have an account yourself. Having upward of eighty friends was not exceptional, particularly for a teenager—some members were known to have hundreds, even thousands, of "friends" in their friend space, most of whom they'd never even chatted with. But a lot of "friends" in Lainey's network would potentially mean a lot of legwork tracking everyone down if the kid didn't resurface, even though chances were she didn't actually know 90 percent of the people she had friended. "Let's see who Mom can ID from this. And let me look for a more recent picture of our girl." Under "start" Bobby ran a Find Files search to look for jpegs—electronic photos—on the computer's hard drive.

"Whoa," said Zo, as dozens of tiny pictures swarmed the screen.

"'Whoa' is right," Bobby said as he clicked on one of the images. A picture of a girl dressed in tight jeans and a midriff-baring, see-through white T-shirt, a sexy smile on her bright red lips, filled the screen. Her long brown hair, the color of coffee ice cream, was blown sleek, and straight. Her big, brown, made-up eyes flirted coyly with the camera. Long red fingernails beckoned Bobby and Zo to come a little closer.

"She sure don't look thirteen," Zo said with a low whistle.

"That's the idea," Bobby answered. "There's about thirty of these on here."

"A photo shoot?"

"Yup."

"For who?"

"That's the question that needs an answer."

"The boyfriend Mom insists she doesn't have?" Zo asked.

"Bingo."

"Great," Zo said with a chuckle. "I'll let you be the one to tell her that she doesn't know shit about her daughter. She already doesn't like you."

"She's in good company. Let me look at those MySpace friends again." Bobby went back to the first page of Elaine's MySpace. Most of the names under her top six were recognizable as friends from the neighborhood that her mother had told him about: Molly B., Melly, eRica, Teri, Manda-Panda. Each had a picture of a teenage girl accompanying the name. Only one name on the top six was missing a picture. Only one name stood out from the rest and caught his attention.

"I think we might have found our boyfriend," he said slowly, spinning the chair around to face Zo. "Looks like little Lainey's been making nice with someone who calls himself El Capitan."

15

Lainey's head hurt so bad. It felt like someone was inside her skull, pounding away with a hammer on the bone, just trying to get the hell out. The more aware she became of it, the worse the pain got.

Tap, tap, tap.

Louder, louder, louder.

Bang, bang, bang.

Somewhere, someplace not too far away, she could hear the sound of humming. Pleasant, do-the-dishes humming. And a TV. The chatter of a TV. Louder, louder, louder, as if someone were turning up the volume very slowly.

The Israelites have saved the women! And Moses, well, he says, "So you've spared all the women? Why? Why, when they're the very ones who have caused a plague to strike the Lord's people! Why did you spare them?"

Then, the shuffle of heavy footsteps across the room. Across creaky wood floors. Coming closer. Coming toward her.

Lainey lay very, very still. Could the person see her? Where was she? She tried to open her eyes. They were so heavy.

. . . She smells good. She sure looks good. She doesn't seem evil. What man would not be tempted? Like many of us in our everyday lives, Moses must make a difficult decision. A terrible decision . . .

She tried again. Something was wrong. Very wrong.

Her eyes would not open.

Was she dreaming? Was she blind? She reached to touch them and couldn't. Her arms would not move. She struggled, but they would only tug. She felt the burning in her wrists and realized her arms were bound.

She was tied up.

. . . He tells them, "Slay, therefore, every male child and every woman who has had intercourse with a man. But you may spare and keep for yourselves all girls who had no intercourse with a man . . . "

She could sense the flashes of bright light and she heard the familiar click of a shutter lens. Over and over and over. Someone was taking pictures of her.

"Help me," she tried, but only a croaked whisper escaped. Her words were as heavy as her eyelids and her throat burned. The footsteps slowed, circling her. Closer, closer. Like a cat might approach a wounded bird, studying it, watching it.

Playing with it.

The shaking started first in her knees, then like a fast-moving electrical current, the fear traveled up her spine, to her arms, her neck, her head, her teeth, until her whole body was trembling uncontrollably. She thought of the time in fifth grade when she had caught the flu and couldn't stop shivering even under a dozen blankets. Her mom had let her watch Scooby-Doo cartoons all day in her bed, and gotten her wonton soup from the Chinese restaurant.

Mommy, Mommy, I'll be good, I swear. I won't do anything bad ever again. Ever. I'll take care of Bradley. I'll never complain. I'll get straight A's again. I'll listen. Just let this stop. Make it all go away, Mommy, please, please, please . . . please, oh God, let me wake up!

She felt him standing there, maybe inches away, maybe a foot or two at the most, watching. Then he sat down next to her, and the mattress or cushion she was on sunk just a little under his weight. The smell of his cologne was nauseating. Paco Rabanne again. Was it Zach? Her mind raced. Was it the same person from the car? Could there be more than one? Could there be more than one person in the room right now, watching with him? Who had taken the pictures? She could hear him breathing hard but trying not to, the feel of his warm breath as it fell on her face. His breath smelled like . . . Spaghet-tiO's? She wanted to turn off her senses, just hear and smell and feel nothing. She wished everything were black again. She wished she could cry.

The TV began to scream. *Remember that! We are watching you! Are you pure in both thought and deed?*

Then his hand reached out and gently stroked the hair off her forehead. His trembling fingers were moist and warm.

"Ssshh now, pretty girl," said the Devil in a singsong voice. "You're home now. Right where you belong."

16

It was his gut that told Bobby something was wrong. More wrong than just a troubled teen from a dysfunctional family not wanting to come home anymore.

Bobby knew the stats all too well: Every forty seconds in the U.S. a child is reported missing. That's 800,000 kids a year; 2,185 each and every day. Most of them were runaways. And those were just the kids lucky enough to be *reported* missing. The National Runaway Switchboard put the actual number of runaways—often called "throwaways" because nobody cared if they didn't come home—closer to somewhere between 1.6 and 2.8 million a year.

Faced with overwhelming statistics like that, it wasn't too far a leap to the conclusion that Elaine Emerson had run away from home. She fit the classic profile: a dysfunctional family, a history of running away and truancy by an older sibling, a family history of alcohol and drug use, a recent drop in grades and cutting classes, a recent relocation away from friends, and a tumultuous relationship with her parents, one of whom was a step. Her disappearance had taken Mom almost two days to finally get herself worried enough to call in, which—translated into cop language—meant this was probably not the first time little Lainey had decided not to come home. Add in the sexy photos and a Web space where the kid rants about her "asshole" stepdad, "bitch" mom, and how she wants to "get the hell away from here," and the missing-juvi classification in NCIC was certainly justifiable. Statistically speaking, little Elaine should be walking back through that front door in the next twelve to twenty-four hours.

Bobby leaned back in Elaine's desk chair and looked out her bedroom window. The skateboard contest down the block had moved and was now in the street right outside. Given the neighborhood, he figured one or more of the kids had recognized the Crown Vic, Taurus, and Grand Am as undercovers and had edged the game closer to see what was happening. Maybe they knew about the troubles with Liza Emerson. Maybe they knew of some troubles with Lainey. He made a mental note to talk to them as soon as he finished up with the computer.

Of course, not every kid who went missing in the night left on his or her own volition. Bobby closed his eyes and rubbed his temples. He'd spent the past decade working those very cases. The worst of the worst. The cases that turned parents into zombies, lives into nightmares. While most of the 800,000 kids reported missing each year turned out to be runaways, approximately 8 percent—69,000— were classified as abductions. Although the great majority of those ultimately figured to be parental abductions—like when a parent skips town with a kid in violation of a custody agreement—a sobering 12,000 kids who disappeared were identified as victims of nonfamilial abductions. Nonfamilial, as in taken by an acquaintance, a family friend, or—in the more remote and more terrifying cases for the public at large—a complete stranger. Plucked off of school buses or snatched from busy malls. Those were the cases that instantly made headlines and triggered AMBER Alerts. And for good reason. While the stereotypical kidnapping was statistically rare, it was almost always deadly.

With the explosive growth of the Internet over the past fifteen years, Bobby had seen a rise in nonfamilial abductions. Bad guys didn't need to lurk around corners anymore or peek in windows in the middle of the night. Now they walked straight through a kid's front door in broad daylight. Right past overprotective Mom and Dad and into Junior's bedroom via the computer. There they could exchange pictures, chat, play video games, and discover all sorts of neat things about the "distant" teen whose parents didn't understand him. The World Wide Web had spawned a new hunting ground for predators. Trolling kiddie chat rooms and adolescent networking sites at their leisure, they picked off their prey from the millions of profiles offered on MySpace and Facebook, where smiling victims provided as much scrumptious detail about themselves as dinner entrées on a menu. Sitting behind a keyboard and monitor, this new breed of predator could pretend to be anyone: An eighteen-year-old boy; a twelve-year-old girl; a talent agent; Eminem's best friend. They took advantage of the naïveté of kids and the ignorance of their parents—gaining the former's trust, and then slowly, carefully exploiting the relationship, subtly grooming their victims for the ultimate, devastating high: a face-to-face meeting. And then, with just the simple click of a button, disappeared forever back into the black abyss of cyberspace once lives were destroyed and the police were finally called in.

Bobby looked around the pink bedroom with its typical teenage decor. Lainey hadn't lived here long, and she'd moved under protest, but she *had* hung up her posters and wall art, which meant she considered this room home. She was definitely a slob, but although her clothes spilled haphazardly out of drawers and boxes, they hadn't been packed up into a suitcase. It would be hard to figure out what was missing, but, perhaps more important, *if* anything was missing. And then there was the faceless photo in her friend space. Bobby was willing to bet the bank ElCapitan just might be the intended recipient of all those sexy pictures. And of course, perhaps the most troubling fact that he kept coming back to was also the most innocuous one: The girl hadn't logged back on to her MySpace since the day before she'd disappeared. He knew that, for teenagers, MySpace was their social lifeline. A kid wouldn't just abandon it for a few days—unless she physically couldn't check it.

Obviously with more than 2,000 kids reported missing each day, not every face got slapped on a milk carton and not every kid got his or her physical description launched on traffic message boards across the nation via an AMBER Alert. The system would be critically over-loaded within minutes, and people would quickly grow desensitized and indifferent to the plight of yet another kid gone AWOL. AMBERs were reserved for the most urgent of situations, and a cop had to meet strict, three-pronged criteria to have one issued, and that included: (1) a belief the child was abducted; (2) a belief that she was at imminent risk for serious bodily injury or death; and (3) sufficient descriptive information about the kid, the suspect, and the abduction so that a public broadcast would actually help find her. Bobby tapped his note-pad. He didn't have enough to meet any one of the prongs with Elaine Emerson. He just had that familiar, heavy feeling in his gut.

Somewhere in between the panic-mode AMBER and the runaway code-word "missing juvi" entry in NCIC was a Missing Child Alert. In cases where you didn't have an abduction, but you had enough in-formation to believe the child was in imminent danger, you could re-quest a Missing Child Alert. While it didn't spark the same urgent, national "Oh shit!" response as an AMBER, it did trigger notifica-tions to the local media, neighborhood businesses, and community law enforcement agencies. But again, other than his agita, Bobby had no concrete reason to believe Elaine was in danger. An alert would definitely be a stretch. And based on the info they had right now, it would be much easier to just OK the missing-juvi report that Coral Springs had put into NCIC, grab his golf clubs, and call it a day.

"Veso just showed up," Zo said, popping his head back into the room from the hall, where he'd disappeared for the past ten minutes. "Fucking numb-nut got lost."

"Obviously a great detective," Bobby replied, not bothering to look up from the screen.

"Be nice."

"Fuck that. You be nice. I don't need a pet. Or an understudy."

Zo shook his head. Diplomacy was a tough tightrope to walk, and he was a shitty acrobat. "You almost done here?" he tried. "I got tick-ets to the Dolphins game at four."

"Just writing down a few things. I'm gonna try talking to some of these friends while I'm out here. And the step, too. See what the hell's up with him."

"OK, bro. You're the expert."

"Can you tell your boss that, please?"

Zo stepped into the room and closed the door behind him. He waited a long moment before he finally spoke. "I don't know how you deal with," he started, looking around, "this shit every day. Every day. Let me be honest with you, Bobby, my friend. I don't know how you do it. Especially after Katy. I don't know how you can function. It's like you're locking yourself in a freaking torture room every second of every day and forcing yourself to look at all the shit on the walls. It ain't healthy." He sat down on the edge of the bed and waited till the pregnant silence caused his friend to finally look over at him. "None of these cases, none of them, have a happy ending, man. None of them. You know that better than anyone. You bring 'em home, Bobby, that's true, all these . . . these kids. Dead or alive you bring 'em home, but what kind of life is that? I mean, what kind of career is that? 'Cause it's never a happy ending, even when it's supposed to be. And you know it. It's just the beginning of years of therapy for those who do make it home. I've worked a lot of squads, you know, in my years, a lot of different cases. Violent Crime, Terrorism, Narcotics, Organized Crime. You name it, and I've probably worked it. And I'm not saying they're easy, but you know, when you're working something like homicides—it sucks, there's blood and brains and bad shit—but at least you know the guy you're working for is dead. I mean, there's never any *hope* of finding him alive. It's depressing and all, and it's a dead body, yeah, yeah, yeah, but you never get that fucking *hope* ripped out of your chest, like you do in these kid cases. Over and over and over. What I'm saying is, why don't you look at the changes Foxx wants to make as a way out? As a long-overdue, I don't know . . . vacation? A chance to move on? Ain't nothing wrong with pushing some paper and taxiing governors around when they come to town. I know you don't want it. Hell, we all know—the director included and every suit in Tallahassee, too, as well as the freaking Fibbies—we all know that no one else can do this job as good as you. You're the best at what you do, man. But—well, fuck the Vesos of the world and Foxx if you think they're trying to squeeze you out—but, for LuAnn, for your own sanity, let someone else try."

Bobby said nothing. The whoops and hollers from the skateboard contest filled the strained silence. "Look, you brief the guy if you want to," he replied finally. "I already know he's a fuckup and I don't want him in here." Then he turned his attention back to the screen.

Zo let out a slow breath. "Whatever. I'll meet you outside when you're done."

After Zo walked out, Bobby leaned back in the desk chair and rubbed his tired eyes.

Not all of them. I don't bring them all home, Zo. And that's the problem. That's why I don't sleep anymore. I don't bring them all home and we both know it . . .

He flipped open his cell and dialed.

"Florida Missing Endangered Persons Information Clearing-house. Travis Hall."

"Hey there, Travis, it's Bobby Dees down in Miami."

"Hey, Agent Dees. I haven't heard from you in a while. I thought you wasn't working these cases no more, after, you know, well, after what, um, happened . . . " Travis's voice had slowed and stumbled off, like he'd just gotten the memo that it wasn't such a hot idea to be saying what he was saying.

"Don't believe everything you hear, Travis." Bobby sat up. "I'm still alive and well down here in the Conch Republic."

"Glad to hear it. You doing OK, Bobby?"

Bobby ignored that question, because any idiot with half a brain and knowledge of the hell he'd been through the past year wouldn't have asked it in the first place. "Listen, Travis," he said dismissively, fingering the two pictures of Elaine Emerson he had printed out on the desk. Before and After. The Geek and the Lolita. Stretch or not, he'd learned over the years to listen to his gut. It was the one partner that never let him down. "I'm gonna need you to put out a Missing Child Alert on one Elaine Louise Emerson. White female, DOB 8/27/96 . . . "

17

"So you don't have any idea where she might be?" Bobby asked the skinny girl with the mop of wet, dark blond curls. Just past the sky-blue foyer where he stood, an arched entryway led into the kitchen. Plastic grocery bags were piled on the countertop and he could see something was boiling on the stove. The house smelled like meatloaf and onions.

"Nuh-uh," the teen replied, rubbing her head with a Scooby-Doo beach towel. Her identical twin sister, the mirror image standing next to her in the same exact bathing suit and shorts, just shook her head.

"Her mother called here last night at almost eleven o'clock looking for her," Mrs. Weber added with a frown. "I told Debbie I didn't think the girls had seen Elaine in a couple of weeks. They were at their dad's Friday and Saturday and they had a swim meet this morning. They just got home." She rubbed the shoulders of either Melissa or Erica. Bobby couldn't tell the difference. "Do you think she ran away? Is that it?"

"Do you think that might be the case?" Bobby countered.

Mrs. Weber shrugged. "Elaine's mother parents differently than me, let's just say that. Her older sister is a mess, you know. A mess. Drugs and boys. That's why I don't like the girls over there. There's no supervision. Elaine is very sweet, but . . ."

Bobby waited.

"The apple never falls far from the tree, is all I'm saying."

"Mom! Lainey's not like that!" one of the girls protested.

"Mo-o-mm!" Mrs. Weber said, mimicking her daughter. "We'll see," she added softly, casting a skeptical glance over at Bobby.

"Well, give me a call if you or the girls or their friends hear from her." Bobby handed her a business card. "Or if you come into any ideas on who this Carla or Karen might be. Any at all. My cell's on there." He turned to the twins. "Before I forget, do you two email with Lainey?"

They even nodded in unison. *It must be weird to have two girl-friends who are identical in every way*, Bobby thought. It might be a grown man's fantasy, but a little overwhelming on a kid; you were always outnumbered. "Can I get her address from you? Her mom didn't know it."

Mrs. Weber rolled her eyes.

"Sure. It's LainBrain96@msn.com," the one with the towel said.

"Thanks. Your other friend, Molly—I stopped by her house, but no one's home."

"Her grandma died. She's in New Mexico," Scooby-Doo offered.

"Nebraska," her sister corrected.

"Nuh-uh. It's New something."

"New York?" Mrs. Weber asked. "New Jersey?"

The first one shrugged. "Maybe. She's there till Monday, I think. Or maybe Tuesday."

"Does she have a cell?" Bobby asked.

"Yeah, but she got caught texting in science lab on Friday. Mrs. Rohr took it and she can't get it back till she does detention next Wednesday."

"What's that number?"

Mrs. Weber's eyes rolled once again.

"It's 954–695–4229."

"One last question. Does Lainey have a boyfriend?"

Both girls giggled, embarrassed. "No."

"Another last question, then: Does she like boys?"

"Well, yeah, she's not a lesbo or anything."

"Erica . . ." Mrs. Weber scolded.

"But she doesn't have a boyfriend. The boys we know are idiots. She likes Rob Pattinson," finished Melissa.

Bobby slid the notepad into his jacket pocket. "All right. Thanks for your time, girls."

He'd no sooner stepped out the door when it closed behind him with a thud. Amelia Weber wanted to keep whatever bad germs Bobby was carrying far away from her kids. A cop at her door on a Sunday afternoon inquiring about her daughters' friend was not in the parenting plan.

He climbed into the Grand Am and looked at the dashboard clock. It was 2:24. Almost fifteen hours since Elaine Emerson had been reported missing, and more than fifty-four hours since she'd been dropped at the corner to wait for the school bus by her mother. If she didn't surface by tomorrow morning, he'd visit Sawgrass Middle, talk to her classmates, and try to track down every Karen or Carla on the register to see who Lainey might've gone home with.

But right now, it was time to go car shopping. He slipped on his sunglasses and pulled away from the curb, as Lainey's identical friends, standing side by side, watched expressionless from the living room window.

18

Even though Bobby had never met the guy before, or even seen a photo, he already had an idea what the CarMax regional salesman of the month looked like. Maybe it was the used-car profession that had him drawing mental pictures, or Todd LaManna's choice of a spouse, but stocky, short, temperamental, and balding were the first four adjectives that came to mind.

Bobby stepped through the automatic glass front doors, and there he was: stocky, short, temperamental, and balding, dressed in a blue CarMax polo shirt and khakis, a clipboard in hand and a slippery smile on his ruddy, full face. Like a shark to chum, he rushed over to Bobby before one of his clipboard-carrying brethren could get there first.

"Hey there, guy!" Todd called out in a booming voice. "Thinking about helping out the economy today?"

"Todd Anthony LaManna?" Bobby asked, reaching for his badge.

The apple cheeks deflated. Even if he wanted to, he couldn't deny it. There was a big "Todd" patch sewn on his polo. "What's this about?" he asked, the self-assured boom reduced to a decibel above a whisper.

"This is about your stepdaughter Elaine, Mr. LaManna. Do you have a moment?"

"Not really," he replied, looking around. Besides salesmen, there was no one else in the showroom. "I'm kinda busy."

"Make one."

They stepped into a glass-enclosed cubby that looked out onto the showroom. It was a room where deals were made. Where sales managers, in full view of the anxious customer back on the sales floor, but without the sound effects, finally "gave up" their lowest price after bullshit haggling with the tenacious salesman of the month. It'd been a while since Bobby had bought a car, but the games were always the same, whatever dealership you were in or car you were buying.

But there was no dealing today. "I guess she's not home yet," Todd said quietly as he closed the blinds.

"And I'm guessing you're not too worried about that," Bobby answered.

"Oh, man, don't make this about me. Debbie said she's at a friend's house. She's probably having a good time, is all, and doesn't want to come home and do shit around the house all day. I know I wouldn't." He chuckled. "Why do ya think I work weekends?"

Bobby didn't laugh back. "Any idea where Elaine might be?"

Todd shrugged. "She's Debbie's kid. She told her mother she was going out with some girl from school. I don't know who her friends are; I don't ask. I tried getting involved with the other one, Liza, ya know? To be a good parent and all. Lot of damn good it did me. That little—" He cut himself off. "She's constantly getting in trouble and me worrying about her don't do no good. She doesn't listen to anyone. I've had the cops in my life ever since the first time I caught her smoking weed."

"When was the last time you spoke with Elaine?"

"I've been working a lot lately. I haven't even seen her since, I don't know, like, maybe Wednesday? It's gotta be, I'm thinking here, maybe Wednesday morning before she went to school. That's when I talked to her. Told her to clean her friggin' room up."

"What's your relationship with Elaine?"

"What?" Todd replied, his face crimson. "Fine, great. Normal."

"Normal?"

"I'm feeling trapped here. Like you're asking me questions for a reason."

"There's no reason to feel trapped," Bobby replied. "She's a teenager. Just trying to figure out what kind of relationship you two had. Why she might have gone running, if that's what she did do."

"Well, you said it. She's a teenager. It was, our relationship was, well . . . normal. She was pretty busy with school stuff and friends and she was, ya know, a real bitch sometimes, but aren't all women?" He laughed uneasily. "You know, when they get on the rag."

Bobby looked at him a long time. "I don't think so."

"Whatever. I don't want to say no more." Todd shook his head.

"I ran your name through a couple of systems, Todd," Bobby began. "And guess what? I caught a fish. Domestic battery. Solicitation. And a really interesting arrest just last year. L & L. You know what that stands for, Todd?"

"That was dropped to a fucking disorderly, man!"

"Lewd and lascivious conduct," Bobby continued.

"I was, you know, peeing against a wall when this dyke cop walked up! That's all it was! I was taking a leak!" Todd ran his hands through the few strands of hair he had left on his head. His round face was shiny with sweat.

"Less than twenty feet from a playground?"

"I'm no child molester, man! They overcharged me! It was a disorderly!"

"Where were you Friday night?"

"What? What's that got to do with anything?"

"Where were you Friday night?"

Todd began to tap his shaking hand against his thigh. "I was, I was, well, out with the boys, ya know? We went out for a beer."

"Your wife doesn't know where you were. Not a clue, Todd."

"Fuck this! I don't need this shit. When the—when Elaine gets her ass home, her mother can deal with her. I don't need this bullshit from any more of her fucking kids!"

"I'll need the names of those boyfriends of yours. And the name of the bar"—Bobby paused deliberately—"or other fine establishment you were holed up in."

"If I'm not under arrest, then I'm going back to work," Todd declared as he headed toward the door. "I know my rights."

"I'm sure you do. I'll need those names, Todd."

The cubby walls shook as the glass door slammed behind him and an angry Todd LaManna stormed back out into the showroom.

19

The FDLE Miami Regional Operations Center—a three-story, cluttered, chaotic maze of squad bays, secretarial pools, Formica cubbies, and conference rooms—was normally bustling with activity. Home to more than fifty special agents—plus analysts, lawyers, and support staff—there was always a handheld radio squawking, a cell phone ringing, or a meeting being held somewhere in the building.

At eight o'clock on a Sunday night it was empty.

Bobby looked up from the stack of crap on his desk that never seemed to get smaller and out his open office door into the deserted squad bay. Ten metal desks, each stacked with their own case files and clutter, sat abandoned in the darkness. It was so quiet he could hear the traffic buzz by outside on the Dolphin Expressway. The light from his office spilled across The Board, the montage of missing-children flyers that covered a corkboard on the far back wall.

He was supposed to be "flexed-off" till the first of the month—meaning he had already worked his 160 hours for October—but the Emerson girl had given him a reason to drop in, write a report, and finish up a few things. Once that happened, he couldn't just ignore the stack of case files on his desk. Even when command told you to go home because the state was too broke to pay overtime, you were never really off, anyway. He had a charging conference Friday with the State Attorney's

Office on a multi-agency child-porn investigation, a depo on an upcoming murder trial, and a complicated search warrant to walk through Legal. Whether FDLE paid him or not, each case had to be attended to. So a thirty-minute stop-in had slipped into a four-hour-and-counting layover. He rubbed his eyes and downed the rest of his Red Bull. Guaranteed to have him pacing floors at four a.m., but he didn't want to nod off on the drive home. Insomnia was a vicious cycle: dog-tired when you couldn't afford to be, wide awake when the rest of the world shut it down. He logged out of AIMS, the Automated Information Management System he was working in, and shoved the stack of files into his briefcase. Then as the computer started to shut down, a thought came to him. He logged back in, hopped on the Internet, and clicked onto Elaine Emerson's MySpace. She still hadn't logged back on to her profile. He went to her My Friends space and clicked on the only friend that was missing a picture.

ELCAPITAN
Headline: JETS SUCK!
Orientation: Totally Straight
Here For: My Peeps and Bettys
Gender: Male
Age: 17
Location: Jupiter, Florida.
Profile Updated: October 18, 2009

Bobby scanned the Web page, set against a backdrop of an animated Rolling Stones tongue logo that kept licking provocatively at the computer screen. Although the profile was public, like Lainey's, which meant anyone could see it, unlike Lainey's, the personal info was pretty scant. His name was Zach, he lived in Jupiter, and he played high school varsity football, basketball, and baseball. He also played bass guitar. That was it. Musical tastes, gauging from the album covers that dotted a corner of his page, ranged from Nine Inch Nails to The Fray. Most kids spilled every detail of their lives on MySpace. This looked like the one kid who'd actually listened to warnings about personal data going out over the Internet . . .

Who was this Zach? That was the question that Bobby's gut still demanded an answer to. That and where the hell Todd LaManna had spent last Friday night. The used-car salesman of the month was definitely a creep and he was definitely holding back. Whether that had anything to do with his missing stepdaughter or the prospective demise of his marriage had yet to be seen. As far as finding out more about the lone boy who had made it to the top of Lainey's friend space, even with a subpoena Bobby wouldn't be able to get the email registration info from MySpace corporate till probably Tuesday or Wednesday at the earliest. Unless it was an absolute emergency, even favors took a few days. But with a little ingenuity and help from the World Wide Web, he figured he could maybe beat out the lawyers and find the kid himself.

A few searches on Google led him to Jupiter high schools and the Jupiter High Web site. From there it was on to their athletic programs and then a click on football. There was no player roster, but there was a link to a *Palm Beach Post* news article about high school football stars.

And there he was. Zachary Cusano. #17. A Jupiter High Warrior to Watch. Position: Wide Receiver, Team Captain. Class: Senior. A 6′1," 190-pound, blond-haired, blue-eyed, smiling All-American Warrior. Bobby then Googled "Zachary Cusano basketball Jupiter High School." And there he was again—#17, saving the day last January when the Warriors basketball team tromped the Boynton Beach Tigers. Another search under baseball found Zachary Cusano, a pitcher, expected to start this spring for the Warriors. An accompanying article named some of Zach's favorite hobbies besides sports. Jamming with his band on bass guitar was first up.

Same description, same picture. Same kid.

No wonder Lainey was taking sexy pictures of herself. The kid was good-looking, no doubt. There was also no doubt he was seventeen. Bobby wondered if the star high school football player knew his cyber pen pal was jailbait.

He ran an Autotrack using the kid's name and birth date and . . . *voila!* Zachary M. Cusano, son of Violet and Thomas Cusano, residing at 124 Poinciana Lane, Jupiter, Florida. Social security number, school records, driving history, and a very brief employment history that consisted of a two-month stint at a CVS pharmacy popped up on the screen. No accompanying juvenile criminal history. That was good.

He printed everything out, including the pictures from the *Palm Beach Post* article, and slid them into the Emerson folder. He'd still subpoena the kid's MySpace registration info, but at least he had something—someone—to start with, if necessary. If Lainey didn't come home.

With his briefcase in hand, he headed out the door. Dinner was probably past cold and LuAnn beyond pissed. He'd pick up flowers and a bottle of her favorite wine from Publix on the way home. Maybe a couple of glasses would help bring him down from the Red Bull. At The Board he stopped, raised a finger to his lips, and then ran it over a picture in the center of the sea of flyers. Over the beaming, beautiful young girl with long, straight, dusty blond hair and baby-blue eyes, and a smile that took over her whole face. KATHERINE "KATY" ANNE DEES. DOB: 06/13/1992. MISSING FROM: Fort Lauderdale, FL. DATE MISSING: 11/19/08. AGE AT DISAPPEARANCE: 16 years, 5 months. The red-inked caption on the top of the flyer read MISSING CHILD/RUNAWAY.

Bobby kissed his little girl goodnight, flipped off the lights, and headed on home.

20

"Phone's dead," said Clint Fortune, the FDLE tech agent. "Dead or off."

"Her mom says she never charges it," Bobby replied into the Nextel as he pulled up to a light.

"That makes sense, then. It's dead. It can't pick up a signal from the cell towers."

Bobby took a slug of coffee. "When was the last phone call? In and out."

"Um, hold up," Clint replied through clenched teeth, his lips obviously wrapped around a cigarette, which they always were. There was a rustle of papers in the background. "OK. Last call out was 23rd October at 5:31 p.m. to a 954–695–4229. Lasted forty-five seconds. What was the 23rd? Friday?"

"Yeah."

"Last incoming was from 954–914–5544. That was also on the 23rd. Came in at 5:15 p.m., lasted two minutes. I have back to October 2nd, which was the end of the last billing cycle."

"How about texts?"

"Yup. Sheets of 'em. Good luck on that. You'll need to hire a fucking teenage girl to help you translate all the BFFs and OMGs into sentences." Clint laughed so hard he started to cough.

Bobby closed his eyes. It felt like someone had just punched him in the chest. "Yeah."

"What's this kid? A runaway?"

"Looks like it."

"Well, I told Candy, my contact at Verizon, that it was a possible abduction. Real urgent. That's how she got me this shit so fast. Probably gonna bitch if she doesn't see something on the news tonight."

"I appreciate the help, Clint. I just didn't wanna wait a week or two. And anything's possible. I did put a Missing Child Alert out on the kid."

"I thought you said she was a runaway."

"Probably is, but some things just aren't sitting right with me."

"You go with that, then, Shep."

Shep stood for Shepherd, an old, old nickname that Bobby didn't want to hear anymore. But it was hard to tell people that without opening up another can of worms. "Thanks, Clint."

"Any word on your kid?"

Damn. The can was open and wriggling all over the fucking floor. He should've expected that question; he heard it at least every couple of days. "Nope. Nothing new. Thanks for asking."

It was hard to believe it was almost a year since that miserable Friday afternoon when Katy hadn't come home from school. The rainy day a week before Thanksgiving when life stopped having meaning. Every day he relived every second of the fight he and LuAnn had had with her the night before she left—what he could have done differently, what he should have done differently. Why he hadn't. Clint had pulled cell records for him that night, too. And for months after, just in case Katy turned her phone back on.

"Hey, you need me to do anything for you, Bobby, I'm right here for ya."

"Yeah. I appreciate that, Clint. Look, I'll swing by the office this afternoon to pick up the rest of those cell records."

"Isn't that new guy from Pensacola, Veso, working with you now? I can give them to him if you're gonna be seeing him today. He's a shortie, man. Wears his pants too high, too. Hope he don't have one of those Napoleon complexes."

"Haven't met him," Bobby replied quietly. Obviously yesterday's little heart-to-heart with Zo hadn't meant shit—Veso was still hanging around looking for something to do. "I wasn't planning on it, either, Clint. Just leave them on my desk."

"I promised Candy a subpoena."

"On second thought," Bobby replied, as he pulled into a parking space, "tell Veso to get you that subpoena. That'll give him something to do."

Clint laughed again. "Will do."

Sawgrass Middle was so close to the Everglades, Bobby half expected to see a few gators running around the lawn with the hundreds of kids who were pouring off of buses and out of cars, lethargically making their way up the roundabout and through the school's double doors. Kids were everywhere. It was like working a wiretap, he thought as he waded through the herd, catching snippets of conversation along the way: *Skating soooo sucked Saturday . . . Meghan told Alexis that Joanne's brother was a pervert and now she won't talk to . . . Cesar is grounded because he told his grandma to fuck off, so he . . .* Just as he made it to the hall where the front office was, the bell rang overhead. Bodies scattered in a dozen directions. Thirty seconds later there was apocalypse quiet in the white maze of stuccoed outdoor hallways.

Mr. Cochran in Guidance had the school records ready and waiting for him. All fifteen hundred students were alphabetized by their first names and organized by grade and class. One hundred and seventy-four Carries, Carlas, Courtneys, Karens, Katherines, Kristys and Christines. Seventeen were in Lainey's classes. All of them were called to the front office. Only four of them even knew who she was. No one had gone to the movies with her.

Next were the teachers. Elaine had attended all her classes Friday. No one had noticed anything strange. She had made no new friends that the teachers could recall. No boyfriends in the halls or lunchroom. She also had no enemies. A loner. Underachiever. Sweet. Lazy. Unmotivated. Shy. Invisible. One sour-pussed teacher's observation was "troubled," but couldn't or wouldn't say why. All were saddened by her disappearance. None were all that surprised.

A check with Lainey's afternoon bus driver proved fruitless. With three different afternoon bus routes for elementary, middle, and high school, over 150 kids to drop off and four dozen stops to make, she was lucky to remember her own name at the end of the day. She had no idea who Lainey was, much less whether she had been on Friday's afternoon bus.

Bobby thanked each of the teachers for their time, put the records in his briefcase, and a half-hour later pulled into the Ring-A-Ling Answering Service parking lot in Tamarac. It was a little after twelve. He waited in the reception area for almost ten minutes until Debbie LaManna could officially take her break and join him outside under the concrete overhang. The cement patio where they stood was littered with cigarette butts and gum stains.

"I don't know. Could be any of these. Did you talk to them all?" she asked, exasperated, as she combed through the list of Sawgrass students and puffed away on a Marlboro.

"We talked to the ones Elaine had classes with. No luck."

"Well, talk to the others."

"Do any of them pop out at you?"

She shook her head.

"What's your husband's cell phone number, Debbie? I spoke to Todd yesterday at work, but I have some follow-up questions I'd like to get with him on, and I'm betting he doesn't want me asking them at the dealership again."

She took a deep drag of her cigarette and her eyes narrowed. "He told me you were there. He said you told him I didn't know where he was on Friday. That I told you to ask about him and Elaine, how they got along and all."

"You don't know where he was on Friday," Bobby replied.

"That's none of your business, though. I'll handle that."

Bobby sighed. "What's his cell, Debbie?"

She blew out a plume of smoke. "It's 914–5544," she answered begrudgingly.

He didn't have to look at his notes. He remembered the numbers Clint had spewed over the phone this morning. The outgoing call Lainey had made at 5:30 was to Molly Brosnan's number. He'd recognized that right off. The incoming call fifteen minutes earlier was from one Todd Anthony LaManna. The same person who had said he hadn't seen or spoken to his stepdaughter for two days before she disappeared.

"So where was he?" she asked finally.

"Don't know yet. Did Lainey ever talk to you about their relationship?" Bobby looked at her hard.

Her eyes narrowed. "Todd told me you'd try that, you know, try and bring in the time he was arrested. Todd's not like that. He wouldn't do that stuff, you know, with kids." But she hesitated before she made the last statement.

Bobby folded the list from Sawgrass back up and slid it into his pocket. "OK. I'll be back in touch," he said, as he started toward the car. "I still haven't heard from your other daughter, Liza."

"She said she doesn't have any idea where Elaine is or who her friends are."

"I still need to hear it from her."

"That's it? That's all you're gonna do?" Debbie yelled after him as he crossed the parking lot. "I called that detective from Coral Springs, you know. He said Elaine's a runaway. Said if I want her home, I may want to hire a fucking private detective!"

Bobby turned and looked back at Debbie LaManna's drained face, her hard, tired eyes. How do you tell a mother that there just isn't enough time or manpower to look for all the troubled kids who don't want to be found? That the grim runaway statistics he was so intimately familiar with say that if her kid's not back home in thirty-six hours, then there's a frightening reality she's not ever coming back? That with every passing hour her daughter's on the street she's more and more likely to become a victim of sexual exploitation, prostitution, child porn? And how do you tell a wife who doesn't want to hear it that there's a chance her latest husband just might like her adolescent daughters a lot more than he likes her? That maybe, just maybe, he's the reason they don't want to come home?

You don't. Not yet.

"I'll be in touch when I have something more," he replied.

"Damn cops!" Debbie barked. Then she flicked her cigarette at the ground by his feet and marched back inside.

21

Bobby pulled up the drive of a palatial, apricot-colored, Tuscan-style house. Massive stone lions greeted him as he passed through a dramatic arched entry, covered in plum-colored bougainvillea. Under the porte cochere sat a black BMW and a Land Cruiser. Hand-painted Spanish tiles above the doorbell confirmed he was at the right place: 124 Poinciana Lane. He rang the bell. Through the beveled glass and wrought-iron doors he caught the bright-colored flashes from a TV playing somewhere in the house.

A tall, good-looking teenager with sun-streaked blond, wavy hair that just kissed his shoulders answered the door. He was dressed in jeans and a Warriors T-shirt. The kid was built like a truck. "Zachary Cusano?" Bobby asked.

"Yeah," the teen answered.

"I'm Special Agent Robert Dees with the Florida Department of Law Enforcement," Bobby said, holding up the gold badge that dangled around his neck. "I'd like to ask you a few questions, son. Are your parents—"

"Mooommm!" the kid yelled.

Two seconds later, Mom arrived from the kitchen decked out in an apron. As soon as she spotted the badge, she stopped dead in her tracks and yelled, "Tom! There's a police officer on the porch!" with the same fear and reproach as if there had been a Palmetto bug on her carpet.

Dad hurried in behind her, fresh from the office, wearing a five-hundred-dollar suit, drink in hand. "Officer? What's all this about?" he asked, quickly ushering Bobby into the house and out of sight of the neighbors.

"I wanted to talk to Zachary about a girl he's been communicating with on his MySpace, Mr. Cusano. Her name is Elaine Emerson."

As soon as the door closed, Dad handed Bobby a business card. *Thomas T. Cusano, Esq., Cusano Whitticker Levinsky, Attorneys at Law.* A lawyer. How convenient.

"Zachary?" his mother asked.

"I don't know any girl named Elaine," Zach started.

"Hold on, Zach," Tom Cusano barked, holding up his hand to stop his son from talking. "What's the matter? What happened to this girl?"

"I didn't say anything happened to her, Mr. Cusano," Bobby replied.

"I'm assuming something happened, or you wouldn't be standing in my living room."

"She didn't come home after school Friday."

"Zachary?" his mother asked again, the pitch higher.

"I don't know any Elaine!"

"Maybe you know her as Lainey, then," Bobby offered. "Or Lain-Brain."

The hand was up again. "Zach, hold on. Don't answer that."

"Zachary?" Mrs. Cusano was furiously wiping her flour-dusted hands on the apron.

"I don't know what this guy's talking about, Dad. I don't know any Lainey!"

"Do you have a MySpace?" Bobby asked.

"Yeah," Zachary answered slowly.

"Why don't you pull it up so we can look at it?"

"Zachary?"

"Mom! Stop! I don't know this girl!"

"I don't think so," said Tom Cusano, shaking his head. "I'm not liking where this is going. No computer. No way. If you have some sort of proof my son knows this missing girl, then let us know."

Lawyers always messed up everything. "Listen, Mr. Cusano," Bobby replied, his tone polite, yet firm, "you're right. It's not going anywhere. But it will. Remember, I'm here because I've already seen Zachary's MySpace."

Zachary didn't wait for his father to answer. He ran into his room, grabbed his laptop, and brought it into the dining room. With shaking fingers, he clicked onto MySpace. "Zach's Page" appeared in green block letters over a screen filled with dancing surfboards. A running blog took up over six pages, as did pictures of partying teenagers. He had 485 names in his friend space; over 65 in his top.

"Who are all those people?" Violet Cusano asked, confused.

"I dunno, Mom," Zach replied with a shrug. "Kids from school, people I met online. Friends, you know."

Bobby scanned the Web page. There was no LainBrain. No reference to an Elaine or Molly or Liza or any other name that had crossed Lainey's MySpace. No pictures of Lainey or her friends. "Is this yours, too?" he asked with a frown, as he clicked onto the Rolling Stones profile of the Zach from Jupiter who played football, basketball, baseball, and guitar.

"No," said the kid, with a shake of his head. "It's not mine and I don't know this guy. Or that Lainey girl you were talking about."

"Where were you Friday night?" Bobby asked.

"Zach," his father cautioned.

Zachary looked back and forth at his parents. "I . . . I . . . I don't know. I was . . . Wait! I was on that field trip, remember? You picked me up at school at eleven when the bus came in. We—Ms. Grainger, my science class—we went to Cape Canaveral to see the space place. NASA, you know?"

"That's right!" his mother exclaimed giddily. "You were on a field trip!"

"He wasn't even home," his father said matter-of-factly to Bobby. But relief betrayed his don't-fuck-with-me lawyer voice. "It wasn't him," he added with a smile.

As if Bobby hadn't already figured that out.

22

The graphic crime-scene photos were carefully arranged across Bobby's desk, alongside the three clear evidence bags sealed with red tape that he'd signed out of the evidence locker that morning. He fingered the smooth outer edge of the bag that contained the crumpled Trojan wrapper, dotted with flecks of blood, his cell phone cradled between his neck and cheek. "Calm down, Belle," he said into the phone. He motioned to Zo to start putting everything back into the cardboard trial box marked State v. Marcus Stahl.

"Damn it, Bobby, it's ten o'clock and she's not home! I . . . I can't take this anymore. I really can't!" LuAnn replied, her voice cracking. He knew she was already pacing the floor, twisting her long blond hair over and over and over in her slight fingers. That's what LuAnn did when she was nervous.

"Where did she say she was going after school?" Bobby asked. He rubbed his eyes and tossed the evidence bag into the trial box.

"The library, for some project. Social studies—it was a social studies project. I let her go, even though she's supposed to be grounded. But she should have been home hours ago!"

"Did you check there?"

"It closed two hours ago."

"Maybe she went home with Lilly. Maybe Lilly's mom picked them

up." Across the desk from him, Zo was mouthing, "What's happening?"
in between bites of his burger. Bobby shook his head.

"I called, Bobby. Lilly went to the library with Dahlia. Not Katy.
Katy wasn't there."

He started to shove the reports and crime-scene photos into an ac-
cordion folder. "Maybe she's with—"

"Don't! Don't even say it!"

"I'm gonna have to call him, LuAnn."

"I'll kill her. She better not be with him." She started to cry.

"OK, OK, Belle. Don't worry. Try her cell again," he said as he
stuffed the accordion folder under his arm, grabbed his briefcase, and
rushed out the squad bay, past Zo and the other task force members.
He took the stairs two at a time, his stomach churning like someone
had poured acid down his throat. Something was wrong. He could feel
it. He pushed open the doors into the MROC lobby. "I'm coming home.
I'm coming home, honey . . . "

The semi in the middle lane next to him blasted his horn. Bobby
looked around at the cars flying by him on I-95. He'd drifted again. He
sped up, forcing himself to focus on the present. He crunched two
Pepcids and downed the chalky taste with a dose of hot coffee. He
shook the terrible memory out of his head and passed the trucker.

"Give it time, Robert," LuAnn's shrink had said the first and last
time Bobby had seen him, swallowed up in the executive leather
chair he was sitting in, a patronizing smile on his thin, pasty face. "It
really does heal all wounds." Bobby had wanted to pummel him. As if
it was all that simple. *Just give it time and all will be fine.* Each night
was longer than the one before; each day an emotional battle to get
through. And the not knowing was pure hell. He'd worked Crimes
Against Children for too long and knew all too well just what the
worst-possible-case scenario looked like. It was a reality far darker
than any nightmare Dr. Give-It-Time could ever imagine.

He slugged down another jolt of caffeine as his thoughts returned
to Elaine Emerson. While he still had to confirm the field trip with
Jupiter High, he already knew Zachary Cusano wasn't lying. The kid

had never heard of, much less met, Lainey. So either he had the wrong seventeen-year-old Zach from Jupiter who played varsity baseball and basketball, was captain of the football team, and strummed the bass guitar, or . . .

That person did not exist.

That would potentially present a host of other problems. But, even if it were true, even if this ElCapitan proved to be an Internet phantom, he still had no evidence that Lainey had ever met the guy. Or that the sexy pictures she'd taken were for him. Kids chatted with hundreds, sometimes thousands, of people from all over the world on the Web. People whose paths they never crossed outside of an Internet connection.

It was almost eleven by the time he got home. Nilla, Katy's Australian shepherd mix, greeted him at the door with a yawn and a stretch, then followed it up with a few kisses and tail thwacks. Nilla was a Humane Society survivor—Katy had rescued her from death row when she was just a pup. Out of the dozens of sad, woeful eyes, Katy had picked Nilla as her birthday present and the dog had never forgotten. From the second they'd brought her home, Nilla was Katy's pooch. They played together, swam together, slept together. Even when Katy turned into a teenager and found friends and boys and parties more interesting than racing her dog to the end of the pool, Nilla was there—just like tonight—waiting patiently at the door for Katy to finally find her way back home.

LuAnn had to be at work at seven a.m., so chances were she'd popped a Xanax and was out like a light. "Come on, girl, let's get us some salami," Bobby whispered as he headed into the kitchen with Nilla at his heels. The Nextel chirped just as he excavated the makings of a sub from the fridge. "Dees."

It was Zo. "You need to turn on the TV."

LuAnn walked into the kitchen just then in her pajamas. "Hey, Belle," Bobby said softly. "I thought you'd be sleeping."

"You really need to see this," she replied, flicking on the kitchen TV.

On the television screen, Debbie LaManna, Elaine's mom, was wiping tears off her cheeks. " . . . I asked them to call the FBI, you know?" Bobby recognized the pink bedspread that she sat on, the movie posters that decorated the walls behind her. "Those cops all told me to hire a private investigator if I want to find her. Can you believe that? A private investigator? Don't ask me what the police are doing. They're doing nothing! Nothing at all!"

The picture then cut to the lobby of MROC. "Debra LaManna only wants to find her little girl," said the handsome reporter with the salt-and-pepper black hair and piercing blue eyes. His manicured dark eyebrows were deep-set in a concerned *V*. "A little girl who loves her friends, her teddy bears, her family, vampire movies, and love stories. Yet no one wants to help her look. That's because Lainey is just like any one of the hundreds of other Florida runaways that Channel 6 has discovered listed on the Florida Department of Law Enforcement's Web site."

The reporter moved through the empty, sun-streaked lobby, over to a wall-mounted glass case that held FBI wanted posters, along with a montage of missing children/endangered runaway flyers. The piece had obviously been filmed that afternoon. Bobby's jaw clenched. *Why had no one called him?*

"Here at FDLE headquarters in Miami, an entire squad of special agents investigates what's known as Crimes Against Children. Those crimes specifically include missing and exploited kids. Posted right here in their lobby are pictures of some of the missing." The camera panned across the faces as names were read aloud. "Eva Wackett, Shania Davis, Valerie Gomez, Kathleen Thomas, Gale Sampson, Nikole Krupa. And there are more, not posted here in the lobby, but still listed as missing on the FDLE Web site. Dozens and dozens of missing kids, right here in South Florida. Right in our own backyard. Some have been missing for months; some for years. And no one's looking for them. Now there's one more name to add to the list. Only this time, one mother has had enough and is speaking out."

The reporter held up the fifth-grade picture of a bespectacled young Lainey sitting at her school desk two years ago. Bobby shook his head. He knew how bad this was sounding. "Thirteen-year-old Elaine Emerson. Debra LaManna can only wait and hope. Hope that perhaps Lainey is more important than the dozens of other kids South Florida law enforcement have written off and thrown away. Reporting for Channel 6, WTVJ, I'm Mark Felding."

"Son of a . . . ," Bobby started.

"I'll make the coffee," LuAnn said quietly, reaching for the bag of Dunkin' Donuts.

"How about them apples?" Zo asked with a loud sigh before Bobby could finish his sentence. "Tell LuAnn to brew a pot. I'm coming over. I do believe, Shep, that the shit has just hit the fan."

23

The man leaned forward and stared hard at the TV. He was on the news! Not just any news, but the eleven o'clock news! Prime-fucking-time news! He looked at his watch and thoughtfully rubbed his jaw. It was only 11:07. Maybe not *the* top story, but *a* top story! He did it!

He sipped at his warm milk and rubbed his tummy. He thought about how many people saw the news. Hundreds of thousands? Definitely. Much more than that. This was no time to be modest. Millions! Millions of people were sitting in their beds right now, watching this sniveling excuse for a mother boo-hoo about the daughter who just last week she couldn't give two shits about, and wondering what might have happened to her. Where she might have gone, why she might have left. If she was dead. Crying just so she could squeeze off a few more seconds from her fifteen minutes of fame, maybe tape it so she could critique with her friends how good she looked on camera.

Then the camera slowly panned down the FDLE hall and across the sweet faces of the others.

He fell back into his recliner. The names—they didn't matter. But those . . . faces. He always remembered a pretty face. Every detail, every curve, every line, every dimple, every perfectly misshapen freckle.

He felt himself getting excited at just the thought of what he had done and he closed his eyes. The sweat began to gather on his forehead and the back of his neck and he licked his dry lips as his hand went to his pants. He clutched at the tweed upholstery on the chair's arm with his free hand, twisting it in his clammy, shaking fingers.

No. This was not the way. This was not the time. He opened his eyes. There was work to be done. He sat up and reached for the canvas roll-up bag of paintbrushes on the side table next to him.

On the television, a photo of his pretty little princess flashed on the screen. Only it wasn't really her. He stuffed the bag of brushes into the back pocket of his jeans. Lainey was much, much prettier than that. She'd made herself that way for him. She'd made sure she was special. Different than the rest.

The piece ended and the dramatic music ushered in a commercial break. He stood and brought the empty milk glass and cookie plate over to the sink. He hummed the catchy music as he washed the plate and glass and set them out to dry. Then he turned off the TV and reached for his utility case and the Jullian French easel that sat by the cellar door.

That's when he heard her. Loud and nasally, piercing the delicious quiet.

"Noooooo . . . somebody . . . please . . . "

He covered his ears with his hands. He'd have to go down there and stop that. All that noise, noise, noise, noise! It was disappointing, no doubt. The spoiling process had already begun. Like a perfect, round red apple set out on a countertop couldn't just sit there and be perfect forever, but instead had to rot slowly, from the inside out, until the peel bruised and darkened, and the inside decomposed to a mealy, tasteless mush. Annoyed, he shoved the easel under his arm and reached for the basement door handle. On the outside his little princess still looked perfect and red and ripe, but on the inside she was already moaning, whining, complaining.

Rotting away.

It was a fucking shame. The pretty ones never lasted long.

24

"Why wasn't an AMBER Alert issued, Agent Dees?"

The Miami Regional Operations Center training room was only maybe half-filled with reporters, but every eye in it turned to SAS Bobby Dees, who was positioned as far away as possible from Regional Director Trent Foxx, his entourage of yes-men—headed by none other than recent Pensacola transplant Frank Veso—and half the brass of the Coral Springs Police Department on the makeshift press dais. Bobby and his Stepford replacement had finally met that morning, exchanging forced pleasantries in the elevator before rushing off to a series of frenzied "damage control" meetings, run by public relations department heads and people who didn't have a clue about missing-kid protocol. Clint was right—standing at about five-three with lifts in, Veso was a shortie. With a scruffy white beard, oversize ears, and his pants pulled up practically under his armpits, he looked like a gnome. All that was missing was the pointy red hat. Probably on directive from Foxx, Veso had followed Bobby around from useless meeting to useless meeting like a silent shadow all morning, frowning and scribbling pages and pages of notes on a legal pad but saying nothing. Now here they all were, gathered together in a noon knee-jerk press conference that Bobby had not recommended and wanted no part of. He had hoped all questions would just be directed at Foxx, a media hound who had taken command of the podium the second he saw it, but once again, luck was not on his side.

"As I already explained to y'all, Agent Dees and Detective Dagher did not feel that was necessary," Foxx started, irritation beginning to fray his hospitable Panhandle twang. The forced soft smile was melting. The director liked the limelight well enough, but he had no use for the obnoxious Miami media. Up where he came from, cops told the press what was a good story, not vice versa. Last night's investigative-report bullshit would never have happened in Santa Rosa. But Foxx was new to the area and he was no fool—you caught more flies with honey than you did vinegar. He was only a couple of weeks into a long five-year commitment in this city, and he knew if you didn't want every news channel and paper in town looking for ways to make you sound like a moron, you smiled when you took their questions and you bitched when the door closed on their tails. "You see now—"

"No, I'd like to hear from Agent Dees, please," interrupted the reporter. It was the guy who had done last night's interview with a teary Debbie LaManna. His curly hair was even fluffier in person, and of course the on-camera makeup gave him a deep tan any tourist would envy. "Mark Felding, Channel 6. I'd like to hear from Agent Dees, if we could. He's running this investigation, is he not?"

Foxx shrugged and stepped back from the podium. The smile was gone.

"Elaine Emerson did not and does not meet the strict protocol to issue an AMBER. That is reserved for abductions," Bobby responded as he leaned over into the mike.

"But you issued a Missing Child Alert, so you had to believe Elaine was in some sort of danger," Felding persisted. "What made you think that, Agent Dees? Did you have any additional information?"

The Missing Child Alert had been the domino that notified the local media that Elaine was missing, which caused Channel 6's Felding to follow up on-air with her sad sack of a mother yesterday afternoon. That led to the tears at eleven, followed by the barrage of phone calls from frantic parents and slick reporters chumming for a juicy link back to the Makala Jarvis mess, which ultimately brought on the shit storm that Zo had predicted. Hours had been wasted and nothing had been accomplished. "I did that in an abundance of caution," Bobby replied.

"Doesn't a Missing Child Alert mean a juvenile's in imminent danger?" Felding repeated. "So what is it about Elaine's disappearance that made you believe she was, or is, at risk of bodily harm?"

There was a reason why they didn't let Bobby head up the press conferences—he was no good at either the smiles or the sugarcoating. "I know you're looking for a story here, Mr. Felding," he replied testily, "one way or another. Either law enforcement did too much, or did too little. But there's nothing to report. The investigation's ongoing, we are pursuing many avenues, which I'm not going to comment on, and hopefully with all the attention you have now focused on it, Elaine will see herself on the news and call home."

"Channel 6 has been conducting an investigative report on runaways in South Florida," Felding continued. "The first installment ran last night. There are literally hundreds of missing kids across the state that I've discovered on the FDLE Web site that nobody is looking for, Agent Dees. Hundreds. And over the years, I'm sure, thousands. My question for you, then, as the supervisor of the Crimes Against Children squad, and as a recognized national expert on child abductions, is why do some kids' disappearances get a full-blown investigation, with AMBER Alerts and organized volunteer searches, while other disappearances—like Adrianna Sweet, Eva Wackett, or Nikole Krupa—don't get the time of day?"

"Every case is different, Mr. Felding. There are many factors—the age of the child, the circumstances surrounding the disappearance—"

"Well, Eva Wackett went to the Dolphin Mall to meet friends and never came back. That never got any attention. Adrianna Sweet didn't come home from a friend's house in Miami. That never got any attention either. Of course Eva was in the foster-care system and Adrianna had a juvenile record for drug possession and a family that didn't give a damn. Maybe that's what mattered. Could that be it?"

"FDLE didn't work those cases, Mr. Felding." Bobby knew exactly what this asshole was trying to do, and his blood was beginning to boil.

"My point exactly. When is a case bad enough—or, rather, a kid important enough—to get turned over to the Crimes Against Children unit of FDLE?"

"A kid's socioeconomic status is not a determining factor in issuing an AMBER or starting an investigation, and you know it. Neither is race or heritage. You're breaking this down to a sound bite for the second installment of your investigative report, Mr. Felding. More than a million kids run away from home every year in this country. A million. There's just not enough manpower to go looking for teenagers who don't want to be found, is all."

"But why do some runaways—like your own daughter, Agent Dees—why do those kids get a full-blown investigation at taxpayers' expense, and others, like Elaine Emerson, get only a couple of perfunctory phone calls to the morgue and the hospitals?"

A buzz ran through the crowd.

Bobby gripped the podium with both hands, so hard his knuckles went white. The room was spinning. "Who the hell do you think you are, asking me that question?"

"That's enough! This is over," broke in Zo, pushing forward and wedging himself between Bobby and the podium. He clasped a firm hand on Bobby's shoulder and waved over the public information officer. "Thank you for your time, everyone. Please direct any further questions to our PIO, Leslie Mavrides."

Leslie hesitantly moved toward the podium.

"I knew that was gonna come up," Foxx grumbled to Matt Donofrio, the Coral Springs police chief, as the two of them quickly stepped off the dais and exited into a back hallway. "Jesus Christ . . . what a mess. That's all I need."

"I just want to know why some kids are being ignored!" called out Felding, looking around at the agents who were coming at him from the back of the room. "What if something more sinister is happening to these kids? What if they're not all just runaways? We'll never know, 'cause no one's looking for them!"

"Who the hell is this guy?" Bobby demanded, as Zo moved to get him off the dais. "Who the hell does he think he is?"

"I have a list," Felding shouted, waving a piece of paper above his head as the agents closed in. The cameras spun on him. "Nineteen girls—all fitting the same general description or same strange circumstances of disappearance! Nineteen, and I've just started to look! All local runaways on your Web site! I think they deserve an investigation, Agent Dees! They deserve someone to go looking for them," he said as he shook off the agents who ushered him toward the door. "Just like your daughter, Katherine. Don't you think?"

25

"I found out when I got to class this morning. Melissa told me, but, I mean, everyone knew. Everybody was asking me, you know, what happened to her. Then my dad called the school and said you wanted to talk to me." Molly Brosnan sat on the edge of her seat in the Ramblewood assistant principal's office, twisting her long Strawberry Shortcake locks through frosted blue fingertips. She chewed on a chapped lip.

Bobby leaned forward in the chair across from her, elbows resting on his knees. It was a little over an hour since he'd left the circus back down in Miami. Five minutes after he'd finally told a pissed-off, bitching Foxx to fuck off, Mark Brosnan had called to say Molly was back in town, so he'd jumped in the car and headed north to Coral Springs. There was no time to stop, no time to think about the bullshit that'd gone down that morning, and really no reason to stick around to see what squad or field office he was going to be reassigned to—assuming he still had a job at all after Foxx made a phone call to the commissioner. What a fall from grace. Exactly a year ago he had a great marriage, a beautiful daughter and was a "nationally recognized expert on child abductions," assisting everyone from the FBI to the Georgia State Police with missing kid cases. *Time* had done a piece on him as the 2007 recipient of both the Officer of the Year

Award for Missing and Exploited Children and Florida's Law Enforcement Officer of the Year. *People* had even named him a "Hero Among Us."

Look, Daddy, you're on the same page as Beyoncé! Katy had said in amazement when the tabloid came in the mail. *You're famous! You're a hero!*

But am I your hero, Kit-Kat?

Always, Daddy . . .

Now his marriage was crumbling, his daughter was gone, and he just might be in need of a job. "Molly, when was the last time you saw Lainey?"

"Saw her? Um, well, not this weekend, 'cause of my grandma, but I saw her last weekend. I went over to her house Saturday."

"And the last time you spoke with her?"

"The day before I lost my cell phone."

Mark Brosnan, Molly's dad, was standing across the room next to the assistant principal, his arms folded across his chest. He frowned and shot her a look.

"Well, I didn't lose it. My teacher took it on Friday," she added sheepishly. "I get it back tomorrow."

"What'd Lainey say? Did she tell you about plans she had over the weekend?" Bobby asked.

"We were gonna go to the mall, but then my grandma died and I went to New Orleans."

"What about a boy? Was there any boy she was dating?"

"No. Lainey wasn't dating anybody. There was a guy she liked, but, you know, she'd never even met him."

"Who?"

"I don't know. Just some guy she talked to on the Internet. I only know his name's Zach and he plays football. He's really cute, too."

"Is that the boy Lainey took the pictures for?"

Molly's face went beet red and she looked down at her shoes.

"I know about the pictures. Did you take them for her?" he prodded.

Molly nodded.

"What pictures, Molly?" her dad demanded, puzzled.

Molly shook her head. "Just Lainey looking pretty."

"How did Lainey communicate with Zach?" Bobby asked. "I've checked her AOL email account, but I didn't see any messages from either a Zach or ElCapitan."

"She IM'd him."

"On her cell?"

"No, 'cause her mom would check that sometimes and she didn't want her reading her messages. They IM'd on the computer, like we did. On Yahoo."

"This boy, this Zach"—Bobby tapped the file folder on his lap— "you said he's cute, but yet you never met him."

"He sent Lainey a picture. He's blond and, like, a surfer-looking guy."

Bobby opened the folder and found the picture of a casual, T-shirted Zachary Cusano he'd downloaded from the Internet baseball news article. "This him?"

Molly nodded. "That's the picture."

Bobby felt his heart speed up. He'd already verified that the real Zachary Cusano was looking at space shuttles a hundred or so miles to the north the night Lainey disappeared. "Was she going to meet him?"

"No, no. He lived, like, real far away. It took all of Lainey's nerves to even IM the guy a sentence. There's no way she'd go meet him."

"How'd she get along with her mom?"

Molly shrugged. "OK, I guess."

"Stepdad?"

Both Molly and her dad made a face.

"Lainey and Mr. LaManna don't . . . well, she doesn't really like him. Is it OK to say that?" Molly asked, looking over at her dad, who nodded. "He's just, he's hard on her and he can be really weird. Lainey avoids him. They had a big fight Thursday. She wasn't talking to him."

"Really?" Bobby asked. "Do you know what it was about?"

"He's just weird. He flipped out on her room, 'cause she locked the door on him."

"Would she run away from home?"

She shook her head. "Where would she go?"

"Molly," Bobby said quietly, "I pulled Lainey's cell records and they show her last call out was made to you Friday night. That was the last communication anyone has had with her."

"I didn't talk to her," Molly replied, her small voice catching. "I didn't have my phone. But she did leave a message. I checked my voice mail from my grandma's house. I guess it was kinda weird . . ." Her voice trailed off.

"Do you still have it?" her dad asked.

"No, but I remember it. She said I'd never guess where she was. She sounded real excited. Then someone called her name and she whispered she had to go and said not to call her back, that she'd call me." Molly looked over at her dad, as tears ran down her cheeks. "But she never did, Daddy. She never did."

26

"The email address used to open the MySpace account was elcapitan17@msn.com. The name was Zachary Cusano, with a street address of 69 Lollipop Lane, Jupiter, Florida," Clint said into the phone, taking a long drag on his cigarette. It was Thursday morning. Almost a week since Lainey hadn't come home.

"What the hell kind of address is that?"

"MySpace has over five million users, Bobby. They don't verify names, addresses, or ages."

"Let me guess," Bobby said, pulling in front of the white ranch. "The address is bogus."

"Of course."

"ISP?"

"No good, either."

"What about the connectivity history?"

"MSN says the connections are always from free WiFi locations. Coffeehouses, the Fort Lauderdale Airport, libraries. He's untraceable, Bobby. It's a ghost."

"Shit." Bobby slapped the steering wheel. "All right, Clint, I just pulled up to the kid's house. I got Zo and a tech behind me and a warrant in my pocket."

"That's a nice way to say, 'Good morning.'" Clint laughed.

"Let's just pray little Elaine didn't actually try to hook up with this guy. That would definitely not be good."

He walked up to the weathered door and knocked. Debbie opened it, leaning against the frame in her robe, blocking the barking golden retriever behind her from getting out. Or maybe Bobby from entering. Lainey's brother, Brad, watched wide-eyed in his pajamas from the kitchen as he slurped down a bowl of cereal. The circles were so bad under Debbie's eyes, she looked like someone had punched her. Given the history on the house and the husband, that was a definite possibility.

Bobby handed her a copy of the warrant. "We're here for the computer."

"So you're finally gonna do something? That shook you up the other night, I bet," Debbie snapped, her voice scratchy and slightly slurred, probably from lack of sleep and drinking too much.

"Again, permission would've made it easier."

"The freaking computer . . . what the hell you want with that? Waste of time. You should be out looking for who took her!" she yelled as Bobby, Zo, and the tech pushed past her and headed down the hall.

The bed was made, the room all prettied up. No doubt for the cameras that had been in here two days earlier. Bobby flipped on the computer, burned the hard drive onto the zip evidence disk, and sealed it in an evidence bag.

He didn't want to wait for a lab in Orlando to look for what he knew he could find himself in a matter of seconds. While he still had no concrete evidence Lainey had gone to meet this ElCapitan, he figured if he could just get a look at her last IMs, he'd know for sure. Unfortunately, most of the time on most of the search engines, IMs were gone the second you closed the program or shut down the computer. But on some Yahoo IM accounts, the default system would automatically save the last ten days' worth of Instant Messages.

He navigated Yahoo Messenger over to Lainey's My Yahoo. He launched into her IM settings and checked the date for archived messaging. Ten days. But the archive default was real-time sensitive, like the voice mail feature on a cell—it only went back ten days from the current date. Today was Thursday, October 29th. That would mean he could access stored IMs sent or received only through October 20th.

He launched into Lainey's account. A bunch of texts appeared. The screen name ElCapitan was everywhere. He quickly scanned through the chatter till he hit last Tuesday, October 20th, and his eyes fell on the texts he knew he was going to find.

ElCapitan says: have to meet u.

ElCapitan says: what about friday nite? wanna c Zombieland?

ElCapitan says: ill pick u up at school. weve played CS High b4. stay late and meet me @ 5:30 in the parking lot in back by the baseball field. ill b in a black BMW.

"Oh shit," said Zo, who was reading over Bobby's shoulder. "Her last phone call to her friend was at what time Friday?"

"5:31."

"That's not good. Maybe she didn't go through with it, though. Maybe she never showed. What's the last IM say? Is it from this piece of shit?"

Bobby scrolled down to the end. "Last IM was Thursday, October 22nd at 9:47 p.m. from . . . " His voice trailed off.

On the screen was the last message Lainey had received right before she disappeared.

ElCapitan says: c u 2morow ☺

27

Lainey was with him. No doubt about it. Now the question was, who exactly was he? And the even more important question, how do you find him, this faceless phantom who wreaked havoc over an Internet trafficked by millions of people each and every second of each and every day? A cyber-ghost who's smart enough to not just cover his tracks, but leave none at all?

Bobby watched the kids playing scrimmage on the Coral Springs High School football field. Everywhere he looked there were signs of life. Teenagers running track, reading books, hanging out in their cars. A completely different scene on a sunny Thursday afternoon than it apparently had been at dusk last Friday night, when no one had been around to see anything. He'd checked the storefronts on Sample, the homeowners across the street on Rock Island. He'd had security search the school's video surveillance tapes, and even the Coral Springs PD pull traffic cams, but there was nothing. Nothing at all.

Bobby had worked Internet abductions before—the endings were never good. Statistically, most violent crimes are perpetrated by someone the victim knows, either intimately or casually, so starting with the victim will usually lead you back to the bad guy. *Where did she hang out? What were her hobbies? Who were her friends? Who were her enemies?* But Internet stalkings didn't play by conventional rules. Most often, they began as random hunts in invisible chat rooms or through social-networking sites, where no one was who they said they were, witnesses didn't exist, and whole identities simply disappeared with the click of a mouse. Trails were electronic, not physical, and if the bad guy was experienced enough to know how not to leave one, then there was no way to track where he'd been or where he'd come from. It was like a masked stranger sneaking into a random home in the middle of the night, who leaves no fingerprints, no trace evidence, and no DNA behind. Short of someone squawking, the case was almost impossible to solve.

Bobby looked out on the expansive field, home to the Coral Springs Colts. Blue-and-green-skirted cheerleaders giggled and laughed as they practiced on the sidelines, oblivious to the guy with the badge and sport coat watching on the other side of the fence. Before she'd met Ray, Katy had been a cheerleader, too. Varsity St. Thomas Aquinas High School. She'd started out in gymnastics soon after learning how to walk, and then sometime before she was eight or nine, switched to cheering. The competition schedule was grueling, with meets that lasted entire weekends in cities all across Florida. Standing in the bleachers, his hand wrapped in LuAnn's, they'd watch with their hearts jammed in their throats as their only child flipped and twisted atop a pyramid of bodies. It was at one of those meets, watching one of those back tucks twenty feet in the air—watching as someone else caught his little girl as she spiraled with a smile to the ground—that Bobby first confronted perhaps the most frightening reality of all about parenting: He had no control.

"Every guy with a badge is looking, Bobby. Key West to Boynton. There's nothing."

"She can't just disappear, Zo; she's a sixteen-year-old kid. She's got nowhere to go, and—what?—maybe a few hundred bucks in her pocket from working at the fucking Dairy Queen?"

The Dairy Queen. That's where Katy had met that loser, Ray. Reinaldo Coon. The moment Bobby had met him—hovering over his daughter like a second layer of skin while she cleaned the Blizzard machine, watching her every move—he knew the kid was trouble. Barely eighteen, he had the confident swagger of either a rock star or a gang member, and the smirk of someone who just didn't give a shit who you were or what you wanted. Bobby knew even then that it was too late, that the spell had been cast and Katy was falling hard. Her baby-blue eyes followed badass Ray and his mop around the store like an obedient puppy. Perhaps she found his tattoos sexy, his defiance exciting, his cockiness assuring. If Bobby could go back and do one thing over in his life, it would be to tell Katy that she couldn't work at the fucking Dairy Queen.

Zo chose his next words carefully. "Looks like the two of them maybe thought it out, Bobby. There's no trace of the boy, either. Mom's still saying she hasn't heard from him in weeks. Says he moved out in November and she doesn't want him back."

"Bullshit." Bobby ran his hands through his hair. "She's lying. I'm gonna go over there and talk to her again . . . "

"No. No, you're not. She's already screaming lawsuit over you breaking her shit last week. You can't threaten 'em, Shep. No matter how good it feels to wrap your hands around her throat, or punch out her car window, you just can't do it. Scum like her is looking for a way to make your life hell."

There was a long, horrible silence. "It worked, Zo," Bobby said softly as he looked out the door of his office at the smiling faces on The Board across the hall. They were no longer photos of Somebody Else's Kid. "My life is hell now . . . "

The sun was starting to slip out west. The football players had trudged inside; the cheerleaders had stopped cheering. Across the street and down the block, porch lights were coming on. A couple of homes had already lit the jack-o'-lanterns on their stoops, and tremendous blow-up witches and ghosts were puffing to life on green lawns sprinkled with leaves. Halloween was just a couple days off. He'd almost forgotten, or maybe tried not to remember the fun, kid-friendly holiday that used to be his favorite. It wasn't so long ago that Katy had been a princess in a sparkly Sleeping Beauty costume, stepping out the door with no front teeth, giddily swinging her trick-or-treat bag. He kicked the fence and turned back toward the car and the emptying parking lot. He was no closer to answers than he had been yesterday. On either case.

"But why do some runaways—like your own daughter, Agent Dees—why do those kids get a full-blown investigation at taxpayers' expense, and others, like Elaine Emerson, get only a couple of perfunctory phone calls to the morgue and the hospitals?"

That asshole reporter's words from Tuesday kept repeating in his head, as they had all day. Who the hell did that guy think he was? Maybe he shouldn't let it get to him—Katy's disappearance had triggered a Missing Child Alert and had made a blurb in the local section of the *Herald*. Everyone in the South Florida media knew she'd run away. Even *People* ran an update in its MailBag section. And the guy did have a point, even if it stung to hear it. Why were runaways right up there with barking-dog complaints on a department's priority list? Why were the final case disposition stats for them so dismal? Why were so many teens not even reported missing? And why was that somehow acceptable?

Nineteen girls so far, all fitting the same general description.

His Nextel beeped as he climbed into his car. "Dees."

It was Zo. "Yo, Bobby, listen up. I'm sitting here at MROC at my desk, getting ready to head on home, when Duty puts a call back from someone who you won't believe is looking for you."

"What? Who?"

"That dick reporter from the other day. Felding. The guy's all freaked out. I ask him what he wants, and, well, you really ain't gonna believe the weird shit he's telling me . . . "

28

Mark Felding sat anxiously on the edge of his seat in front of Zo's desk. The hands that held the oversize manila envelope on his lap were shaking; the deep makeup tan was gone, the color completely drained from his face. Bobby had noticed before that on-air person-alities always looked a lot smaller in person than they did on the Sony in your living room. TV had a way of making even a midget seem larger than life.

"I got the mail late today," Mark said, fumbling for words. "I was in editing on my special-report piece and then went to my mailbox. I'm not sure when it came in. I didn't know who to call at first, to tell you the truth, but then I saw the slip of paper with Agent Dees's name on it . . ." He stopped himself, as if he didn't want to go any fur-ther. "I put it back in there. In the envelope."

"How do you know this has anything to do with what you're working on?" Zo asked, shooting a look over at Bobby, who stood at a distance in a corner, holding up a wall. Present, but removed. Chan-nel 6 Super Reporter might not have been that far off base when he'd said what he'd said Tuesday morning, but that didn't mean Bobby wanted to be in a room again with him.

"The note that was paper-clipped to the top of the picture said, 'Nice piece, Mark.' The South Florida runaway story is the only thing

I've been working on. And of course," he said, nodding at the envelope as he passed it to Zo across the desk, "it has a young, you know, girl in it."

The mailer had already been torn open. Zo flipped it upside down and, with latexed fingers, slid out a folded piece of what looked like stiff cloth or canvas. A strip of newspaper gently fluttered to the desktop. He picked it up. "It's cut from the paper," he said, passing it to Bobby. "It's your name."

Bobby slid on a glove and held up the thin slip of newspaper.

FDLE SPECIAL AGENT SUPERVISOR ROBERT DEES

Zo carefully unfolded the cloth canvas. Thick, colorful paint covered one side. He took a step back. "What the hell?" he snapped in disgust.

"I told you it was sick!" Mark piped up, pointing at the picture. "I told you! I mean, Jesus Christ!"

Clumsy streaks of yellow colored a happy-face T-shirt, indigo blue filled in the skin-tight jeans the model—or whoever she was—was wearing. She was seated on what looked like a metal stool, coils of rope dangling from each wrist, just above her outstretched hands. The palms were smeared with streaks of red paint. She was a brunette, with dark waves that spilled over her shoulders, and a long platinum streak that ran down from the center of her head, like the comic book character Alexandra from *Josie and the Pussycats*.

But it was the face, or lack thereof, that made Bobby's blood run cold.

The mouth was open and contorted, just like in the disturbing Edvard Munch painting, *The Scream*. Two gaping black holes existed where her eyes should have been; red drops of paint dripped down her cheeks.

Bobby knew what it was right away.

It was a portrait.

29

"The paint's oil based. That much I know," Zo remarked.

"Art major?" Bobby asked, surprised.

"Nah. I dabble. Hoping to retire with my paintbrush to a fishing shack and an eccentric life in the Keys one day. Also, until it completely dries, you can smell oil a mile away."

"You never really know a person," Bobby commented. "That makes you more of an expert than me, then. I don't even color. So, what's your opinion?"

"He's no Picasso, but he's also no paint-by-numbers novice. My guess is he's had training. Art school or classes."

"We'll get it to the lab and see if we can get a brand on the paint. Maybe pick up some trace evidence. Same with the newspaper clip and the note."

Mark sat there looking bewildered. "Has this guy done anything? I mean, is this girl real? Is she a real person?"

Bobby stared at the painting. "Don't know, Mr. Felding. Hope not."

"Do you recognize her? Is she missing?"

"How the hell can anyone recognize that?" Zo asked. "She has no freaking face. It's probably just a Halloween nut trying to shake your station down for some airtime. The freaks come out in full force this time of year."

"Well, it's not going to work. I'm not letting that get on the air," Mark replied quietly.

Bobby stared at him. "A reporter with a spine and a set of morals? That's novel."

"We get a lot of dements looking for airtime, Agent Dees. You'd be surprised how much garbage we don't broadcast." Mark gestured toward the desk. "Even when it is news."

"Well, I'm not comfortable with just sitting here and saying it's nothing," Bobby remarked after a minute, turning his attention back to the painting. "I want to know it's nothing. Look behind her, here, Zo. There's a window, right? You can see the top three towers of what sure as hell looks like the CenTrust building. The blue water of the bay, and this white curve here? What's that? A building? The American Airlines arena, maybe? If this is a portrait and the artist painted it as he saw it, including what he saw out the window, then where the hell is he?"

"He's gotta be downtown Miami," Zo muttered. "Real close to the arena. From this angle and height, it looks like he's on a high floor, which would make him northeast of the CenTrust."

Bobby thought for a second. "The room itself's a bust. Tan paint. No pictures on the walls. What's that white thing on the floor behind her?"

"Looks like a mattress," Zo replied.

"A mattress? So it's gotta be either an apartment or—"

"A hotel," Zo finished. "Hey, isn't there a Days Inn or Best Western on Biscayne that's slated to come down one of these days? Close to the arena?"

Bobby nodded and reached for his jacket. "It's the old Regal. It's been on the demo block now for six months, held up in litigation. It's about fifteen stories, totally abandoned, and in a shit part of town. In other words, it's perfect."

30

The Regal All-Suites Hotel sat at an odd angle, in an odd part of downtown Miami, wedged in between the massive American Airlines Arena and desolate Bicentennial Park, which probably explained why it was being torn down. Slated to be reinvented as luxury condos, when and if the housing crisis finally abated, the fourteen-story building was surrounded by temporary chain-link fencing with signs posted NO TRESPASSING—DEMOLITION ZONE every ten feet or so. The recent downturn in the housing market had all but brought an end to new construction, and many builders were stalling to pull permits and begin projects, especially in a city with a glut of overpriced brand-new luxury condominiums.

It took a couple of hours for Bobby to track down somebody with a key and a clue. The property had already been transferred from Regal to the builders, New Bright Construction, and since New Bright was tearing the whole thing down, no one there really cared if they ever opened a door at the property again. But protocol was protocol, and except for a wild guess farmed from a creepy painting, there existed no exigent circumstances that would let them enter the property without either permission or a warrant, and they didn't have enough for a warrant. As for permission, it would definitely have been easier to wait till morning, when Susie or Barbara or whatever secretary was finally in to answer a phone at New Bright, but Bobby didn't want to wait that long. He might not have enough for a warrant, but he definitely had a feeling. A feeling that was gonna gnaw at his gut and his thoughts all night anyway, so he might as well get this done tonight and hope to God he was wrong. The worst he had to lose was a couple of hours of shut-eye, which was a rare happening nowadays, anyway.

It was almost ten by the time they tracked down an owner and the property manager and got inside the building. They—as in Zo, Bobby, and the four officers borrowed from the City of Miami to help execute the search. The Regal's electricity had been turned off when the security fencing went up, and the first-floor windows had all been boarded to keep out the homeless and the crackheads. The smell of mold and must hit them the second the doors opened onto a pitch-black foyer. Each cop took in the room. Beams from a half-dozen flashlights probed the two-story lobby for signs of life, falling on mostly nothing but cockroaches and a few brazen rats that stood their ground for a minute or so before finally scurrying out of sight.

The furniture was gone, the fixtures stripped from the walls. A Dumpster full of broken sinks sat where the reception desk had presumably once been. All that was left from the original hotel was the streak of royal red carpet that ran the length of the lobby, from the glass front doors to the bank of elevators, tucked away in a back corner. That's where Bobby spotted the pile of dirty blankets, empty snack bags, discarded syringes, condom wrappers, and a couple of burnt Coke cans on the floor nearby. "Jenna is HERE!" was spray-painted on the wall. A crack den. *So much for keeping out the vagrants,* he thought uncomfortably as he shone his flashlight into the empty elevator car that had been propped open with a broken sink, and the bank of numbers that ran up the car's wall. The hotel had fourteen floors and over two hundred rooms. While there was no telling if this crack campsite was abandoned or fresh, Bobby knew that, just like rats and cockroaches, where there was one, there were usually more.

One of the uniforms flashed his light on a closed door that led to the stairwell, and they started upstairs. Even though the painting looked as though it'd been sketched from a higher floor, for safety, all rooms had to be searched. Fortunately, the property manager had informed them that the electronic door locks were all inoperable due to the lack of electricity. The doors, if closed, were supposed to just open when pushed on.

They went floor by floor in teams of two, clearing each room after they entered with a shout-out of "Clear!" followed by the room number searched. Most of the suites had been stripped down to the wallpaper. No carpet, no fixtures, no sinks, no toilets. Pieces of broken furniture or discarded mattresses had been left behind in others. It was definitely unsettling to walk the pitch-black halls of a shuttered-up, deserted hotel, pushing in doors to see if there were any more unwelcome squatters taking up residence. Or worse—any dead young girls waiting to be found, their tethered hands outstretched, their black eyes pleading for help. This part of the city was pretty desolate at night, too, unless there was a Heat game happening next door or a concert going on across the street at Bicentennial Park—neither of which was the case tonight. It made Bobby think of the horror flick *The Shining*. As he and Zo went from room to room, checking closets and closed-off bathrooms—a flashlight in one hand and a Glock in the other—he half-expected a deranged maniac to hack his way through a bedroom door to greet them with an ax and a cheery smile.

On thirteen, they spread out in the usual fashion—one team went left around the corner to the end of the hallway, and one team went right, eventually working their way back to the stairwell and elevator bay. Bobby and Zo worked the rooms across the hall, on the other side of the building. The ones that faced southwest, toward downtown. In the interior hallways, without a flashlight, it was impossible to see even the hand in front of your face. It would suck to run out of batteries all the way up here.

"Clear! 1310!" shouted a team down the north hall. Lopez and Carr.

Bobby went to push on 1381. It didn't open.

"Clear! 1340!" yelled another team. Weiceman and Quinnones.

Bobby tried the knob. "It's locked," he said quietly.

Zo drew his gun up to his chest and nodded, as they both silently moved into position in the hall, flanking the door frame. Later, Bobby would come to think they probably both knew what they were going to find inside. And if either had spent any time at all thinking about it, neither would have ever wanted to open that door. They'd both been cops long enough to know that certain images, once witnessed, could never be erased from the mind, no matter how much time passed or how hard you tried to forget them.

Bobby nodded back. He could hear the other team from the north hall coming back their way, their gun belts jingling, their heavy shoes clunking on the thin carpet, wondering perhaps why they hadn't cleared a room yet. With each floor they had climbed, the anxiety had grown. "Agent Dias?" Carr called out. "Dees? You guys OK back there? You find something?" The beams of light from their flashlights danced against the hallway walls.

Bobby sucked in a breath. "Police!" he shouted.

Then he kicked in the door and the screaming began.

31

"Body is that of a black-haired, white female Jane Doe, sixty-three and a half inches tall, approximate weight 110–120 pounds, approximate age between twelve and twenty-one years." Gunther Trauss, the Miami–Dade County medical examiner, spoke softly into an Olympus digital handheld recorder as he circled the body of a young woman splayed out like da Vinci's Medicine Man on a dirty white mattress in the center of the stripped room. The black handle of a carving knife protruded from the middle of her yellow happy-face T-shirt. Dark blood and other fluids had pooled under her back, seeping into the mattress and spreading out beyond the outline of her body. Pinkish watery fluid leaked from her nose and mouth. Portable forty-eight-watt lighting towers lit the suite like a Hollywood movie set. More towers lined the thirteenth floor and the entire stairwell, where a parade of crime-scene techs, ME assistants, and dark blue uniforms trudged continuously up and down thirteen flights of stairs.

"Eye color is"—Dr. Trauss frowned and paused for a moment—"unknown. Eyeballs have been removed from their sockets; their location is unknown. Injury appears to be inflicted postmortem. Rigor is resolved. Date and time of death is unknown. Decomposition has begun, right lower abdominal quadrant shows green marbling, skin is slipping. Body is in stage two, putrefaction. Contusions around both ankles and wrists are observed, as are what appear to be ligature burns." He looked across the room at his assistant, who was fiddling with the disposable mask that covered his mouth and nose. "Sil, get a picture from this angle, please. Also, you and Joe be careful when you bag her, cause she's slipping and I want to try and get an impression of those rope burns back at the lab. Make sure you get a picture of the butterfly tattoo on her left foot. I don't want to lose that, either."

Bobby crouched beside the ME, a rag to his nose. Decomps in Florida were the worst; the smell was horrible. The heat and humidity in a building that hadn't seen air conditioning in months accelerated decomposition. So did the rodents, flies, and all those tropical super-size bugs. "OK, Gunther, what've we got?"

"A dead girl."

MEs never had a sense of humor at a party. Put them around a dead body and suddenly they think they're Dane Cook. "No shit," Bobby replied. "You wanna tell me how long she's been that way?"

Gunther smiled, which in itself was disturbing. It took a different kind of person to be a pathologist. You had to wonder what happened in their childhood. "Don't know," he replied. "Awhile. Definitely a day. Maybe longer. I'll know more in the morning after I've done the autopsy. But don't expect a second hand."

"Cause?"

Gunther looked at Bobby as if he had three heads. He blinked hard and nodded at the body behind him. "I won't know for sure till I do the autopsy, but I'll venture a guess it probably has something to do with the rather large knife stuck through the middle of her heart. Again, just a guess."

Bobby sighed. "You're in a fun mood. I wanted to know if you see something else. Drugs? Blunt trauma?"

"Not yet, but your guy is very theatrical, with the scene he staged all the way up here, and that painting you showed me that he sent you. I wouldn't be surprised if he's done some other nasty things to your poor Jane Doe. My guess is he's had her for a while."

"What makes you say that?"

"The contusions on her ankles and wrists. Some of those have already begun to fade, and that has nothing to do with her dying. She was tied up for a while before he killed her."

Zo walked back in the room then, a jar of Vicks VapoRub in one hand, a sealed evidence bag in the other. His nostrils were slathered in shiny goo. "Crime Scene had a jar in the truck. Want some?"

Bobby smeared a gob under his nose.

"No, thanks. The smell doesn't bother me," Gunther replied with another smile.

"You're doing a kit, right?" Zo asked.

"Of course. Based on the sexually provocative positioning of the body, I won't be surprised to find she was raped. You have an idea who she is?"

Bobby shook his head. "Not yet. There's nothing outstanding that matches her description."

"Maybe she's a tourist. Welcome to Miami," Gunther quipped. "That'll make for some good press. You've got a crowd downstairs already, I see."

"I don't have to tell you not to say anything."

"No, you don't. OK, we're ready, Sil. Bag her hands and feet."

"Particularly about her eyes. I don't want every freak in South Florida trying to claim responsibility," Bobby said. "Or worse, copycat. I also don't want a panic."

"I've worked homicides for twenty years," Zo remarked. "I've seen everything from Colombian neckties to wannabe cannibals, but I never saw this shit before. What's with the missing peepers?"

"Like I told Agent Dees, I believe that injury was, mercifully, inflicted postmortem—after she died."

Zo shook his head. "OK. So she's dead and he takes her eyes out. Obviously it's not 'cause he's worried she'll ID him, then."

"I was going to be a psychiatrist before I decided to go into pathology, so I'll give you my opinion, for whatever it's worth," Gunther replied. "The mutilation is symbolic. In the picture you showed me, he painted her without eyes while she was still alive. Rather than hoping she won't ID him, he doesn't want her to see him. He doesn't want anyone who looks at that painting to see him. By taking out the eyes of the one witness who was in the room with him, he's showing you what happened in there, but making a statement that no one will be able to see but him, and only through his eyes, the way he wants you to see it. The whole scene is very controlled. The guy probably hates how people see him. Probably hates himself, if that means anything. He could be physically deformed. Anything more than that, go get yourselves a good profiler."

Sil opened the black body bag. "What do you want me to do about the knife, Dr. Trauss? She's pinned."

"Excuse me," Gunther said as he turned back to the body.

"We could have a real psycho on our hands," Zo said with a low whistle as he looked out the window that faced southwest, onto the skyscrapers of downtown Miami. All three upper levels of the famed CenTrust skyscraper, aka the Bank of America building, were lit purple for Saturday's macabre holiday. "She was right where you said she'd be."

Gunther carefully pulled the carving knife from Jane Doe's chest and bagged it.

"Our guy knew it was you who was gonna find her, too," Zo added as he fingered the clear evidence bag in his own hand. Inside was the folded white eight-by-ten piece of paper that had been found at the foot of the mattress when they first entered the room, propped up for all to see between Jane Doe's legs, like a place card at a fancy dinner. He handed it to Bobby. "Looks like you've got yourself a secret admirer, Shep."

Bobby took the invitation meant especially for him. Glued across the front were thin strips of newspaper that, once again, spelled out only one name:

FDLE SPECIAL AGENT SUPERVISOR ROBERT DEES

32

"My source said he heard it's a gang shooting. They're keeping it off air because Miami PD has him cornered up there. They don't want to start a war tonight," said a voice in the thickening crowd that had formed outside the chain-link fence in front of the Regal All-Suites.

"They're up there high. Maybe it's a jumper," said another, staring up at the blinding lights that lit the thirteenth floor of the otherwise dark hotel.

"It's bullshit when they keep it off the radio. Waste of my fucking time to stand out here and pick my fucking nose for a jumper. Who the hell cares?" fumed a reporter from Channel Seven, WSVN.

"I think it's a kid. Someone said that FDLE's in there. Bobby Dees does Crimes Against Children. He's been in the news lately. Maybe it's a dead kid! Matter of fact, Channel 6 did a piece on his case the other day. Hey, Mark!" a crime reporter with the *Herald* called out. "Felding! You know what's going on?"

Even though he was the man with the ultimate scoop, Mark Felding wasn't saying a word. Not a single one. He'd waited a long time in his career for a moment like this—when he had the answers everyone was looking for. The inside skinny. It was so hard to keep quiet, but when the Miami–Dade County Medical Examiner's van pulled past the chain-link fence and disappeared into the parking garage below, he resisted the urge to go live with all he knew. Not long after, his cell rang.

"Mr. Felding, this is Bobby Dees."

Mark instinctively looked up at the blob of bright lights. "I'm in front of the building," he answered with a short, nervous laugh. "It's funny, I got a call from my producer asking me what the hell was going on at the Regal and if I was covering it."

"You didn't say anything, did you?"

"No, no, of course not. You said not to. I mean, I said I was here, but I didn't say anything. I . . . I saw the coroner's van pull up," he blurted. "Is it the girl?"

"We need to meet, Mr. Felding. I'd like to talk to you about some things."

"Yeah, yeah, sure, sure." Mark pulled his hand through his thick hair. "I need a drink, though. Bad. Can we talk in a bar? Is that OK? Or does it have to be, like, in your office?"

"A bar's OK with me. No cameras, no mikes, no one else. It's not a press conference. There's a dive on First and Flagler. The Back Room. I have to finish up here. Let's meet up in an hour or so."

"What do I report down here?" Mark said, looking anxiously over at his clueless colleagues.

"Have I told you anything?"

"No . . ."

"Well, I guess there's nothing to report." Then he added after a second, "Here's a bone: Your photo op's coming out of the south garage in about three minutes."

It was past one by the time Bobby finally got to the Back Room. Aside from the bartender and the lone drunk swigging Jack on a corner stool, the place was dead. He found a disheveled Mark Felding nursing what looked like a scotch in a back booth, puffing a Cowboy Killer and spinning an oversize pack of matches on a heavily shellacked pub table that was dotted with cigarette craters.

"I thought bad news was good for your business," Bobby commented as he sat. "You look worse than me."

Mark glanced up from his drink and crushed out his cigarette. He managed a strained smile. "Long day."

"Yeah? Me too." Bobby grabbed the spinning matchbook. "That's distracting." Then he called out to the bartender, "I'll take a Bud, Chief."

"I'm not a virgin, Agent Dees," Mark said quietly, running a hand through his curly hair, "but, well, let's just put it this way—I've never been, well, involved before. Forgive me. It's almost two in the morning and I'm waiting for the happy juice to finally find my brain and numb it. But I'm already on number two, and unfortunately, it just ain't happening. I'm still seeing that girl's face from that painting. Or lack thereof."

"It'll take more than two drinks to not see that anymore. Hope you're not driving. Thanks," Bobby muttered when the bartender dropped off his beer.

"Was it her? Was it the girl in the picture?"

"It was a girl. But we don't know who she is. She was wearing the same happy-face T-shirt, though."

"Is it Elaine Emerson?"

"No."

"Did she look like she did in the painting? I mean . . . how'd she die?"

"It's an open investigation. Suffice it to say it was bad. Bad enough that I'm sitting here in a bar with an asshole reporter whose throat I wanted to rip out just the other day, asking for help."

Mark just stared at him. "Me?"

"You see any other asshole reporters in here?"

"Look," Mark said, nodding slowly, "I was out of line bringing in your daughter. I shouldn't have. I know that. But I still can't figure out why some kids make headlines and some don't even raise an eyebrow. I just was looking for an explanation."

"Looks like you got yourself a headline now."

"I'm sorry. Again. About your daughter. I hope we can be . . . friends."

Bobby sipped at his beer. "You have no idea what it feels like to hear her name."

"Is there anything new? I reported on it when she—" Mark caught himself. "When it first happened. We—everyone—we were all hoping it would just be a kid thing, you know, a couple of days and then she misses home."

Bobby shook his head. "We're not going there tonight. Nope."

Mark reached for another Marlboro. Bobby slid the matchbook across the table. It had a picture of an old house on the cover and the words "For a little taste of home . . . and a little taste of Grandma's cookin'!" The bottom was stamped THE HOME SWEET HOME INN. It made Bobby think of the little bed-and-breakfast that he and LuAnn had stayed at in Vermont on their honeymoon. It had snowed so much, they'd stayed in bed for two straight days 'cause they couldn't get out.

"Kids are tough. No doubt about it. They'll break your heart," Mark mused.

"You have any?"

"A girl. She's eight. Lives with her mom back in LA. But, like you said, let's not go there tonight."

Bobby tapped his finger on top of the matchbook, which Mark had begun to spin again. "For some reason, this guy sent this portrait to you, Mr. Felding. I don't know why. And it had my name in there. The obvious connection is the story you ran the other night."

"Please call me Mark. Look, I don't want to be a part of this, Agent Dees. I always thought I would, that I would love to be in the middle of a big story, but I don't want to climb the ladder this way. It feels wrong, exploitative."

Bobby was quiet for a long while. "I appreciate that. I really do. But it's too late. And . . . I think there's more here. More than just the one girl."

Mark downed the rest of his drink just as the bartender announced last call.

"I need your help, Mark," Bobby said quietly. "I need that list."

33

The first step in working a homicide was to identify the body. Once you ID'd the victim, you worked backward and found out the last person she spoke to, the last places she went, where she was living, who she was dating, where she was working, who her friends were, who her enemies were, etc. In practically every criminal investigation, starting with the victim eventually led you back to a suspect. When you had a dead body with no personal ID and no one actively looking for them, like Bobby did, the normal course was to turn to a list of open missing-persons investigations and work from there. The real problems started when either (a) the person was never reported missing, or (b) was reported missing from a jurisdiction other than the one you were looking in. It was a big country with a lot of missing people. The four counties that composed South Florida alone had more than twenty different police departments.

FDLE's Missing Endangered Persons Information Clearinghouse (MEPIC) was supposed to be the central repository of information for all of Florida's missing children. The MEPIC Web site, intended as a resource for both law enforcement and the public at large, broke down missing persons into various categories: missing, endangered/involuntary, disabled, parental abduction, disaster victim, and runaway. Of the hundreds of names and faces posted on the site, the great majority fell under the category of runaway. Most were teen-agers. Some had been missing for hours. Some for years.

Bobby knew that the MEPIC Web site was only as good as the information that went into it. Hundreds, possibly thousands, of missing kids never made it onto the site because nobody gave a shit when they didn't come home. Especially teens in the foster-care system. Estimates put the number of throwaway children around the country to be as high as two million. Then there were the runaways who were reported missing to law enforcement, but not to the Clearinghouse. It took an affirmative act by a cop to not only enter the kid in NCIC as a missing juvi, but then pick up the phone and call MEPIC. For a lot of cops in a lot of jurisdictions, that was just too much effort for a kid whom (a) nobody gave a damn about anyway, and who (b) was just gonna run off again if and when she did get her ass home. At the end of the day, a cop on the beat couldn't fix all the reasons why a kid took off. Sometimes, the view simply was, the kid was better off on his or her own anyway.

That meant the list on the MEPIC Web site was flawed.

Flyers and police reports covered Bobby's dining room table. Jane Doe matched none of the outstanding runaways on MEPIC. Of course, the girl was missing half her face, she'd started to decompose, and the descriptions on MEPIC were limited, to say the least. Recognizing that the MEPIC list was not comprehensive, Bobby had had the squad analyst, Dawn Upton, download all of the current MEPIC runaway flyers from just Broward and Miami–Dade County and put them into book form. There were 127 names—79 of which were female. Most had pictures on their flyers. Some did not. Late this afternoon, Dawn had begun the painful process of collecting the hundreds of missing-person reports from every police department in Broward and Miami-Dade going back one year. Each report would then be cross-checked against both the NCIC missing-juvenile entries and the MEPIC Web site, to make sure that every kid who had been reported missing to the police had either been found and reunited with family or entered into the MEPIC site. It was a tremendous amount of work, and it still wouldn't yield a full list of every missing teen, since it wouldn't account for throwaways, but at least it was a start. Because as he stared at the mess that was his dining room table, the one thing Bobby knew for certain was that, without an accurate list of potential victims, it would be impossible to ever identify Jane Doe. And without a confession, physical trace evidence, or a miracle, it would be impossible to find her killer.

Sitting beside his now very cold cup of coffee was Mark Felding's list. The "revealing" list the reporter had begun to compile for his Channel 6 investigation. Emphasizing it was still a work in progress, Mark had taken the 127 names of Broward and Dade runaways from the MEPIC Web site and, through public records requests, had already obtained the individual missing-person police reports for about 70 of the names. The reports offered much more detail than the MEPIC postings. Mark had then broken down the information about the victims in the reports by race, religion, age, criminal history, family background, identifying body marks, clothing descriptions, location of disappearance, and circumstances surrounding the disappearance. Obviously, the intent was to prove a discernable pattern of discrimination by law enforcement against certain victim types—a charge that would be sure to make a lot of noise on the news.

Bobby had spent most of the weekend at his dining room table, carefully combing through each police report and MEPIC flyer looking for details or a description that matched the dead girl at the Regal. He hadn't found Jane Doe, but he had found something weird. Allegra Villenueva, a sixteen-year-old from Hialeah who'd been missing since August, was described as "last seen wearing a yellow happy-face T-shirt and blue jeans." At four-eleven and 145 pounds, Allegra wasn't Jane Doe—even if she'd lost a ton of weight in the months she'd been missing, she sure wasn't gonna grow four inches. And there was no indication of any tattoos on her body. Was it just coincidence, then, that Jane Doe had on the same unusual T-shirt? Then there was Gale Sampson. Seventeen years old, missing from Hallandale. She did have a butterfly tattoo on her right ankle, and at five-three and 115 pounds, she matched Jane Doe's physical description, but in her picture she was blond. The picture of another girl, Nikole Krupa from Riviera Beach, had a streak of blond running down the center of her dark hair like Jane Doe, but she had four tattoos.

He leaned back in his chair and rubbed his tired eyes. Besides being one of the more gruesome murders he'd ever worked, it was already clear that, for Bobby, Jane Doe was going to be much more than just another homicide. It was already part of him, the brutal details burrowed deep in his brain, spawning question after question. Whoever this animal was, he wanted Bobby's attention. And he'd gotten it. But why him? You didn't need a psych degree to see the obvious message on that placard: The killer was inviting him into the investigation. Bobby had worked a couple of serials before in his career; he'd assisted on a half-dozen more outside of FDLE. Some frightening truths applied generally to society's most feared murderers: They wanted an audience. They wanted people to notice them. And oftentimes they wanted to show the police that they were smarter than them. Death, to a psychopathic serial or spree killer, is a game, and like every good game, it's more fun to play against a worthy opponent. While there was no evidence yet to confirm Jane Doe's killer was a serial, Bobby had seen enough homicides to know that the scene at the Regal wasn't the hand of an amateur. And while Bobby didn't yet know if Jane Doe's murder was connected to Elaine Emerson's disappearance, it was definitely a frightening possibility.

It was time to try and get some sleep. As the laptop shut down, he gathered together the crime-scene photos of Jane Doe. That was the last thing in the world LuAnn needed to see when she came down for breakfast. That and pictures of missing teenagers. She was already living on a ledge. This just might push her over. He shoved the crime-scene photos into his briefcase, and his eyes fell on Katy's flyer, right there in the middle of his dining room table. Photos of her filled every wall in the house, but this was the one that forced him back in his seat as a wave of nausea threatened to bring him to his knees.

He remembered the day he found out LuAnn was pregnant. She'd come out of the bathroom in their tiny one-bedroom apartment in Whitestone, a look of complete surprise on her flushed face. In her shaking fingers was the stick with the big pink line through it that Bobby could see from five feet away.

They were so young. He hadn't wanted a kid yet. He was only twenty-three. LuAnn was only twenty-two. They'd only been married nine months. They had student loans to pay off and parties to go to with friends who hadn't even gotten married yet. At her first doctor's appointment LuAnn found out she had an enormous fibroid; the pregnancy was high risk. Everything changed. Every priority. Suddenly the focus became having this baby. They named her Katherine, after Bobby's mom, this precious little perfect baby with pink skin and a full head of blond hair. Two hours later, doctors rushed LuAnn into surgery. Her uterus had ruptured and she was bleeding to death. Bobby could remember sitting in that ultra-quiet hospital room, rocking this newborn life that he could no longer remember not wanting with all his heart and soul and praying to God to please save his wife. Praying that he wouldn't have to raise this little girl all alone, because he just knew he'd screw it up. He knew without LuAnn it would never be good. Six hours later, someone finally came in to tell him that his prayers had been answered. LuAnn was going to live. But she could never have another child.

He'd promised God he would do the best job any father had ever done. That he would never let Him down. But he had. Somewhere along the line, things had gone bad. The fairy tale had changed endings.

"You're high, Katy," Bobby said as she started up the stairs to her room.

"No. No, I'm not, Daddy."

"Don't lie to me, Katherine Anne. I'm a cop; I know high when I see it. What the hell are you on? What does he have you on?"

"Nothing!" Her bloodshot blue eyes suddenly flashed with anger. "It's not about him. You always make it about him!"

"This isn't you!"

"It is now. It is me. Deal with it."

"Look at you," LuAnn broke in quietly. "Your grades are plummeting, you're staying out late, you're not cheering anymore. You're talking back. You're lying to us. You're lying to yourself. This is not you."

"I'm going to bed. I'm tired." Katy pushed past LuAnn to go up the stairs.

"Don't walk away from your mother!" Bobby grabbed her by the arm and pushed up the sleeve on the Hollister sweatshirt that she now wore every day—even in eighty-degree weather. Katy squirmed and tried to pull away, but he held her fast. The tiny needle marks started just below the elbow.

"Oh my God!" LuAnn screamed. "Oh my God!"

Bobby felt like someone had taken his heart and thrown it on the ground. He was so incredibly angry he feared he might throw her into the wall if he didn't let go. "It's over," he said quietly. He released her arm and fell back against the railing.

Katy's eyes filled with tears. "I hate you!" she hissed as she marched up the stairs.

"You can if you want," he replied, his eyes closed. "But it's over, Katherine. This time, it's over. You will never see that boy again."

Then the door to her room slammed and the yellow "bear crossing" sign fell to the floor, tumbling down the stairs with a loud clang, until it finally stopped at his feet.

Bobby rubbed the tears away before they started. He felt hands, then, warm on his neck, rubbing his shoulders. He reached up to touch them. It was LuAnn and she was staring at the flyer of Elaine Emerson alongside that of her own daughter.

"You'll find her," she said softly as she kissed his head. "I know you will this time."

34

He was watching her.

Even though Lainey couldn't see him, she could feel him. He was somewhere very close by, yet far enough away that he didn't think she knew he was still in the room. He liked to play games like that. He'd come to give her food, and unlock the metal cuffs that chained her to the wall. Then he'd sit and silently watch her while she ate God-knows-what, wiping her face when she was finished with a scratchy rag that smelled like a mix of mildew and old-lady perfume. Then he'd lock her back up and take the food bowl away. He'd say goodnight or goodbye or whatever, and close the door real hard so that she would think he was gone when he really wasn't. Instead, he would just stay and watch her, sometimes for what seemed like hours. Why, she didn't know. Maybe he was waiting for her to do something bad, like rip the strips of surgical tape off her eyes, or move a creaky floorboard to reveal the escape tunnel he thought she might be burrowing. Or maybe he wanted to watch her go to the bathroom in the metal pot he had set up in the corner. Whatever it was he was waiting for, Lainey knew he was there. The freak had never fooled her. At least she didn't think he had. She could still smell the faintness of his nauseating cologne, the dirt on his shoes, the musky scent of his body odor, mixed with . . . rain, maybe? The smell reminded her of the time she and Bradley had gotten caught in the thunderstorm at Mrs. Ross's and had run all the way home together. The smell of rain had stayed in her hair and on her skin even after she'd changed clothes. She pushed the memory out of her head. It hurt to think of good times.

She didn't dare say a word. He didn't like it when she pleaded or cried or tried to talk to him. He got very angry—embarrassed, probably, that she was on to his stupid Peeping Tom game and he wasn't fooling anyone. Like the red-faced boy caught peeking through a hole in the wall of a ladies' bathroom wasn't sorry that he did it, only sorry that he got caught, and the best defense when you're caught doing something bad, her mom liked to say, was a good offense. That meant no food or water for her for a really long time.

So she said nothing and she did nothing while he watched her in the dark like some freak in a horror movie—his creepy eyes rolling over her, thinking horrible thoughts. But just because she couldn't see him in the pitch-black world she now lived in, it didn't stop her knowing he was there. She had other senses. Senses that had sharpened like a superhero's since she'd been in this smelly, dank, cold room. She now heard every creak, every whisper, every little whistle of wind, or rustle of paper. Sounds she never, ever appreciated before. Sounds she was never scared of before. And her sense of smell was crazy good. Like right now. Never before would she have smelled dirt on somebody's shoes, and yet without a doubt that's exactly what she knew she was smelling. He'd tracked in mud on his shoes, and the rich smell of earth, mixed with maybe a little dog shit, was as strong and familiar as the stink of gasoline at a gas station or popcorn at a movie theater. And the sound of his breathing, slow and measured through his mouth, was as loud and clear as if he were whispering right there in her ear. She could hear him, breathing heavier sometimes . . .

Lainey liked to think she was becoming a superhero. That every day, every hour, every minute she was locked up here, chained up against her will, she was getting stronger. That her powers—powers she didn't even know she had until this real-life horror movie began—were growing. Every time she recognized a scent from across the room or heard the wind blow under a doorjamb, she imagined she was morphing into a superhero—like Claire, the ordinary high school cheerleader who was anything but ordinary in her favorite TV show, *Heroes*. And just like Claire, one day her powers would fully come to her, and she would be able to break the chains that bound her to the wall. Then she would stand up and she would see again, and with her superhuman strength she would find him, watching her there in the corner, like that snotty schoolboy, making his weird snorty noises as he thought bad thoughts. And he would be surprised at first. Really surprised. Because she had caught him. But then he would be scared. More scared than he had ever been in his whole horrible life. Because she had all her powers now. And she would fly across the room and beat him till he stopped making those noises. Till *he* couldn't see anymore . . .

"Do you know I'm here?" came the whisper in the dark.

Her heart stopped. It was the voice of the Devil and he'd just read her mind. She started to shake. "I want to go home, mister. Please. I want to see my mom."

He sighed, annoyed.

"Please! I won't tell anyone about you. Just let me go home!"

She heard him get up from the chair or the floor, or wherever he was. The joints in his knees popped. And he walked slowly over to her, the stink of him filling her nose and throat, making her gag. She tried to crawl away, but there was nowhere to go. Nowhere to hide.

He knelt down in front of her and reached out, stroking her hair behind her ear. He leaned closer. "Time's up," he whispered in her ear as he unlocked the chains on her ankles and wrists. His warm breath smelled like old coffee. He pulled her to her feet.

It was time to die. She only hoped it wouldn't hurt. "Please, mister," she pleaded as he pushed her forward, her arms outstretched, grasping at nothing. She had no idea where she was going, what was in front of her. If there were a flight of stairs or an open window. "Please! I'll be good. I won't tell anyone!"

A door opened with a creak. His hand was suddenly on the back of her head. He shoved it down hard and pushed her forward. She fell into a wall and then onto a hard dirt floor.

"I know," was all he said.

Then the door closed behind her, followed by what sounded like maybe the sliding of a bolt and turn of a key. She heard his footsteps cross the wood floorboards in the other room where she had been. Then another slam of a door, and the faint patter and creak as he climbed the stairs. She heard him walk above her somewhere. The heavy click of his heels on the creaky wood floors. The jingle of his keys. Then there was silence.

The room or closet, or wherever she was, was really, really small. Her back was pressed up against a wall, and her feet practically touched the wall across from her. The ceiling felt really low, too. There was no way she could stand up. It smelled musty and earthy, like the crawl space under the house she'd lived in before her family had moved to Coral Springs when she was five. When she and Liza used to play hide and seek, Liza could never find her, because she would never look in the crawl space. She said there were bad things that lived under there, out of the light.

She was so scared. She pulled her knees up tight against her chest and started to rock back and forth, back and forth. She needed her superpowers to happen right now. There was no more time to wait. "Mommy, mommy, mommy . . . ," she whispered in the dark.

Then she heard the sound that made her breath suck in and her blood run cold. A faint scratching somewhere. Right next to her. Only inches from her, maybe. And coming closer.

It was in the walls.

Liza was right. There were things that lived in crawl spaces, far away from the light and the living. Horrible things. Rats or snakes or bugs. Or worse.

Zombies.

She'd never believed in vampires and ghosts and all the horrible freaks she'd seen in horror movies until she found herself living in one. Now she knew monsters did exist and even the worst things were possible. Like zombies, who scratched their way through walls with long yellow nails, their dead hands reaching to grab her and drag her back to hell with them . . .

"Nooooo!" she screamed, her hands over her ears. "Nooooo!"

The scratching stopped. Lainey stopped rocking and held her breath, every muscle in her body frozen stiff with fear. Her ears strained to listen, to make sure the zombie was really gone and not in there with her, having broken through the wall while she screamed, now ready to come up behind her with his putrid breath and eat her alive . . .

Time froze. For how long she wasn't sure. It might've been hours that she sat there not moving, not breathing, praying that she was all alone in the dark.

When the walls began to whisper, she knew she wasn't.

35

"It's Gale Sampson. I got a positive ID twenty minutes ago," Gunther Trauss said into the phone in between bites of his breakfast sandwich. "The DNA swab you got from her mom on Saturday came back. It's definitely her."

"Damn. I had a feeling." Bobby waved at a Florida Highway Patrol officer who was pulling out of the Miami Regional Operations Center complex just as he was pulling in Monday morning. "But she's blond."

"You know kids," Gunther returned. "They change hair color like they change belts. It's just an accessory. I have a seventeen-year-old. She's been every color in the rainbow. Her mother says it's normal. I just nod and hope."

"I'll go talk to the mom this morning. I have a charging conference at the State Attorney's on another case I'm working that's gonna take up my afternoon. You have anything else for me?"

"The contusions on the ankles and wrists are shackle indentations. They look like Wonder Woman cuff bangle bracelets that were put on too tight, but given how she was found and that there were matching contusions on her ankles, I'm going with restraints. If you get me the shackle, I can maybe match it. She also has rope burns on both wrists. Again, get me a standard and I'll see what I can do for a comp."

"So she was held for a while?"

"Looks like it. When did she disappear?"

"June 12th."

"That's going on five months. A long time to be held by a nut. Poor kid," Gunther said. In the background somewhere Bobby heard the sound of a saw.

"Can you step out of the lab for a sec, Gunther?"

"That wasn't me. That was Motte."

"Whatever," Bobby replied when the buzzing had stopped. "How old are the bruises?"

"Can't tell you that, but she's had them for a while. At least a week or two. The burn marks take longer to fade. She could have had them a lot longer."

"Shit."

"And there's more."

"G'head."

"Eyes were removed, like I said, postmortem. But she has adhesive on her temples, and on the only remaining section of left lid I found cyanoacrylate."

"What's that?"

"An acrylic resin better known as Krazy Glue."

Bobby immediately thought of the infamous Miami serial killer, Cupid, who would glue the eyes of his victims open before he cut their hearts out, forcing them to watch their own death. "What the hell? Why would he Krazy Glue her lids? Is he a Cupid copycat? A wannabe?"

"Well, she still had possession of her heart, it just had a rather large hole in it. I have no idea why he would Krazy Glue any part of her, and I can't tell you if he actually put the stuff in her eyes, because he kept the specimens. Just thought I would keep you advised. I told you that I expected your boy to be nasty. After twenty years of cutting people open, you get a feeling about the bad ones."

"Was she raped?"

"What did I say on Wednesday? I repeat, you get a feeling about the bad ones."

"Damn . . ."

"Good news is, it looks like he did that, too, after she was dead. But if he held her for a while, there's no telling if he was so chivalrous the whole time he had her chained up."

"Damn . . . anything left?"

"Nah. This guy's too good to maroon any swimmers. Oh, and one last thing. She had what looks like dog food in her stomach. Kibble. I'll call you when I get the rest of the results from toxicology. I had them test it, too. Maybe it's a weird brand. You never know."

Bobby hung up the phone and sat in his car, staring straight ahead at the four-story building that for years LuAnn had joked was his home away from home. For a number of reasons, he didn't want to go in there today, the first of which was he had a feeling Gunther's good morning wake-up call was just the beginning of a day filled with more shit news and surprises. And then there was Foxx. The regional director was scheduled to be back from his weeklong jaunt to Tallahassee, where he'd been palling with his very good friend, the FDLE commissioner. Bobby hadn't seen Foxx since he'd told him to fuck off last Tuesday.

A loud bang sounded on his driver's side window. It was Zo, looking spiffy in a suit and tie. He either had court or a meeting. It seemed the circus was coming to him.

"You just gonna sit there all day, or you gonna do some work?" Zo yelled at the glass.

Bobby lowered the window. "Do I have a job?"

"That I don't know. But I haven't heard them pull your number off the radio yet. That's good. The girls in dispatch will know you're on the dole before you do."

Bobby grabbed his laptop and stepped out of the car. "I just talked to Gunther."

"I just talked to Lou Calderon at the lab in Orlando. You first," Zo said as they started across the lot.

"We have an ID: Gale Sampson, seventeen, out of Hallandale. The rest can wait till I've digested breakfast and have had lots of coffee. You go."

"Serology has the Picasso. Calderon thinks he's got a brand on the paint: Winsor & Newton Professional Artist. The bad news is it looks like it's sold in every artsy paint store in the U.S." He held open the front glass door and waited till Bobby had waved at the duty officer and was committed to the elevator before dropping the next bomb. "Now for the bad shit. Remember the red smears on the girl's hands and the red drops on her cheeks in the picture?"

"Yeah," Bobby replied slowly as he hit the button for three.

"That's not paint. It's blood."

Bobby shook his head. "After speaking with Gunther, notice how I'm not all that surprised?"

"Well, now that we have an ID on Jane Doe, maybe one of the smears will turn out to be hers."

"One of?"

"That's the kicker, Shep. The DNA's back and the blood droplets on the cheeks are different than the smears on the hands. It's two different people's blood."

"Maybe one of them is our bad guy. That'd be nice. It'd be even nicer if he's already banked a sample in Tallahassee."

"No such luck," Zo replied as the elevator opened. "Both samples are female. That means we have at least one more victim out there."

36

"Bobby, you got a minute?" Chris Turan, the resident FDLE computer geek extraordinaire, popped out of his office on his rolling chair as Bobby and Zo passed. "I got some info for you on your case."

The day kept getting better and it wasn't even nine. "Is it on Emerson?" Bobby asked.

"That's the one. The runaway."

"Follow us to my office," Zo said with a nod. "I got a chief's meeting in a half-hour, but I wanna hear this, too."

"It's just like you figured, Bobby," Chris said as the three of them walked down the hall. "Somebody tried to erase files from the hard drive. Good thing for you it was a somebody who didn't know what they were doing."

"Talk to me," Bobby said, waving at Zo's secretary, who was busy cursing the copier in Russian as the three men stepped into Zo's office.

Chris closed the door. "You know, just hitting 'delete' doesn't erase a file completely. I ran a REDS program. It goes back over computer files that once existed. It's like looking at a blank piece of paper on a notepad. There are no words, but if you shade it in, you can detect the words that were written on the piece of notepad paper before it. The impression of the words still exists. The only way you get rid of those words is to either destroy the whole pad or keep writing over it enough times that the impression is no longer readable."

"I love my job," Zo said with a smile.

"So when this guy tried to erase files on the 25th, it told him they were deleted, but they weren't," Chris continued. "The impression was still there. And it was not written over enough to be unreadable. The point is, I got back what it was he was trying to erase."

"The 25th was—what?—last Sunday? That's interesting," Bobby remarked. That was the day he'd talked to Todd LaManna down at the dealership. "You keep saying 'he.' You know who he is?"

"I'm pretty confident it's a he. And my money's on the dad. I found lots of porn jpegs. He also forgot to delete his cookies. This guy's been to all sorts of bad sites. Younghotties.com, sluttygirls.com, real-voyeur.com, whosyadaddy.com, to name a few."

"'Who's your daddy?' What the hell?" Zo snapped.

"Hence the jump to Dad," Chris said.

"You got anything else?" Bobby asked. "It's not enough to know that someone went to those sites. I need to know who. The computer was in Lainey's room, under her care and control. His argument's gonna be that it was his stepkid's curiosity that stroked the wrong keys. Or her inquisitive little brother. To pin that on the scumbag stepdad, I need something more than just whosyadaddy.com."

"OK. He used a prepaid card to pay for access, but he linked into the site through the email account RoosterTAL@operamail.com."

You didn't need to be a detective to figure out the double entendre. Or that the initials TAL following it stood for one Todd Anthony LaManna. This changed everything. "Bastard," Bobby muttered. "I knew the guy was a creep."

"He's a used-car salesman, isn't he?" Zo asked.

"With an L & L on his résumé."

"Nice," Zo commented.

"Is the porn kiddie?"

"You'd have to get an expert to give you an official opinion. They look like teens, but it's hard to say how old. Sometimes these slugs dress up a twenty-year-old in a Catholic-school plaid mini and put her hair in pigtails. Tracking down the girls is impossible. But, no, there are no real young ones."

"It's enough to bring him in for a chat," Zo offered. "Let's see how he tries to talk himself out of it."

"He also forgot to mention the blowout that he and his missing stepdaughter had the night before she disappeared. Or that he was the last person to call her cell phone that Friday evening."

"Alzheimer's?" Zo asked with a raised eyebrow.

"Selective," Bobby responded.

"Did they have a convo?" Zo asked.

"Don't know. The call lasted two minutes, but there were no messages on her cell. She could have talked to him, or deleted his voice mail. She's not here to tell us."

"What does he say?"

"He's been busy ducking me. And I've been busy with Jane Doe—Gale Sampson. I was beginning to think there was a connection between the two, but maybe not."

"Or maybe yes. Maybe he decided to take his fucked-up fetish outside the family," Zo offered. "The mutilated body of some other kid would take the heat off his stepdaughter's disappearance."

Bobby nodded. "I'll bring him in. I have to talk to Sampson's mom first. I want to find out her story. Maybe she can give us a connection to Todd LaManna."

"There's one more thing, Bobby," Chris said slowly, "something I think you might find interesting. I found a backdoor Trojan."

"What's that?" Zo asked.

"A virus, usually 'wrapped' in a program or sent through email," Chris answered. "It's called a backdoor Trojan because it comes in through a wrapper that's disguised as a desirable program, like the 'Whac-A-Mole' game, or through an innocent email, from what the recipient believes is a trustworthy source, but it's really a Trojan horse. Once the program is running, it tries to hide itself in the applications. It doesn't show any icon or indication that it's running. It just sits and listens on a port until the computer—"

"Connects to the Internet," Bobby finished, nodding slowly. "It allows the person who planted it to control the recipient's computer over the Internet. So whenever she's on, he knows it."

"Control? Like how?" Zo asked.

"Record keystrokes, move the mouse, view files, open and close the CD-ROM. Whenever the computer is on, the Trojan rider has almost complete control over the computer and the recipient never even knows he's there," Bobby replied.

"Well, this Trojan was customized," Chris said. "Whoever sent it to your missing teen definitely liked to watch."

Bobby and Zo stared at him.

"It operated the webcam."

37

Bobby sat across from Todd LaManna at the small table in the interview room, his fingers tapping the folded manila folder in front of him. He let a fraction of the disgust he felt bleed into his words. "We already know you like to watch, Todd."

"That's not true," Todd said, shifting in his seat. Tiny beads of sweat had suddenly sprouted all over the top of his head, shining under the bright lights through the thinning strands of hair he had left. He looked around the room for a friendly face, but there were none to be found. Zo stared at him, arms folded across his chest, as if he'd just peed on the carpet.

Bobby waved a computer printout in the air. "I'm looking at an arrest for lewd and lascivious. Twenty feet from a playground, Todd. A playground full of kids."

"That was a mistake! I already told you I was taking a piss!"

"And now we have Lainey's computer, Todd. Tell me, before we start talking about all the dirty pictures we found, is that gonna be a mistake, too? Just like the cell phone call you made to her the day she disappeared that you forgot to mention, or the fight you had with her two days before?"

The color drained from Todd's face.

"We have the phone records. What did you talk to Lainey about the very day she disappeared, Todd?"

"Nothing. I never talked to her," he stammered. "She, um, she didn't pick up. I forgot I even called her."

"Two minutes is an awfully long connection for someone who didn't pick up. Try again."

"I don't know—I didn't talk to her, I said. Maybe the phone didn't hang up right or something."

"What did you want to talk to her about, Todd?"

"Can't remember."

"Maybe you wanted to apologize for trying to bust in her room the night before?"

Todd shook his head.

"Yeah, we know about the fight. And we know you tried to erase the Web sites you've been to. And we know you tried to erase the dirty pictures. Before you tell me it's all a mistake, that it didn't happen—we know, Todd. We already know." There was a long pause. Bobby opened the folder and slid three pictures across the table. "They sure look young to me. I'm betting that they're no older than fifteen."

Todd looked up at him, his eyes as wide as saucers. His hands were shaking. "They only make them look that way . . . ," he mumbled.

"And you like to look at them young, don't you?"

"You're twisting this."

"Whosyadaddy.com? Real-voyeur.com? I don't think I'm twisting it. Then we find the backdoor Trojan you put on your old computer that you gave to Lainey, the one that operated the webcam. What—so when Lainey wouldn't let you in her room, you could watch her from the computer down the hall? Or at work? Maybe on your iPhone, as she's getting dressed in the morning, you could get off in your Rice Krispies?"

Todd's eyes looked like they were gonna pop out of their sockets. He stood up and pounded his fist on the table. "I never did nothing to her, man! I never put nothing on that computer! I swear it! I swear to God! Oh my God, oh my God, oh my God . . . OK. I had some pictures. Big fucking deal. Ain't nothing wrong with that. My wife, Debbie, she doesn't look like that no more," he said, pushing one of the pictures back at Bobby. "Let's face it, guy, Madonna may look good for fifty-one, but she's still *old*. She doesn't look like that, no matter who's stuffing and stitching her back up. Nothing wrong with using a picture to fantasize. *Playboy*—ya know, Hefner—he built an empire doing that. It's OK to look at young, pretty girls. So fuck you is what I'm saying. I know my rights."

"Not when they're underage, Todd. Then it's a felony. For every single picture." Bobby paused deliberately for a long while but never broke his stare. "Where's Lainey?" he demanded.

"What the fuck?" Todd said, pulling his hands through the two thick tufts of brown hair left on the side of his head. "You think I took my stepdaughter? That I did something to Lainey? That's sick . . . Oh my God, oh my God . . ."

"Enough with the 'oh my Gods,' brother. Where were you the night of the 23rd?" Zo asked.

"We already know you got off work at five," Bobby added. "Lainey was meeting somebody at five-thirty. Coincidence?"

"You fucking guys . . . I was with a girl, OK?"

"What girl?"

"Lori. I don't know her last name. I met her at a bar after work. With the boys, you know? And we, you know, shot some pool and drank and fucked around in my car. And then I went home. I swear it. I should've told you last week, but I didn't. I thought Lainey would come home again, like her sister always did."

"You've been doing a lot of that, Todd. Swearing," Bobby said, shaking his head. "Then I catch you and you swear it's something else. Lori No-Last-Name is not good. You're gonna have to do better."

Todd looked around the room again. "I want a lawyer," he said, reaching for his cigarette pack in his windbreaker. "I need a lawyer."

"There's no smoking in here," Bobby replied, swiping the Marlboros from his hand. He slid them into his pocket and walked out.

Stephanie Gravano, the Miami-Dade assistant state attorney, was across the hall in the MROC monitoring room, watching the show on closed-circuit TV. She shook her head when Bobby walked in. "There's not enough. What'd they find at the house?"

Bobby sighed and slapped the wall in anger. "This is such bull-shit . . ." As if on cue, his Nextel chirped. "I guess we get to find out," he said to her as he clicked in. "What ya got, Ciro?"

Ciro Acevedo was a CAC agent in Bobby's squad. One of the best. "We're still here, Bobby. Chris burned the hard drive on the other computer. He's been looking, but no matching program that would work the Trojan on step-pop's Dell. More pictures, though. The guy's into hardcore, ya know? But I don't know how old the girls are, which is the next question I know you're gonna ask me. We'll have to get an opinion from McBride."

Damn. Bobby didn't need Chris or Ciro or Stephanie to point out what he knew already. Without a victim to testify she was a minor when the picture was taken, to make a child pornography possession case, the kid had to look ten minutes out of diapers. Any older than that and you had to get an expert to look at the pictures and render an opinion on age based on the physical development of the child that he or she was under the age of sixteen. It was impossible to make an exact call, so if the photos were of a developed teen, you were pretty much out of luck. If she looked fourteen or fifteen, the foresee-able defense argument was going to be that she very well could be seventeen, and that makes possessing a picture of her in a sex act not a crime. Bobby could hear yelling on the other end of the phone. "Who the hell is that?"

"That voice you hear screaming behind me is the witch, Wifey Dearest, going off on Chris. She's none too happy that you're chatting up her good-for-nothing husband. She must've told me ten times already how she's gonna own my badge when the day is done. I feel like I should just give it to her with the inventory and copy of the warrant when we leave." Ciro chuckled. "No wonder your car salesman went shopping someplace else."

"Did she give you his uniforms?" The Friday Lainey disappeared was a workday. If it was Todd who picked up Lainey, he'd most likely still have been in uniform. If things went bad, if Lainey was dead or hurt, he'd possibly have some trace evidence on him. Bobby had found DNA in the cuffs of a jacket before, and blood spray in between the links of a watch. You had to sometimes think out of the box. But because the new search warrant was based on the porn found on Lainey's computer, agents were limited in what they could look for—which was, namely, more porn. Or equipment to make, manufacture, or transmit more porn. Getting the uniforms was only going to happen via permission from Mrs. So-Far-Uncooperative.

"Done. And the shoes. Don't ask me why she said yes, but she did. Nothing noticeable that I can see, though. Chris is taking the computer out to the truck now. He says he'll pick it apart back at the office. But while I was looking around in this guy's closet, I found something else, Bobby. It's not named in the warrant, but I thought you'd find it mighty interesting, considering you're working Picasso, too, right?"

Bobby turned and looked back at the pudgy car salesman on the closed-circuit TV. An uneasy feeling began to spread through his bones. *Always expect the unexpected,* a veteran NYPD homicide detective had advised him many years ago. *A rabid dog doesn't always look dangerous and a madman doesn't always look mad.* "Yeah. What've you got?"

"I found a back room, like a pass-through door that must have been part of the garage before somebody converted it. I opened it up and took a peek. Found a whole friggin' studio. And a bunch of—get this—paintings. Trees, flowers, street scenes, that sort of shit. Asked wifey who the *artiste* is. And she says she can't even draw a stick figure. That's when Junior blurts out it's his daddy. Says he likes to paint on the weekends. Says it relaxes him."

38

On the flat-screen TV that was mounted above the bar, the perky, pretty blond Channel 6 anchor tried hard to look concerned. She furrowed her brow and leaned in toward the camera, but it was impossible to conceal the glint of excitement in her blue eyes as they tracked the teleprompter. The man seated at the semi-crowded bar nursing his J & B looked down, swirling the amber liquid in the cheap glass. He couldn't help but smile as he listened to the newscast, but it would be really bad for anyone to see him doing that here, now. It would be inappropriate, to say the least. So instead, he bit down hard on the inside of his cheek till warm blood filled his mouth. It didn't really hurt, but he knew it would keep him from smiling. A bloody vampire grin would definitely attract attention and raise some eyebrows.

"The body of a young woman discovered last Thursday in downtown Miami has finally been identified as that of missing seventeen-year-old Gale Sampson of Hallendale. Our own Mark Felding, who was at the abandoned Regal All-Suites Hotel earlier this afternoon, reports," said the anchor.

"The identity of a young female found by police in this condemned all-suites hotel last Thursday remained a mystery until just this morning, after DNA testing identified her as seventeen-year-old Gale Sampson of Hallandale. One reason why the identification took so long? Well, while officials with both FDLE and the City of Miami won't comment, sources who were at the grisly scene confirm the body was mutilated. Now this case is certainly one for the bizarre books. Although I've vowed to cooperate with police and not compromise their investigation, the mutilation that sources have described to me does seem to match the injuries inflicted on the female subject of the gruesome painting that was sent to me at WTVJ 6 just last week. In fact, this piece of 'art' looks like it is the work of Gale Sampson's killer. Sampson, a troubled teen with a troubled past, has been described by officials as a habitual runaway. She'd been living in the foster home of Guy and Tootie Rodriguez for almost a year before she disappeared last June. She wasn't reported missing to DCF, though, until September 16th, almost three months later, when a truancy officer contacted the Rodriguezes to find out why she hadn't been in school. Now we've been out to the Rodriguez residence, but no one is answering the door and no one is returning our calls. Agents with FDLE are also investigating the recent disappearance of another troubled South Florida teen, thirteen-year-old Elaine Emerson of Coral Springs, who went missing October 23rd. Elaine has been listed on the FDLE's Web site as a runaway, but now authorities are trying to determine if the disappearances of these two young women might somehow be related. Let's hope not. I'm Mark Felding. As part of my ongoing special investigative report into the troubling, dark world of South Florida's runaways . . ."

The man signaled the bartender for another as the news went to commercial. Finally he was getting face time. He was getting noticed. Even though the intense media coverage threatened to expose him, even though he was officially living out there on the edge now, it felt good. For too long he'd been all alone with his strange thoughts, doing things that even he sometimes thought were . . . not right. But now, the decision to show the world who he was and what he was capable of was strangely liberating. And the danger, even here in this bar filled with strangers, listening with them, alongside them as they learned of the horror he was capable of inflicting . . . it was, well, exciting. He was not a homosexual, but if he were, he imagined it would be a similar feeling to coming out of the closet. Or at least *deciding* to come out of the closet. Especially if he were, say, a famous ballplayer or a rock star, wrapped up so tight in a handsome, masculine, commercial package it was suffocating him—just the decision to be who you really were, no matter the consequence, would be . . . well, cathartic. Even if you never actually stepped out beyond that closet door and into that pink, poofy new world, just the *decision* to do it was a heavy weight off your shoulders.

The bartender brought him over another drink and a bowl of peanuts without saying a word. The man loved Dave & Buster's. The food was great, but the concept was what kept him coming back. An eclectic family-themed restaurant emporium with an attached arcade, complete with pool tables, *Nothing But Net!* basketball hoops, batting cages, *Dance Dance Revolution*, Derby simulators. Any game—from *Pac-Man* to *Ghost Squad*—if you wanted to play it, it was there. And it wasn't just kids' stuff. The arcade had an enormous, fully stocked bar in the middle with all sorts of fun drinks, like the Melontini or the Snow Cone. He looked around him at the half-empty bar. At the girls sipping blue drinks with umbrellas and pineapple wedges. Getting looped on blue curaçao and Bacardi Limón before doing the nasty in the backseat of a boyfriend's car, never realizing just how potent the blue sweet stuff could be, till the next morning when they woke up wearing no underwear, with their shirts on backward.

He spotted her then at the far end of the Skee-Ball lanes, just like she said she'd be on her blog. Long pink neon ringlets framed her pale face, contrasting with her otherwise straight, jet-black mane. Tall and, as his mother would politely say, "big-boned"—which was a euphemism for chubby. An Amazon. Not his normal choice of fare, but he sometimes liked to switch things up to keep it all interesting. He definitely had a weakness for blondes, so it was time for another brunette. And while Shelley didn't sport a supermodel waist, that could be fun, too. He could invent a whole new series of games to play just with her. She was certainly no Lainey, that was a fact. But Lainey was special. She was different, so there was no sense comparing. Earring hoops ran up Shelley's ear; one hung from her lower lip. He could see her tramp stamp, even from across the room. The brilliantly colored butterfly that ran up her back, and down into her too-tight jeans. Everything about Shelley screamed, "Notice me!" And he had. His hand began to tremble, sloshing the liquor onto his thumb. He licked it off and glanced at his watch. A little late, but at least she was here. Just like she'd said she'd be.

She looked exactly like her profile page. It wasn't all that surprising—at sixteen or seventeen there was nothing yet to hide, no image that needed a desperate makeover from a rough past. That was why he loved this age; it was so very honest. In the future, he suspected Shelley Longo would want to run from her piercings and tattoos and easy reputation that he was sure she'd justly earned. She would look back on her troubled childhood and, like so many others, creatively rewrite it. Here it was, approaching midnight on a Monday and young Shelley was out partying hard, sneaking a sip of cocktail from one of her hoodlum friends, high as a kite on some shit, flaunting her tats and not a parent in sight. He knew the type, he could spot them in an instant in a chat room, at the mall, in an arcade. It was almost like he could smell them. Vulnerable loners, left alone to grow up, looking for friendship anywhere they could find it and from anyone who would offer it. Even from vultures like him.

He watched her bend and pick up the balls, laughing and throwing her mane around, wrapping her lips seductively around the beer the horny bartender had just sent over with a smile. He felt himself getting hard, and wondered if she would recognize him from their little chat yesterday in the *World of Warcraft* White Wolf chat room. He imagined what she would look like as an addition to his collection. If she'd fit in. He imagined himself painting her full face, how he would capture on canvas the shaking of that nasty silver ring on her lower lip when she screamed.

But tonight was not about mistakes or acting on impulse. He was here to look, that was all. And even that was real risky. Being out at all now was risky, with all the attention he was getting. When the media announced a bad guy was on the loose, the public at large saw that bad guy everywhere, calling out their own boss or grandpa if the description fit. The hard-on disappeared. That was how the best got caught—being stupid. He was probably being paranoid thinking people were watching him. Or narcissistic. The anchor had already moved on to Terrible Tragedy Numero Quatro. He sipped at his drink and casually looked around, out at the world that was just beyond that closet door. No one was looking at him. No one was staring to see if they knew him. Or recognized him. To see if his face was famous or infamous. No one gave even a second thought that the person one barstool over, sharing a smile and a drink with them, might actually be . . . not right. That he might just be a psychopathic murderer who had a weakness for, well, pretty little things. No one worried that the hand they had inadvertently touched en route to the peanuts was the same hand that had made news tonight.

He grabbed his coat and put a very nice tip on the bar. He took one final glance around and downed his drink with a mouthful of warm, coppery blood. Nope. No one was looking at him. No one was even looking at the TV.

He held the smile in check as he headed through the late-night crowd and passed by the busy Skee-Ball lanes. The tips of his fingers lightly brushed the warm wings of her brilliantly colored butterfly as he made his way through the narrow swathe of young bodies and headed out the door. He felt the electricity run up his arm like a current. He mumbled an apology for his indiscretion, but she didn't even acknowledge the slight. She just kept on laughing.

No one cared. No one at all.

Not yet.

39

Lainey lay on the dirt floor, curled up in the tightest, smallest ball possible, her hands covering her ears. Her favorite song played over and over in her head. "The Sweet Escape" by Gwen Stefani. How she wished her mind could just escape, could just re-create a whole new world, like the song said. If only she could leave this tomb that reeked of old earth and mildew and human rot that she was trapped in, even for a few minutes. But there was no escape. Even her dreams had been replaced with terrifying nightmares.

She wasn't sure how long she had been lying there, singing the same song over and over again. Time had no meaning anymore. Minutes could be hours. Or even days. Or weeks, maybe.

Slowly she sat up, listening hard. Silence. There were no footsteps. No creaking floors. The ghostly scratching had finally stopped. And the voices . . . were they real? She shook her head, reaching cautiously in the darkness to feel where she was. To make sure she was, indeed, alone. She was so hungry. And thirsty. Her hand fell on something in the corner. Something smooth and bulky and large. It felt like a stuffed bag. Her hand felt around till she found an opening. She dipped her hand inside. It was filled with little, hard . . . pebbles?

"Are you still there?" whispered the voice. It was coming from the wall.

Lainey immediately curled up again on the floor and started to cry. "No, no, no . . ."

"Listen! Listen! Don't start singing again," commanded the voice in the wall. "Just talk to me."

Lainey sucked in a sniffle.

"Talk to me. It's OK. It'll be all right." It was a girl's voice. "Don't cry. I'm here, too. You're not alone."

"What?" Lainey whispered back.

"Just talk to me. I need to talk to someone. I'm going crazy here. And then you were singing . . ."

"Where are you?" Lainey placed her hand upon the cold wall.

"I don't know. In a closet, I guess. A room, like you. Right?"

"Right," Lainey said softly. She pressed her face up against the wall.

"Who are you? What's your name?"

"Lainey. I'm Lainey. My name's Lainey. He took me." The moment completely overwhelmed her and she started to cry again.

"He took all of us. He's bad. He's a really bad man."

"Us?"

"Yes. There are more of us. Down here, somewhere. I hear them in the walls."

"I can't see," Lainey blubbered. "He did something to my eyes. I think I'm blind!"

"It's just bandages. Bandages and tape. You can try and take it off, but you won't see anything anyway. There're no lights down here. And you'll rip your lashes out. If he finds out you peeked, he'll use glue."

A shiver ran up her spine. Just when she thought words couldn't get more horrible, they did.

"I don't care, though," the girl said defiantly. "I took mine off. That's what I'm saying—you can't see anything anyway."

"But you said he would hurt you . . ."

"I don't care anymore. Let him try. At least I'll see him coming at me. I won't be a sitting duck, like . . ." But she stopped herself.

"How many of you are there?" Lainey asked.

"I don't know. I only know the girls I've heard, like you, in the walls. I've talked to three others. Eva, Jackie, Adrianna."

"Where are they?"

There was a long pause. The girl sounded like she was choking up, but holding it in. "I don't know. I haven't talked to them in a long time. What's your sign?"

"What?"

"When's your birthday?"

"Um, August. August 27th. Why?"

"You're a Virgo. I knew it."

Lainey didn't say anything back.

"He's been gone for a while this time," the girl continued. "When he puts me in here, he's gone for a long time, but this time it's been really long."

"I'm hungry."

"He leaves a bag of food in the corner. Have you found it? And water bottles. Feel around."

"What is it? It feels like the bags my mom buys Rosey. She's my dog. It feels like dog chow."

"It is dog food. Have you found the water bottles?"

There was no way she was eating dog food. No way. She felt around some more. "Yeah. I feel them. There's a stack of them. How long have you been here?" Lainey asked, twisting off the cap and sniffing it. It smelled like nothing.

"Don't know. Longer than most, I think."

Lainey took a long drink of water. It tasted so good. She practically finished the entire bottle in one gulp. It reminded her again just how hungry she was. She raised a piece of kibble up to her nose and sniffed. It didn't smell that bad. "Who are you?" she asked finally, as she tried a little taste with the very tip of her tongue. "I mean, what's your name?"

There was a long pause. "Katy," the girl replied softly. "My name's Katy."

40

Mark Felding slugged down the last of his cold coffee, grabbed his script and research pad from the desk, and hurried out of his cramped office and down the hallway to makeup. His producer, Auggie, had only booked an hour of precious studio time, and Mark was, as usual lately, running way behind schedule. Not that he was complaining. In fact, Mark was feeling pretty damn good about himself these days. As he should. News ratings at WTVJ had shot way up since last week, impressively beating both CBS4 and WPLG Local 10 night after night in the eleven o'clock news slot; his investigative piece on South Florida runaways had generated a lot of buzz; and he was being considered for a couple of projects at the station, one of which was headlining a weekly three-minute crime prevention segment. What a 360. Just a few weeks ago the rumors were flying fast and furious at the station as to when the next round of pink slips was coming and just whose names might be on them. YouTube, Internet news groups, and SmartCams—robotic studio TV cameras that operate without cameramen—meant fewer and fewer warm bodies were needed to put on a news broadcast, so every day you had to worry if you were one of those bodies that producers could do without. Mark knew it wasn't hard, though, to connect the dots and figure out why ratings had shot skyward and his career had experienced a sudden resuscitation. The Picasso murder, as Gale Sampson's homicide was being called, had definitely been good for the business of news, and Mark's bizarre, intimate connection to the case was drawing crowds.

It was perhaps exploitative to personally benefit from such tragedy, but Mark also knew you had to strike while the iron was hot in the television business, because it didn't stay hot for long. In fact, producers didn't care what you did last year or last month or even last week—it was what are you doing right now? And right now, Mark Felding was riding a ratings surge into his own crime prevention segment, and maybe one day a shot at weekend anchor.

He knocked on the makeup room door. Nothing. He tried the handle. Locked. *Damn.* It was his first shot at hosting "Ask Mark" and HD was no one's friend. He dialed Auggie to find out where everyone in makeup had disappeared to. With the way station cuts had been going, it wouldn't be completely inconceivable to learn that makeup artists were some of the warm bodies that management had decided could be done without. He got Auggie's voice mail. Great.

"Felding! Yo, Mark!"

Mark recognized the voice behind him. It was Terry Walsh from the mail room, who was standing at the mail cubbies next to the elevator down the hall. Mark turned, waved, and motioned a thumb toward the door. "Hey there, Terry. You know where everyone went?"

Terry shrugged. "I don't know nothing important, Mark. But I got a package here that won't fit in your box." Dressed in a worn work shirt, tie-dyed tee, and too-long jeans, with his frizzy gray mane and super-size specs, Terry was a dead ringer for Jerry Garcia. He was also a fixture at the station, hiding out with the mail and eluding pink slips for years. Next to him was a loaded gray mail cart. He waved an oversize manila envelope in Mark's direction. "You want me to just put it on your desk?"

Mark's heart began to pound. He stared at Terry for a long moment. He *was* expecting some videotapes from archives on other self-help segments. Maybe that was what Terry had in his hand. "What's that, Terry?"

Terry waved the envelope again. "I don't know, dude. It came in today. Must've been hand delivered. It's got your name on it, but it won't fit in your box, 'cause you got a lot of other stuff in it already. It doesn't want to really bend." He tried to fold the envelope to demonstrate.

"No! No!" Mark yelled, running down the hall, his hand outstretched as if Terry was holding a bomb and playing with the red and blue wires. "Don't! Don't touch it!"

Terry stepped back. "OK, man," he answered with another shrug, handing the envelope over.

It felt like his heart might explode. Scenes from his two favorite crime shows, *CSI* and *Law & Order*, flew through his head. *What should he do?* He shouldn't flip. That's what he shouldn't do. He should look at the envelope, that's what he should do. He turned the mailer over in his hand. No special markings. Just a plain computer-printed label that said "WTVJ 6 Investigative Reporter Mark Felding" stuck on the front. He squeezed the package slightly. It felt stiff and bulky. Bumpy in spots. He sniffed at the flap. It smelled like paint.

He looked at his watch and pulled out his cell again. He ran a hand through his hair and dialed his producer as he headed back down the hall to his office. "Auggie, it's Mark again," he said when it went to voice mail. He tried hard to tame the excitement that was building in his voice, but it probably didn't work. "Cancel that concern about makeup. I'm afraid I won't be able to tape today anyway." He slid his fingers under the flap and opened the mailer. "Something's come up. Something really big."

41

The two girls were seated face-to-face on the floor, pressed close together in a twisted embrace, their wrists chained together at their sides, their butchered faces turned to face the artist. Black sockets existed where their eyes should have been. Red tears flowed down their cheeks to their distorted open mouths, forever immortalized with thick strokes of paint into bone-chilling screams.

The macabre painting of two screaming blond females had been made into a poster-size crime-scene photo that was now tacked onto a new corkboard that completely dominated a wall in the Crimes Against Children squad bay. Hung next to it was the picture of the Gale Sampson painting that had come in last week. Below that were photos from the Sampson crime scene taken at the Regal All-Suites. Two MEPIC flyers were thumbtacked below the screaming blondes, but there were no crime-scene photos posted there. Not yet. As of ten a.m. Friday, all they had was another brutal portrait.

"The painting's at the lab," Bobby said to the men seated at the conference table that had been set up in the CAC squad bay: Zo, Frank Veso, and CAC special agents Ciro Acevedo and Larry Vastine. If this latest work of grisly art turned out to be a painting of another crime scene, assembling a task force would be his first priority. But even without two more bodies, Bobby knew that was exactly what he was looking at—a crime scene. So he figured it would be in the public's interest to get the best brains in on the investigation now. With that in mind, he'd brought in Vastine and Acevedo and contacted the Miami-Dade State Attorney's Office for legal assistance. ASA Stephanie Gravano was now officially assigned part-time to assist the soon-to-be formed task force with legal matters, like warrants and subpoenas. If more bodies were found in jurisdictions outside the City of Miami, where Gale Sampson was found, then members of those police departments would join the task force as well, along with members of departments where the victims had gone missing from.

"Here's to hoping you don't need a bigger wall," Zo commented. "I see you think you have an ID," he added, nodding at the MEPIC flyers underneath the screaming blondes.

"We're getting DNA from birth dad out of Dayton, Ohio, but it looks like Roseanne and Rosalie Boganes, eighteen and seventeen, from Florida City. Two sisters who disappeared last August from their aunt's house after their mother died of a heroin overdose. Dad's getting swabbed as we speak. When and if we get a body—or bodies—we'll at least have a genetic sample to compare."

Zo shook his head. "Sisters? Never even heard they were missing. How do runaway sisters not make the freaking news?"

"Runaway siblings aren't all that unusual. Abuse in the home usually means more than one kid's being abused. Or maybe Mom and Dad have drinking or drug problems and the kids want a way out besides being separated in foster care," Bobby replied.

"Kids think there's safety in numbers—you know, the 'I'll jump, if you will' mentality. Or maybe one sibling doesn't want the other to be on her own. I call it the 'Little Momma syndrome,'" offered Larry Vastine.

Bobby nodded. "Both Boganes girls are habitual runaways, according to the aunt, who never wanted custody anyway. I talked to her today. She still thinks Rosalie and Roseanne hopped a freight train and finally went to Vegas, like they were always threatening to."

"Can Auntie ID if we get a body? Or rather, bodies?" Zo looked over at the photos of Gale Sampson and thoughtfully rubbed the scruff on his face, obviously remembering the gruesome scene he had walked in on last week. "Probably not," he murmured, answering his own question. "So how do you figure it's them? These sisters?"

"Since last Thursday I've been combing through Clearinghouse photos and Dawn's been compiling a list of South Florida kids that aren't on MEPIC, trying to come up with some kind of comprehensive list of runaways to work with. Mark Felding at Channel 6 had started making his own list, too, categorizing similarities in victims and disappearances. There are other missing sibs, but only two blond sisters. The deciding factor was Rosalie Boganes was described as having a disfigured thumb in the Florida City police report. Daddy sliced off half of it when she was three, which is why he lost custody. Look here," Bobby said, pointing below the chained wrist of one girl in the painting. "Half a thumb."

"Shit." Zo exhaled a deep sigh. "Another whacko trying to give this city the reputation it deserves. Now this Felding. Talk to me. What the fuck's up with that guy? I get to find out there's another painting by watching the motherfucking news? What's that about?"

"Felding's an asshole," Bobby replied. "Claims he got the package and was calling us when his producer walked in, saw the painting, and went live at five. Says all he mentioned on air was that there was another breaking development in the Picasso murders."

"Yeah, and I about choked on my hot dog when he said that breaking development was another fucking painting of two dead girls that had been sent to him," Zo grumbled.

"That whole 'I would never compromise a police investigation!' bullshit was just that—bullshit. He's a paparazzo and this Picasso is his meal ticket. Being the first to blab that he's just received another painting is sure to keep the ratings up and confirm Mark Felding as the new star in the neighborhood."

"He's a vulture," Ciro said. "They all are, every one of those reporters. Just ask a celebrity."

"Can we charge him with obstruction?" Zo asked.

"Don't I wish, but no," Bobby answered. "The painting went to him. I don't think we have any grounds. For whatever reason, this

Picasso psycho has picked a washed-up Channel 6 field reporter to be his mouthpiece to the world and the guy is doing a helluva job. He's no fool—I'm sure he sees the potential career opportunities. He did eventually call and he did eventually hand the painting over. But I'm gonna ask Stephanie to try and have a judge gag him. It's an on-going criminal investigation that his antics are compromising."

"If a judge doesn't wanna do it, tell Stephanie I'll shove a gag in his mouth," Zo replied. "Anything on the package?"

"Nope. Untraceable adhesive label. Dime-a-dozen Office Depot envelope. Prints everywhere, from the mail room to the executive producer, I'm sure. It's going to Trace and Serology. We'll see what we get, but I'm not hopeful, unless they can pick up DNA on the label."

"Let me guess—your name was somewhere in this package?" Zo asked Bobby.

"Same as before. A string of newspaper clips glued together," Bobby replied.

"Well, it's obvious this guy wants your attention, Shep. After he makes the five o'clock news, that is," Larry commented.

"Fortunately, Felding didn't broadcast the actual painting," Bobby said. "At least we have something to screen the loons." For some reason no one could ever rationally explain to him, high-profile crimes always attracted a large number of false confessions. Weeding out the nuts from among the leads could be very time-consuming.

"If this is the same sort of deal as Sampson, then these two are already dead," Larry said. "Based on Sampson's autopsy, she'd been held for a long time before he offed her. If he had her since she disappeared, that was five months. These sisters—how long you say they've been gone?"

"August," Bobby replied.

"That's three. And that's a helluva long time to be housing live girls, if that's what he's doing. Was there anything on Sampson's body that might help us out in figuring where he's keeping them?"

"Everything on her person is going through Serology and Toxicology. You know that can take weeks, sometimes months if they don't know what they're looking for," Bobby answered with a sigh.

"What the hell is bringing this guy out now?" Ciro asked. "I mean, if he's been keeping and offing girls without anybody bothering him, why is he coming out now? What does he want?"

"Just what he's getting—publicity. His face on the tube. Infamy."

"So where are they?" Veso asked quietly.

"That's the million-dollar question," Bobby replied with a sigh, forgetting for the moment that the guy was still gunning for his job. He moved to the photo of the girls. "Here, out this small round window behind them is clearly blue water. And two boats sitting there. I had Forensics enhance the photo they took, here." He slid an eight-by-ten out of a folder and tacked it up on the corkboard. "It looks to me like he's painted the beginning of a name on the boat. *The Emp*. Then it cuts off. And this here? Is this maybe the outside of a house? Looks real fancy. Maybe Star Island or Sunny Isles. Could be any real nice waterfront."

"Maybe they're on a boat? Ya know, the round window?" Ciro said. "Larry, you're the yachtsman. What does it look like to you?"

"Could be a boat. If, like Bobby says, he's painting what he's seeing, he's looking at those two docked boats and probably a house or restaurant. I don't recognize it either."

"Search all registered boats from Palm Beach to the Keys to see if we can get a match, Larry," Bobby said. "And see if there's a way we can find out about visiting boats. You know, those registered someplace else but holed up in South Florida during season."

"Done," Larry replied with a nod.

The room went quiet for a long moment. All eyes were on the corkboard. It was Bobby who broke the somber silence. "I think he's put some other clues in here for us to find, guys. Very subtle clues. And that's why I think it's time for more than one set of eyes to look for them."

Bobby pulled out another eight-by-ten and pointed at a necklace on one of the blondes. A bright neon pink heart within a heart. Then he pulled out an MEPIC flyer. "This necklace is seen on a picture of one of the Clearinghouse girls. Here—Nikole Krupa, a fifteen-year-old brunette out of Riviera Beach. It's a very unique necklace, you know? And the Led Zeppelin T-shirt worn by the other sister matches the clothing description of another runaway, Adrianna Sweet. We also have the happy-face T-shirt that Gale Sampson was wearing that matches the clothing description of what Allegra Villenueva was last seen wearing. Then here," he said, pointing to the far-off corner of the painting, "look at this." He pulled out a third enhanced eight-by-ten. The top of a math textbook poked out of a khaki-and-pink book bag.

"What does that say? 'What if I'm Not the Hero?'" Larry asked.

"Looks like it," Bobby replied. "It's a reference to a line spoken by Edward Cullen, the vampire character in the *Twilight* movies."

"Didn't that whacko mom say her daughter had a *Twilight* book bag?" Zo asked.

Bobby nodded. "She did."

"He's got the Emerson girl . . . "

"Yup. He's got Lainey," Bobby replied. "And I think there are others. I think that within these paintings are hidden clues. Like a *Highlights* magazine. Remember them? The 'Can you see the hidden pictures?' puzzles? The T-shirts, the necklace, the different hairstyle on Gale Sampson. The two different DNA blood samples on the Sampson painting. Hell, we may not even recognize all the clues because we're not looking for the victims. We may not even know they're missing."

"Holy shit . . . ," Zo said, rubbing his stubble again.

"He's not just taunting us, guys," Bobby said quietly, staring hard at the painting. "He's showing us his collection."

42

"What about the stepdad?" Ciro asked as the room stared at the photos in silence. "I mean, if it wasn't interesting before that he liked to paint pretty pictures in his secret room, it sure as hell is now. Now that we know there's definitely a link between Lainey's disappearance and this Picasso."

"Exactly. Only it's a little too obvious, I'm thinking," Bobby replied. "If LaManna is Picasso, why would he send us a painting that potentially linked him to the disappearance of his stepdaughter? He already knows we're looking at him for that."

"Could be he thinks it will throw suspicion off of him," Ciro mused. "Could be he thinks that if we think this psycho Picasso is the one who has his kid, then we won't look at him no more. That we'll go away, go looking in another direction, at other people. You know, reverse psychology? Like he's duped us by putting up a sign with an arrow that says, 'Bad Guy that-a-way!'"

"I've interviewed the man and I just don't think he's that smart," Bobby replied. "But he might be that stupid. And I agree that we have to check him out. That means surveillance, twenty-four-seven."

"Have you talked to his other kid? The older girl? Maybe she can shed some light," Zo asked.

"According to Debra LaManna, she's been continuously, quote, 'unavailable.' End quote. Not sure if that's with a little assistance from

Mom—the family wagons circled after Hubby became a person of interest. But Sis has a runaway history herself, so it is quite possible she took off and Mom is not reporting it so we stay out of her life."

"The kiddie porn on LaManna's computer wasn't enough to pop him, huh?" Larry asked. "At least get him off the street while we look for more?"

"He's denying it's kiddie, and the girls are not prepubescent," Bobby replied. "Finding an expert who'll testify that they could be under sixteen will be difficult and will inevitably lead to another saying they're not. That's reasonable doubt. Stephanie won't even consider an arrest on that. As far as the webcam, there's no evidence he's the one who sent the Trojan. Chris Turan can't ID who sent it. The secret studio is what's going to get us another search warrant and a much closer look at that house. I want clothes, paint, canvas, brush hairs, fibers—anything and everything that could possibly link him to these paintings. I also want to get in his car. He had to transport these girls from wherever he met them to where he kept them, to wherever he dumped them."

"And wherever he might be holding them still," added Zo. "If what you're thinking is right, Bobby, if this pink necklace and the different T-shirts and DNA means he's planting a clue garden and there are more victims—and, like Gunther speculated, this nut has been chaining them up for a while before he kills them—then that also means he has to have a place to be keeping them. Let's pull whatever we can on properties that LaManna's got access to. That includes relatives. We also have to consider that maybe this guy isn't working alone."

Bobby nodded. "Another reason why I don't want him picked up just yet. If he is involved, if he is Picasso, then he can bring us to these other girls, who might very well still be alive. Gale Sampson was only killed a day or two before we found her. I'm not holding out much hope for the Boganes sisters, but I am for the others—if there are others. Whether LaManna is Picasso or it's somebody else, the question we have to ultimately answer is the one that will lead us to his victims. Every indication so far is this guy is targeting runaways and throwaways—the kids nobody wants. How? How is he meeting them? And what kind of music is he playing to get them to follow him out of their houses like some Pied Piper in the middle of the night? If we find out where he's hunting from, we might just find him." Bobby's cell chirped just then. He picked it up when he saw the number. "Dees."

"Agent Dees, this is Duty Officer Karin Koehle with FDLE in Tallahassee. I'm calling to advise you that the juvenile you had flagged in the system was run this morning by the Coral Springs Police Department responding to a residential burglar alarm. Liza Ashley Emerson, DOB May 10, 1992, is being transported to Coral Springs, pending an interview and parental notification. Would you like me to contact the arresting authority on your behalf to advise them of the flag, or would you like the contact information yourself?"

43

"We've been looking for you, Liza," Bobby said with a smile when he and Detective Bill Dagher opened the door and stepped into the detective's office at the Coral Springs PD.

The thin, disheveled girl with the long, tangled brown hair squeaked, jumped in her chair, and dropped her cell phone, which she'd obviously been busy yapping on. It hit the thin carpet with a thud and ricocheted into three pieces around the room. "I . . . you . . . I didn't hear you open the door. I thought you were my dad," she managed as she stooped down to pick up the pieces. She cleared her throat. "My step—"

Bobby picked up the battery and handed it to her. "Stepdad? No. But that's who I want to talk to you about, Liza. I'm Special Agent Bobby Dees. I work for the Florida Department of Law Enforcement. I'm investigating the disappearance of your little sister, Elaine."

"Oh." Liza's eyes darted around the room. She sat on the edge of her seat, like she was getting ready to run.

"I've been trying to talk to you for two weeks now, but you're not at home, you're not at school. You're not working at the bowling alley anymore." He leaned casually against the edge of the metal desk in front of her. Dagher stood guard by the door. "What's up with that? Are you in trouble, Liza?"

She looked down at her lap, where she was shredding a tissue. "No. No trouble. I just don't want to be home right now, that's all."

"Why?" Dagher asked.

She shrugged.

"When was the last time you saw Lainey?" Bobby asked.

She shrugged again. "Dunno. The day before she didn't come home, I think. At breakfast."

"What're your thoughts on your sister's disappearance? Any reason she might not want to go home, either?"

Liza said nothing for a long while. She continued to shred the tissue into little white shards of fluff. "I saw the news at my friend's house. I saw that there's a guy killing teens, you know? Painting weird pictures of them dead and all. And that Lainey . . ." Her voice broke. "Oh God, that Lainey might be with him, you know? Then my mom told me the police were at the house, taking things like the computer and stuff, and that they were interrogating Todd at the police station."

Bobby nodded. "Well, I'm not at liberty to discuss everything with you, but we have a couple of investigations going, that's true. And your stepfather has definitely been questioned about some things— some things I want to talk to you about."

She turned red and looked back down at her lap. "There was no way I was going home after that, you know? With him still there."

"Todd?"

She nodded.

"Tell me why."

She shook her head and sucked in a sniffle. When she finally spoke, her small voice was just above a whisper. "She's a good kid, Lainey. A good sister. I didn't tell her that. I thought she just left for a few days to get away from him and all, you know? To get him to stop trying to come into her room. Like me—I didn't take that shit from him, you know? The fucking perv. But then she didn't come home at all and now he's back at the house. And I'm not going back there." She started to cry finally. Full force. Bobby handed her another tissue from the box on Dagher's desk. He said nothing while she tried to catch her breath.

"So me and my friends, we just crashed at this house we thought was empty. You know, like the people couldn't pay for it no more? I forget what they call that. We weren't burglarizing nothing. I just didn't want to go home, is all. He's a creep and an asshole and a perv, and . . . oh God, I think, I think he might have done something to Lainey . . ."

44

"So you think this might be the guy, huh?" Judge Reuben Sullivan said with a cocked eyebrow as he signed the warrant that would allow them to search Todd LaManna's home once again—this time for evidence in the Gale Sampson homicide and the Boganes sisters' disappearance. The judge had already signed one for Todd's 2001 black Infiniti Q45. "Picasso, hmmm? Is that what they're calling him in the press?"

"The name seems to be sticking," Bobby replied, looking around at the dozens of celebrity charcoal caricatures that covered the walls of the judge's chambers. With his enormous curly, leprechaun-red head, Karl Malden–size noggin, and small body, Judge Sullivan kind of looked like a caricature himself.

"Great. Another South Florida serial killer with a catchy nickname. Look what Cupid did for tourism in Miami; they're still taking pictures on the MacArthur Causeway," the judge remarked, shaking his head. "Stopping traffic to get a picture of nine-year-old bloodstains that aren't there anymore."

"Don't forget the dead celebs, judge," Stephanie chided. "They still stop buses on Ocean Drive in front of the Versace mansion. And that's over a decade. Wasn't Anna Nicole Smith handled in this courthouse?"

The judge grimaced, as if he'd just sucked on a lemon. "Don't remind me. You couldn't drive down Third Avenue for a month. I hope
that circus fever doesn't spread north, now. Keep your bloodthirsty
tourists and their cameras in Miami." The judge slid the warrant
across the conference table to Bobby. "Hope you boys find what
you're looking for this time." Then he slipped on his black robe and
headed out the door and back to his courtroom.

With the warrant in hand, Bobby and Stephanie stepped out into
the chaotic hallways of the Broward County Courthouse. Babies in
umbrella strollers whined and cried while being pushed by teens who
looked far too young to be moms outside the fourth-floor courtrooms, alongside tired, middle-age women who looked far too young
to be grandmas. Broward Sheriff's Office deputies escorted cuffed defendants to their courtrooms. Witnesses and out-of-custody defendants, some in baggy long-shorts and wife-beater tees, mingled
around the wooden doors, either waiting to be called into court or de-
bating whether to run before they were. God rest his soul, when
Bobby's dad was on the bench in New York, he would've held somebody in contempt for wearing shorts in his courtroom. And whether
it was a defendant or a witness wearing them, contempt would've
meant jail.

"We've got a signature on both. I'm headed to the house now,"
Bobby said into his Nextel as they followed the cheesy black strip of
electrical tape on the floor that led pedestrian traffic from the newer
criminal court wing to the older part of the courthouse and the bank
of elevators that went down to the lobby. He hated the Broward
courthouse. It was like a rat maze.

"Was that Zo?" Stephanie asked.

Bobby nodded. "The guys are sitting up on the house. The car's at
CarMax Pompano, along with its owner. Zo and Veso are gonna seize
it there. The Sheriff's Office is assisting, since we'll be using their lab.
Thanks for being so quick with this, Steph. And thanks for coming
up here with me. You didn't have to make the trip."

The line for the elevators was four persons deep, so he led her by
the elbow to the stairwell.

"It got me out of calendar with Judge Spencer, so thank you," she began as they headed down, the click of her high heels echoing through the empty stairwell. "But I'm warning you, Bobby, we still may have a real problem with the paints that Ciro seized from LaManna's studio. The brand looks like a match with the paint used on the Picasso paintings, and that's good and all, but Ciro should never have seized them without a warrant. He should never have been in that room."

"But it's because Ciro was in that room and saw what he saw that we just got warrant number two signed. Remember, the wife gave consent to search and seize."

"We may be OK on the search part, but as far as the seizure, the room was Hubby's and Hubby's alone. Debbie LaManna's claiming she didn't even know it existed. If this guy is our Picasso, the argument that LaManna's slick defense attorney will eventually make is that the wife didn't have authority to consent to the seizure of her husband's things that she clearly had no control over. I don't mean to be argumentative or rain on your search-warrant parade, but . . ."

A senior prosecutor with over a decade of trial experience—including a couple of years experimenting on the dark side with criminal defense—Stephanie definitely knew her way around a case and a courtroom, and she was pretty damn good at guessing what was coming at her around every corner. She never tried to sugarcoat shit, either. Some cops—a lot of cops, actually—didn't like it when a pretty girl was smarter than them. And they really didn't like it when that pretty, smart girl let them know just how smart she was without at least stroking their egos first. But that's what Bobby appreciated about Stephanie—he always knew where she was coming from. And unlike his colleagues, he was smart enough himself to listen.

"Well, there's no unringing a bell," Bobby said with a shrug. "LaManna's on twenty-four-seven surveillance now. If he is our guy, the hope is he'll lead us to the Boganes sisters and anyone else he's holding."

"You mean Lainey," she said as they reached the first floor.

"And any other missing girls that we think he may be keeping," Bobby said quietly as he held the lobby door open for her.

Stephanie stopped walking and stared at him. Then she shut the door with her hand, so that they were alone again in the stairwell. "Bobby," she said softly, "I've known you for a long time. You're one of my favorite agents. I'm thrilled that you're working this case, because I know it's in the best of hands. But"—she took a deep breath—"I gotta ask—are you OK with all this? I mean, this is real close to home."

Stephanie and he had worked together long enough and closely enough on a couple of cases that they'd developed not only a good working relationship, but a friendship as well. Stephanie knew all about Katy. She'd been one of the very first to offer help in those horrible days right after Katy had run off.

"You corner me in a dark, empty stairwell to tell me I'm your favorite? I'm blushing," Bobby joked with a wry smile.

"Ha, ha," she returned. "You don't make this easy on a person, do you?" She shook her head. "Cops, you know, they're so big and strong that nothing and no one can break them. I'm just saying that . . . well, look, I won't pretend to know what you're going through, but I know that it must be hell, Bobby."

"It's a party, sweetheart."

"We haven't talked much in the past year."

"Not much to talk about."

"How are things at home, then? Can I ask that?"

Bobby shrugged. "Sure, you can ask."

She looked hurt. "Sorry. I didn't mean to stick my nose where it obviously doesn't belong. My bad." She turned to walk away and open the door.

He gently grabbed her arm and pulled her back to him. The smile was gone. He ran a hand through his hair, trying hard to pull his thoughts together. "Things are . . . tough, Steph. I'm not gonna lie. Look, I appreciate you asking, but this year has been, like you said, hell. Pure hell. My wife has not recovered. Neither have I. I don't think we ever will. No, I *know* we never will."

She nodded but said nothing, waiting for him to go on.

He took a deep breath. "Everything's changed. Everyone's different. Sometimes I feel LuAnn and I are like two strangers in this little boat just sailing the world all alone, hoping to find our way back home, but in the meantime just trying to find some land. A place where we can stop paddling and searching and just . . . be. And every day we don't find home, every day we don't even find that little patch of land, we forget more and more what it is we're looking for. I mean, we remember home as Utopia, right? But meanwhile, maybe we're passing by a lot of smaller opportunities to just . . . be. To just make it." He shook his head. "I'm an asshole. I shouldn't be saying nothing. That's all the Red Bull talking on no sleep. But you asked, Counselor."

"I did ask," she replied softly. "Look, do you really think you're the only one in the world to have relationship issues? Especially after a—for lack of a better word—tragedy? Don't be such a guy."

He smiled. "You must have a way with getting people to talk, Counselor. That's why all those defendants are afraid to take the stand. Afraid of what you're gonna get them to say."

She blushed. Stephanie was pretty, no doubt, with long, thick dark red hair and fiery blue eyes that lit up when she was angry or got an idea. He'd heard more than one cop fantasize about what she looked like underneath her fitted suits. Bobby had wondered once or twice why she'd never gotten married.

"Thanks for the compliment," she said. "So where do you go from here? I mean, with your daughter?"

"I keep looking. I've had some sightings in California. San Fran and Venice Beach. I've been to the runaway hot spots in Jersey, New York, Vegas, Detroit. Nothing. Then last month Covenant House sent me a picture of a girl out of New Orleans that could've been her, but it was so blurry there was no telling for sure. By the time I got there, she was gone."

A couple of clerks walked down the stairs past them and out the stairwell. Neither Bobby nor Stephanie said anything. "Do you think there's a possibility he has her?" Stephanie asked quietly when they were gone and the door had closed again. "That Picasso has Katy? Is that what I'm sensing here?"

Bobby sighed and slapped his hand on the wall. "I can't go there. That was the first thought that crossed my mind when I realized that there might be more victims. But no, I can't go there. There are thousands of runaways out there. And some don't come home because they don't want to. Because they're not ready, is all. Anything else, and . . ." He closed his eyes. "Well, I just can't go there, Stephanie."

She grasped his hand, her warm fingers wrapped tightly in his. He squeezed back. It felt good. It was a weird sensation, though—one that immediately had him feeling guilty. The other night at the dining table covered with MEPIC flyers was the first time LuAnn had spontaneously touched him in months. Like he had just blurted to Stephanie for some unknown reason, since Katy had run away, things had slowly but surely gotten more and more distant between them. He was sure LuAnn blamed him for Katy leaving. No doubt she harbored resentment that it was *his* final words to cut Ray out of Katy's life once and for all that made her leave. *His* initial indiscretion in letting her date the boy they both knew right off the bat was bad news. *His* failure to recognize that Katy was doing drugs long before track marks appeared on her skinny arm. Over the past eleven months he'd watched as LuAnn withdrew into her world—working more hours, going out with friends when she did have free time. He probably had, too, to be fair—but work for Bobby was no escape. It provided no relief. Looking for someone else's missing kid while staring at a wall with his daughter's smiling picture on it just made him that much more aware of his failings as both a father and a cop. And now, feeling the way he was feeling, with Stephanie's hand in his, the smell of her perfume filling the small space between their bodies, made him that much more aware of his failings as a husband. He pulled away and opened the lobby door.

"You know, I'm here if you need me," Stephanie said softly as she stepped past him. "That's all I'll say. I'm here for you if you need an ear. Good luck today."

He nodded slowly. Then he watched as she walked out into the bustling lobby and disappeared into the crowd.

45

Walter "Wally" Jackson was tired of getting the shit beat out of him. Having lived on the streets for so many years he'd lost count, Wally knew the dangers that came with resting your head under a bridge when the sun went down. It used to be that cops were your biggest worry—hassling you from place to place when the neighborhood started to complain, messing with your nest when you went out to rustle up a little change during the day. While sitting in a jail cell might fill the stomach and keep you out of the rain, a loitering arrest all but guaranteed that when you finally did get CTS—credit time served—all your shit would be long gone. Now, partying with the wrong person, getting jacked while you were high, pissing on someone else's nest, or fucking with someone's lady—those were all things that any fool could tell you would bring trouble. Homeless or not, you can't lose your common sense just cause you don't have a crib and a job. But lately, living on the streets presented a whole new set of fucked-up dangers to look out for. The rules of fair play and survival had apparently changed, and twice in the past six months—twice— Wally had had his skull split open by punks with peach fuzz on their balls and too much time on their hands. Macho teenage faggots who took to beating up guys like him with baseball bats just for fun. "Bum bashing" was what it was called, and it was apparently now some sort of fucked-up sport all over the world, someone at the hospital had told him the first time they'd put his brains back inside his head. It could be worse, that same someone had told him. In Miami, a guy had been lit up like a birthday candle with his own bottle of Popov vodka while he slept off a big one. But Wally hadn't listened to all the dire warnings. He'd gone back to his nest in Birch State Park. This time, though, when he woke up with another sixty staples on the other side of his dented melon, he'd decided it was time to take the warnings a bit more seriously.

With a brown paper bag full of all the shit he owned in the world under his arm, Wally had walked out of the hospital Monday afternoon, gotten on a bus, and tried to figure out where the hell he was gonna go now. Since his aching head was still wrapped in bandages, a shelter was what the discharge nurse had suggested. But Wally knew from previous encounters at the Homeless Assistance Center that there was more of a chance of getting into a fistfight there than under a bridge with an acne-faced bastard and his friend, Louisville Slugger. Besides, Wally liked his space. He liked doing as he pleased. He didn't need no one telling him how to live just because they fronted you a pillow and a hot meal.

He remembered his old friend Bart, who he'd chummed with for a while before Bart dropped dead last summer. Bart used to have great ideas on where to crash when things were getting hot with the cops or you needed to stay dry. Fort Lauderdale beach was full of second and third homes, owned by old people who didn't like to come down to Florida till it got real cold up north, like January and February. Great places to crash. Course, the penalty was a lot stiffer if you got caught in someone's crib rather than in a park after hours—Bart had showed him the scar from the bullet that had hit his chest, courtesy of a trigger-happy cop who'd caught him sneaking in a window. You could be looking at prison time, too. Of course, Wally thought, as he stepped off the bus at Las Olas and Hendricks Isle, those were things you only had to worry about if you got caught.

Like a lot of older homes on the swanky isles off Fort Lauderdale's Las Olas Boulevard, almost every other house on Hendricks seemed to be in some state of construction or deconstruction. Old houses were being torn down, new mansions were being built, and towering dockside condos were going up on both sides of the street. Mixed in with all the new construction were a few old houses farther down the block that were shuttered like bomb shelters—at least until winter officially arrived in a couple of months. Homes that were too old for alarms.

With the sun almost down now, the construction sites were all abandoned. Even so, Wally knew that limping like a zombie down the middle of the road with a mummy-wrapped head and stitched-up face would definitely attract the attention of anyone who might be out for a jog or walking her dog, so he ducked inside the concrete bones of a half-built mansion and cracked open a cold one while he waited for it to get dark. When the lights came up on the houses and their matching yachts on the isle across the waterway, he slipped out through graveyards of landfill, broken concrete, and rusted rebar to the crumbling seawall, following it along till he found the house Bart had told him about: The flamingo-pink ranch with the hurricane shutters on the back door and the extra key hidden in a magnetic hideaway box behind the dead flowerpot. In just a few minutes he'd be inside and out of sight, hopefully enjoying some AC if he could get the darn thing to work.

Except the hideaway box was gone.

Damn. The windows were all sealed with metal accordion shutters. Wally looked around. His head was killing him. Maybe he should just make camp here in the backyard and look for a new place in the morning. Then he spotted the old forty-foot sailboat docked behind the house. If the owners obviously weren't here till at least next month, then they just as obviously would not be needing their boat, which didn't look to Wally like it had seen much sea time lately anyway. *Crown Jewel* was the faded name gold-scripted on the back. With no intimidating shutters to worry about, Wally figured it would require a lot less effort to get inside the *Crown Jewel* than the Crummy Abode. He limped down to the sailboat and climbed aboard. It would be too much to hope for some food down below, but you never knew.

Maybe there'd be a couple of cans and some bottled water. A few brews would be nice, too. That would hold him for a couple of days till he felt up to going back out on the street and raising some cash.

It was too easy. A quick jimmy with the pocket knife he kept in his sock and he was in. The wood door led to a cabin below. As he climbed down the skinny stairway into pitch blackness, he hoped that Bart hadn't blabbed to a few dozen other guys about this place. He didn't need to get his ass kicked again.

It was the smell that had him thinking that perhaps his first hunch was right, that maybe someone else was living aboard the *Crown Jewel*. It was a rancid smell, like of really bad BO, or maybe of old, rotting garbage, but it was not overpowering. It was more like it had been really, really bad and was fading away. And it was mixed with the stink of mildew. The owners had probably left the freaking fridge open with food in it. Without electricity, the food had gone bad. He hoped there were no bugs. He hated flying roaches. Wally stuck a cigarette in his mouth and reached for his lighter. Time to see what tonight's accommodations would look like.

He lit his butt, then held out the flame in front of him to see where he was going. He was standing in the middle of a living room, with chairs and a coffee table and a dining table, too. Off behind him was a galley kitchen. So far, so good—and no monster bugs. If he opened a couple of windows, he could probably get rid of the stink. What a life. To have enough money to own a house you don't use and a forty-foot boat you don't sail. He walked a little farther, down a few more steps, and opened the door right in front of him. The one that led, presumably, to the sleeping quarters. The flame went out and he shook the lighter and flicked it again, squinting in the darkness to see what was in front of him.

When he saw the two bodies sitting up in the middle of the round captain's bed, their arms wrapped around each other, his first thought was that his hunch had been right—someone else had gotten this great idea long before him and he'd just walked in on two people doing the nasty. He mumbled "sorry" and took a step back, but he stumbled, catching himself with the edge of the bedding and pulling it with him. The bodies tumbled forward on the bed. The flame went out. And no one said a word.

That's when Wally realized that the bad, rotting smell was all around him and the two people he'd just walked in on in the inky darkness were very, very dead.

46

"Larry, what've you got?" Bobby started as he walked into the CAC squad bay Tuesday morning. "Anything on Lori No-Last-Name?"

"No luck on the girl," Larry replied, looking up from his laptop. He picked up files, following Bobby into his office. "I did find the two losers Todd LaManna met up with the night of the 26th at the Side Pocket Pub: Jules Black and Alex Juarez. They work in CarMax service. Both say Todd hooked up with them about eight and left about eleven with a lady nobody knew. Some brunette. Best description is she had a rack on her and looked to be more than of age. They didn't know her name. She just talked to him at the bar and they walked out together a few minutes later. It's not the secretary, 'cause she's a redhead and we checked, although he was banging her, too."

"Anyone know where he was from five to eight?"

"Nope."

"That's not so good for our boy."

"What about the lab?" Ciro asked as he walked in, coffee cup in hand. "Anything back yet?"

"The car was clean," Bobby replied. "No blood, but they did find three strands of Lainey's hair in the trunk." He waved a piece of paper in the air. "Lab report—hot off the fax."

"In the trunk?" Ciro asked.

"They pulled hairs from the brush we seized in Lainey's room and matched them. Is that fresh?" Bobby asked, nodding at Ciro's coffee.

"Kiki just made some. It's a little strong, but you know, she's Cuban. So things are really not looking good for our boy." Ciro shook his head. "Scumbag. How do you think they got there?"

Bobby shrugged. "Could be he threw her in the trunk. Could be from the beach bag she threw in the trunk last summer. Impossible to say where or when or how, and it's potentially explainable. But there is more news: The manufacturer is a match on the paint. Winsor & Newton. We just can't ID an actual color match, because both the Sampson and Boganes portrait paint was blended. The lab can't differentiate pigment colors once they're blended. Canvas is white stretched linen, no discernable weave. Untraceable." Bobby picked up his empty Mickey Mouse mug and fingered an oversize ear. It was a gift from Katy years ago for his birthday. "I think I'll see if Kiki wants to share."

"So we got one sis saying Stepdad's a fucking octopus and that the younger one, who's now missing, was busy trying to fend him off. He ain't got no alibi for the time his step goes AWOL, and her freaking hairs are in his trunk? Oh, and the paint's a match," Larry said, scratching his head. "When can we move on him, Bobby? I mean, we can pop him for L & L on the older kid—at least get him off the street."

"I don't want him off the street, Larry. We have at least one missing girl that we know for sure is still out there—his stepdaughter. If he's working alone and he's popped, who the hell's gonna take care of her?"

The twisted facts of a case out of Kentucky a couple years back that Bobby had verbally assisted on immediately came to mind. Chad Fogerty was a suspect in a series of disappearances of at least ten girls. Kentucky police figured Fogerty's victims were long dead, so they trumped up some charges just to get him off the street while they tried to make a case, thinking they had potentially saved another parent a heartbreaking tragedy. When the trumped-up charges fell flat some three months later and Fogerty finally got out of jail, persistent detectives followed him to a remote farm outside of Bowling Green. A farm nobody ever knew he had. In the underground tornado shelter, shocked detectives found the caged bodies of all ten missing girls—girls who had slowly starved to death while Fogerty was sleeping peacefully on a cot in the county jail. No way was Bobby gonna let that happen in this case. He'd never forgive himself. Even though he still wasn't completely convinced that LaManna was Picasso, he wasn't taking any chances with a kid's life.

"If she's still alive, Bobby," Larry tried.

Bobby shook his head. "I want to see where he's going. Zo did some checking. Found relatives in Tennessee and LaManna's mother in Port St. Lucie." Port St. Lucie was a small, super-quiet city on the eastern shore of central Florida, about an hour and a half south of Orlando. It was a haven for retirees. "I'm gonna head up to see Mom tomorrow. I'll have the Chattanooga police check on the other relatives. What about the boat angle, Larry? Anything?"

"There are eighty-nine boats registered in Miami and Broward counties that begin with the words 'The Emp.' And the Coast Guard doesn't track boats registered in other states that come to sail our blue waters—they only keep tabs on boats coming into the country."

"Shit," Bobby replied. "All right. Eighty-nine is doable. Let's start with that. We'll divide each county and each take twenty—"

Frank Veso stuck his head in the CAC squad bay. "Hey, Bobby," he called, obviously out of breath. "You need to turn on a TV. Looks like your case—our case—is on! Put on 6."

Bobby could feel his chest tighten. He flicked on the portable behind him, just in time to see WTVJ's Mark Felding standing in front of a pink house, the sails of a large sailboat rising over the roofline behind him. Blue and red lights from more than one police cruiser spun all around him, visible even in the bright sun. Uniforms crawled on the lawn, which was sectioned off with yellow crime-scene tape. Underneath Felding ran the boldface graphic:

BREAKING NEWS: TWO BODIES FOUND IN BOAT IN FORT LAUDERDALE BELIEVED TO BE MISSING MIAMI SISTERS . . .

" . . . no one knows more than that, or at least they're not telling us, Sue," Felding was saying. "But from speaking with sources who *have* interviewed Walter Jackson, I'd say this could well be the work of the very dangerous killer known so intimately, unfortunately, to both myself and the police as Picasso. And if, once again, *if* these are the missing Boganes sisters, which has yet to be confirmed—well, Sue, all I can say is that law enforcement has previously classified these two girls as runaways, just like they have with missing thirteen-year-old Elaine Emerson, and that could very well mean that a serial killer is operating right here in South Florida. Right here, Sue. Right in our own backyard . . ."

47

A smug Mark Felding stood on the side of the Channel 6 news van, smoking a cigarette and yukking it up with his chubby cameraman and a pair of Fort Lauderdale uniform cops. "Are you fucking kidding me? Do you want to go to jail?" Bobby yelled when he spotted him.

A surprised Felding held his hands up as Bobby rushed toward him, probably to defend himself from the punch he thought was coming. "You had me gagged, Agent Dees!" he started. "No discussing what I saw in the paintings that were sent to *me* and any future paintings that are delivered to *me*. I got it, I got it. But nowhere in your gag order does it say I can't talk about the news, thank you very much. You see, that's my job. I'm a reporter. That's what I do. Sorry you didn't like my report."

The cameraman and uniforms backed away. "You go live with this sort of bullshit before I'm even called out? Why the fuck didn't you tell Fort Lauderdale PD I was working it?"

Felding's eyes grew dark. "That's not my job, now, is it? To tell people what your job is? It's not my problem if the left hand doesn't know what the right's doing. I'm here to get information to the people. That's what I do. That's my job."

"Bobby!" Zo called.

Bobby turned and walked away before he hit the man.

"What about the car in the garage?" Felding yelled after him. "A records check shows that it was purchased at CarMax. Is it true there may be a link between this scene and Lainey Emerson's stepdad, Todd LaManna? Are you gonna arrest him soon?"

Bobby turned around and charged back over. The uniforms scattered. He brought his hand down over the ENG lens, lest the cameraman get any ideas that it was a good time to frame a shot. "Listen, Sherlock," he snapped at a suddenly pale-faced Felding, "I know you really want to be a cop. I can feel it. You couldn't cut it in the academy, maybe didn't pass the background check, whatever. But I know your type. And now this is your one really big chance to make a name for yourself and prove to everybody who thought you were a loser that you should've been the detective on this. But let me tell you—you don't know shit. You are a two-bit, dime-a-dozen field reporter who for some fucked-up reason was singled out to be a madman's messenger. You're not a real reporter. You're not a great detective. You're nothing but a puppet in all this, and you are in way over your head. So do what the nice judge has ordered you to do and shut the fuck up, or so help me, Mark, I will come down on you like I should've weeks ago—with an iron fist and no mercy."

He turned and walked past Zo and the yellow crime-scene tape that cordoned off the driveway and strode up to the house. As he passed the two chatty uniforms who had scampered off, he shouted, "Anyone gives that little shit so much as the time of day, you'll be on midnights till you retire. Got that?"

In the backyard he found what looked a lot like chaos. Crime-scene techs were everywhere, as were a couple of ME techs and uniforms—crawling like ants all over the boat, stomping all around the backyard. Supervising the offload of a single black body bag from the sailboat was a jumbo-size detective sucking on a death stick, dressed in khakis and a sweat-soaked white dress shirt with yellow pit stains.

"Detective Lafferty? I'm Agent Robert Dees, FDLE. We spoke on the phone."

"You got here quick," Lafferty replied, exhaling a plume of gray in Bobby's face.

"That's a good thing. Didn't I ask you not to remove the bodies before I got here?"

"You did. But these boys can't wait around all day."

"It's been twenty minutes. Do you mind?" he asked, walking up to the body bag and unzipping it before the detective had a chance to respond. The picked-over face of what was once a human being stared up at a cheerfully blue sky. Chunks of decomposed black flesh clung to the skull and neck, like a chicken wing nibbled down to the bone and left out in the hot sun beside a park trash can. Thick pieces of long blond hair rested underneath her skull, where her scalp had slipped off. Around her neck was a bright neon pink heart-within-a-heart necklace, which lay against the collar of a black *Got Milk?* T-shirt. Bobby looked down. Blackened fingers rested at the body's side, but the thumb on the right hand was missing its tip. He zipped her back up. Overhead, he could hear the buzz of a helicopter approaching. It was a news chopper. With a telephoto Bobby knew they could catch the tonsils in the back of his throat if they really wanted a picture of them. "Don't move the next body," he said to Lafferty.

"Now, don't be telling me what to do, son," Lafferty began in a testy voice, following Bobby's stare and looking uneasily up at the sky.

"This is an FDLE investigation now. I won't need to tell you what to do anymore, because you're to do nothing but type up your report on how you fucked up my crime scene." He turned to the ME techs, who stood there looking uncomfortable. "Put her in the truck. Don't transport her till I tell you. And don't move the other one."

Zo walked up just as Lafferty stormed off under a date palm and had a hissy fit on the phone with his chain of command. "Now that's how you win friends and influence people. I'm sure glad I'm the boss."

"Who leaked it?" Bobby asked.

"Don't know. It was all over the radio. It didn't take a genius to pick it up off a scanner. To be fair, no one figured it for Picasso till your friend and his camera crew showed up."

"Did you call?"

"Yup. Miami-Dade's in and so is BSO." BSO was the Broward Sheriff's Office, the largest law enforcement agency in Broward County. "Two guys each. I think you can kiss off Fort Lauderdale, but the City of Miami is contributing one man, too. You officially have got yourself a task force, Shep."

48

Years before handsome George Clooney romanticized the ER, Denzel Washington and Howie Mandel were making rounds on *St. Elsewhere*. That was when LuAnn Briggs, a young and impressionable teenager in search of an exciting career after high school graduation, decided to become a nurse. And not just any "stick your tongue out and say 'ah!'" hand-holder in white, but a nurse who made a real difference every day—saving lives and running central lines and riding gurneys, pounding hearts till they started to beat again. Even back then, she knew that there was no way her daddy—who was watching the same medical drama she was on the same couch in Shreveport, Louisiana—would send her to med school, even if he could afford to. Her grades were stellar, but being a doctor was no job for a woman. Nursing, on the other hand, was a respectable profession and the best she should ever hope for. Except LuAnn didn't just want respectable. She wanted exciting. She wanted death-defying. She wanted thrilling. She wanted to be one of the nurses in Boston's St. Eligius, hanging with Howie and Denzel as they smoothly and courageously put the Humpty-Dumptys back together again. So she picked emergency medicine and she picked crazy New York City to practice it. A city she had never even been to. Ten days out of Northwestern State University, she found herself in the middle of hell.

Gunshot wounds at Jamaica Hospital were commonplace; stabbings were routine. There were no funny, tension-relieving jokes being exchanged inside the ER when things went from bad to terrible. No cute, young, carefree doctors hanging by the coffee machine. The patients weren't nice and the hospital administration wasn't forgiving. But for the two-year commitment and sign-on bonus, LuAnn probably never would have lasted even the week.

But then she never would have met Detective Bobby Dees.

Nineteen years had passed since that horrible night when Bobby had been wheeled into her ER on a blood-soaked gurney with a fading pulse, accompanied by about two dozen frantic NYPD officers. It was a twist of fate that had her working a double that day, another that sent a terrible rainstorm to prevent her from going out on break for a cigarette, and yet another that steered her future husband into her trauma room. LuAnn hadn't expected the first real love of her life to come searching for her on a stretcher, covered in blood, his brachial artery shredded by a drug dealer's bullet. She hadn't expected that it would be she who had to save him. But maybe it was because she had met Bobby this way, maybe because something so powerful and so good had come out of working a double shift in hell that rainy day, that LuAnn had passed on the zillion opportunities since to go into other less pressurized areas of nursing.

Now, more than ever, she was thankful that she'd stayed put. Now the high stress of working in a chaotic Level 1 trauma hospital thirty minutes outside of Miami was a welcome distraction from the rest of her life. And as selfish as it would sound if she said it aloud, right now she needed to be around people whose lives were more tragically devastated than her own.

So she worked as long and as hard as she could, and then signed up for double shifts and holidays—drowning herself in emotionally exhausting work, much as an alcoholic would with a bottle of booze. And just like a drunk the morning after a binge, she, too, felt bad. As if she had let everyone down once again. First her daughter had run away from the very home she had created, and now she wasn't even looking for her every waking second of every day, like her husband was. Instead she was working again, pulling another double. But the truth was, she couldn't do what Bobby did. In fact, LuAnn tried her hardest during the day not to even think of Katy, although she'd never tell Bobby that. Because to think about her only child, the little girl who once wanted to cheer for Florida State and go to vet school, and wonder under what bridge she might be resting her head at night, what crap she was shooting into her arms, what vile things she might be doing for money—it was just too painful. So she didn't. Instead, like the lush with a bruising guilt hangover who heads for an open bar, LuAnn sought solace in accepting another shift and fixing somebody else's tragedy.

She tossed her latex gloves and blood-splattered gown cover in the biohazard bin, finished up her cold coffee, and stepped out into the packed waiting room. "Elbe Sanchez?" she called. A frail-looking older woman stood up in the back of the room and, with the help of a walker, began to make her way over. On the overhead waiting-room TV that usually blared *Judge Alex* or *Dr. Phil* or the girls from *The View*, LuAnn saw the news was on. She would never have paid it a second's attention, but for the fact it was that same reporter from the other night on the TV, the one who had gotten Bobby all upset. He had reported on that runaway teenager from Coral Springs.

"We don't have a positive ID yet, but like I reported earlier, Sue, this is a developing story. FDLE is on scene. They've been here all day. Now, they're not releasing details other than what we learned this afternoon, but it's definitely looking like those two sisters from Florida City. The biggest concern is this: Are we looking at a serial killer? Certainly law enforcement doesn't want a panic—Miami is still cringing from the notoriety that the brutal Cupid murders brought to the city a few years back. No one wants that publicity again, but two gruesome portraits, three dead bodies, and multiple missing teens . . . No one can ignore what this is shaping up to look like."

"I'm Elbe Sanchez," said the little woman.

"Do we have a serial killer . . . " Felding continued, holding up a fistful of runaway/missing children flyers and waving them around.

The room began to spin. Slow at first, then faster.

" . . . that is targeting teens or, perhaps more particularly, teenage runaways?"

And faster.

"If so, just how many victims might this Picasso have?"

"Nurse? Can I see my son now? Is he all right?"

And faster.

"Nurse? Are you OK?" Elbe asked again.

Until it spun completely out of control.

"Jesus!" screamed someone in the waiting room crowd.

"Oh my God! Roger! Roger! I need a crash cart! LuAnn's down!"

Then the voices faded off and the darkness mercifully settled in.

49

"Miami, the city for which William Bantling, the serial killer better known as Cupid, forever made love synonymous with brutality, apparently has a new depraved killer on the loose and this one, too, has earned himself a catchy nickname."

The man stared at the TV. No shit—MSNBC. He took a deep breath. *MSNBC.* He looked at the bottom of the screen. MIAMI POLICE FIND THE BODIES OF TWO SISTERS BELIEVED TO BE VICTIMS OF SUSPECTED SERIAL KILLER PICASSO. He was ticker-tape news on the bottom of the MSNBC screen . . .

Cute anchor Chris Jansing was yapping about *him*, her pretty little pouty mouth trying so hard to look serious. And it wasn't just MSNBC covering the story—although it was by far the biggest station he'd seen so far today. He was the top story at six on every local channel, too. People all around the country, from hokey Indiana to bustling LA, were standing around their water coolers right now, maybe, talking about *him*. Looking up at the bright lights of Broadway and reading about *him* as he ticker-taped his way around Times Square. The magnitude of the situation was a bit overwhelming, but . . . The smile slipped out, taking over his whole face. It was easy to understand now the addictive, seductive appeal fame held. And why it was that starlets who complained the loudest about the paparazzi's invasion of their precious privacy took it the hardest when the cameras weren't camped outside their front door anymore and their sweet faces weren't gracing covers every week.

Picasso. Not a bad comparison. Jeesh, he'd take that any day. Although anyone who knew anything about art knew that their two styles of painting couldn't have been more different. Picasso was a surreal cubist—he painted choppy, abstract art that only mentals and geniuses professed they could understand. He himself favored expressionism—a distortion of reality in art for emotional effect. But no matter—Pablo Picasso was more famous than Munch or Kandinsky anyway. As for nicknames, he hadn't honestly given a thought as to what the press or the police might call him one day, or what his new moniker would sound like alongside others whose names lived in infamy: Jack the Ripper. Zodiac. The Green River Killer. The Boston Strangler. The Sunday Morning Slasher. Son of Sam. The Night Stalker. Cupid.

And now, Picasso.

Some men made an indelible impression on history. Some names you never, ever forgot. He wanted to be one of those men.

He was already feeling, however, the effects of notoriety. The police paparazzi were out in full force looking for him now. No matter if they were looking in all the wrong places, they were still out there looking, and he had to be very careful. But he'd never been away from his collection for this long before, and he hoped none of them had, well, expired. That would really suck. Unless they were real pigs and had scarfed down everything he'd left out for them, they should be fine. But he was finding that raising his fragile, eclectic collection was a lot like tending a garden—some flowers required more TLC, while others pretty much took care of themselves. Some bloomed early; some fell apart like an orchid when you touched them. After all the nurturing, the feeding, the watering—after all the motherfucking loving care you showed them day in and day out—sometimes a puddle of pretty petals and an ugly, scrawny stem was all you had left to show for your efforts at the end of the day. He definitely didn't want to come home to that. Especially since he'd have nobody to blame but himself if his precious petunias dropped dead; neglect was strictly his fault. He needed to get back to them by the weekend. No matter what, he had to find a way.

He was probably overthinking his situation. By trying very hard not to underestimate his opponent, he'd succeeded in giving them way too much credit; Miami's finest were turning out not to be so exceptional after all. It had taken a homeless drunk to lead them to what they should have found with just a smidgen of due diligence, which most likely meant they weren't picking up on any other clues, either. It was disappointing. FDLE Special Agent Supervisor Robert Dees was supposed to be the crème de la crème. The Shepherd everyone runs to whenever a lamb goes missing from the flock—so says *People* had even named him a Hero Among Us in 2008. Bobby Dees was the man who was supposed to make the hunt a little more interesting, a little more exciting because he was sooo good at what he did. Well, so far he wasn't impressed. Not at all. It was like playing chess against the latest NASA computer and always winning. Either you were really, really smart, or the mythical, magical, all-powerful computer was a lot dumber than you'd given it credit for.

He dunked an Oreo into his warm milk and turned his attention back to the computer. He was feeling lonely, all dressed up with nowhere to go. It was time to see what mischief big-boned Shelley and her pretty pink butterfly were up to. With just a few clicks of the mouse, he opened the gates to the tank and surreptitiously swam out onto the Internet, navigating past parental controls and protective firewalls. All around him, scrumptious little fishies were IMing and sending pictures and swapping OMGs. He could practically hear their squeaky chatter. Millions of excited young voices, screaming and squealing and yapping—spreading their new wings over the big, bad Internet. Out to prove to Mom, Dad, Grandma, and themselves that there was nothing to worry about on the World Wide Web. No sexual predators on their buddy lists; they'd be able to spot a poseur a mile away. All they were looking for was to make some new friends and have a good time.

Within moments he'd found exactly who he was looking for. With invisible hands he unzipped her dress, unhooked her bra, and slipped undetected inside her computer, his skilled fingers probing through her applications till he found just the right switch. Then he sat back in his seat and finished his cookie just as sweet Shelley walked across his screen in her pink polka-dot Jenni jammies, her hair twisted in a towel turban, yapping away on a phone. Her bed was unmade and clothes were strewn all over her messy lilac bedroom. He picked crumbs out of the hair on his tummy and leaned over the keyboard.

ElCapitan says: hi shell. r u online?

A few seconds later he had her undivided attention.

He smiled. He just loved home movies.

50

"How long do you think he'll be gone for? I mean, do you think he's ever coming back?" Lainey asked, her cheek pressed to the cool, mildew-smelling wall. She was losing her voice.

"Don't know. Maybe he had an accident," Katy answered back. "I hope to God it hurt." The thought had occurred to Katy that the freak might not be coming back at all. That he had just left them in this hellhole—wherever it was—to rot and die. At first she was OK with that because it was better than what she faced if he came back. It was better than listening to the screams down the hall. Or smelling the nauseating stink of paint. Or feeling his sticky fingers on her skin. Now all she heard was quiet; all she smelled was her own stink in the corner. Then she got to thinking about the possibility that he really might not be coming back. She started to think about slowly starving to death in the darkness and how that would feel. And while death seemed preferable to living her life out in a blind dungeon, if he never came back, and she did die here, she'd started to consider the possibility that no one would ever find her body. Would her poor mother ever know what had really happened to her? Or would her parents think for years that she was living it up in Vegas or LA or New York? Would she rot like a mummy and wither to bones, only to be dug up in a century or two and studied by some dinosaur hunter who would wonder aloud why the hell she was buried where she was?

"How's your tunnel coming?" Lainey asked. "Can you feel the other side of the wall?"

"I hit rock."

"Oh. Are you quitting?"

"No way." Katy lightly clenched her fists. She felt her raw fingertips rub against her palm, the nails broken, jagged stubs. They'd been bleeding for what felt like days. "I'm just going around it. This may be our only way out if he doesn't come back. How's your tunnel?"

"I stopped. My fingers hurt too much."

"Lainey . . ."

"I wanna go home, Katy. I don't want to dig tunnels I'll never fit through."

"Think positive."

"Don't you want to go home, Katy?"

Katy closed her eyes. She didn't like to talk about home. It hurt too much. "Yeah. That's why I'm digging. Wishing you were home, warm in your bed, doesn't fly, Lainey. There's no wizard here to grant you your wish when clicking your heels doesn't work." She sighed and sat back against the wall. "Tell me about your brother again. What's it like to have a brother? And why was he called Bradley Brat?"

"I don't remember any more. I don't remember why I called him a brat," Lainey whispered back. "Or why he made me mad so much. I just miss him. I can't believe I'm saying that. I miss Brad. I miss him coming into my room and stealing my comics because he's scared of the thunderstorm and he wants to read them under the covers. I miss his stupid, snorty laugh when he thinks something's really funny. I used to think he was faking, but now I know it's real."

"And your mom? Tell me about your mom."

"She's probably really upset but not telling anyone, you know? She's gotta hold it in. She always does. We weren't getting along, you know, like I told you, when this happened. And Liza—you know, my sister—she's run away before and my mom was really pissed. She told her once not to bother coming home anymore if she did it again. And Liza, well, you know, she probably doesn't even know I'm gone, she's always so busy. She has lots of boyfriends and stuff, so . . . " Lainey broke off and rubbed her bandaged eyes. "She's probably still mad that I took her jeans and her makeup."

"I wish I could redo things," Katy said softly. "Do a do-over, you know? I thought things were so bad at home. Isn't that funny? But sometimes you have to see the really bad to know what's good. I fucked things up at home. It was my fault. It's just too late to do anything about it."

"Don't say that!" Lainey yelled at the top of her lungs.

There was a long silence.

"Do you think anyone is looking for us, Katy? Do you think anybody even cares?"

Katy rubbed away the tears on her cheeks with her shredded, bloody fingertips. There was no way she was gonna answer that, either in her head or out loud. She felt around for the hole she had started long ago. Her fingers caught on the rough limestone and she followed it with her hands till she felt the sharp drop-off into what she hoped was just plain dirt. She dug her hands in and began to feverishly tunnel, ignoring the pain in her fingers, the ache in her back, the grumble in her stomach, the fear in her heart. "That's why we need to get the hell out of here, Lainey," she whispered. "And we need to get out of here now."

51

"Where is she?" Bobby asked as soon as he opened the front door to his house. Charlotte Knox, a close friend of LuAnn's from the hospital, was sitting on a chair in the dimly lit living room, a *People* magazine on her lap, waiting for him. Nilla met him at the door with a tail thwap and a howl.

"She's sleeping in the family room, on the couch," Charlotte replied, with her finger to her lips. She stood up and gathered her purse. "She's not so good."

"What the hell happened, Charlotte? They won't tell me anything at the hospital. I flew here as soon as you called—"

"She's gonna be OK, Bobby. They did a dozen tests, and it looks like she just fainted. But she hit her head on a chair on the way down, so she'll have a shiner and a nasty headache when she wakes up. She whacked it hard enough for a concussion, so she has to take it easy for a couple of days and see the doc before they let her go back to work."

"Fainted? Jesus . . . what?"

"Don't know. One minute she's plucking asphalt out of the back of a motorcycle accident victim, the next she's down in the middle of the ER waiting room. She was only out for a few minutes. She didn't want to alarm you while they did tests." Charlotte's voice lowered. "I see you're on that big case. It's been all over the news today."

"This was her idea not to call me?"

"She didn't want to scare you, is all."

Bobby, it's Deirdre. Dispatch just put a call through from someone at Broward General looking for you. I picked up. I . . . I don't know how to say this. Something's happened to your wife, Bobby.

He shook his head and looked past Charlotte in the direction of the family room. His hands were still shaking. "Too late, Charlotte."

"She's gonna kill me when she finds out I called you. I just didn't want her to come in tomorrow like nothing ever happened. She's been working way too much. I think the girl's plain exhausted."

"You did the right thing, Charlotte," Bobby said, walking her to the door. "She's been under a lot of stress."

"Obviously," Charlotte said as she headed down the front walk to her car. "Take care of our girl. Goodnight, Bobby."

The family room was dark. In the kitchen, which opened onto the family room, only the light above the stove was on. Still, with the moonlight filtering through the palm trees outside, he could make out her small frame on the oversize navy blue chenille couch. She was curled up like a baby. A cotton ball was taped to the crook of her elbow. Another was on her wrist, presumably where they'd taken blood and run an IV. Right below that was her hospital patient ID.

"Hey there," he said in a hushed voice as he knelt beside her, pulling the old knitted throw back up over her shoulders. He stroked a piece of her long blond hair off her cheek and saw the black stitches over her left eye, which was swollen and already bruised. A raw-looking red scrape ran across her cheek. It must have been one hell of a fall.

LuAnn opened her eyes and looked at him. "She told you," she murmured.

"You should've called me, Belle. What happened?"

LuAnn's eyes welled up and she suddenly started to cry.

"Honey, honey. What is it, Lu?" he asked as he scooped her up in his arms and held her head against his chest. "Is it bad? Jesus . . . Did the doctors tell you something bad?"

She shook her head.

"Then what is it, honey?"

She shook her head again.

"You're gonna be OK, Belle. Everything'll be all right." He stroked the hair off her face and tried to find her eyes. "Why didn't you call me?"

"I saw it on the news. I know, Bobby," she managed, her voice barely a whisper.

"Saw what?"

"That reporter on the runaway case you have. I saw him."

"LuAnn . . ."

"I want the truth. I want you to tell me. Does he have her? This killer, Picasso?"

"What? LuAnn . . ."

"Does he have her?" Then she buried her head in his shoulder. "Does he have my girl?"

LuAnn was normally so composed. So much so that she could come across as cold to some, especially since Katy left. Bobby knew it hurt for her to talk about their daughter—about what had gone so wrong in between the bottle feedings and adolescence—so they never did. But seeing LuAnn break down this way was awkward, not because he didn't want to hold her, not because he didn't want to listen and tell her to get it all out, not because he didn't want to tell her he had the same exact fears as her, but because he knew she didn't want him to see it. He knew tomorrow she would likely regret her indiscretion, and cold might turn to freezing.

"No, Belle. He doesn't have her. She ran away, is all. She's somewhere with Ray, but I know she's safe. I know she is. She's been gone far too long to be a victim of this guy. She's too smart. And I don't know where this reporter is coming off, saying it's a serial or that our bad guy is targeting runaways. He's trying to make headlines, is all. He's trying to make a career for himself."

"Bobby, it can't be her."

"She ran away with Ray. She's with him."

"Tell me I'm not a bad mother. Oh God, tell me it wasn't me. Lie, if you have to. I just need to hear it . . ."

"Jesus, Lu, it wasn't you. Why would you think that?"

"It was me she ran from, Bobby. Me. I was too strict. I made her cheer and she didn't like it. I made her study and kept her home on Friday nights sometimes. I told her I hated that boy. I told her he was no good for her, that he was a loser and trailer trash and a druggie, and she left. She left because of me . . . "

He lifted her face to make her look at him. "Don't be crazy," he said firmly. "She left because she made a choice to leave. She wanted to be with Ray and she was doing drugs. She made the choice. It was never you. You're the best mother. The best. And I'm not lying. Every time I saw you with her, whether it was walking her in a stroller or sitting on the sidelines, it was perfect. And until that piece of shit came into Katherine's life, everything was good. She loved cheering. She told me she wanted to try for a scholarship. I asked her once if she wanted to stop, because of all the homework and stuff, and she said no. She said she loved it. So it wasn't you."

There was a long silence. He closed his eyes as he rocked LuAnn in his arms, with her head against his chest, still kneeling beside her on the couch. "I should've seen that she was trying stuff," he began quietly, whispering into her hair. "I know the signs. I should've checked her arms sooner, gone through her backpack or her drawers. I should've tested her. I'm the cop, LuAnn, I should've seen this, not you. I didn't want to think she'd do it. I didn't want to think *my* kid would do all the things I told her never to do. Things only bad kids do. Ray . . . goddamn it, I knew he was bad news. I knew he was a banger . . . I never should've let her work at the fucking Dairy Queen. I should've told her she didn't have to get a job. I should've just given her more spending money. It was me, LuAnn, not you. It's me who should be crying and asking you to forgive me for not doing my job."

She pulled his face down then, close to hers, her fingertips wiping away the tears that had welled in his eyes before they even fell. Then she kissed him on the lips, her warm tongue finding his, pushing deeper into his mouth. It had been a long time since they'd kissed. Even longer since they'd kissed passionately. LuAnn had the most beautiful mouth, with warm, full red lips that quivered slightly when she kissed you.

He pulled her closer, his hands buried in the tangles of her long hair, pressing against her back. He wanted to feel all of her, all at once—her warm skin, the curve of her cheeks, the arch of her back. He wanted to touch all of it, take it all in, because he knew the next day it would all be over, and he had to savor every second of this feeling before it left him again.

She didn't move away. Instead, she pressed close to him, her hands moving over him as his did with her. She pulled his dress shirt out of his pants and ran her hands underneath it and over his back, her nails tracing his skin, moving to the front of his chest, finding his nipples, moving lower, over his abs. With both hands she pulled his shirt up and over his head.

He looked at her lying on the couch before him, feeling a bit like a teen on a date who has just gotten the signal that tonight's the night. He was excited, hungry to touch her, to feel himself thrusting inside of her, but hesitant, wanting to make sure this was the decision she wanted to make. Wanting to know that she was sure of the next step. As though she'd read his mind, she sat up on the couch and pulled her sweater over her head. Then she reached back behind and unhooked her bra. It slipped off onto her lap, exposing her beautiful, full breasts, her erect nipples. She reached out and took his hands and placed them on her.

"Make love to me, Bobby. Please."

He had never needed her more. He stood up before her and undid the Velcro keepers on his belt that held his gun holster in place, and set it on the coffee table behind him. LuAnn reached over, undid his buckle and unzipped his pants, pulling them, along with his briefs, slowly down over his thighs till they fell on the floor. He stood there, exposed before her, his penis erect.

Then he climbed on top of her on the couch and did as she had asked.

52

When the sun came up, LuAnn was there, sleeping on his chest, where she had stayed all night. She had fallen asleep on the couch after they had made love, and Bobby had carried her upstairs to the bedroom, careful not to wake her as he gently laid her head on the pillow and slipped in beside her under the covers. He hadn't wanted their time together to end even one moment sooner than it had to. But the painkillers they'd given her at the hospital had knocked her out pretty good. Of course, that didn't cure Bobby's insomnia. In fact, LuAnn's concussion was just one more worry to keep him up counting sheep all night. He'd made sure to check on her every two hours, to make sure her pupils were dilating, that she was responding to stimuli, that she was safely beside him, breathing on his skin . . .

Now the morning was here, and they were still one beneath warm sheets, legs tangled together, wrapped in each other's arms. It was a place he had not been in so long he could not remember the last time he was. He just knew that when things were good—before Katy left— he had taken for granted the feeling of LuAnn's breath on his chest at night, the sweet smell of her hair under his nose, the curve of her waist in the palm of his hand. Even though they had gotten married relatively young—much younger than most of their friends and certainly younger than what their families would have liked—for almost eighteen years Bobby had believed they had a great marriage. A lot of ups, a few downs when money was tight, but nothing that he ever felt was insurmountable. Nothing that ever made him wish for something better. Being a cop meant nine out of every ten friends were divorced, in the process of divorcing, or cheating. For myriad psychobabble reasons, unstable marriages and affairs seemed to just come with the job description. But not him and LuAnn. They were always so good together. And now that he had tasted again what he took for granted all those years, he didn't want the morning to come. He didn't want to go back to yesterday, although the choice, he realized, might not be his to make.

He slid her head gently onto the pillow and left her sleeping while he went in to shave and take a shower. No matter the fragile status of his personal life, he had a young girl to find, two bodies to positively identify, and a madman to catch. It was barely eight a.m. and he already had ten messages on his cell, which he'd turned off for the first time in a long time last night. If it was bad enough, the right people knew how to find him.

He watched her sleep while he quietly got dressed. Nilla had taken his spot, curling up beside LuAnn, her head on a pillow. The dog watched him back with her big brown eyes, while he clipped on his cell, slipped on a sport jacket, and then stood there for a long, long moment. He was unsure of his next move. If he woke LuAnn to say goodbye, the spell might well be over. She might look at him like a girl with a roofie hangover stares at the stranger smiling at her on the other side of the mattress. The how-did-I-get-here-and-what-did-we-do-last-night? look. Maybe it was better to just leave . . .

Of course leaving and not saying goodbye was offensive. Then she really would have reason not to talk to him when he got home. He decided to take his chances. He sat on the edge of the bed and gently brushed the hair off her face. "I've got to go in. No work today; just stay in bed," he whispered.

LuAnn opened her eyes and squinted at the sunlight that streamed in through the blinds. "OK," she said with a nod.

"How do you feel?" he asked.

"How do I look?"

Her left eye was black and blue and swollen shut, her scrape even more raw than last night. She looked as though she'd just gone a few rounds with Tyson. "Beautiful," he said.

"Liar."

He smiled. "I'll call you to make sure you're OK. And you better be in bed. Doctor's orders." He kissed her on the cheek and rose to leave.

She touched him on his arm. "That's it?" she asked.

He shook his head. "I hope not," he replied. Then he leaned over and kissed her on the lips. She kissed him back, her tongue meeting his, her fingers on his neck. He held her in his arms and she didn't pull away. "Hold my spot?" he whispered in her ear.

She nodded.

"I have to go catch a bad guy now. I'll be back."

She nodded again.

"How do I look?" he asked as he rose, straightening his jacket.

"Beautiful."

"Liar," he answered with a smile. Then he leaned over and kissed her one more time before he slipped out the door.

53

"Like I told you people already, the last time I seen them, they were going to a friend's house, or whatever. They were bad kids." Gloria Leto blessed herself and looked up to heaven. "It's bad to say things like that about the dead. God forgive me. But they had no guidance, you know? My sister, their mama—bless her soul—she was on the junk. It ate her bad. Her body, her soul—it took everything, right down to nothing but bones when she died. Before that asshole got her hooked on smack, she was a good mother, you know? Made a living, took care of her family, but . . . when she was on smack, she had no time for those girls no more. They went wild, you know? And the different men in that house every night . . . " Gloria sighed and folded her arms across her chest. "I don't know. I don't want to say no more. It's not right. But when my sister, when she died, you know, last year? When she died, I tried to take those girls in and fix them. Raise them proper, take them to church, teach them to be good girls. I sacrificed for them, you don't know. But that Roseanne, she was always talking back. She didn't come home at night sometimes. When she did, she brought boys back with her, snuck them into my house. Then Rosalie, the little one, she started shit, too. When I found the drugs—the baggies in their purses—I said, 'Enough! I don't want no crack whores in my house!' How could they do that junk after what it did to their mother? And I don't know, maybe two days, maybe a week later, I can't remember exactly—they left. Went out somewhere—they didn't tell me—and they never come back. I took their clothes and I got rid of them maybe a month later so I could rent the room. I just threw everything out."

"Ms. Leto, did your nieces have access to a computer?" Bobby asked.

"I let them use mine. I let them borrow it a few times, you know, for school. Then when I found the drugs, I hid it because I was afraid they'd take it and sell it like a junkie."

"Can we see it?"

She shook her head. "Someone broke into my house and took the stupid thing. Along with my TV and my jewelry. Everything—gone. All of it. Even the drink in the kitchen cupboard."

"I'm sorry to hear that," Zo said.

She shrugged.

"Well, thank you for your time, Ms. Leto. And, again, we're sorry for your loss," Bobby added.

Gloria shrugged again and crossed herself. "I don't have to pay for their funerals, do I? I'm not, like, responsible for the money, am I?"

"I don't know, ma'am. You'll have to check with a lawyer about what your financial obligations are," Bobby answered.

"That reporter said he didn't have to pay me to talk to me, but that ain't right. I mean, they pay people to talk to Oprah, don't they?"

"Did you speak to the press, ma'am?"

"I thought he was gonna pay me. Wanted to ask me questions 'bout the girls and why they ran away. I said sure. But now I think I should get money."

Felding, probably. Or any one of the other camera-ready sharks out there chumming the murky waters for scoop. Time to bite back. "I agree, Ms. Leto," Bobby said. "I don't think you should talk to anyone from the press unless they pay you. Crime victims get paid big bucks to talk to the media. We're talking thousands. You should hold out."

They left Gloria Leto pondering her finances on the front porch of her duplex and headed down the broken concrete path. Kids playing hula hoop and jump rope in the street eyed them suspiciously.

"She's a trip," Zo said with a shake of his head.

"Was that Ciro on the phone before?" Bobby asked.

"Yup. He's back from CarMax. Bob and Mary Bohner, who own the house on Hendricks, did buy the Buick in the garage in 2005 from CarMax Pompano. The salesman was a Karen Alfieri. Larry talked to her—she knows nothing."

"But we have a link to where LaManna works."

"Yes, we do," Zo replied, whipping out a cigarette.

"I thought you were off those."

"Nope. I've officially failed at two things in my life: quitting smoking and quitting drinking. I'm out of the closet about it, too, so I don't want to hear no more shit. I've already got Camilla yapping in my ear."

"I never thought the toothpick and patch thing was gonna work. You know, I'm still not convinced LaManna's smart enough for this," Bobby said with a shrug. "But maybe I'm wrong."

"What about the two different blood samples on painting number one? The one of Sampson?"

"We know for sure neither sample belonged to Lainey. As for them matching the Boganes sisters, I'm hoping the lab will say they both do. We should know by today. If not, then . . . " Bobby didn't finish his sentence. Both of them knew what "if not" meant. More victims.

"LaManna's under surveillance, twenty-four-seven. Let's see what he does," Zo said.

Bobby's cell phone chirped just as they climbed into the car. "Dees."

"Agent Dees, this is Duty Officer Craig Rockenstein with FDLE in Tallahassee. I'm calling to advise you that the juvenile you had flagged in the system—Reinaldo Coon, white male, DOB July 7, 1990—was run at 11:32 last night by the Palm Beach County Sheriff's Office, terminal OR1 26749, Detective Greg Cowsert. Would you like me to contact the Palm Beach County Sheriff's Office on your behalf to advise them of the flag?"

Jesus Christ, Reinaldo Coon. Ray Coon. They found Ray . . .

He left Zo in the car and stepped back out into the street. "No, no. I'll call," he replied quietly, trying hard to think through the train wreck of thoughts piling up in his brain. His heart began to pound. *Was he with Katy?* "What's the contact number?"

His fingers shook so hard, Bobby almost couldn't hit the numbers. A tense excitement was building in his chest. The only feeling he could equate it to was one he felt at Christmas as a kid—the adrenaline-fueled anticipation as you walked down the stairs, hoping you saw exactly what you'd asked for all year long under the tree. And the heavy, dread-filled fear that you wouldn't.

"Detective bureau. Richards."

"Detective Cowsert, please."

"Can I help you with something?" asked the woman.

"This is Agent Bobby Dees with FDLE down in Miami. Detective Cowsert ran a history on somebody last night that I had flagged."

"Oh. Hold on a sec. Hey, Greg," she yelled, obviously across a room, "FDLE's on the phone."

Bobby listened to the background noise of the squad bay for what seemed like a lifetime. Choppy bits of conversation and snippets of laughter. Finally someone picked up. "Cowsert."

"Detective Cowsert, this is FDLE Agent Bobby Dees out of Miami. I had a flag set up on a subject that you ran last night, Reinaldo Coon. Is he in custody?"

"I guess you could say that," Cowsert replied with a laugh. "He certainly ain't going nowhere."

Bobby suddenly imagined Katy lying in a hospital bed, hooked up to IVs and tubes, unable to speak. Or maybe sitting dirty and disheveled in a jail cell, too ashamed to call her mom and dad. He ran a hand through his hair, trying to rein in his thoughts. He closed his eyes. "Why's that? Was there an accident? Is he in the hospital or something?"

"Don't look much like an accident, Agent Dees. The kid's got two bullets in the back of his head. Some Boy Scout camping out in Belle Glade found what was left of him. From the looks of it, he'd been there awhile, too. I hope you didn't need him for nothing, 'cause your boy Reinaldo is dead."

54

"You OK?" Zo asked when he stepped back in the car. He flicked his cigarette out the window.

"Nope," Bobby replied, pulling away from the curb.

"What's up? Who was on the line?"

"Palm Beach Sheriff's Office found Ray Coon's body last night."

Zo stared at him. "Ray Coon? As in your Ray?"

"Yup."

Zo rubbed his jaw. "Jesus . . . Katy?"

Bobby shook his head. "Don't know."

"How?"

"Shot in the head and dumped in Belle Glade. He'd been there awhile, too."

"Shit. Suspects?"

"He was a banger. Everyone wanted him dead. I sure as hell wanted to kill him. PBSO is working it."

"I'll get with them. We'll take care of it, Shep. We'll work it."

There was a long silence. The Grand Am pulled up to a light. Across the street was a playground full of kids, yelling and screaming in the early afternoon sun as they slid down slides and swung on swings. Not a care in the world. Bobby stared off at it. "I thought she was still with him," he said softly. "They were supposed to be in New

Orleans or San Francisco or LA, making it somehow. Maybe she was a grocery clerk or waitressing, you know? Maybe she was getting her GED. Maybe they were Romeo and Juliet and I was the asshole for not believing in the two of them. Maybe she had a baby and was embarrassed to come home, is all . . . ”

“Bobby . . . ”

“But now he’s dead. The one guy who was supposed to protect her is dead and she’s still not home and now we have a psycho out there who likes to cut up teenage runaways. So where the hell is she, Zo? Where the hell is my kid?”

55

Angelina Jolie shook out her gorgeous dark hair. "Have you been selling big guns to bad people?" she asked the terrorist breathlessly. Even on the small portable DVD, her pouty red lips looked larger than life.

Larry Vastine yawned and reached for his coffee, which was really liquid mud. His wife had made her normally bad coffee twice as strong for him, for moments just like this. Moments when even Angelina Jolie—decked out in black patent leather with a whip in hand and mounting a terrorist—wasn't keeping the dreams from starting the second he so much as blinked. Larry's clubbing days were years behind him—most nights he was lucky if he made it through all of *The Tonight Show*. It'd been a while since he'd done all-night surveillance on a target, and that was in Narcotics, where a lot of exciting things went down long after dark and you had no chance to get tired. But being the eyeball in suburbia at three a.m. was the worst. Most of the bars and clubs closed in Florida at two, so it was too late for the revelers to be out and too early for the commuters to be heading in. If he'd spotted three cars drive down the quiet, tree-lined street in the past hour, it was a lot. Even Pauline's sludge wasn't cutting it. It was time for some real shit. Larry reached for a Monster energy drink from the cooler on the passenger-side floorboard. His son in high school drank the stuff like water, which meant Larry would probably be up till Christmas.

Just as he cracked open the drink, took a sip, and sat back up in the driver's seat, he saw it—the quick-second flicker of light thirty yards off in the distance, coming from the target house. More like the *reflection* of a flicker of streetlight, he realized, bouncing off of the target's glass side door just as it was opening. If Larry hadn't looked up at that exact moment, he would have totally missed it. And then he would have missed the husky figure dressed in a hooded black sweatshirt and dark jeans slipping down the ficus-lined side of the house into the backyard of the neighboring duplex and disappearing out of sight.

Larry wiped the sleep and surprise from his open mouth and started up the car. Without putting his lights on, he drove around the block to 115th. He cut the engine and watched as Todd LaManna emerged from the darkness and hopped into a car parked in the lot of a two-story apartment complex. He started it up and backed out onto the street. Larry ducked as he drove past. Then he got on his radio.

"You better not be looking for company," Ciro answered with a throaty growl. "We just got the baby back to sleep."

"He's moving."

"What?"

"LaManna. He's dressed all in black, driving a black Acura, heading north on Coral Ridge toward the Sawgrass."

"A black Acura? Where the hell'd he get that?"

"He either borrowed it or he stole it. That don't matter none right now. I just don't wanna lose him. You're a Parkland boy, which means you're not far away. Get your ass up and get dressed. Let's see where this asshole's going in such a hurry at three in the morning."

56

"Where the hell are we? Bum-fuck?" Ciro grumbled as he climbed in the front seat of Larry's SUV. "Are we still in Palm Beach County? I didn't even know Lyons Road went this far north."

"Me neither," Larry replied, peering through a pair of night-vision binoculars at the back of the dark gray, two-story building across the street. "He went inside ten minutes ago, through a door on the far north side. Used a key."

"What is this place?" Ciro asked, looking around at the deserted parking lots and a string of hulking, mainly windowless buildings.

"Looks like a warehouse to me."

"No shit, Sherlock. A warehouse for what, though? You see a name?"

"The small sign in the front said 'C.B. Imports,'" Larry replied. "I just checked online at the Florida Division of Corporations. President is a David Lee, agent for service is Sam Rice. That's it. The Web site doesn't tell you what kind of business it is. Can't see nothing through the front glass door except what looks like a waiting area with a couple of chairs and some cheap paintings. I can have Dawn run it in the morning."

"Fuck that," Ciro replied. "I'm up. We're here. We're going in there tonight."

"That's what I was thinking."

"Bobby said it," Ciro remarked. "He said it would be some remote place, big enough to hold girls without anyone knowing."

"Ain't nothing out here past State Road 441," Larry said, putting the binoculars down. "Just some horse farms and a couple of sprawling retirement communities a few miles up. The adjoining space next door is for lease. He could have God knows how many girls locked up in there somewhere. They could be screaming right now and nobody'd ever hear 'em."

"So what do we do now? Do we get a warrant?"

"We don't need one," Larry answered as he unclipped his Glock and pulled the slide back to make sure he had one in the chamber. "He could be hacking girls up in there, Ciro. He could have hostages. If we wait around for a judge to sign a fucking piece of paper, it could be too late. Exigent circumstances, my man. We find out he's cutting dope, not girls, then we secure it and call in the state and the suits."

Ciro nodded and looked back across the street. The Acura was parked about thirty yards from the back of the warehouse, near a green construction Dumpster. Far from the door where LaManna had gone in. "Why the fuck did he park all the way over there?" he asked.

"Surveillance cameras for the glass company in the next building over, I'm thinking. He doesn't want to be seen. He'll go in, do his dirty work, and get out like a fucking ghost."

Ciro had a bad feeling in his gut. Going into any building in the middle of the night was a risky proposition. Going into a sprawling warehouse searching out a potentially armed serial-murder suspect sounded over the top. It sounded like a bad Saturday morning headline, is what it sounded like. He thought of the new baby he had just put to bed. Then he thought of what might happen if he and Larry didn't go in. If LaManna did have those girls. He thought of the paintings that he had seen and the Boganes sisters' crime scene. "What about backup? SRT?" he asked quietly. SRT was the Special Response Team, FDLE's acronym for SWAT.

"I thought you were my backup." Larry cracked a smile. "Look, if we call in Lake Worth or PBSO and wait for a response, it's another twenty minutes before we get an authority out here, and another cook in the kitchen, and we gotta deal with turf wars. If we call in SRT, you're talking at least another hour before they're here and set up. I just don't think we have that much time to dick around."

Ciro nodded slowly. *Sometimes you gotta just make a decision*, his dad, a former police captain in Chicago, had once told him. *That's what makes the difference between a cop and a hero.* "All right. Let's do it," he answered.

Larry drove across the street and parked next to the door he'd seen LaManna slip through just minutes before. He called in their position to Miami dispatch and requested uniform response from Lake Worth PD. That would mean at least more bodies on the way if something went wrong inside. Then they got out of the car and took up tactical positions alongside the metal door.

Ciro tried the knob. Locked.

Larry pulled out the Halligan tool, wedged it into the jamb, and popped the lock. Ciro banged on the door with the butt of his Glock. "FDLE! Police!" he called out, just as Larry kicked the door in and the two of them rushed forward into pure darkness.

57

"Lainey! Lainey! Did you hear that?"

Lainey was dreaming again, wasn't she? Or maybe hallucinating. Brad was in her room and he was trying to take her covers but she was so cold, she was shivering. She wanted to yell at him but was too tired to form the words.

"Lainey? Are you OK over there?"

She tried to pull the covers back over her . . .

"Lainey! Get up!"

"I'm here," she managed with a whisper. She tasted the dirt on her lips from where they had been pressed up against the floor, and realized she had only been dreaming. It was the nightmare that was real. "I'm awake, I think," she called back into the darkness, wiping her mouth with the back of her hand. She had finally removed the bandages from her eyes, but Katy was right. It didn't matter. She couldn't see a thing anyway.

Or could she? She blinked twice as she sat up. She could make out the faintest, dull outline, of . . . maybe her foot? There was light, coming from somewhere . . .

"I can see my foot, Katy," she whispered. "I think that's my foot."

"Someone's here, Lainey," Katy called out. "I heard something!"

He's back. Oh my God, he's back . . .

Lainey began to tremble. It started in her core, and slowly worked its

way out to her extremities until her whole body was shaking uncontrollably. Since he'd been gone, since she'd finished off the last of the water
and was down to only a few chunks of kibble, she had begun to wonder
what it would feel like to starve to death. If it would take a long time. If
it would hurt at all. If she would ever stop being hungry. The thought
had completely terrified her. But now, just the thought of him coming
back, opening that door with his heavy chains in hand and the stink of
SpaghettiO's and old coffee on his breath, she realized, terrified her far
more. She started to cry. This time she could feel the tears, wet on her
cheeks. She pulled herself into a fetal position and began to rock.

"Lainey! Don't! Stop! Maybe it's someone else! I heard noises up
above! Noises I haven't heard before!"

Lainey cried even harder.

"No! Don't cry! Maybe someone's here to save us! And if we don't
make noise, they'll leave and we'll never be found. Yell! Yell with me,
Lainey, so they can hear us! We're underground somewhere. They
won't find us unless we yell! Help!" she screamed.

"Help . . . " Lainey started softly. "Help!" she shouted as Katy's
words sunk in. The only possible thing worse than starving to death
was starving to death knowing you could have been saved. "Oh God,
help us! Help! Help!"

Katy started to bang on the wall with her fists and Lainey joined
in. She heard it now. The loud clanging from somewhere not too far
away. It wasn't the clinking of the chains, it was more like a hammer-
ing sound. And the light was getting brighter. Maybe it was a flashlight! Maybe it was the police with a flashlight, looking under doors
and into far-off windows for them. She banged harder. It didn't matter that her hands throbbed. She could feel the skin begin to chafe
and bleed. She wished her superpowers would start to work. "Help!
Oh God, help us!" she screamed till there was no voice left in her.

The outline of her foot grew more pronounced. Lainey stopped
pounding and stared at it in disbelief.

"Hello?" a voice called out from somewhere. "Where are you?"

"We're here! Oh God, we're in here!" Katy yelled. "We're in here!"

Then the door opened and the light poured in.

58

Ciro moved slowly along the wall of stacked cardboard boxes, his gun out before him at the ready. He turned a blind corner and shone his flashlight straight into the snarling face of a hulking werewolf, its yellowed fangs dripping with blood. He jumped back.

"It's like a fucking horror movie in here," Larry whispered, coming up behind him and reaching over to touch the fur on the enormous werewolf mask that sat on a Styrofoam wig head atop a cardboard box. "Look at all this weird shit. It must be a Halloween outfitter or something," he said, his eyes darting in every direction. "I almost put a cap in the fucking Grim Reaper back there . . ."

The narrow walkway they were headed down was lined with stacks and stacks of more boxes, precariously piled high atop one another, so that when each stack reached the ceiling, some twenty feet up, it leaned across the aisle to kiss the other, blocking the moonlight from the sky-lights above, and making it virtually impossible to see more than a couple of yards in front of you. Larry's flashlight scanned the stacks of boxes like a searchlight. Stuck to the sides of some were modeled color pictures of the contents inside: witches, vampires, sexy nurses, devils, cops, clowns. A little farther up, Ciro could make out a life-size Santa sitting in a rocking chair set atop a box, and a shimmery, skinny silver Christmas tree beyond that. Along a rickety metal shelving system was a pile of wreaths, stacked like tires at a Goodyear store. Plastic seasonal lawn decorations—from Rudolph and his gang of friends, to red and blue gnomes and pink flamingos—dotted shelves alongside plastic plants and palm trees. Everything looked more than a few seasons past its freshness date.

The place smelled old and dirty, with an underlying hint of mildew, like it had been in a flood at one time and no one had fixed the water damage. It reminded Ciro of an ancient Woolworth's that he used to work in as a stock boy when he was a kid in downtown Chicago. A faint slice of dull yellow light emanated from underneath a door at the end of the aisle, back by a far wall. They moved toward it. When they reached the cheap door, Ciro stopped and motioned for Larry to listen. Far off, as if it were muffled by something or someone, was the sound of someone screaming.

Larry nodded. They took up positions next to the door. Ciro's hands shook slightly, and the tip of his Glock tapped his chest. No matter how much training you got, you were never really ready for some things. They should've waited for backup is what they should've done. He turned the knob quickly and together they rushed into an empty office, which led out to another hallway. A half-empty cup of coffee sat beside an open *Hustler*. Ciro touched the cup. It was warm. The screaming started up again. It was louder—no, it was closer. It was still muffled, or maybe buried, but it was definitely closer.

They stepped out the pass-through door and into another hallway, this one lined with more closed doors. Offices, most likely. Ciro counted four on either side, eight altogether. Lights were on underneath three of them.

Which door? Which one do they pick? If LaManna wasn't alone, and there was more than one bad guy, with more than one victim, busting in one door would signal the others. It could set off a deadly chain reaction. They'd have to hit each door quickly and quietly.

Larry signaled to Ciro this time, to take up a position on the very first door. It sounded like the muffled screaming was coming from somewhere inside that room.

It was too late to go back out. Too late to wait the stupid fucking ten minutes for backup to arrive. Ciro said a silent prayer and blessed himself. His heart was pounding and he could hear the blood rushing in his ears. He thought of his new baby girl, Esmerelda. Just an hour ago, he had been mad that, at six months old, she was still getting up in the middle of the night. Now he would do anything to be home in bed, wide awake and feeding Essie a bottle.

His hand shook as he tried the knob. It turned in slow motion in his sweaty palm. God, he hoped Larry had picked the right friggin' door.

Then he pushed open the door, stepped inside, and pointed his Glock right at the back of Todd LaManna's head.

59

The light was not only blinding, it was painful. It felt as though someone had stuck a knife straight into her eyeballs. Lainey shut her eyes tight and scurried into a dark corner.

And then it was gone.

As quickly as it had opened, the door slammed shut and darkness enveloped her once again. Tiny white spots danced across a smoky black canvas. Before she could think about what had just happened, Lainey heard the screech of metal on metal, the sound of a lock turning.

"I'm in here!" she heard Katy shout. "I'm in here! Oh God! Thank God!"

And then the heavy creak of a door opening.

"It's so bright . . . I can't . . . I can't see. He had my eyes taped . . . " Katy was saying.

There was a long silence. Too long.

"You've been busy," replied the Devil. "Very, very busy, I see."

He was back.

"No, no, please . . . " Katy whimpered.

Lainey shut her eyes tight. She got on her hands and knees and frantically searched the dirt floor for the eye patches. *Where were the patches?*

"Didn't you know I'd come back for you?"

"No, no . . . Oh God, no . . ."

"You were trying to get away from me, weren't you?"

She found them on the floor, the thin discs of plastic and tape. She felt around her eyes for the track of adhesive where she'd ripped off the duct tape. She remembered what Katy had told her about the glue.

"No . . ." Katy said again.

"Look at the mess you made," he hissed.

Lainey put the patches back on her eyes and pressed the tape down hard, but part of the tape had stuck onto itself and much of the stickiness was gone. She could feel it lifting off her skin and she knew he would know. She wet herself.

"You know what happens to bad girls, Katy."

"You know, fuck you, you freak of nature! Fuck you! I'm not gonna let you scare me anymore! I'm not gonna be scared anymore!"

"Oh no?"

Katy screamed then. A long, bone-chilling scream that Lainey feared might never, ever end.

She rocked back and forth, her knees to her chest, her thumbs in her ears, her sweaty palms pressing down the strips of tape to her temples. She whispered the nite-nite prayer her mom had taught her when she was little. Over and over again. It was the only prayer she knew.

> Now I lay me down to sleep.
> I pray the Lord my soul to keep.
> And if I die before I wake.
> I pray the Lord my soul to take.

Minutes, maybe even hours, passed, for all she knew. Hesitantly, Lainey pulled her thumbs out of her ears and listened to the deafening sound of silence.

The screaming had finally stopped.

Katy was gone.

60

"There's a whole ring of pervs here," Ciro said to Bobby as he stepped out of his car. "Larry's talking to one of 'em, some Dutch business-man who suddenly claims he don't know English, even though we got him saying lots of interesting slang words on the video he was barking into. What a rush," Ciro added, holding his hand out to show Bobby. "Damn, I'm still shaking."

Uniforms from PBSO and Lake Worth PD were everywhere. At least a dozen cruisers were in the parking lot, which was ablaze with red and blue flashing lights. "Where'd you find him?" Bobby asked as the two of them headed inside and through the towering maze of cardboard boxes. Even with the lights on full blaze, the werewolves, vampires, Grim Reapers, and old Santas waiting around every end cap were pretty freaky.

"Back here. We followed a light underneath the door that led to what we thought were back offices. Turns out they were playrooms. We found LaManna behind door number one, buck-naked with a whip in his hand and about to have his way with some screaming fif-teen-year-old. Mind you, she don't look fifteen. Lorelei Bialis. Told us at first she was eighteen, but when the first couple of names she gave didn't check out, she finally came clean. Works for a fucking escort service, Tender Love."

They stepped into the pass-through office. "This is where the bouncer from Tender Love was supposed to be," Ciro continued, "but he had stepped into the john, which is all the way in the back, when we came through. That's why he didn't spot us outside on the video surveillance."

"And the others?" Bobby asked.

"We found four girls and three pervs, inside these three rooms," he said, motioning to three open doors off the hall. "One of the guys doubled up. All of the girls are under eighteen. The pervs range from mid-thirties to Grandpa, a banking exec in his sixties. Haven't verified names or exact ages on two of the girls—they're not talking. Yet. One who is, is a Theresa Carbona, a fifteen-year-old runaway from Dallas. Hooked up with Tender Love through her boyfriend, a thirty-eight-year-old mechanic from Waco. It's an underage prostitution ring, Bobby. You call in and order what you want, and they deliver after midnight every Friday and Saturday. The back offices are all outfitted to your personal, fucked-up fantasy: chains and whips; videos and televisions; school desks and blackboards. And the girls are, from what we can tell so far, all consenting."

Bobby stopped walking and shot him a look. "There's no kid who consents to this shit at fifteen, no matter how hard they are. Pick a different word."

"Sorry. They're prostitutes, Bobby. I meant to say none of them are drugged or forced here, or nothing. They show up at the escort service for work, and the company van brings 'em here. Customers park far away from the building and each other and avoid cameras. The operation's been going on for some time—months, maybe even years. You gotta be screened first to be let in. I wouldn't be surprised if the Fibbies were already looking at 'em."

"Lew Wilson, head of the bureau's Miami office, is on his way," Bobby commented as he looked off at one of the rooms, closer to the end of the hallway. "He said he's got guys up here who're gonna work it with you and Larry. Should be here within the hour. It may be best to let the feds take it. If they have jurisdiction, they'll get more jail time."

He spotted three girls sitting on a ratty blue couch in a dimly lit room. Two whispered anxiously to each other, but the third sat off by herself on the end, her arms wrapped around her elbows, as if she were incredibly cold. She was dressed like a cheerleader, in a short skirt, tight tee and high-heeled white patent-leather boots, her long blond hair up in curled pigtails. Black mascara streaks stained her fresh cheeks. It was, for a painful split second, like looking at a ghost. "The word *forced*, Ciro," Bobby remarked softly, taking off his jacket, "is, again, a matter of interpretation." He walked into the room and handed it to the blonde. "Take this," he said when she looked up. "It's gonna be OK." Then he walked back out.

"According to his passport stamps, the Flying Dutchman has been to Miami six times in the past year," Ciro said, looking around uncomfortably when Bobby stepped back out into the hallway. It was too late to take off his own jacket, so he just buttoned it.

"And LaManna?"

"Looks like he's a frequent customer, too," Ciro replied, heading back down the hall. "Claims this is where he was the night Lainey disappeared. After he left Tweedledee and Tweedledum in the Side Pocket Pub, he came here. The girl, Lorelei—aka Lori—confirmed it. That was her, the blonde. She's a little fuzzy with actual dates, but they used the video room that night, so I'm assuming there'll be a date/time stamp. Tape's at Tender Love offices, which is in Palm Beach, and currently surrounded by PBSO. Like getting your picture taken at Disney: the snapshot's free, but the actual picture's gonna cost ya. In this case, the nookie's five hundred, the tape's double that. Todd hasn't ponied up the ching yet, though." Ciro stopped in front of another office door. This one was closed. The red plastic nameplate stuck in the middle of it said THE BOSS.

Bobby pressed his hand against the door as Ciro went to open it. "You know coming in here by yourselves was stupid, Ciro."

Ciro said nothing.

"You're shaking for a reason. Don't let a good outcome cloud that judgment of yours. And for God's sake, don't ever fucking listen to Larry. That was your first mistake."

Ciro nodded with a smile and opened the door to a back office, where a sweaty, tear-faced Todd LaManna sat handcuffed to a desk. He looked up when Bobby entered and started bawling.

"I told you I didn't do it, Dees! I told you it wasn't me who took Lainey!" He looked at Ciro. "You told him, right? You told him I have an alibi?"

"Now we know where you were that night, Todd. We still have a problem with where you were from five to eight."

"Jesus Christ . . . you guys are . . . " His voice trailed off. "I don't know. I got something to eat, then met up with Jules at that bar I told you about. I just didn't want to go home because then Debbie wouldn't let me go out again. And I had, you know, paid half up front already."

"Is Lainey involved in this, Todd?" Bobby asked, leaning against the desk.

"No, no, no . . . " Todd shook his head fervently. "Swear to God. I'll take a lie detector, I'll drink truth serum, you know, whatever. Anything. 'Cause I didn't do it!"

Bobby looked across the hall, where crime-scene photographers were busy snapping pictures of the video room. "You're a pig, Todd, you know that?"

"It's a mistake! She told me she was eighteen! How the fuck was I supposed to know?"

Bobby shook his head. "You're gonna swear to that, too? You're a piece of work. Now, how am I supposed to believe anything you say?"

"It's on tape, man," Todd shouted. "I have an alibi on tape! Just look at it. Tender Love—Ricky, the owner—he'll tell you I was here. I didn't take Lainey and you all damn well know it!"

The blonde walked by then in Bobby's jacket, along with her two friends, escorted by PBSO uniforms. Her head was hung low, but Bobby could still see the black stains on her pale cheeks. She didn't look up.

"You're a pig, Todd," Bobby repeated, turning to leave. "And right now, the only thing I find comforting about having to sit and watch any part of that tape is knowing that it is gonna put your fat, twisted ass away for a few dozen years."

61

It was a fucking shame. A real shame, the man thought. You weed them, you feed them, you water them and give them love, and in the end all you got left with was a thorny stem that wasn't even pretty to look at anymore.

Katy was his "prize" and joy, he liked to say. She was one of the very first. He had taken such a long, patient time to cultivate her. And when the time had come, as it had with the others, he simply could not bring himself to paint her portrait. He was never ready. There was something so intriguing about her. She was not like the others. In the beginning, she was more like . . . his Lainey.

But Katy had disappointed him more than any other. It wasn't that he didn't think she would try to escape one day, because he was definitely not that naive. It was . . . well, the ingratitude. She knew he favored her. She knew the others had not enjoyed the things that she had. She'd manipulated him into giving her privileges, like letting her have a little company when he was away on business. Or giving her special food. Or letting her listen to his sermons with him. With her pretty face and pretty long hair . . .

He felt himself growing hard and he brushed away the tears of anger from his face before they even had a chance to fall.

Are you pure in thought and deed?

I am not, Father. I am not pure in either thought or deed. In fact, I've been very bad.

He chewed on the end of his paintbrush, till the ragged plastic stub cut his tongue. While it was now necessary to finish her painting, he was not happy about it. And that's what was really making him so upset. That's what he knew a shrink would tell him was the root of his incredible anger right now. Katy had forced him to do this. She had forced him to pick up his paintbrush, and he was just not enjoying it like he should. She had robbed him of that pleasure and made it instead a sad, laborious chore.

He mixed his palette on top of the morning's *Miami Herald* headline.

PALM BEACH CHILD PROSTITUTION RING BROKEN UP; FATHER OF MISSING CORAL SPRINGS TEEN ARRESTED

He blended just a bead of ebony into the smoke gray. A drop dripped from his Filbert brush onto the face of FDLE Special Agent Supervisor Robert Dees. Didn't he just look so smart? Grabbing headlines—no, hogging headlines—once again? Even the fat dimwit dad who got arrested didn't get his picture on the front page—he'd been banished to page 3.

He took his paintbrush and smeared the droplet all over Special Agent Supervisor's headline-hogging face. He'd show the *Herald* and the *Sentinel* and MSNBC who should have the headlines once again. It was he who'd brought the local Hero Among Us into this fame game for a little sport, and it was he who could knock him right out. Right out of the fucking ballpark, he could. Because the truth was, Bobby Dees was in way over his handsome special-agent head. And the whole fucking world would get to see that soon enough. For a second he almost felt bad for the man, for the pain that he was about to experience, but the feeling quickly passed. He smiled to himself and took his brush to the stretched, primed white canvas. The rich smell of oils was intoxicating, and the smooth feel of the brush handle in his fingers, heavy with paint, was cathartic.

"Now sit still," he said in a singsong to the ugly, thorny disappointment seated across from him. She had finally stopped pulling on the chains, and her head had lolled perfectly to the left. The lighting was just right.

"Just like that," he cooed. "Now, open that nasty little mouth of yours and let me see you scream . . ."

62

"White male, between the ages of twenty-five to fifty. Probably employed in a white-collar profession," Christine Trockner, FDLE's resident profiler, said to the crowd of detectives and special agents gathered around the conference table in the Crimes Against Children squad bay. As promised, Miami-Dade PD and the Broward Sheriff's Office had each sent over two homicide detectives. The City of Miami PD had sent one. Together with Larry, Ciro, Veso, and Bobby, the Picasso task force now officially had nine warm bodies. Ten if you counted Zo, who was seated next to Bobby. Technically, Zo was running MROC while Foxx was off rubbing elbows and jetting to Tallahassee to meet with the commissioner; he wasn't supposed to be involved in tactical squad operations or task forces. But while Zo might have passed his ASAC interview with flying colors, the stiff suit didn't fit quite right. A squad bay was where he really belonged.

"He might be working part-time," Christine continued. "He's probably gone to art school or taken art lessons, given his work with oils, use of professional products, and advanced skills. But I think he's a closet painter, meaning I don't think he does it as a profession. He has a problem with how he relates to women, so he targets younger women, namely adolescents, before they can fully mature and reject him. He may be impotent. He may have been beaten or abused as a child, and probably has a bad relationship with his mother, if she's still alive. He may be married, and if so, would be very submissive. My guess is that he's single. He is likely to be a loner. No friends, isolated at work. Unsociable."

"Let me get this straight," Larry said slowly. "We're looking for an unsociable white male between twenty-five and fifty who doesn't like his mommy and prefers younger women? That's supposed to narrow it down? Drop the art appreciation and you just described, well, all of us."

The room laughed.

"What did you expect, a picture and an address?" Christine returned. "Profiling's not a science, you know. It's a psychological, behavioral analysis that might help you narrow down your pool of suspects. Have you looked at art schools? That's a good place to start."

"Oh yeah," Bobby answered. "And art galleries to see if anybody can recognize maybe the style of painting. We've got an art aficionado with the FBI up in NY looking at high-resolution pictures of both paintings, too, to see what, if anything, he can tell us. But we're kind of stuck, Christine. The paintings are evidence—graphic, disturbing evidence—and I have to be real careful who I show them to; you've got to save a few things to identify the nuts and false confessors. And there's the media. They sure would love to get a hold of those paintings and blast them all over the news just for kicks."

"I'm sure that Channel 6 reporter—what's his name? Felding? I'm sure he has pictures squirreled away on his laptop," commented Jeff Amandola, a Miami-Dade detective. "I bet Picasso is the best thing that ever happened to that guy's career."

"I'm sure. That's why we had him gagged," Bobby answered. "What about a pedophile history, Christine? Should we look for that?"

"He's not a pedophile," she replied with a shake of her head. "He targets teenage women who are physically developed. It's the emotional maturity of an older woman that I believe he fears, but he doesn't target young kids. And given the pictures you showed me of Lainey that you suspect she sent him over the Internet, she certainly doesn't look thirteen, either. Most likely she told him she was older. I don't think you'll find a history of pedophilia or even a sex-offender history. This guy is very brazen, much more than any serial I've ever seen. He's taunting you to find him, even going so far as to send you the evidence that he himself created, without fear that it could one day be used to find and identify him. So I don't think he's been caught before. In fact, I believe this guy's been doing this for a long time. Like a killer who targets prostitutes, if you're right in your theory, Bobby, he has purposely selected a very transient segment of the population—one that's notoriously difficult to identify and track: teenage runaways. There are hundreds of missing teens in South Florida alone; hundreds of thousands around the country. Many more who are never even reported. So he has had a relative smorgasbord of victims to whet his appetite and experiment on. Perhaps even going back years. We know from the old contusions and chain marks on Gale Sampson that he's restrained his victims for a period of time. We can surmise that if he has had them from the date of all three girls' disappearances, that that time period is substantial—months, even. That means he has the facilities to restrain these girls, perhaps multiple girls at a time, and the confidence to know he can brutalize them. I also look at the fact that he is accomplished at torture, which means he's done it for a while. As you well know, generally speaking, serials escalate in brutality, starting oftentimes with animals, and escalating to humans. With a sexual serial, often there is a Peeping Tom phase that escalates to home burglary, and then rape. From there he may escalate to kidnapping so that he can have more time to play out his fantasies of torture and ultimately murder."

The room was quiet. Bobby blew out a pent-up breath. "So that means," he said, pointing to the crime-scene photo of Gale Sampson splayed out on the bed, a knife through her happy-face T-shirt, "he's done this before."

Christine nodded. "He has other victims. Go back and look for unsolved homicides that perhaps involved dismemberment, although he might have recently escalated to that."

"We're already doing that," Zo said. "But there's more than a few Jane Doe cold cases on file with the police departments going back over the past five years. We're talking at least thirty, and that's just looking at four counties. And Picasso's not the only bad guy in town, unfortunately."

"Don't forget, he could be transient himself. He could be mobile, although serials favor areas they are familiar with," Christine responded.

"Why now?" Bobby asked. "Why has he come out now all of a sudden? And with two portraits in two weeks? He's been at this awhile under the radar, you're saying, and he's just exploded? Why? Normally there's a downtime between crimes with serials."

"I think the fact that you haven't recognized his crimes before is what has drawn him out. Many serials want to gain attention from what they've done. They want to fantasize about their crime, then finally act on it, and then relive it all again by reading about it and watching the news coverage on TV. Oftentimes serials will be one of the first faces in the crowd at their own crime scenes, because they like to watch others react to what they've done. It feeds them. But perhaps no one noticed this guy for a while, or his 'accomplishments,' and so he is reacting now in part to the explosive attention he's gotten from the press and national media. He doesn't want it to end. That would explain the short time span in between sending the two portraits. Like I explained, his time line between murders has already had an opportunity to escalate over months or perhaps even years of not being caught. Now he's gotten cocky and has moved on to the next step—finding you and forcing you to recognize him."

"Why Bobby?" Zo asked. "I get the reporter, because that gives him a jump start on the media fanfare, like you said. But why Bobby? Why has he directed the paintings to him? Left his name at the crime scenes? Should we be looking at enemies here? Guys Bobby has put away in the past? Should we focus on anything in particular?"

"That's a good question. He obviously has singled you out, Bobby, for a reason," Christine replied. "I don't think it's an archenemy, necessarily, or someone who you put away, although that is a possibility worth exploring. I think it's more likely a challenge."

"A challenge?" Ciro asked.

"Your reputation, Bobby, precedes you. You've garnered national attention on missing children and abduction cases. You've been the recipient of many prestigious awards; your cases and your work have been on the cover of every paper and magazine from the *New York Times* to the *Enquirer*. And most recently, *People* magazine wrote a special-interest article about how you are a hero and how you are nicknamed the Shepherd by colleagues because of your outstanding work in solving the most baffling abductions and bringing these victims home. Cases like this. In Picasso's eyes, it's like David challenging Goliath to a duel. He's challenging you."

"Any idea when he might strike again?" asked Raul Carrera, another Miami-Dade detective. "What we can expect?"

Christine started packing up her stuff. "Oh, I would imagine he has already struck again. Unless something or someone is preventing him from acting out his disturbed fantasies, he's just going to go and pluck another victim out of his storage unit, wherever that might be, and paint you a picture of his latest and greatest accomplishment. Expect it to be even more brutal. Expect a shock to the conscience. This guy has tasted infamy, gentlemen, and like a genie, it's going to be impossible to get him to go back inside his bottle. He likes what he does way too much to ever stop."

63

Around the Palm Beach headquarters of LEACH—Law Enforcement Against Child Harm—veteran Sheriff's Office Special Investigations Detective Mike Hicks's nickname was "The Dick Magnet." And for good reason. Nine times out of ten, within just a few minutes of his logging onto the Internet and entering a chat room, pervs were on Mike like flies to shit. His record was forty-five seconds for a full-on proposition, faster than any other computer decoy on the LEACH task force.

At five-ten, 211 pounds, and forty-nine years of age, Mike certainly didn't look the part of a fourteen-year-old girl who LOVED Joe Jonas, the color fuchsia, M&M's, rainbows, Weimaraner puppies (soooo cute!), and riding roller coasters all day and night. Or, for that matter, one who HATED all things Miley Cyrus/Hannah Montana (go away now, PULEEZ!!), social studies (who really cares WTF happened 500 years ago??? Talk to me about TODAY ☺), smelly guys (Get AXE. Use it!), and plastic people who didn't even know HOW to tell the TRUTH. And he looked absolutely nothing like his perky, long-locked, brunette, blue-eyed MySpace profile picture.

When LEACH was formed almost ten years ago in response to the then-nouveau crime of Internet trolling by innovative sex predators, the computer age was already up and running, but, like most befuddled middle-agers with a new-fangled gadget that technologically changed every two weeks, Mike wasn't. Looking back, he probably would've been content just marveling through the next few decades at what a cell phone could do, but Mike had two really pretty girls who just so happened to turn into teenagers in 1999. Unable to vote, drink, smoke, or even swear, at twelve and thirteen, Sherry and Lisa already knew far more about how to work the foreboding lump of metal and disk drives that sat on a desk in the family room than he did. And what really bugged him was that they knew it, too. They knew the secret acronym text jargon, and had AOL Instant Messenger accounts before he even knew what the hell Instant Messenger was. Because he was a cop and because he vividly remembered all the shit he'd done as a kid that his parents still knew nothing about, when his own offspring became teens, he'd vowed he would never be so willfully ignorant. So when LEACH formed and requests for techie decoys made the rounds through the Palm Beach Sheriff's Office, he signed up for the war without even knowing what OMG stood for. It was supposed to just be a short stint to get him up to speed and through the rest of adolescence. Ten years later, here he still was. His kids were grown and long gone, yet every year he seemed to get a little bit younger. Eleven was the new thirteen. But of course, no one could've imagined back then that farty Mike Hicks would be a more believable teenager than he was a middle-age cop and soon-to-be grandpa.

Today his name was Janizz, but her friends all called her Skittles. She was almost fourteen—blowing the candles out on December 16!—lived in Riviera Beach, and loved to meet new people. Janizz entered the hot tub, a local South Florida chat room on TeenSpot.com. The topic of conversation was simply "Have fun and relax in the hot tub. Everyone's welcome." There were thirty-one members chatting.

Janizzbaby: what up all?

Within seconds, a half-dozen responses erupted at lightning speed on the screen. Mrpimpin16, lowtone, sykosid, drinkpoison, nastyboy, zzzzho. And within a minute, a small gray window opened at the top.

TheCaptain is requesting a person to person chat with you:
. . . what up there? long time, no c janizz. where u been?

The Captain. Mike knew that screen name. He'd chatted with him in a few rooms before, under different names, of course. The guy was pretty aggressive, if he remembered right. He checked his log. Sure enough, Janizzbaby had chatted with The Captain before, too. He clicked the chat button.

Janizzbaby: grounded ☹

TheCaptain: sux. Y?

Janizzbaby: tell me bout it. came home at midnight

TheCaptain: bad girl

Janizzbaby: no. usually im really good ☺

TheCaptain: oohh. good girls gone bad. 12AM. how old r u again?

Janizzbaby: 14. blowing the candles out in december. u?

TheCaptain: 17. blew them last month. ur bad - 12AM w/ao special?

Janizzbaby: i wish

TheCaptain: they call me the dreammaker

Janizzbaby: where u been? waiting on me 2 come back 2 the tub?

TheCaptain: playing

Janizzbaby: at least ur honest

TheCaptain: kiddin! i wuz missin u ☹ . . . now that i know ur looking 4 s/o special . . .

Janizzbaby: i never said that

TheCaptain: didnt need 2. u shudnt b out by urself @ nite. psychos r everywhere

Janizzbaby: oohh. do i look scared? jus having fun

TheCaptain: i seen ur pix. hot. psychos b looking 4 u!

Janizzbaby: thanx. i think

TheCaptain: ur hot, is all im saying. u need 2 b protected

Janizzbaby: and who's gonna do that?

TheCaptain: im looking 4 work ☺

Janizzbaby: hmmmm . . .

TheCaptain: ill make sure u don't get in no trouble. have u home and in bed rt on time. mom will luv me ☺ all moms do

Janizzbaby: f* her. there r others?

TheCaptain: not if i got u. im a 1 woman guy

It was an interesting, delicate dance of words. To successfully prosecute a person under the Computer Pornography and Child Exploitation Act for luring or enticing a minor to engage in sexual conduct over the Internet, certain magic lingo had to be said and it couldn't be said by Mike. The number-one defense to an 847.0135 charge was entrapment. In simple terms, the "Boo-hoo! I wouldn't have said all those nasty things, but for the coercive, manipulative undercover cop making me say them!" defense. Mike knew to be careful. And patient. No inducing, encouraging, soliciting, persuading. The invitation to hook up had to come from the bad guy.

Thirty minutes and a whole lot of BS later, it came.

TheCaptain: have 2 meet u ☺

Janizzbaby: ha

TheCaptain: serious

Janizzbaby: what u want?

TheCaptain: u 2 b mine

Janizzbaby: thats it?

TheCaptain: nope. TTA. being honest again

TTA was text for "Tap That Ass," which was street slang for "I want to fuck you." That qualified as magic lingo.

Janizzbaby: im a virgin

TheCaptain: even better

Janizzbaby: maybe not. im a good girl, remember?

TheCaptain: i could turn u. its amazing what my hands can do

Janizzbaby: u could try ☺

TheCaptain: thursday. i gotta meet u

Janizzbaby: cant. gotta babysit

Being too available or too pushy might spook him. It could be a tip-off Janizz was a cop.

TheCaptain: friday?

Janizzbaby: have track till 4

TheCaptain: after

Janizzbaby: maybe

TheCaptain: what school u @? bak?

Bak stood for Bak Middle School. He had obviously found Janizzbaby's profile.

Janizzbaby: yup

TheCaptain: MCD on australian @ 45. that by u?

MCD stood for McDonald's; 45 was 45th Street.

Janizzbaby: i know it

TheCaptain: ill b in a new black bmw. 4:30

Janizzbaby: ooh - dinner. you have to do better than MCD

TheCaptain: i will. i got a special place we can get to know each other

Janizzbaby: wheres that?

TheCaptain: they change the sheets

Janizzbaby: ill wear s/t nice

TheCaptain: not 2 much

Janizzbaby: ur bad. got 2 b home by 9. no joke there

TheCaptain: plenty of time

Janizzbaby: i told u—im a virgin. nervous to give it up

TheCaptain: ill be gentle, like i said ☺ nice and slow. u need s/o w/experience 1st time

Janizzbaby: GTG. TLK-2-U-L-8-R

TheCaptain: r we on?

Janizzbaby: yeah. k. u better not bring no friends, though

TheCaptain: jus me

Janizzbaby: no cameras, either

TheCaptain: ☹ k

Janizzbaby: k. bye

Mike left the chat room and notified the rest of the task force about Friday's setup on McDonald's. He subpoenaed the registration info for TheCaptain's screen name from TeenSpot.com but didn't expect much. More often than not, cyberpredators used a fake email with an untraceable ISP address; the only way to find them was to lure them out into the light and catch them red-handed. But a live catch also helped refute the "it wasn't me on the computer saying all those vile things" defense. It also helped nix any entrapment defense, because showing up to meet the fourteen-year-old virgin pretty much demonstrated independent thought. As he wrote out his report, Mike got to wondering who this Captain might be. Just who might step out of that new Beamer Friday afternoon? He'd seen just about every walk of life pull up in every car imaginable—from Ferraris to jalopies—and nothing and no one ever surprised him anymore. Just a few years ago, it was the Miami TV weatherman, Bill Kamal, arriving at a restaurant with a smile and a glove compartment full of condoms to pick up the fourteen-year-old boy-toy he thought he was meeting for a romp in the hay. A couple of months back, it was a federal prosecutor from northern Florida who showed up at the airport in Michigan to meet a five-year-old with a Dora the Explorer doll and a jar of petroleum jelly in his pocket. Mike knew it could be anyone on Friday, from his own lieutenant to a bank CEO.

He finished his report and went to navigate out of TeenSpot. In another chat room, he watched as the sexually charged, drug-referenced acronyms flew back and forth. No one was who they said they were. One guy, makeitfit12, just kept asking for single hot girls who liked to party hard to respond—"The younger the meat, the sweeter the flesh." There was no beating around the bush. Not even a little friendly word-foreplay. Even sexting—sending sexually explicit text messages and pictures in the hope of hooking up—was becoming more and more impersonal.

He popped back into the hot tub to see if The Captain was still there. He wasn't. But a new name, babygurldee, had logged into the chat room. Mrpimpin16, drinkpoison, and sykosid raced to say hello.

Like flies on shit . . .

Mike sure was glad his girls were all grown up.

64

Mark Felding sat at his dining room table and with a trembling hand poured himself another scotch. Every light in the two-bedroom apartment was on, the closet and cabinet doors flung open wide, the shower curtain pulled all the way back in the bathroom. Before him on the table sat an oversize mustard-yellow mailer. A mailer that had the strip of newspaper with his name on it glued to the front. A mailer that smelled of paint.

He ran a hand through his hair, trying to reel in his thoughts.

"I'm not letting that get on the air."

"A reporter with a spine and a set of morals? That's novel."

"We get a lot of dements looking for airtime, Agent Dees. You'd be surprised how much garbage we don't broadcast. Even when it is news . . . "

Mark wiped the sweat off his lip. *When had he said that?* Weeks ago. Eons ago. A few lifetimes ago.

Even when it is news . . .

Mark stared at the mailer before him. Without looking, he knew full well what was inside. He threw back his drink in one gulp.

It was more than news inside. It was Big News. Big, Shocking News that had captured the attention of a city. Big, Shocking News that had suddenly turned an aging, invisible field reporter into an expert on crime prevention and quite possibly the station's next weekend anchor. Those young, lost lifetimes had changed the rules, grayed the lines, if they'd ever really existed in the first place.

Of course, Mark owed his recent catapult to success to another. He realized that. Those few young lifetimes back he was just a Friday or so away from a pink slip, and now he was being recognized in the toilet paper aisle at Walgreens.

Mark flipped the mailer over and fingered the metal closer on the flap. His covenant with the Devil.

We get a lot of dements looking for airtime . . .

Decisions, decisions.

He wiped the sweat that had gathered again on his upper lip with the back of his hand and picked up the phone. Given their acrimonious recent history, Mark wasn't expecting Special Agent Bobby Dees to actually pick up, though.

He was right. "Agent Dees," Mark said at the tone. He strained to keep his voice calm and professional. He looked around his empty apartment, with its hiding spaces wide open and all its lights ablaze. "This is Mark Felding with Channel 6. I know it's late and I know that we've had, well, some issues recently, but I think it's time to make peace because I have another package here. Here, as in *at my house*. I just returned from the studio to find it under my door. I'm calling you because . . . well, you know why—as you said, you're running this show. And I'm thinking that it's pretty messed up that this guy knows where I live. Call me as soon as you get this. Or I guess I'll call Agent Dias or . . . I don't know. Just call me, please."

The apartment was perfectly still. The only sound was the kitchen clock a full room away, loudly ticking off the seconds. Mark pinched open the metal closer and tore the flap back. The unmistakable scent of oil paint seemed to fill the apartment.

He poured himself another drink and just waited for the phone to ring.

65

Bobby looked over at the cell phone on the nightstand, his right arm wrapped protectively around a sleeping LuAnn in the darkness. He spotted the name MARK FELDING on his caller ID.

Why the hell would that jerk be calling him at almost midnight? Was he drunk?

Bobby thought back to that night in the bar after the grisly finding of Gale Sampson's body at the Regal All-Suites. Mark Felding had been pounding down the hard stuff before they'd met up. It was entirely possible he was drunk and dialing Bobby's digits in the middle of the night just to harass him with some question or a new "theory" of the case. A madman's seemingly random choice of a washed-up field reporter to be his messenger boy had not only revitalized the guy's career, but had also emboldened the idiot into thinking he was the next Bob Woodward. It was as if he were competing with Bobby to solve the case. He stared at the phone, waiting for it to do something.

Why the hell would he be calling at this hour?

Maybe he had something important to tell him. Maybe there was another painting.

Bobby closed his eyes. Another victim. *Please, God, no . . .*

It was late. Another mailing would have come to the TV station a lot earlier than midnight, right? So it must be the midnight ramblings of a drunk, or time for Let's All Play Detective.

Bobby rubbed his eyes. *Please let that be it. Let the madness end . . .*

The phone blurped, indicating a new message.

"You better get that," LuAnn whispered in the dark. She was wide awake, too.

Bobby nodded. "Let me check my voice mail. It may be nothing."

"Who is it?"

"You don't want to know." They both knew it was never good at this time of night, no matter who was calling. He sat up on the edge of the bed and went to his voice mail.

"This is Mark Felding with Channel 6. I know it's late and I know that we've had, well, some issues recently, but I think it's time to make peace because I have another package here. Here, as in at my house. I just returned from the studio to find it under my door. I'm calling you because . . . well, you know why—as you said, you're running this show. And I'm thinking that it's pretty messed up that this guy knows where I live. Call me as soon as you get this. Or I guess I'll call Agent Dias or . . . I don't know. Just call me, please."

Bobby stood up and walked to the window.

"I heard," LuAnn whispered, her soft voice shaking. "I heard what he said."

"I have to go out," he replied, dialing the number back. "Try and sleep."

"That's not going to happen." She sat up in bed, her arms wrapped around her knees. He knew what she was thinking. He wanted to comfort her, but he couldn't. He still hadn't told her about Ray. So he said nothing.

"It's Dees," he said when Felding picked up on the first ring.

"I was just about to call 911. He's been to my home, Agent Dees."

"All right. I'm on my way. Where are you?"

"In Tamarac. At the University Apartments on University and Hiatus. Um, 304. That's apartment 304 in Building C." He paused for a split second before adding, "It's bad. It's really bad . . . "

"Don't touch anything, Mark! Don't open it."

"It's too late for that. I saw. I had to see."

"Just put it down and leave it wherever it is right now! Just leave it. I'm on my way!"

"He came to my house!"

"I'm on my way!"

Bobby hung up the phone and rushed to get dressed while he chirped Zo and the rest of the task force.

Expect it to be even more brutal. Expect a shock to the conscience. This guy has tasted infamy, gentlemen, and like a genie, it's going to be impossible to get him to go back inside his bottle. He likes what he does way too much to ever stop.

How could one top kidnapping, torturing, murdering, and dismembering two young sisters together? What could this psycho possibly do that would, as Christine Trockner warned just a few short days ago, "shock his conscience"?

Bobby couldn't even begin to imagine.

66

Tamarac wasn't too far from Fort Lauderdale—just fourteen miles to the west. It took Bobby fifteen minutes from the time he pulled on pants, strapped on his badge, and raced out the door. Of course there was no one on the road and he was doing eighty.

The first thing he spotted as he pulled into the parking lot of the University Apartments wasn't a cluster of cop cars with sirens sounding and lights ablaze. It was the WTVJ 6 news truck. His chest tightened. The truck must've just pulled in, because he watched as the driver and passenger—who were watching him back—scrambled to get out and grab their equipment. Just as Bobby pulled to the curb and stepped out, the uniformed response he'd called in from BSO arrived in two cruisers.

"Keep them down here," he directed a young uniform as the cameraman and his assistant hurried across the asphalt, frantically trying to make it across the finish line and into the elevator before they were tagged. They got as far as the Coke machine. "Unless they have a badge, no one goes upstairs!" Bobby called out, heading for the outdoor staircase.

At 304, he rapped on the door. "Felding, it's Bobby Dees. Open up." Bobby heard several locks open before a weary and worn Mark Felding opened the door. Bobby could smell the scotch on his breath before he even said, "Hey."

"Where is it?" Bobby asked, walking in. Somehow Zo was right behind him, rushing down the hall.

"You all right, guy?" Zo asked Mark as he entered, looking around the apartment with a frown. He walked into the back bedroom and bathroom, looking for anyone hiding with either a weapon or a camera.

"I checked already. There's no one . . . ," Mark offered.

"Thanks, but I think I'll take a look myself. You know, your boys from Channel 6 are downstairs. They said to say hello, but they won't be coming up to join you. Tsk, tsk . . . calling them out here. You know the rules."

"It's my job, guys. I just called and told my producer that I had another one. You know, to be ready. I don't know what he did or who he called with that information."

"Who'd you call first this time?" Bobby asked sarcastically.

"You," Mark answered wearily. "But the public has a right to know . . . "

"Yeah, yeah. Spare me. Where is it?" Bobby asked again. Then he spotted the manila envelope on the kitchen table, next to a pile of magazines and mail. Pasted in small, boldface newspaper strips across the front was the name MARK FELDING. The top had been ripped open. Right next to it was a folded piece of canvas, lying face-down. On top of the canvas was a small white place card, like the type you see at wedding receptions. Even from five feet away, Bobby could make out what it said in pasted letters cut out from the newspaper.

FDLE SPECIAL AGENT SUPERVISOR ROBERT DEES

The distinctive squawk and chatter of police radios was making its way down the hall, along with the sound of rushed voices. In just seconds, the room would be full of people.

"Tell me you wore gloves when you opened this," Bobby said.

Mark shrugged again and looked down.

Bobby shook his head. He couldn't even look at the idiot anymore. "Zo, make sure they don't touch the door. Have them secure the hall-way and start looking for witnesses." He reached for the canvas.

Mark looked up at him then, with bloodshot, tired eyes. He shook his head. "It's bad, man . . . "

Using gloves, Bobby carefully unfolded the canvas. His stomach tightened, as it did when he went on a roller coaster. The bad drop was always the one you didn't prepare for, the one you never saw coming.

Expect it to be even more brutal.

Expect it to shock the conscience.

"Bobby, we're here, man. I'm gonna have Crime Scene start dusting . . . ," Ciro called.

"There's video on premises, but it's broken in this building, go figure. I'm pulling it anyway, and the other buildings . . . ," someone barked.

"Do you want to think about releasing a statement?" another called out. "They're already asking for one downstairs . . . "

Dozens of voices chattered around him, but all Bobby heard was the whoosh of blood as it rushed to his head. He stared at the twisted image in front of him. Of the girl in the baby-blue T-shirt and striped Abercrombie sweater, her chained hands raised up toward the ceiling, the slight fingertips whittled to raw, bloody stubs. Her eyes, like the others, were black, empty sockets. Her cheeks were dotted with teardrops of blood. Her mouth was contorted in a horrific scream. Long dusty blond hair spilled over her shoulders, some caught in the coils of shiny chains wrapped around her slight neck. Hanging right below them, resting on her creamy, white skin dotted with freckles was a shiny round silver pendant with a scripted *K* engraved on it.

Bobby knew that necklace. He knew that dusty blond hair, the T-shirt and sweater. He could smell her breath, still sweet with bubble gum, hear her melodic voice as it called out to him to watch her on the playground, watch her dive in the pool, watch her climb a mountain of cheerleaders to get to the top.

Time stopped and everyone moved about him in slow motion. He watched as Mark Felding just shook his head back and forth, his red eyes tearing up.

"Bobby? What is it?" Zo asked quietly, walking up behind him, his hand on Bobby's shoulder. "Shep? What's the matter?"

"Jesus Christ, Zo," Bobby replied slowly, his voice shaking. His knees felt like they were going to give way. He couldn't tear his eyes off the macabre painting in his hands. "It looks like Katy . . . "

67

"OK. It looks like a cement floor here, so it's a structure she's either in or next to. But behind her, there are clearly flames . . . "

"A furnace, maybe?" Jeff Amandola offered.

Don McCrindle, a detective with the Broward Sheriff's Office, sipped at his coffee and scratched his head. "But over here it's sunny. A furnace would be in a basement, right? And Florida don't have no basements, right?"

"Is he going out of state?" Ciro asked.

Larry piped in. "Doubt it. How the fuck are we gonna find her, then? He wants us to find her, doesn't he? That's what the shrink said."

"Profiler," corrected Roland Kelly, a big, burly homicide detective with the City of Miami. "So maybe it's religious. Fire and brimstone," he offered.

"You need to turn off the freaking televangelists, Kelly," quipped Don. "And stop giving them all your money. The world ain't coming to an end now."

"Very funny."

"So where do you see flames and sunshine at the same time?" asked Larry.

"How about the Port? They've got incinerators."

"That's real tight security, but yeah. We'll check it out," Don replied with a nod. "I don't know if they've got incinerators. And we'll check out Port Everglades, too. Anything with smoke or fire."

The Crimes Against Children squad bay was still filled with bodies at three a.m. They surrounded the conference table, standing over the graphic portrait—now preserved in a clear plastic evidence bag—like surgeons working on a body, trying to save her with their questions.

"You don't need to be here," Zo had cautioned Bobby more than once. "You should go home. We'll tell you if we come up with anything."

Bobby had nipped that idea right in the bud, the last time in the hallway of the University Apartments, before the task force headed over to the command center at MROC. There was no way he was abdicating control of this case. If, God forbid, it was Katy in that picture, he would make sure she was brought home proper. He would make sure justice was served. And he knew from experience that that couldn't and wouldn't be done watching from the sidelines. So he stood at the head of the table, throwing ideas around with the boys, listening to their measured banter and all the while trying very, very hard not to look at the terrified painted face on the table in front of him.

By four a.m., the consensus was to get back together in the morning, after everyone had had some rest. It took the coaxing of all eight men and an actual order from Zo to get Bobby to leave the building, though. Because all he wanted to do was figure it all out—in his office, in front of his computer, staring at his corkboard, like he had with hundreds of other cases over the years. He didn't want downtime. He just wanted to find out for himself that it was Somebody Else's Kid in that painting. As horrible as it would be for someone else, he wanted it to be anybody else but Katy. Anybody else but My Kid. And he didn't want to go home.

But he didn't have a choice.

"You know what today is?" he asked Zo as they walked across the empty lot to their cars. The sun was still far from coming up, but the birds had started to chirp in the palm trees overhead. At the far end of the lot were the administrative offices and Troop E station of the

Florida Highway Patrol. Bobby could see a Christmas tree twinkling in the lobby through the front window. FHP troopers always started early in putting up the holiday decorations; it seemed every year they moved it up another week. Thanksgiving was just a week out. Exactly a year ago today was the last time he had heard from or seen his daughter.

"Yeah, I know," Zo replied quietly.

"You think it's coincidence?"

"In this business, nothing's coincidence. He knows what buttons to push, though, Bobby, so I'm not gonna jump the gun. What she was last seen wearing was posted on the fucking Internet, for Christ's sake. Anybody could have seen it. He could very well be playing you, Shep."

Bobby nodded.

"Let me drive you home . . . ," Zo offered.

"I'm not drunk. I'll get myself home," he said, climbing into his car. "I'll see you in a couple of hours."

Bobby pulled out of the parking lot and swung on to the turnpike northbound. The silence in the car was deafening, so he turned on the radio. But that didn't help, either.

"What was she wearing, LuAnn? Think."

"Um, um, she had on her blue T-shirt. The one she got from Abercrombie with the matching striped sweater. I just washed it. It covers her arms, that's what I was thinking this morning, Bobby. I was thinking, 'It covers her arms.' Oh my God . . . "

"OK. I'll get a description in right away. They'll check the hospitals, bus stations, Amtrak, TriRail, and airports. How much money does she have, Belle?"

"Um, I don't know. A couple hundred, maybe, from her birthday and confirmation and work? No, wait—what am I thinking? She's working a lot. She's been saving up for a car, so maybe it was more. No, it was more. She was looking at a car, so she had at least a thousand. Maybe she had more. I don't know. I don't know, Bobby!"

"What about a suitcase? Did you check her closet?"

LuAnn began to scream, banging her fists on the counter behind her. "No! She did not run away! No! You have to find her! You have to bring her back home, Bobby! You have to bring her back home to me!" Tears streamed from her panicked face. "I want to say I'm sorry! I want to do it over! I want another chance!"

He rubbed his eyes. How was he going to act normal in front of Lu-Ann? How was he supposed to not completely drop to his knees and fall apart? And if it was true, if it turned out that it really was Katy in that horrible portrait, how in God's name was he ever supposed to tell his wife that?

His mind raced, flipping between the alternate personalities of dad and detective. He tried his best to shut them out, but bittersweet memories flooded his brain. The last time he saw her, the last time he kissed her cheek, the last words she said to him . . . Much like how he would remember someone as he headed off to their funeral.

He shook the images out of his head. *Focus. Find her, whoever she might be. If it's Katy, bring her home. And don't think about what he's done to her. Don't go there, whatever you do.*

It was useless going home. Bobby sat at the kitchen table and drank more coffee until the sun finally came up. For all he knew, Lu-Ann was above his head, still wide awake and rocking with her hands wrapped around her knees. She had known something was up before he left. Call it instinct or a premonition or whatever, but she knew something was not right. She knew something was very, very wrong. And he didn't want to walk into that bedroom and confirm her worst suspicions with just one look.

He took a quick shower in the guest bathroom—Katy's bathroom—grabbed some clean clothes out of the laundry room, and headed back into the office somewhere around eight-thirty.

And, of course, he hadn't slept a wink.

68

Bobby stood up from behind his desk and stared out the window at the endless stream of cars headed west on the Dolphin. The sun was just starting its slow descent into the Everglades and roadwork crews were packing up for the day, which only helped thicken the congestion. "Anything?" he asked into the phone.

"We combed every bay like we were looking for lice on Carrot Top's head—nothing," Larry replied. Bobby, Zo, Don McCrindle, and an army of BSO uniforms and Customs officers had spent the day at Port Everglades in Fort Lauderdale. Larry, Ciro, Veso, Roland, and MDPD had covered the Port of Miami. Both teams had come up empty.

"Ya know, all day long I've been thinking, trying to figure where it was I might've seen that scene before," Larry continued. "It's been bugging the shit out of me, 'cause it looks familiar. And I was thinking, maybe Kelly's right—maybe this guy is getting real profound, you know? Maybe the flames are symbolic and instead of leading us to a site, he's maybe trying to send us a message."

"I'm listening . . . ," Bobby replied quietly, still staring out the window. Traffic looked the same as it did five minutes ago. As it did that morning. As it did yesterday. In fact, but for the Christmas trees strapped to the roofs of some cars, everything outside looked exactly the same as it did every day. Construction workers in T-shirts and sheikh caps packed up their coolers, smoking cigarettes and goofing off, while others finished up for the day expanding the same stretch of highway they'd been working on for the past couple of years. Down the halls of MROC, the same secretaries gossiped about the same people, the same agents worked at the same desks on the same cases. Everything looked and sounded exactly the same as it did yesterday or last month or last year, but with the simple unfolding of that canvas—with a quick sniff of nauseating oil paint—the whole world as Bobby knew it had changed once again. No longer did he have even the comfort of his imagination that his kid was fine and defying every cold, hard runaway statistic. No. Today his only child might be dead—the victim of a sadistic serial killer, perhaps kidnapped and tortured and raped all those days and weeks and months while everyone's life on the other side of that window went on as normal. And now, as he looked out on Miami, wondering where the hell Katy was, he couldn't stop the incredible anger that was swelling inside of him. Anger at Picasso, at himself, at every person on the other side of the glass. And he secretly wished—like he had for the past 365 days—that he was one of those mindless, faceless drivers stuck in traffic, banging on his steering wheel in frustration because he was going to be late for his kid's recital or miss dinner with the family. He wished to God he didn't have to feel the incredible pain he was feeling right now—a burning ache in every fiber of his being, as if he were coming apart at the very seams that held him together as a person. It was an indescribable pain that he could not imagine could get any worse, and yet he knew most definitely would, when and if his worst fear was finally confirmed—when the phone rang and the terrible words were finally spoken: "It's her." Like a death-row inmate already living in abject hell who'd vowed he'd rather die than live his life out in a six-by-eight cement box, Bobby stood waiting with anxious hope as the clock ticked its way down to midnight to hear if he'd won an improbable last-second, last-chance reprieve. He'd told himself since Katy left that the not knowing was the worst, but he knew now that was wrong. And as he listened to the warden's footfalls slowly approach his cell with grim news of his appeal, he realized that living in hell was much better than the alternative.

" . . . that's when it popped into my head! I have some dope I've got to drop off in a case that closed out years ago, when I was in Narcotics," Larry was saying. "The guy pled to twenty and the two keys are just sitting there, waiting to get destroyed, right? I have the court order and everything, but it's just freaking sitting there in the evidence room and I really have to get rid of it. Anyway, I'm driving across the MacArthur and I'm thinking about this dope and I'm thinking it's a Broward case, so I'll have to drop the dope up in Broward, and I don't know when I'll be there again. The last time I had to get rid of smack, it was at the dump. You ever had to dump dope, Bobby?"

"No."

Zo walked in the office, a frown on his face. "You look like shit. What're you doing?"

"Thanks," Bobby replied, rubbing his temples. "Waiting for Larry to get to the point." He put the phone on speaker. "Zo's here. You're on the air."

"Hey," Larry answered. "So I haven't been there in years myself, to the dump, but I start to think about it, Bobby. When you drop dope, you know, to destroy it, they have to burn it."

Bobby froze.

"The burn pit, it's outside. You can be standing in the sunshine while this sanitation worker's getting high off your leftover nose candy. Now, I haven't been there in years, so I call to see what time they're doing burns, 'cause it used to be they'd only do it by appointment and only on certain days of the week. But they're freaking closed! Like closed, closed. Now burns are done at the Wheelabrator facility off 441 and Interstate 595. The administrative facilities are still out there in the fucking Everglades, but the site's been shut down for a couple of years, and the landfill's been closed. That's when I started thinking—shit! That might be it! The burn site at the dump!"

He's taunting you to find him, even going so far as to send you the evidence that he himself created. He's challenging you.

It made sense. Where the police dumped and burned their evidence, Picasso would dump his. It would be very symbolic, like Roland

Kelly had suggested. Bobby looked at Zo. "Larry, is every burn site like Broward? You know, Miami, Palm Beach?" he asked.

"I don't know. I only had to get my stuff burned in Broward. I would think there's at least a procedure in each county, because you need a court order. Checks and balances, you know? To make sure we don't take it home and smoke it ourselves." He laughed. "Or sell it. Now that's capitalism."

It would also be symbolic to get rid of that evidence in the county in which it was seized. Bobby lived in Broward.

Bobby was already on the radio. Within minutes he had uniforms from a half-dozen departments responding to secure both the current and closed narcotic evidence burn sites in Miami, Palm Beach, Monroe, and Broward counties.

"You're not going," Zo said quietly as Bobby grabbed his sport jacket.

"The hell I'm not."

"You didn't sleep last night."

"Neither did you."

"Maybe. But this is way too much." Zo hesitated, as if he'd almost said the wrong thing, and closed the office door with his foot. "Listen, I want to say I'm sure it's not her, I want to tell you that, but I can't. And neither can you. Today's one year since she ran away. This psycho's addressing these portraits to you, and the clothing in the painting matches Katy's description to a T. If Larry's right and he's dumping the evidence at that site . . . " Zo trailed off and lowered his voice. "It's just not looking good, brother. And I don't think you should be there to see it."

"That's exactly why I am gonna be there, Zo. It isn't looking good. I know exactly what it looks like. It looks like this is gonna turn out to be my daughter. And if it is, well, I'm gonna be the one to find her, and I'm gonna bring her back home." He willed both the tears and the fear back as he opened the door and stepped into the squad bay. "And then I'm gonna find the sick fuck that did this to her, and when I do, when I'm through with him, he's gonna be begging me to fucking kill him."

69

LuAnn knew something was wrong. She felt it in every joint in her body. She felt it in her gut, and she felt it in her heart. Something was wrong. Something was very, very wrong.

Bobby was holding out on her.

At first she thought it was another woman. And that made sense. She'd been away from him for so long—emotionally, physically—that she'd often thought one day he'd decide he'd had enough and go find someone else. Or someone else would find him. At times during the past year she'd actually wished it would happen—so that it would be over with, so that she could finally be completely alone in the world, so that nothing and no one would matter anymore. She could stop silently blaming him, and he could stop silently blaming her and it would be done—their lives could go in different directions, without even the bond of a child to bring them back together at a future graduation and wedding. She could just curl up into a ball and wallow in self-pity until life was over. And the waiting for it to happen—to finally find out about the affair, to confront him, to see her marriage end, to watch him move out and start a life with someone new, to find herself completely alone—well, the waiting was too exhausting. She'd just wished the inevitable would happen already.

So it was no doubt unfair of her to think that a few nights together might close the expansive emotional void that had grown between them, no matter how great or tender the sex was, or how much she might will it to be so. No matter how close they'd seemed for a few days, or how much it felt like the "old days" of their marriage, when everything was normal and people called them lucky. She'd made a mistake shutting him out for all these months, she knew that now, but she was finally ready to heal. She was finally ready to come back. But should she expect him to still be there waiting? The truth was, no. A year was a long time.

The past few days had been, in a sense, worse than the previous eleven months: The void seemed now a chasm, but it was Bobby who was shutting down this time. When the midnight phone call came that he uncharacteristically didn't answer, she'd laid there beside him in bed, her heart pounding, thinking, *This is it. This is how I will find out. And no matter how much I thought I wanted it, I'm not ready to know. I'm not ready to watch everything I had unravel, and at the end of it all blame myself. I'm not ready for him to leave . . .*

She'd pretended to be asleep, lying there, waiting for him to sneak downstairs and call his mystery lady back, and wondering what she should do next. Should she hire a PI? Or perhaps get the number from his cell and call the woman back herself and confront her? Bobby hadn't moved, either. She could hear his heartbeat quicken, she could feel his body tense. But when he played back the message in the dark bedroom, and she heard the panicked whispers of that reporter on the other end, she knew it wasn't another woman that she'd lost her husband to—it was this case. This case that had consumed him from the second he'd picked it up. It was too close to home. For both of them. It was too close to Katy.

He had rushed out and she had waited up all night, trying to shush the horrible thoughts that were now running unchecked in her brain, only to hear him finally come home, but not come to her. She knew there was a reason, but she wasn't sure she wanted to know what it was, and so she'd stayed upstairs, waiting. Waiting for him to come. Waiting for him to leave. Waiting for the day that had just begun to finally end.

They had not spoken about today—there was no note on the

fridge to remind either of them of the significance of the date. But of course neither of them needed a reminder. November 19 was an anniversary LuAnn had never expected to pass. One last Thanksgiving, Christmas, or Mother's Day, she could never imagine having. An anniversary. For couples and jobs and tragedies, an anniversary was the mark to make. *Wow, it's been a whole year! Look where we are!* More than just the passage of 365 days, it was the symbolic turning of an event into a permanent part of time—a day of remembrance. And LuAnn wanted no part of it. Ever. Before the concussion that had laid her up now for almost a week, she'd volunteered to work a double.

She could only imagine how hard the day would be on Bobby. Like a firefighter who's called to put out a blaze in a downtown Manhattan skyscraper on September 11, he had to focus on the emergency while the world held vigils and the ghosts of fallen comrades screamed in his head. After her husband had quietly slipped back out of the house when the sun came up, she'd turned on the TV for company, only to shut it right off. Bobby's case was already all over CNN, Fox News, MSNBC. Another brutal painting. Another possible teenage victim. Another runaway. Another Miami serial killer. Another frantic manhunt under way.

So she'd flipped on satellite radio and wandered about the house all day, doing busy, mindless things, like watering plants and dusting bookshelves and mopping the floors. She almost welcomed the distraction when the doorbell rang, tempered by the fear that it was a neighbor who perhaps had marked the date on her calendar and wanted to make sure LuAnn was OK with a plateful of cookies, a sad face, and a few intrusive questions.

All she saw when she opened the door, though, were flowers. Red and white roses and white lilies—an enormous bouquet of flowers.

"I have a delivery for Mrs. Dees," the deliveryman said, passing a clipboard to her.

"From who?" she asked as she signed the receipt and watched as he placed the vase on the hall table. There were at least two dozen roses in the bunch.

"Don't know, ma'am. There's a card, though."

She stared at the flowers, but he stood in the foyer and didn't leave. "Oh," she said after a moment, digging into her pocket for a couple of dollars. "Here you go."

He smiled. "Sure do appreciate it. Have a nice day, now."

"Thank you," she said absently as he headed down the front walk. Normally she hated the short days of winter, but today she welcomed seeing the setting sun and the long shadows of afternoon. She flipped on the front light and turned to head back inside. The heavy perfume of fresh roses already filled the living room, and the smell was making her nauseous. This was not the day for flowers.

Who the hell in their right mind would send her flowers on the one day of the year she would most like to forget?

"Enjoy them, ma'am," the deliveryman called out just as she closed the door. "They sure are pretty. Just like you."

70

There were no hills in South Florida, so the two-hundred-foot mound of green grass rising out of the sawgrass to the west of Interstate 75 stood out like the Statue of Liberty on the Hudson. An inconspicuous and almost impossible-to-find entrance off of U.S. 27 led to a forgotten paved road that wound through the heart of twenty acres of what was once the South Broward County SWT Landfill and Incinerator #8, aka the Dump. A ten-foot-high chain-link fence with a rusted, broken lock surrounded the property. A sign warned that trespassers would be prosecuted.

One wouldn't think that the dump would get a lot of trespassing, but as the cliché went and as fans of *Antiques Roadshow* could attest, one man's trash could very well be another's treasure. Everyone wanted to discover that diamond ring in the rough, even if it meant wading through twenty stories of garbage with a metal detector to find it.

The dump was completely deserted. Even the scavenger birds that at one time feasted by the hundreds, if not thousands, atop the refuse were gone. Removed from the expressway by more than a mile, and set far back from any community, the parking lot was eerily quiet. And no matter how old it was, or what chemicals the city used, or how much they tried to insulate it with tarps, the air still stunk like garbage.

"I'm going in with Larry and McCrindle," Zo said as he walked around the back end of his Taurus and over to where Bobby stood with Larry, BSO Detective Don McCrindle, and three uniforms in front of a cement rectangular building that looked like a 1970s double-wide trailer. Boards covered every window. He looked at Bobby. "Don't even try to fucking argue with me. I'm a fool for letting you come here."

"The incinerator pit was out in the back," Larry said. "You had to show the order to the clerk inside, then get your shit inventoried and get a receipt. Somebody would escort you through to a secured area outside where they'd burn it in front of you. If you stood close enough, you'd feel no pain for a week or so."

Zo looked at the uniforms and nodded toward Bobby. "Make sure he stays at the car. You got light?" he asked Don.

Don nodded and waved his flashlight.

"All right. Let's do this."

Within a minute they were in. Flashlight ribbons sliced like light sabers through the inky darkness. Bobby stood by the front end of his car, counting down the seconds with the cooling tick of the engine, holding his breath, praying this was another dead end. Praying for good news from the warden, whose footfalls had finally reached his cell . . .

Moments later, radios crackled to life.

"I got her," Zo said.

Time stopped. Bobby held the radio up to his face with two hands. "Zo?" He could feel the cold fear racing through his body to his heart, threatening to shut it down. "Zo?" he asked again. "Dias?"

Zo came back out the door, a handkerchief to his nose. Radios erupted all around him, everyone chattering at once. He heard Don McCrindle call for Crime Scene and the medical examiner.

"Is it her?" Bobby asked, rushing over to his friend on legs that threatened to betray him.

Zo held his hands up like a stop sign. "You're not going in there."

"That wasn't the deal."

"Is it her?" It was Ciro, calling in on Zo's radio. Zo didn't respond.

The fear hit its target. Bobby shut his eyes tight to stop the world from spinning. A weird line from *The Godfather* suddenly popped into his head, from the scene where Vito Corleone goes to the funeral home after his son has been shot.

I want you to use all your powers and all your skills. I don't want his mother to see him this way. Look how they massacred my boy . . .

"Is it her?" he asked again.

"It's bad, Shep, I ain't gonna lie—"

"Don't fucking call me that!" Bobby shouted. "Is it her?"

"I don't know!" Zo shouted back. "She's staged, she's—it's bad. You don't need to fucking see it, is all!" He grabbed Bobby by the arm. "I don't know what we have. He's fucking with your head here—"

Bobby pushed past him, running up the cement steps of the double-wide, through the front door, and into the murky darkness that reeked of garbage and death.

The warden had finally arrived. And Bobby could tell just by the pained look on his face that the news wasn't good.

71

LuAnn closed the door and stepped over to the vase. Stuck deep down into the heart of it was a white card clipped tight to a plastic holder.

Was it Jeannie? Would she have sent it?

Her baby sister was well-intentioned but could be thoughtless. Sometimes LuAnn wondered when she went on and on about her own kids and their piano lessons and school plays if she remembered that Katy was still missing.

The girls from work?

Maybe it was a belated get-well bouquet. Maybe they didn't realize the significance of today's date . . .

Who the hell would do such a terrible thing?

She reached down into the bouquet and found the card. People always thought they were saying or doing the nicest things during a life-altering event, but sometimes those were the words or deeds that left the deepest cuts.

"She probably left to get her head clear, Lu. You know? Stretch her wings a little!"

"Maybe you were too tough on her. I always say I'm not going to be Lauren's friend, but it's so hard nowadays to get them to tell you anything . . . I guess you have to be tough, though."

"Being a parent isn't easy, LuAnn. None of us knows if we're doing

it right. Don't be too hard on yourself. Did I tell you that Jonathon just got into FSU? He's so excited!"

Now the same well-intentioned friends were sending her roses on the anniversary of her daughter's running away. Then they would go home tonight and talk about their great deed over dinner with their own kids, and everyone at the table would gossip about how it's been a whole year already, and why it was they supposed Katy left in the first place, and the current suspected state of LuAnn and Bobby's marriage. The smell of the flowers was beyond nauseating now. All LuAnn wanted to do was throw them out. Shred the petals and throw the fucking things out . . .

She turned on the hall light and opened the card.

What words of comfort could someone possibly say to her today?

She slid out the small white card with the yellow happy-face emblem at the top. A piece of paper fluttered to the ground.

She stared at the words in disbelief.

HAPPY ANNIVERSARY!! HOPE IT'S MEMORABLE!

Then she looked down at the floor. At the small black-and-white picture of a smiling Ray Coon from his high school yearbook, right there on her floor. His eyes had been blacked out with magic marker. She knelt down and picked it up. It was pasted onto the picture of a tombstone. Taped below the tombstone was a small, two-sentence police blotter cut from the *Palm Beach Post*. It was dated November 14.

BODY FOUND BY BOY SCOUT IN
BELLE GLADE IDENTIFIED

The decomposed body of a young man found shot to death late last week by a boy scout and his father in Belle Glade marina and campground has been identified as Reinaldo "Ray" Coon, 19, of Margate, Florida. No suspects in the slaying have been identified.

LuAnn dropped the clipping and watched as it fluttered gently back down to the floor.

It landed faceup, still smiling at her.

72

The first thing he saw when he rushed into the small back storage room was the crisscrossing beams of light from Larry and Don Mc-Crindle's flashlights. It was catching on something shiny and reflective off the floor.

Then Bobby saw the chains.

They were wrapped around the ankles of the slender body that hung by its arms from the ceiling, spooling beneath her feet into a polished, silvery pile, like the coils of a snake. He turned his own flashlight up. Her back was to him. Long dirty blond hair was caught in the chains that were wrapped around her neck. More chains tethered her thin arms above her to a pipe in the ceiling. She dangled there, facing a window that looked out onto the long-closed burn pit that Larry had described. Someone had removed the boards from the window so she could face out.

Bobby circled around the body and beamed his flashlight up past the thick necklace of chains.

No one said anything. Nobody moved.

It wasn't Katy.

The body was fresh, a day or two old at the most. Most likely she had been killed somewhere else. Her eyes, like the others, were missing, and decomposition had started, but she was still recognizable. At least to Bobby.

It wasn't Katy.

Zo was behind him. Bobby shook his head and took his first breath in a minute. He felt like a thousand pounds had been lifted from his shoulders. "It's not her," he said in a small voice. Then he stumbled back outside to wait for Crime Scene. The tears he'd been holding back, reserving for the worst news, came anyway.

His cell phone rang just as he stepped through the front door. It was LuAnn, calling from the house. He let it go to voice mail. There was no way he could talk to her now. No way he could tell her what had almost happened. No way he could tell her how incredibly relieved he was, without telling her just how scared he'd been. But then it rang again. And again. Which meant it was more than important—it was an emergency. He walked over to his car, wiped his face with the back of his hand, and tried his best to sound normal. "Lu?"

He heard her crying, trying hard to control her breathing. She was hysterical.

The fear was right back.

"He's dead!" she yelled. "Oh my God, Bobby, he's dead!"

"What?"

"He's dead!"

"Who's dead? What the hell are you talking about, LuAnn? Is it your dad—"

Sirens exploded in the background as emergency vehicles made their way up the rotting, winding Florida mountain.

"Ray!" she screamed. "Ray Coon! He's dead! Someone shot him!"

Bobby closed his eyes. *How was this happening now?* He'd known it was only a matter of time before the news of Ray's murder eventually made the rounds back to her. He should have expected this call. He should have told her. "Lu—" he started.

"And now someone's sending me his picture! His picture, Bobby!"

"What? Who's sending you Ray's picture?"

"On a tombstone!" LuAnn screamed.

Zo came over. "What's happening?"

"It came in the flowers," LuAnn said between sobs.

"What flowers? What are you talking about?"

"I don't know! Someone just sent me flowers. I thought it was my sister or maybe the girls at the hospital . . ."

"Jeannie wouldn't send you flowers," Bobby started. None of this was making sense.

"Roses. Red and white roses. This enormous bouquet of fucking flowers, Bobby!"

"Who? Who sent them?" he demanded. "Who the hell would send you flowers today?"

"I don't know!"

"LuAnn, this is making no sense. Help me out here. Someone sent you flowers today, along with a picture of Ray on a headstone—was there a card?"

"It wasn't signed. The picture of Ray was in the card with a news article that said he died—that he was murdered!"

"What exactly did the card say? Anything?"

"It said 'Happy Anniversary. Hope it's memorable.'" She started to sob again. "Who would do this? Who would send this to me?"

Bobby looked at Zo. "LuAnn, how long ago did these flowers come?"

"I don't know . . . five minutes ago, maybe."

"Where are they from? What store?"

"I don't know. It doesn't say on here. It doesn't say anywhere."

"What did his truck say? Did you see his truck?"

"It wasn't a truck. It was a regular car, I think. I don't know! I don't know!"

"What did he look like, LuAnn? What did the deliveryman look like?"

"I don't . . . um, he was your height, I guess. And I think he was blond. He had a cap on. That's all I remember! I wasn't looking at him." She paused, for just a second. "You knew about Ray, didn't you? Didn't you, Bobby?"

"LuAnn, lock the door. Don't answer it for anyone. I'm coming home."

"Why? Bobby, what is happening? Tell me, goddamn it!"

"Get a car out to my house!" he commanded Zo.

"Tell me!" LuAnn shouted.

"What's happening?" asked Zo.

He held his hand over the phone so she wouldn't hear. "He was there. Five minutes ago," Bobby yelled. "At my motherfucking house!"

Radios erupted again.

It would only be a matter of minutes. Just three minutes for a car to be there. Less, if one was in the area. Please, God, let there be a car . . .

"Who was it? Who sent them?" LuAnn screamed.

"LuAnn, listen carefully. This case, this Picasso case I'm on . . . I think it's him. I think he was the one who sent those flowers," Bobby said as he climbed into his car.

She was sobbing. "Oh my God . . . Katy . . ."

He turned the engine on and threw it in reverse. "And I think he just hand-delivered them to you."

Then he raced back down the winding road with his lights and siren on, headed for home at a hundred miles an hour.

73

The man hummed as he sat in the traffic that had pulled over to the side of the road, watching as the police cars whizzed by him, one after the other, lights flashing and sirens blaring, like a scene from an action movie. He knew just where they were headed in such a hurry—if he sat where he was long enough, he could wave at the Super Special Agent as he whizzed by himself. But he would most likely be too busy to wave back. He was, he imagined, in a Super Special Agent rush to get home. Boy, was he gonna have some explaining to do to the little missus when he walked through that door tonight . . .

Something told him that the Hero Who Walked Among Us hadn't yet let his wifey in on the recent and very substantial development in the case of their missing daughter. Like the fact that the sleazy gangsta boyfriend was now officially out of the picture. Whew! Wasn't that a relief?

Only he wasn't so sure the little woman was gonna take it that way. Not after her Hero told her exactly what he'd been up to today at the office, in all its graphic, glorious detail. Not after he spilled the beans about the striking, uncanny resemblance to their pretty little missing daughter in Picasso's latest and greatest masterpiece.

But there was no such thing as coincidence, was there? And the great detective knew that better than anyone. Soon enough his wife would know that, too. No, there was no such thing as coincidence.

SUPER SPECIAL AGENT ROBERT S. DEES
EVERYMAN'S HERO

. . . nicknamed the shepherd by his colleagues in law enforcement, SAS Dees has worked over two hundred missing children/abduction cases around the country since his career with FDLE's crimes against children squad began nearly a decade ago. Of those, only five remain unsolved (see box). While not every case ends happily, dees has persisted in "bringing home kids who should never, ever have been found," Marlon Truett, assistant director of the FBI, told *People*. "Dead or alive, he brings them back home to their families, which is a great comfort. people want closure. They need it. And Bobby Dees—he won't ever stop. He's like a shepherd, and he will see to it that every last one of his flock is found. He'll never stop looking. That's just the way he is." A recipient of the prestigious officer of the year award for missing and exploited children, and Florida's law enforcement officer of the year, Dees says the faces of the missing—the ones he hasn't yet "brought home"—haunt him every day of his life. "I could only imagine, if that were my child, how I would feel."

He rolled the worn, chewed magazine up and tossed it onto the seat beside him. Less than a year after that glowing piece had been written—before dust even had a chance to collect on all of those pretty little awards—Super Special Agent's own daughter had vanished into the dark night.

Pity.

The man smiled.

A good shepherd lays down his life for his sheep. He who is a hired hand and who does not own the sheep, sees the wolf coming and leaves the sheep and flees, and the wolf catches them and scatters them.

John 10:11–18. Right out of the Gospel . . .

The real lesson to be learned? Just like *People* magazine so eloquently put it, there's not always a happy ending to every story. In fact, just like in the Bible, most stories end tragically. The good shepherd either dies or he runs when he sees the wolf coming. Either way, the poor sheep are doomed.

So as much as he was sure Mr. and Mrs. Dees wanted to forget this momentous occasion, he knew it was only right to help them celebrate it. He just wished he could be a fly on the wall of their pretty little house tonight. He wished he could hear their screams. Listen in on the anguish. He closed his eyes and imagined for a second just what the little woman's mouth would look like, open and lush, twisted in pain into an eternal black grin. He thought of how the brush would feel in his hand, heavy with paint, the fragrant smell wafting like a perfume through his secret labyrinth . . .

His hand fell to his lap.

Are you pure in both thought and deed?

He wiped the sweat from his forehead with his trembling fingers. He felt the beads of perspiration run down the back of his neck and into his shirt, making it stick to his skin. Oh, there were so many fun things to look forward to.

The wolf was on his way. The story was finally coming to an end.

Then he flicked on the radio and waited for the news to come on.

74

"It's a hairpiece," Dr. Terrence Lynch, the Broward County ME, said with a smile full of oversize teeth. He held up the long blond wig, stroking it with his stubby gloved fingers, as if it were a cat. Short and stuffed, his pale skin bathed in the reflection of the old mint-green tiles that covered the examining room of the Broward County ME's office, the pathologist looked a lot like Dracula's assistant, Renfield. A recent import from upstate New York, Bobby hadn't worked with Lynch before, but for once in his career, he was missing Gunther.

Zo shook his head and looked across the gurney at Bobby. "An ME who likes his job—go figure."

"Mmmmm . . . ," Dr. Lynch murmured, returning the hairpiece, which was matted in places with dried blood, to the clear evidence bag. "It's not expensive. The fibers are synthetic; the make is cheap. I have a young daughter, and it looks strikingly similar to the Hannah Montana mop she parades around in. Maybe there aren't too many Miley Cyrus fans in South Florida. We can run it through fibers and see if that'll narrow down our search."

"I think we'll find out there are more fans than we feared," Zo replied.

"Do you have an ID yet?" Dr. Lynch asked.

"Her prints aren't in AFIS," Bobby answered with a shake of his head. AFIS was the Automated Fingerprint Identification System.

"She doesn't match a description of any of the missing juvis we've got on our list. At least, we don't think she does." He tried hard not to look down at the young girl on the metal gurney who just yesterday he thought would turn out to be his daughter. A crisp white sheet covered her torso and legs. Thankfully the autopsy was over.

"I understand you had quite a scare, Agent Dees," Dr. Lynch said as he washed up. A tech came over with a large spool of black nylon thread in hand and a large stitching needle. "I'm glad it didn't turn out to be what you had feared."

Bobby was too, but it seemed wrong to agree while he was standing over the mutilated body of a girl with no name, who had no one waiting outside to even claim her body. So he just nodded and moved over to make room for the tech.

"Your Picasso was particularly brutal," the doctor continued. He dried his hands and turned back to face Bobby and Zo. "Besides the obvious missing eyes, she's also missing her tongue. Both injuries were inflicted premortem."

Bobby had seen many things in his career. Many horrible things. Too many things. Some cruelty, though, was beyond even his comprehension. "How can you tell?"

"There was bruising in the skin, muscle, and surrounding soft tissue," Dr. Lynch said, gesturing toward Jane Doe's black sockets. "The dead, gentlemen, do not bruise. So the injuries were inflicted while her heart was pumping blood and she was still alive."

"This is like Cupid all over again," Zo muttered.

"I'll screen for anesthetics and analgesics," Lynch added. "Maybe he showed a little compassion and numbed her up first."

"What's with her fingers?" Bobby asked, looking down at the slender gray hand that lay on the side of the table, protruding from underneath the sheet. The fingertips were black, the nails broken and jagged, the skin severely abraded.

"The skin is beginning to slip and decompose, which accounts for some of the discoloration. But the tips—the pads—they are also severely bruised and scraped—almost ground down to the bone. I thought perhaps an animal had gnawed at them postmortem, but the injuries, it appears, were inflicted, like the tongue and eyes, before she died. I X-rayed the fingers—they're not broken."

"In the portrait Picasso sent us, the fingertips were covered in blood, too. What the hell would he do to her fingers and why?" Zo asked. "Is he trying to tell us something?"

Dr. Lynch shrugged. "I don't have an answer for you."

"Maybe she did it to herself," Bobby answered softly, gently taking Jane Doe's hand in his own gloved palm and carefully looking at it. "Maybe she was trying to get out of wherever it was he had her held. Maybe she was clawing her way out. She still has nail beds, Dr. Lynch. Make sure she's scraped. Look for rock, clay, dirt, pesticides—anything. Screen whatever it is you find. Maybe we can figure out where he held her."

Dr. Lynch nodded. "Done. I took samples of everything. The screens take a while, but I'll try and get a quick return."

The problem with multi-jurisdictional serial homicides was consistency. Three bodies in Broward and one body in Dade meant multiple police departments, multiple crime labs, and multiple medical examiners. "Can you get with Gunther Trauss in Miami and see what he's come up with so that we don't duplicate efforts?" Bobby asked. "Time is of the essence. We need results yesterday, if you could."

Dr. Lynch nodded. The horse-toothed smile was back, which was definitely disconcerting. He slid his hands into his lab-coat pockets. "So, how long do you want me to hold her, guys?"

There was no potter's field in Broward County—no graveyard for the indigent and unidentified like there was in Miami. The bodies of the destitute and unclaimed were simply bid out to the local funeral homes for disposal. The lowest bidder won the prize, which, for economical reasons, inevitably meant cremation and a scattering in the local Dumpster of whatever was left. Unidentified homicide victims were handled a little differently: Their bodies were boiled down and the bones kept in a box on a shelf at the ME's until, barring a screwup, someone, somewhere came up with a name. The hope was that along with that name would be a family, someone to claim the bones and give Jane or John Doe a proper burial.

"Give me time. I'll get you a name," Bobby said quietly as he and Zo headed for the elevator. "Whatever happens with this case, she's not going to auction, Dr. Lynch. I'll take care of it." If they couldn't find a family to go with that name, Bobby would make sure that she was buried properly. No kid should leave this earth unnoticed. Unmissed. He nodded goodbye and the doors closed on the oversize elevator.

"The blond wig, the different sweater. Picasso's fucking with you, Bobby," Zo remarked quietly as the car started its creaky, slow ascent out of the basement.

"It's working. I'm fucked up," Bobby replied, rubbing his eyes.

"You shouldn't be here."

Bobby shot him a look.

"You shouldn't. You look like hell. Have you slept at all in the past few days?"

"I don't sleep anyway. You think I'm gonna start now?"

"How's LuAnn?"

He shook his head. "Medicated. Hopefully she won't have to wake up till after I've found this guy. The ballistics report's back on the bullet that was found in the tree next to Ray Coons's skull. It's a .44-caliber Magnum, left-hand twist."

"Big gun," Zo commented as they stepped out into the hall just past reception. He stuck his head out the back entrance and looked down the long driveway, checking for media; they seemed to be everywhere and anywhere now. Besides being the top story on every channel in South Florida, news of the Picasso murders had made its way overseas as well, piquing the interest of the international media. A flamboyant, twisted serial killer with a taste for young runaways had attracted as much attention as the Cupid serial homicides in Miami had a few years ago. And that had been a complete and utter circus. The parking lot was clear, though.

"It's a gun that a lot of people like," Bobby said with a sigh, slipping on his sunglasses as they headed down the drive and then across the lawn to the lot behind the Broward Sheriff's Office's Tactical Services building. "Particularly gangbangers. Autopsy report says he was dead at least a couple of weeks."

"We've been all over the streets. No one's seen Ray back in Miami," Zo said. "At least, no one who's talking."

"What the hell was he doing in Belle Glade?"

"That's anybody's guess right now. Remember, Bobby, this guy is working you. Don't go crazy thinking Ray's a Picasso victim. We don't know that. And we don't know that Katy is related, either."

Bobby stopped walking. "He came to my house, Zo. My house. He talked to my wife. He's sending these sick portraits for my attention and leaving place cards with my name at crime scenes and he wants me"—he took a breath—"he wants me to believe he has my daughter. Why?"

"Maybe we should be looking at old cases, guys you've put away who may be on the other side of the bars now. Forget what the profiler says—she's just guessing anyway."

Bobby shook his head but said nothing.

When they reached their cars, Zo said, "You're done today. You need to go home and sit with your wife. I don't want you back at the office. At least for a few days. And when you come back, I don't want you on this case."

"Fuck that," replied Bobby. As if on cue, his cell rang. "Dees," he answered.

"Bobby, it's Ciro. I just got off the phone with a buddy who works Computer Crimes up in Palm Beach with the sheriff's office. He's doing a call-out today that the sheriff's office is working with LEACH— you know, the Internet computer kiddie crimes task force? They're setting up on a perv this afternoon who's supposed to do a meet-and-greet with a fourteen-year-old girl at a Mickey D's. One of the PBSO Special Investigations detectives who does decoy caught this fish last week sometime, and they need tactical help to reel him in. Nothing new there, right? Happens every day. Now, there's no guarantee this guy's even gonna show—he's a ghost—and the decoy hasn't heard from him in a few days, so it might be for nothing, but my buddy thought it was real interesting when he found out this morning at briefing the screen name the perv was using. Real interesting, considering he and I were talking about the Emerson case just last week, and this particular info hasn't been released to the public."

"Talk to me," Bobby said, looking at Zo and waiting on Ciro's next words, his body frozen in place, suspended halfway into the car.

"They're waiting on some guy who calls himself The Captain."

75

It was almost comical that in the day and age of sophisticated law-enforcement computer systems and instant communications available via the Internet, email, fax, texting, and cell phones, the left hand still didn't know what the right was doing. The first thing Bobby had done after seeing the Boganes sisters' portrait and realizing that Lainey Emerson was probably linked to Picasso, was send out a BOLO (Be On the Look Out for) teletype via FCIC/NCIC, alerting law-enforcement agencies nationwide to contact him if they had a cyber-predator using the screen name Zachary, Cusano, ElCapitan, or any combination or modification thereof. Of course, just from the number of BOLOs his own analyst received on a daily basis, chances were his BOLO had been printed out, pinned onto a crowded board in a busy squad bay, and promptly ignored.

No department liked their territory pissed on—which was exactly how the Palm Beach Sheriff's Office Special Investigations Unit and LEACH task force members viewed the arrival of FDLE special agents at their tactical briefing in the back parking lot of the 45th Street Flea Market, a couple of blocks from the McDonald's where the meet was set to take place. There was no "Thank God the cavalry is here!" open-arms, high-fiving welcome. Then again, Bobby hadn't expected one. The feds, and more particularly, the FBI—famous for conveniently stealing thunder and claiming jurisdiction on high-profile cases after all the work was done—had made everyone in law enforcement sus-picious. And just like the Rock-Paper-Scissors game, as much as it might burn the locals up, the truth was that FDLE trumped county, city, and municipality, and every ranking officer in that parking lot knew it. So there was definitely reason to be nervous about a hostile takeover. But Bobby didn't want to commandeer a LEACH investiga-tion. He didn't want the glory or the headlines. What he wanted was to end this nightmare and find the bastard as quickly as possible. And so far, the screen name of ElCapitan was the only thing anyone had that might lead somewhere.

Or not.

Like Ciro had said, and as anyone who worked ICAC cases—Internet Crimes Against Children—could attest, there were no guar-antees. You never knew who or what would show up at these illicit meets. Or if anyone would show up at all. Many cyberpredators were well-seasoned; they had multiple victims and a lot of offline experi-ence before they were finally tagged in a chat room. Most could smell cop a mile away.

Although Bobby tried his best to quash it, tensions between the task forces remained high even as everyone took up positions for the meet. Heightened anxiety, though, wasn't necessarily a bad thing. It was like realizing that the porcelain vase you were carrying across the tiled floor was a priceless urn from the Ming dynasty—you were def-initely more anxious, but also much more careful, because you knew the devastating consequences if you screwed up and dropped the thing. Picasso had made horrible headlines in every county, and no one wanted to be responsible for letting him make another.

A petite, brunette undercover PBSO narcotics detective named Natalie, who looked all of fifteen, was set up inside the McDonald's. At four p.m. she would come out and wait on a bench in front of the restaurant and next to the check-cashing store for the approach. Un-dercover eyeballs were set up both in the restaurant and in the park-ing lot behind the McDonald's, which was shared with a strip mall that included a Winn-Dixie supermarket, a Family Dollar, and a host of stores, like a Little Caesars pizzeria and a laundromat. With all the businesses, the parking lot was constantly jammed, constantly moving. Across Australian was a Sunoco gas station and pawn shop; diagonally opposite to the restaurant was a park. Bobby and a couple of LEACH operatives sat in their undercover cars waiting in the Winn-Dixie parking lot; Zo and Ciro were set up on the Sunoco and in the park. An FDLE helicopter was on standby at Palm Beach International Airport, just a few miles away.

It was 3:55. Bobby settled down low into his seat and stared out past the traffic on busy 45th. Without binoculars, it was impossible to see inside the restaurant from his vantage point. And it was impossible to use binoculars without calling attention to himself. He had to rely on the LEACH eyeball. The strip mall was bustling with activity. Moms, toddlers, seniors, businessmen, teens. Men, women. All makes and models. All shapes and sizes.

That was the problem. He could be anywhere. He could be anyone. And everyone looked suspicious, Bobby thought, watching as a young guy unloaded three grocery bags full of nothing but laundry detergent into the back of his SUV. Three rows up, a greasy, middle-age man sitting in a Ford F-150 sucked down what looked a lot like a beer while talking on his cell phone. And of course, he thought, turning his attention back to the McDonald's, they could all be sitting on a dead end. Wasting time while a madman was miles away, painting yet another portrait.

Bobby tapped the steering wheel and looked at his watch again—3:59. There was nothing left to do but wait.

76

The man took a deep breath, letting the fresh, unseasonably warm air fill his lungs. His whole body was tingling, every sense was on high alert, like a hungry, wild animal that hears the soft bleating of lunch far off in a distant meadow. He'd tried dust and acid in high school, but this—this was a natural rush that no high could ever come close to. He sniffed at the air. A dozen scents filled his nose—car exhaust, pine, gasoline, burning leaves, body odor, frying meat, urine. Call him crazy, but he thought he could also smell her. Somewhere out there. Sweet and lovely, probably spritzed down with Pac-Sun's Nollie and sprinkled with a little bit of baby powder. Her freshly washed, dusty brown hair fragrant with Herbal Essence's Red Satin Raspberry.

Janizz. The name was either the product of a kooky, nonconforming mother or a teen who hated the boring, old-fashioned name of Janice. A girl who wanted to be different, like the Parises and Cocos and Demis of the world.

He was thinking door number two. A girl who wanted someone to finally notice her. He smiled. *I can't wait to notice you, sweet Janizz. I can't wait to shower you with attention.*

Janizzbaby. Even her name had a lilting melody to it. He hummed a bar to himself. Slow and sexy it would be, like an H-Town R&B tune. He rubbed his sweaty hands on his pants. Like the Oscars, the anticipation was both the best and worst part of the evening. Would she show? Would she look like her picture, or was she just a fake? Would she come willingly, or would she get spooked for some reason?

It had never happened before—he had never had a problem getting them in the car. But there was always that worry. *There's always a first time for everything*, his mom liked to say. *So be ready for anything.* And he was. He looked in the backseat at his special black bag. It had everything he needed. All he had to do was just get her in the car. Once she was in, she was his.

His hands were dripping now. Of course, she might not show at all. That had happened before. And that'd made him really, really angry. It took a lot of careful preparation to get the house ready for a new arrival. And when it was all for naught—when he was taken for a fool—it took him a long time to trust again.

He stared at the glass front door of the busy McDonald's. Like a freaking revolving door, it was. Lazy mommies and their screaming kids hurried in for another balanced meal of chicken nuggets and fries. Fatties pondered the picture menu like they'd never seen a Big Mac before. Was she inside? Was she looking out that front door, watching for him, wondering what he looked like? Was she as excited to see him as he was to see her? Was she wearing something special, like she'd promised? Was she afraid? Was she nervous?

I told u—im a virgin. nervous to give it up.

His sweaty hands shook like crazy. He lit a cigarette to try and calm his nerves. She would be spooked if he couldn't control himself. If he shook like a Parkinson's patient when he saw her, then she might run. No, she would run. And that would be bad. Really bad.

He wondered if and when anyone would notice little Janizz missing. Now that he was all over the news, making headlines in countries he'd never even heard of, he wondered just how long it would take for someone to make the quantum leap that Janizz was a victim of foul play. And how long it would be before she was known as Picasso's Latest Victim. He smiled. How long would it be before people locked their doors at night just because of him? Or had security walk them to their cars in dark parking lots?

He licked his dry lips, his eyes glued on that glass door, sniffing at the air for the first real scent of her. His little lost lamb.

The door pushed open. A tiny thing—barely five feet, it looked like—walked out and over to the bench by the sidewalk. A sparkly bandana held her long, chestnut-colored hair back off her face. A single streak of vibrant purple ran down one side, just like in her MySpace profile picture. Dressed in a short denim mini and a tight black tank top, she had the stocky, muscular build of a gymnast, and her shapely legs were accessorized with a pair of wedge sandals. She looked all around the parking lot like she was waiting on somebody, but she didn't appear nervous at all. After a minute, she lit a cigarette, and started to text away on her cell, without a care in the world. It was obviously Janizz. From the looks of her, he doubted he was the first boy she'd met up with from the Internet, although he was quite sure he would be the last.

His hands went crazy at the sight of her. He wiped them one last time on his jeans and rolled on antiperspirant. It would be difficult to handle her properly if he had no grip.

Just like the little lamb that's wandered far away from the flock to graze by itself in the meadow, sweet baby Janizz was completely oblivious that just a few steps away, the ravenous wolf watched and waited from his hiding spot.

He flicked the cigarette out the window and smiled. It was time to begin the hunt.

It was time to introduce himself.

77

"What the fuck are you doing?" Bobby asked, tapping hard on the driver's side window.

The window slid down. "Obviously the same thing you're doing," a red-faced Mark Felding answered with a slow smile.

"Are you kidding me?"

The reporter shook his head. "It's a free country. Can't stop the press."

"Are you fucking kidding me?" Bobby repeated. He ran his hand through his hair. "I can't believe this."

"I'm not doing anything illegal, am I? Just following a lead to see where it takes me, is all. Just minding my business, Agent Dees. Just trying to catch some news as it's made. You don't like to return my phone calls unless I got something for you, so seeing as there's no quid pro quo with information, I have to do what I gotta do."

"How did you know?"

"Do you think your boys can walk around without anybody caring anymore? Face it, you're famous now, Agent Dees. You're free game, like Brangelina."

Bobby tried hard to control his anger. It took every bit of restraint to not reach inside that car, take Felding by the throat, and toss him across the parking lot. It wasn't that he didn't want to do it, he just knew it would draw attention, which is the one thing he couldn't have happen. "What the hell is more important to you people? Getting your face on the TV or stopping this guy before he gets his hands on another girl?"

The guy didn't even hesitate. "Frankly, both. And I know you don't like to hear that."

Bobby looked at his watch: 4:07. "You and your camera are going to fuck this up. Get out of here."

"Look, I don't want to fuck this up for you. I don't. I want to see this guy caught. Just let me sit here, I'll be quiet. I'll be good. I won't even pick up a camera," he begged. "Only if he shows. And only if there's an arrest. Fair? If anything goes down—just let me have the story. That's all I want. The story. If it's over tonight, I want to be the one who gets it. He started it with me; it should end with me. It's only fitting."

"I am not making deals with you."

"Can you give me a name? Details? What you know about him?"

"Your face is on the news every night. If he sees you, Felding, it's over."

"Only if he watches Channel 6," Mark added with a smile. "And apparently, need I remind you, our psycho has a thing for you as well, Agent Dees. If he sees your face, I would imagine it's over, too."

"Get the fuck out of here. I won't tell you again—"

The radio crackled to life. "Possible subject approaching. Black four-door Lexus." It was the LEACH eyeball.

"ES," came the response. It was Lou Morick, another LEACH operative. "It's a Lexus ES. Maybe '03, '04."

LEACH, PBSO, and the Picasso task force members were all on the same surveillance channel, so there was no need to go through dispatch or talk radio-to-radio. Chatter came fast and furious.

"Tinted windows. Can't get a look at the driver. Moving slow through the parking lot. Can you get a tag, Mike?"

"Florida tag. X-ray, Seven, Zebra, Delta, Three, Seven. Can't read an expiration date from here."

"OK, 1622, run that," ordered Kleiner, the PBSO Special Investigations lieutenant who was running ops from the northwest corner.

"10–4."

Shit. It was happening now and he was babysitting. "You move from this spot, you pick up a camera, and I will arrest you for obstruction. This isn't *Cops.* This isn't some fucking TV show." Bobby called in. "FYI. I've got a reporter sitting here in front of the Family Dollar."

"What the hell?" It was Kleiner.

"Who's that, Bobby?" Zo asked. "It ain't that weasel Felding, is it?"

The eyeball broke in. "Natalie's approaching the passenger-side window. 10–23."

10–23 meant stand by.

"She's not miked, so watch for the signal," Morick cautioned.

"This better not be on the news," Mike Hicks grumbled over the air. "This ain't *Dateline.*"

"Passenger window's coming down. Still no visual."

"She's talking to the subject."

"Plate's back. It's a stolen tag. Comes back to a black Benz."

"OK. Wait for the signal," Kleiner ordered. "If he runs, stop him, but until then let's see what he does. Let Natalie do her magic."

"I've got a marked PBSO unit turning off westbound 45th into the McDonald's parking lot," reported Ciro.

"Who's that? Is it one of ours?" asked Hicks.

"She's playing with her bandana," said the eyeball.

"That's the signal."

"Is it off? She's supposed to take it off," said another.

"Oh shit, the cruiser just lit him up! What the hell?"

The cruiser had pulled up behind the Lexus and put on his lights. It looked like he was doing a traffic stop.

"Who the fuck is that?" Hicks yelled.

"Perv's gone! Subject just hightailed it out of the lot and is fleeing eastbound on 45th!"

"Shit! All units engage! Do not let this one get away!" Kleiner shouted.

Bobby hustled back to his car, yelling into his radio as he ran. "Ronny, get in the air! Subject's eastbound on 45th in a black Lexus ES. PBSO, 10–9 that tag number!" All he could see was Katy's face.

"X-Ray, Seven, Zebra, Delta, Three, Seven. Copy?" repeated the eyeball.

Her sweet face on the mutilated body of Jane Doe.

"Copy that," came Ronny Martin, the FDLE copter pilot. "I'm going up."

Lying on the metal gurney, chains wrapped around her throat.

"He's turning northbound on Australian . . ."

"Don't lose him!" shouted Bobby into his radio as he reached his car. He hopped into the Grand Am, threw it in drive, and spun out of the parking lot, barely missing a screaming lady pushing a baby in a shopping cart. He joined the undercover units that were racing down 45th and Australian, lights and sirens blaring. The police cruiser must have called in to PBSO dispatch for assistance; he could hear sirens approaching from every direction.

"Shit! Train's coming!" Hicks barked over the radio. "Damn it! FYI, boys, gate's down! I just made it through. If you ain't over the tracks now, it ain't happening! Lou's right behind me—we're gonna need marked units to meet us on the north side at Michigan or Martin Luther King if this guy keeps heading north and don't stop!"

Bobby could see the red-and-white crossing gates some three hundred feet ahead. They were down. If he didn't make it across the tracks now, he'd never catch up. If it was a CSX or East Coast Railway freight train, it could be five minutes or more before all the cars passed and he finally got through. And if Hicks and Morick didn't get the guy to stop, or he got on to I-95 . . .

Rush hour was here. A thick line of cars had already stopped at the gate. He crossed into the southbound lanes of Australian, which were empty, thanks to the closed gate. He could hear the deafening train whistle, warning of its imminent approach.

Do not let this one get away. Not this one.

He cut in front of the Ford Explorer stopped at the gate. He could see the train coming upon him on his right. It was maybe fifty feet off. Maybe less. There was no time to question his decision and no time to turn back. There was no time to even say a quick prayer. With his blue lights on, he gunned the gas. He could almost hear the collective gasp of all the drivers lined up at the crossing.

There was also no time to marvel that he'd made it across. He wiped the sweat out of his eyes. The approaching train had thinned northbound traffic, but he had lost time. Morick and Hicks were a block or more up.

Hicks came on the radio. "He's clocking sixty-five!"

"What's the limit?" Kleiner asked.

"Ah, thirty, I think."

"He's weaving into oncoming! He's freaking nuts!" Lou Morick barked. "It's rush hour!"

"This guy's gonna kill somebody!"

"He just ran the light at Martin Luther!" Morick yelled. "Just totally ran it! Where the hell are those marked units? We're gonna need a roadblock. This guy's not stopping for nobody!"

"Bike down! There's a black chopper in the intersection—he just spun out and he's down!" said Hicks. "Get an ambulance out here to MLK and Australian! Damn, I gotta stop! This guy's pretty bad!"

"That's it." It was Kleiner. "Don't take any more civilians with you, Lou. It's four-thirty in the afternoon, there's too many of them. Terminate the chase. We'll get units at Blue Heron and stop him there!"

Australian ended at Blue Heron Boulevard, a mile or so up. But a left onto Blue Heron led to I-95. The interstate was less than two miles away. It would be open road if the Lexus got on the highway.

High-speed chases were against every department's policy. Civilians or cops inevitably got hurt or killed, property got destroyed, lawsuits got filed. Anything higher than fifteen miles over the speed limit was generally considered high speed, and sixty-five miles an hour through a heavily trafficked commercial area definitely fit the bill. High-speed chases could only be approved by command staff. And they normally weren't.

But PBSO Lieutenant Lex Kleiner wasn't in Bobby's chain of command. He wasn't even in his department. Rock beat scissors and FDLE trumped the county sheriff's office. Morick dropped back. Bobby flew past him.

At the sound of approaching sirens, drivers either pulled over to the right or just stopped where they were, like panicked deer. A crazed driver being chased by a symphony of sirens and flashing lights had turned the already thickening traffic on Australian into a steel obstacle course. Bobby weaved in and out of the cars and oncoming traffic. The Lexus was now in sight.

"I'm right behind him; he's not stopping at Heron," Bobby said as the Lexus blew another light and went right past a marked unit turning onto Blue Heron. "He's gonna go for 95. Have a swarm at both the on-and off-ramps. Do not let him get on 95!" If they could block him in and force him to run, there wasn't far for him to go. Just gas stations and businesses, and those could be locked down.

"Who the fuck is this?" barked Kleiner. "I said terminate. It's too dangerous!"

"I don't work for you," Bobby replied.

The Lexus suddenly shirked sharply to the left and went around a stopped FedEx truck.

Bobby slammed on his brakes and went to follow, but then the world just exploded, right there in front of him.

78

Bobby heard it before he saw it. An incredibly loud bang that went on forever, the sound of metal ripping into metal, glass imploding. Then a thunderous, deafening boom that actually shook his windows. A twisted, thick column of heavy black smoke poured into the air in front of the FedEx truck.

"Holy shit!" came a stunned voice on the radio.

"I've got a fireball rising west of Australian at Blue Heron," Ronny reported. "Heavy smoke. I can't see."

"Dees? Bobby?" It was Zo, calling him over the radio. "Where the hell are you? I'm coming up on Blue Heron . . ."

Bobby was already out of his car, running past stopped SUVs and pickups.

"He hit a fucking tanker!" It was Lou Morick.

Gaping, shocked civilians stumbled out of their cars to get a look. Then ran the other way.

"Oh shit! The truck must've pulled out of a station and he just, wham!" Morick yelled. "He hit him head-on! The tanker flipped! He's on top of the Lexus! There's another car, too, I think. He—God, he's—they're both in flames!"

A wall of thick black smoke had engulfed the roadway. Bright orange flames licked at the sky, thirty feet in the air. The trucker, bloody and stunned, stumbled out of his overturned cab.

The heat was intense, scorching, even ten yards back. Skin-melting hot. A loud pop sounded from behind the curtain of black, sending another fireball into the air. A marked PBSO unit pulled up. Sirens screamed from every direction. It was hard to see through the billowing smoke. Bobby ran around the scene, trying to see past the smoke.

"Oh my God! Look!" a lady screamed. "He's alive! There's a man in the car! He needs help!"

The wind, kicked up perhaps by the FDLE copter above, thinned the black cloud just enough to see the twisted mass of metal and flames. The Lexus was all but gone. The tanker had T-boned and fallen on the sedan's passenger side, completely crushing it. But there in the shattered windshield on what was left of the driver's side, there was a bloody face. A hand was banging on the glass.

Bobby rushed forward into the heat, but a body grabbed him from behind in a firm bear hug and pulled him back. "No way," Zo shouted in his ear. "No way! You can't save him, Shep! You can't do it!"

Bobby struggled against the arms that held him tight and pulled him farther away. The distorted face in the splintered glass got smaller and smaller, obscured by a veil of black smoke.

"It's going up, Bobby!" Ciro yelled in his other ear. "Ya gotta get back!"

Seconds later, the tanker did just that. Flames completely engulfed both car and truck. The screaming face disappeared.

The rest of the LEACH task force and Special Investigations detectives were pulling up, spilling out of their cars now, staring at the inferno that blazed before them. No one said anything. The air stunk of fuel.

"Fire/Rescue is responding. ETA two minutes. Are you requesting an ambulance?" came the monotone voice of the dispatcher over the radio of the PBSO uniform who was standing next to Bobby and Zo.

"Ho, boy. Ambulance? An ambulance ain't gonna help that guy," Mike Hicks said with a chuckle of disbelief. He looked over at Bobby, Zo, and Ciro and shook his head. "Our boy is toast."

79

"Was it him?" Mike Hicks asked.

The entire county, it seemed, had descended on the Wendy's on the corner of Blue Heron and Australian, using it as a staging area for emergency response units, Florida Highway Patrol, Florida HazMat clean-up crews, and investigators with the Florida Department of Environmental Protection. Commandeering the entire back section of the restaurant were the LEACH and Picasso task force members, and the PBSO Special Investigations detectives who had assisted on the now-deemed disastrous meet-and-greet. Reporters from every station, including CNN, Fox, and MSNBC, buzzed around outside, held back by uniforms and yards of yellow crime-scene tape, which seemed to stretch the entire length of the block, where firefighters still worked to put out the tanker explosion, which had claimed another two cars. Mark Felding, of course, was first in line, somberly reporting the breaking developments with a pained look on his face. He had even managed to find some ash, smearing it across his brow and tossing it in his curls, probably in the hope that viewers might think he had barely escaped the flames himself. His ratings would be through the roof.

Natalie nodded her head slowly in response to Mike's question. "I think so. I'll have to say yes. Everything happened so fast. I was looking for a Beamer when he first pulled in, so I didn't even go up to the car. But he stopped and stayed there for a while, parked. Then he lowered his window and called me over and we started to talk. The cruiser pulled in and he got real nervous all of a sudden. Real nervous, looking in his rearview. Then he said he had to go. I tried to keep him, but then the cruiser put his lights on and that was it—the guy ran. Almost took my freaking foot off, too. Five minutes later, he's dead. Whoo," she said, her voice cracking. "What a day at the office."

"Did he use the name Captain?" Bobby pressed. "What about Zach? Did he use the name Janizz?"

"We never got that far. He asked me if I was waiting for him, and I said, 'Guess so.' And he said that's real good, 'cause he's been waiting on me all his life. He said he was glad he waited, too, 'cause he wanted to have some fun. He asked me if I like fun, and I said, 'What do you think?' He said, 'Let's find out.' I asked him, 'You the Captain?' You know, teasing? And he laughed, like he was. Then he asked me if I wanted to go for a ride. That's when he spotted the cruiser and things went crazy."

"What did he look like?" Bobby asked.

"He was white, a white guy between twenty-five and thirty, I think. Light brown hair, not quite shoulder length. Wavy, I think. He was wearing aviator sunglasses, so it was hard to tell. I didn't get the greatest look, to tell you the truth."

"What about the car?" Bobby turned and asked Kleiner, who sat in the back of the booth, with his arms crossed in front of him. "Anything?"

"The car's gone. The tanker was carrying a load of premium. The fire melted the road, it was so hot. We ain't gonna get a VIN, even when whatever's left of the Lexus does cool down enough for us to look at it. The tag came back to a 2006 black Benz C300, registered to a Silvia Montoya of Miami Shores. Car was stolen from her driveway on October 2nd. No leads on that case."

"So we have no idea who the guy driving the Lexus was? Not a clue?" Zo asked.

"Nope," Kleiner returned with a shake of his head. "Not yet. Only thing we know is that he showed up at a scheduled meet, driving a car with stolen plates. And took off as soon as he saw a cop. Sounds like our guy to me. Whether he was your Picasso, I couldn't tell you. That's your investigation."

"Let's get a sketch artist out to see if your decoy can give us a picture. Did you talk to the uniform?" Bobby asked. "Why'd he light him up?"

"He'd run his tag. Knew it was stolen."

"Any reason he ran the tag?"

"To be a ballbuster. Saw the guy on Australian looking like a hot-shot and gunning for lights. So he ran him. You never know what you're gonna find when you do that," Kleiner answered defensively.

"Hmmm . . . case in point. We may never know what we might've found if he hadn't flipped on his fucking lights," Bobby mused sarcastically.

"And if you hadn't been such a hothead and kept up a high speed, we may not have needed a fucking sketch artist to put together a picture of what the guy used to look like. We might have caught up to him nice and easy without three people going to the hospital and one going to the morgue."

"Yeah, just like you had those units ready at Heron and Martin Luther. Nice and fucking easy. Maybe we should have just said 'please' when we asked him to pull over the first time."

"OK, that's enough," Zo spoke up, his hands raised, separating the two men. "So, Lex, if your perv—who's now a stiff—was The Captain, and The Captain was really our Picasso, how the hell we ever gonna know that for sure?" Zo asked.

"When we don't get any more paintings," answered Ciro.

"Or bodies," Bobby said, running a hand through his hair. "Is there enough left of him to do DNA?"

"They pulled him out first," Hicks replied. "But he's mostly gone. Torso's left—it's like a rare steak. You can get DNA, though. If he's been in the system and given a sample, then you might get an ID off that."

Convictions for certain offenses in Florida, as in some other states, required defendants to donate a swab of themselves to the

FDLE DNA bank. Those crimes included any sex offense, burglary, robbery, homicide, or home invasion.

Bobby nodded. "Someone's gotta miss this guy. A mom, a sis, a girlfriend, a brother, a wife. Hopefully that someone will call up the local police department and report him missing. Once we have an ID, we'll work from there to see if we can connect him to either The Captain or Picasso."

"OK. And if he is, or was, Picasso, what about . . . " Ciro's voice trailed off. He caught himself too late.

But Bobby finished the thought for him. "The girls who are still missing? We find them. Fast. That's why we need an ID. We'll take apart the guy's life, piece by motherfucking piece, until we can trace every step he's made since he could walk. If there are any more alive—if Lainey and, well, any others are still alive—then he has them somewhere. And there has to be some sort of connection in the guy's everyday life that will lead us there."

"I don't know what's a better scenario, then," Hicks wondered aloud. "To know Picasso's dead and scattered wherever the wind blows and that the nightmare's over before his body count got close to Bundy's or Cupid's, yet not know where he stashed the rest of his vics—"

"Or to know he's alive and kicking and laughing at us on the news," Zo finished, motioning outside the restaurant's plate-glass windows at the media circus assembled in the parking lot, led by Channel 6's latest and greatest star.

"Some choice," Mike Hicks muttered, rising to leave.

"Yeah, some choice," Bobby repeated quietly, watching as the Palm Beach County medical examiner's van slowly navigated through the mess on Blue Heron, pausing at the red light just long enough for the throng of cameras to come running as it passed by on its way back to the office.

80

When Lainey was little, she never had any playmates. Not because she smelled or no one liked her or anything, but because after her parents divorced and before Todd and her mom had moved out to Coral Springs, she'd grown up mostly living with her grandma in her old-age condo in Delray and there were never any kids around to play with. Her mom worked and there was no time for playdates; Liza never wanted to play with her and she never wanted to play with Bradley. So usually it was just her and her Barbies and their Paradise Pool Playset out behind the condo's clubhouse for hours on end, and that was fine. In fact, Lainey liked playing alone. And she liked reading alone or watching TV alone. She never minded being alone, unlike some of her friends who always had to have somebody standing there next to them like a shadow.

Now Lainey hated being alone.

She was back in the small, smelly room again. He had put some more dog chow and water in the corner, but only a portion of what he'd left last time and she was hungry again. Even though she'd learned from the last time to ration, he hadn't really left much at all— just a couple of handfuls of kibble. And he'd been gone a really, really, really long time. There was no way to tell for sure, but it felt like even longer than before. She had started to think that he might not ever be coming back. Or if he was, he wasn't coming back for her. And like before, she had started to wonder what it would feel like to starve to death.

More than food or Coke or milkshakes, more than sunshine, more than even her mom or Liza or Molly, right now, more than anything or anyone, she missed Katy. She missed talking to her, hearing her voice. She missed Katy making her feel like everything was gonna be OK. She missed her friend. And deep down she knew she'd probably never, ever hear her voice again.

There could be a hundred rooms like the one she was in, a hundred walls with cold, horrible chains on them. A maze of dungeons and torture chambers, like the intricate labyrinth that existed underneath the Roman Coliseum that she'd just learned about in social studies. Like Katy had said, there were others—other girls—somewhere nearby. One, two, twenty—she had no idea how many. Sometimes she could hear their far-off, muffled screams or sobs, but there was no one in the wall next to her anymore. No one to talk to or listen to. No one to help stop her from going absolutely crazy.

And him . . . The Devil. The Freak. He hated her now. He wouldn't talk to her at all anymore—not so much as a whisper or a grunt—and he didn't sit in the room watching her like he used to. That made her happy, but it also made her scared. She hadn't heard from Katy since he'd apparently walked in on her and found the big hole she'd dug. And although she tried not to think about what had happened to her friend, banishing that thought completely from her mind just wasn't working. Every time she laid her head down and closed her eyes, she saw the whole horrible scene play out over and over again in her mind: a pretty girl with dirty hands, her slim body slipping through a tiny, dirty hole into the bright yellow sunshine just on the other side, like Alice in Wonderland. With her legs already through, kicking on the green grass outside, she just had to squeeze her torso and head through and she would be free. But the Devil had found her, and he'd pulled her back into hell with his stubby, filthy, callused hands, covered in wiry black hairs, that crawled over his fingers like a dozen daddy longlegs. And inch by inch, Katy slowly got pulled back in. She kicked and she screamed and she pleaded and she begged, but it was no use. The Devil was too strong and too angry. The hole just got smaller and smaller as she came back through, until finally the sunshine disappeared and blackness filled Lainey's thoughts once again.

He had been so mad after Katy was gone. Scary, scary mad. Screaming and throwing things about everywhere. What would happen if he got mad again? Would he do to her what he had done to Katy?

Lainey didn't want to find out.

So she hadn't dared take off the bandages on her eyes this time, no matter how long he was gone. And she didn't dare dig another tunnel, no matter how close she might be to the sunshine on the other side.

She had given up on superpowers and superheroes that didn't exist. She just sat there, rocking herself in the darkness, missing her friend, and praying for the nightmare to finally end.

81

The fallout from the Palm Beach sting was bad. If the director was looking for a reason to get Bobby out of Crimes Against Children and into pushing paper for the Fraud Squad, he'd found it with a high-speed chase that had ended in a death and three injuries. Even though Bobby and everyone else out there on Friday—including Lex Kleiner and the LEACH operatives—knew that Bobby Dees chasing the bad guy an extra mile hadn't caused the accident, it was just the excuse Foxx needed. Call him what you will—Captain or Picasso or John Doe—the guy was gonna have that accident whether Bobby was on his tail or not, because he was gunning for I-95 and he wasn't gonna slow down till he made it onto the interstate. But a reason was all the regional director needed, even if it wasn't a good one. Bobby had immediately been placed on leave until after January 1. After that, he was probably out of CAC and he was most definitely not going to be a supervisor anymore. Most likely he would be transporting governors for a year or two or chasing down bad checks until Foxx ascended to some throne in Tallahassee and Bobby was released from purgatory by the next RD.

Zo was now heading up the Picasso investigation, assisted by SAS Frank Veso, who was officially numero uno in line for Bobby's job come January 1. But when Foxx found out that Zo had allowed Bobby to stay on Picasso after realizing that Bobby's missing daughter was a possible Picasso victim, the shit had really hit the fan. Zo's future status as a Miami ASAC was now in question. Talk was going around that once Picasso was officially closed, he would be demoted to an SAS and sent to Tallahassee for a year or so to do penance. Even though he insisted he didn't give a shit, Bobby knew he did. And for that he felt bad.

But the worst form of punishment, Bobby quickly realized, was being sent home to do nothing. Nothing at all. The wait for any scrap of information was agonizing, the inability to run leads or interview witnesses beyond frustrating. There had been no further contact from Picasso and the identity of the subject in the car that had tried to pick up the Palm Beach undercover officer was still unknown. That was all the information he got, and it wasn't enough. Because Bobby, of all people, was acutely aware that somewhere out there might be the undiscovered victim or victims of a madman, crying out for help and hearing no reply, and there was nothing whatsoever he could do about it. Bobby could now sympathize with how the parents of the victims on his cases had felt all these years—helpless.

Five days of hell later, on Thanksgiving Eve, of all days, the phone call he'd been waiting for finally came.

"We got a DNA match on our barbecued pervert." It was Zo, calling on his cell.

Bobby stepped into the living room and out of earshot of LuAnn, who had just gotten home. She'd bought a turkey from the supermarket for the holiday but had spent the past ten minutes just staring at it blankly in the kitchen. "What? When?" he asked.

"Don't run for the car, Bobby. Ciro, Larry, and Veso are already at the guy's house. Stephanie Gravano walked the warrants through. Kelly, McCrindle, Carrera, and Paul Castronovo are picking apart the neighbors and employers. Everyone's working here. You're off this. I'm telling you what's going on as a friend, because I don't want you sitting around thinking we don't know nothing. That we're not working it. Counting the ticks on your kitchen clock like it's a bomb. So I will keep you informed, because you are a brother and if the roles were reversed I would want to know . . . I would expect you to tell me."

"Who is he?" Bobby asked.

Zo sighed. "Name's James Roller, a twenty-eight-year-old white male from Royal Palm Beach. He's got two adult priors: burglary of a dwelling in '99 and an attempted sex batt in '05, for which he spent about eighteen months in state prison. The victim in that case was fifteen. He claimed consensual, the victim didn't agree, and the postal worker who pulled him off of her in the deserted alley apparently got there just in the nick of time. The victim had a spotty past, so the state pled him out. He was released from Raiford in early '07. He gave swabs on both crimes, so he popped up in the database as soon as they put him in."

"I want to—"

"I know what you want to do," Zo interrupted. "You're on leave right now, so you're not gonna do shit. Everyone is working on this. Everyone. We'll find her if we can. The boys are picking apart his duplex as we speak and interviewing his baby mama. By five we'll know all there ever was to know about this guy."

"What does he look like?"

"Just like the undercover described: brown hair, brown eyes, five-ten, 185 pounds."

"What did they find at the house? Anything yet?"

"He lived alone. So far there's just mayo and beer in the fridge. No computer at either his house or the girlfriend's, but we think he might've surfed the Web at the local library—which is around the corner from his crib. Or the more likely scenario was he used a laptop, and that laptop was in the car with him and it's now melted into the asphalt."

"Paints? Pictures? Was he an art student? Who the hell is this guy? There's got to be more, Zo."

"We pulled up a work history and he worked at a Sherwin-Williams in Fort Lauderdale back in the late nineties. But give me till five to get you answers. Nothing screams Picasso yet, but nothing eliminates him, either. We're building it up, one piece at a time. He probably had a whole secret studio someplace. We'll find it, Bobby. If it's out there, we'll find it. And if he has Katy, we'll find her, too."

Bobby hung up the phone and punched the wall hard. Unfortunately, the pain in his hand didn't do anything to ease the pain in his heart. And now he had a hole in his living room wall. LuAnn stared at him from the doorway that led into the kitchen.

"They have a name," Bobby said quietly, knowing from the look on her face that she'd heard everything. "He's out of Royal Palm Beach, up in Palm Beach County. James Roller. He's twenty-eight. He's a sex offender."

LuAnn sucked in a breath and her body started to shake. The coffee cup she held in her hand spilled large drops onto the wood floor. "Are you going in?" she asked.

"I'm on leave. I was told to stay away."

"You're not going to stay away, are you? You're going to finish this, aren't you?"

"Yes. Yes, I am."

He crossed the room and hugged her. She buried her head in his chest and started to cry, something she'd done an awful lot this past week.

"I need to know for sure," she whispered. "I don't want someone to just think it was him. I need to know for sure . . ."

"Ssshhh," he answered, stroking her hair. "I'll find out, Lu. We'll know. Either way, we'll know."

"I can't, I just can't . . . I need to get out of here, Bobby. I need to leave."

"If it is him, the boys out front will be sent home and you can go out." Since the flower delivery, there'd been a BSO uniform assigned to watch their house and LuAnn twenty-four hours a day. Even Foxx in all his vindictiveness had not pulled the detail. "You can go back to work, get back to normal." The word sounded strange. Nothing would ever be normal again.

"If they find her . . . if she's . . . dead . . . ," LuAnn said, swallowing the word, "I want to move. I don't want to be here anymore. Here. Around *this*. I want to leave."

Bobby wasn't quite sure how LuAnn meant that. Six weeks ago, he would've thought that "here" definitely included wherever he was. Things had been better between them since LuAnn's concussion, but now, listening to her, he wasn't so sure she felt the same way. He looked at her. "Don't go there."

"I have to. I . . . It's a year she's been missing. A year. This Picasso has killed four girls. I have to be prepared for what I know is coming. And even if you don't find her body, I can't hope anymore. I'm through with it. It tears me apart. And I can't be around"—she paused and looked around the living room—"*this* anymore."

He nodded slowly. "Does 'this' include me?"

She shook her head softly and he held his breath. Everything was collapsing around him. His life was falling apart and there was nothing he could do to stop it. His job, his career, his daughter . . . It was only fitting that his marriage would end here and now, too.

"Just you and me," she whispered. "I want it to be us again. I want it to be the way it was before everything went wrong. I want to start fresh. I can't look at the pity faces any more—at work, on a jog, at the grocery store. I can't look at her room anymore. All I see are ghosts, Bobby."

He clutched her to him, feeling her warm breath on his neck. He kissed the top of her head. There was nothing left to keep him here, either. "We'll make it right again, LuAnn. I'll make it right."

His cell rang. He didn't recognize the number but picked it up anyway. "Dees." LuAnn walked back into the kitchen, wiping her eyes.

"Agent Dees, this is Dr. Terrence Lynch from the Broward County Medical Examiner's Office. How are you today?"

Loaded question, so he ignored it. "Yes, Dr. Lynch. What's up?"

"I wanted to discuss the findings on the fingernail scrapings of Jane Doe that I just got back. In addition to what was found under the nails, there was also a fair amount of debris embedded in what remained of the fleshy pads of her fingertips. I was intrigued by your suggestion that her injuries were self-inflicted—a result, perhaps, of her digging her way out of something or someplace. You expressed that time is of the essence—that your Picasso may be holding other victims, and that the information from Jane Doe could potentially prove very valuable in finding them—so I walked the tests through myself. As you know, lab and toxicology results can sometimes take months to come back."

"I appreciate that," Bobby replied.

"You were correct, Agent Dees, the debris was soil. But that's not a one-size-fits-all definition. Soil has many different characteristics, as you can imagine, depending on where it's from. These characteristics, including texture, structure, and color, are all examined to determine what classification order the soil falls into. I know this is a bit involved—soil study is, believe it or not, a science unto itself. Suffice to say, a specimen was rushed to the Soil & Water Science Department at the University of Florida, which classified it as a histosol—a soil comprised primarily of organic material. Wabasso fine sand, in fact. A sandy, siliceous, hyperthermic Alfic Alaquod."

"You're losing me."

"With a high phosphorus and nitrogen content."

"You're still losing me."

"Phosphorus is a fertilizer typically used in sugarcane production. Sugarcane, as you know, is a big business here in South Florida. U.S. Sugar alone farms some 180,000 acres in Palm Beach, Hendry, and Glades counties. Throughout the state, various sugar companies farm over 400,000 acres. That amount of ground to cover wasn't going to help you very much. So I thought to look for pesticides. Or I should say, I had Dr. Annabelle Woods, our chief toxicologist, look for pesticides that are peculiar to sugarcane farming. While it did require Dr. Woods to bring along a pillow to the office for a couple of late nights, cane is pretty hearty and so there are not too many pesticides that are commonly used. And she found just what I was looking for. Carbofuran and cyfluthrin—two chemicals that remain present in soil for a substantial period of time after application."

"How substantial?"

LuAnn came back in the living room with an icepack and a towel and carefully wrapped his hand, which had started to swell.

"Studies show it can take up to five years for either chemical to break down in histosol. The muck quality of the soil traps the chemicals, not allowing them to flush out."

"There you go again with the fancy words."

"The good news is, usage of either of these pesticides must be registered with the Environmental Protection Agency. So I checked with the EPA for you. Carbofuran, which is used to control wireworm infestations, was applied to approximately 2,000 acres of sugarcane crops last year in the state of Florida."

Dr. Lynch just moved to the top slot of favorite MEs. "So Jane Doe was being held on a sugarcane farm?"

"Or where the runoff was for a sugarcane plant. Finding out which 2,000 acres were treated was apparently a much more involved process for the assistant at the EPA, so you'll have to call them yourself for that. But 2,000 acres is far better than 400,000 acres, I think."

"Much. You're quite the detective, Dr. Lynch."

"Just trying to help out. How's your investigation going?"

Obviously, either the doctor didn't read the papers or he was too polite to ask if the headlines bashing FDLE and its handling of the Picasso investigation were true. "We're looking at a suspect in Royal Palm Beach," Bobby replied.

On that note, LuAnn quietly disappeared upstairs.

"Well, you're in the right area, I suppose. Clewiston is the headquarters of U.S. Sugar, and that's just west of Royal Palm on the Palm Beach–Hendry county line. I believe there are a lot of farms out there. So, where do you want me to fax this report?"

Bobby gave him his home fax and hung up. Then he called Lynch's contact at the EPA to try and track down which farms had the chemicals carbofuran and cyfluthrin applied to them in the past five years. The doctor was right. Specific farm information required searching through certain records—some of which were in storage—by hand. Even with a priority rush, it could take days to get that information.

He looked out the window at the BSO cruiser stationed prominently in front of his house.

I can't look at the pity faces anymore—at work, on a jog, at the grocery store. I can't look at her room anymore. All I see are ghosts, Bobby.

Belle Glade. Sugarcane crops. U.S. Sugar. Royal Palm Beach—where Zo said the suspect James Roller resided—was only a half-hour east of Belle Glade. It was all beginning to come together as a picture. An ugly, horrible picture.

He grabbed his car keys off the coffee table and headed out the door. Like he had promised LuAnn, he was going to finish this. He was going to bring his little girl home.

And he wasn't going to do it sitting on his couch.

82

Outside of those who lived in the county, when people thought of Palm Beach, it was images of opulent oceanfront estates like Lago Mar and the Kennedy compound that immediately came to mind. Maybachs, Bentleys, and hundred-foot yachts. Socialites bejeweled in necklaces that were worth more than companies, shopping along ritzy Worth Avenue, or hobnobbing with other Vanderbilts and Astors at charity functions and debutante balls. Picturesque downtown West Palm, its gleaming high-rises nestled right beside the bright blue Atlantic.

West of the relatively small but famous slice of pricey real estate that ran along Florida's Treasure Coast, there existed the rest of Palm Beach County. And the farther west you traveled on Southern Boulevard, the more removed you became from the socialites and their entourage of champagne- and caviar-toting assistants. In fact, once you passed the upper-middle-class equestrian village of Wellington, there was nothing. Nothing but acres and acres of farmland. Green beans, lettuce, celery, sweet corn, sugarcane. Lots and lots of sugarcane. And, courtesy of nearby Glades Correctional Institution, an occasional chain gang.

Eventually Southern Boulevard turned into SR 441/Route 80. After thirty miles of seeing nothing but green stalks of sugarcane and fields of corn waving in the breeze, Bobby finally spotted life. He had entered the blink-and-you-might-miss-it town of Belle Glade—population 14,906, not counting either the 1,049 inmates housed down the road at Glades Correctional or the illegal migrant farmworkers who had ditched the census-takers back in 2000. Located on the southeastern shore of Lake Okeechobee, at one time Belle Glade was branded with the not-so-distinguished notoriety of having the highest rate of AIDS infections in the United States, and more recently, the second highest violent crime rate per capita in the country. A weathered brown-and-white sign welcomed Bobby to the city that in 1928 had been blown off the map by a monster hurricane:

WELCOME TO BELLE GLADE. HER SOIL IS HER FORTUNE.

How ironic, Bobby thought, fingering his cell phone, hoping it would ring. It just might be a few grains of her Wabasso fine sand—a siliceous, hyperthermic Alfic Alaquod—that would fortuitously bring home the victims of a madman. That might finally lead him to his own daughter. Pam Brody with the EPA had called him back to say that a preliminary record check of the past two years showed a wireworm infestation concentrated in and around farms located near South Bay, South Clewiston, Belle Glade, Vaughn, and Okeelanta. That was still a lot of farmland to cover, but it was also far better than the potential 400,000 acres–plus that stretched across central and southwest Florida. Now he was waiting on the call back with the actual farm names and locations that had registered to apply carbofuran. He knew it wouldn't be a complete list—some companies and farmers ignored EPA guidelines and used pesticides without registering—but it would definitely be a start. Bobby still wasn't sure where he was going, or exactly what he was looking for—he just knew that out here in the sugarcane fields he was one step closer to finding it. And it made him feel like he was at least doing something . . . that he was no longer quite so helpless.

If quiet Belle Glade had ever enjoyed a heyday, it was probably in the forties or fifties. Tired, dated buildings, fast-food restaurants, and half-century-old gas stations abutted Main Street, which ran straight through the center of town. He spotted a few folks on the porch of the local convenience store, sucking down a few Milwaukee's Bests, chatting the day away, probably like they did every day. Down side streets, Bobby could see rundown duplexes, apartment complexes, and single-family homes. For-sale signs littered more than a few front lawns. More than one business had shuttered, and besides the convenience store, most of the open ones looked dead.

He drove to the Belle Glade Marina and Campground, where Ray Coon's body had been found under a banyan tree. If he hadn't had a police report to guide him to the exact location Ray's lifeblood had drained out of him, he never would have known where to look. It was a peaceful spot. Through a tangle of trees, you could see the lake in the distance. Remote enough for a romantic picnic or a brutal murder. Bobby thought of Jane Doe's bloody fingertips. She'd been clawing herself out of someplace. Out of her tomb, as it turned out. Far away from a scenic lake and a shaded banyan tree. And she had been brutally tortured in the most inhumane ways before her murderer finally strangled her with the chains he hung her from. She didn't get a merciful shot through the back of the head. Ray Coon had been a drug dealer and gangbanger with a criminal record. He carried brass knuckles and had bragged to his buddies in the Mafia Boys that he would take out a cop if he was asked to, knowing his own girlfriend's father was an FDLE agent. The anger that swelled within him left a bitter taste in Bobby's mouth. As much as he wanted to exact revenge on Ray Coon for taking his daughter from him, the boy's blood was long gone, his bones sent back to his mom for a proper burial. There was nothing left to see here in this pretty park and, unfortunately, no satisfaction to be gained by seeing it. Meanwhile, Jane Doe sat in cold storage back in Broward, waiting for someone to claim her. For someone to even notice she was missing. Neither life nor death seemed very fair.

He left the park and drove down the winding two-lane roads that wrapped around cane field after cane field, looking for exactly what, he still didn't know. Down U.S. 27 and through South Bay—another blink-and-you'll-miss-it migrant town, population 3,859—and then swinging back north via 827 and Okeelanta, and then back through Belle Glade.

By four p.m. the sun had begun its slow descent over the fields, bathing the sky in a smoky purple hue that was tinged with streaks of tangerine. Pickup trucks filled with dirty, sweaty men and women passed him on the way home to their families and cramped shanties. A few smiled and chatted, but most looked straight ahead at nothing and no one, a completely blank expression on their tired faces. Harvesting the sugarcane would begin in earnest after December, although some farms had begun already. Bobby started back up Main Street, heading toward State Road 441 and, eventually, to civilization. Hopefully the EPA would call him in the morning with more information. Hopefully Zo would call him tonight to tell him that they'd found something at James Roller's house. Something incriminating. Something damning. Something that would confirm that it was this guy Roller all along. Something that would dismiss the nagging, heavy feeling in his gut that told him the nightmare was far from over. He'd tried Zo all day, but he wasn't picking up and he wasn't calling back—probably because there was still nothing to report. Probably because nothing besides a sex-offender past and a job in a paint store screamed "Picasso" yet, and he couldn't bear to tell Bobby that. For his part, Bobby had yet to share Dr. Lynch's findings with him, but that was because he knew Zo would have forbidden him to come out here, just as he had banned him from Roller's house.

He pulled over to find the bottle of Advil in the glove compartment. In addition to the throbbing headache he was now sporting, his hand had swelled considerably. *Damn.* He'd probably hairlined something. He downed three caplets dry. When he pulled back on the road, a rusted tin LODGING sign caught his eye just a few yards ahead with an oversize arrow directing him to turn right. His first thought as he passed was that it was strange to have a hotel right out here in the middle of absolutely nowhere and absolutely nothing. It must have been a leftover from the heyday, because who the hell would stay all the way out here?

Then he saw the name of the hotel, partially hidden from view by a sea of waving green sugarcane stalks, and he slammed on his brakes.

83

Bobby turned down Curlee Road but saw nothing, just acres and acres of lush green. He followed it for a few miles. There were no other signs. So he turned back and then turned down another road, then another, frantically driving through a towering cane maze in the fading light of day, heading deeper and deeper into the heart of nowhere.

Then he saw it, about a mile or so up from the last turn, which, if he remembered right, had put him on Sugarland Road. He stopped the car and got out, staring up at a ramshackle, two-story Victorian-style house that was set back maybe five hundred feet from the road by a long, winding dirt drive that was overgrown with weeds and brush. Surrounding the home on all three sides were acres and acres of sugarcane. In fact, cane stalks had crept up on the house itself, almost completely overtaking the yard, like in, appropriately enough, some freaky Stephen King horror flick. In the light breeze, their rustling leaves sounded like soft, gossipy whispers. There were no lights on, no rockers on the warped wooden wraparound porch, no pitchers of homemade lemonade set up around a late afternoon checkers game. From all appearances, including the boards that covered a couple of the home's many windows, the house had been shuttered for years.

It was like having déjà vu. A cold chill ran up Bobby's spine. He had seen this same house before. A simple black-and-white sign dangled by a single hook, mounted on a post that at one time had been stuck in the middle of a front lawn. It swung with a creak in the wind.

THE HOME SWEET HOME INN

Bobby's mouth went dry and his heartbeat sped up. The matches. In the bar that night after Gale Sampson's body was found at the Regal All-Suites, the matches on the table that Mark Felding was spinning said THE HOME SWEET HOME INN. The picture on them was of this house. The matches had made Bobby think about his honeymoon in Vermont with LuAnn.

Mark Felding.

Bobby's chest grew tight and right then and there he knew. He knew what was in that house. He knew what had happened in that house.

He speed-dialed Zo. This time he picked up.

"It's not five yet. Stop calling me," Zo said.

"I found him."

"What?"

"I found him," Bobby repeated. "It's Felding. He's our Picasso."

"What the hell? What are you talking about?"

"I'm at a deserted bed-and-breakfast out in Belle Glade—"

"Belle Glade?"

"Yeah, Belle Glade. I got a call from Lynch at the Broward ME's this morning. Toxicology traced soil found under Jane Doe's nails to sugarcane fields. Pesticide tests narrowed those fields down to Belle Glade, Clewiston, South Bay, Vaughn, and Okeelanta. I came out here to see what I could find."

"Thanks for telling me."

"You didn't pick up your phone."

"I told you to stay put," Zo said with a frustrated sigh.

"No, you told me to stay away from your scene, so I did."

"You're off this."

"That doesn't matter anymore. I need you and the boys out here now. Are you still in Royal Palm?"

"Yeah."

"It's only thirty-five minutes. You can do it in twenty with lights on."

"How the hell do you know it's Felding?"

"I just do. Do a records check on The Home Sweet Home Inn on Sugarland. There'll be a connection to Felding somehow, I'm sure. Do you have press there now? Is Felding there?"

"We have some stragglers, but most picked up camp and went home after they realized we weren't finding nothing. Felding was here earlier, but I don't see him now. Everyone's shutting it down 'cause of the holiday."

Bobby looked up and down the block, which was defined by sugarcane stalks. No cars in sight. "He's probably back at the Channel 6 studio in Miramar. He's on at six, right? Have BSO pick him up there. That'd be poetic. Arrest his ass on television."

"For what?" Zo asked. "What the hell do we have on him but your gut instinct that he's gonna be connected to this house? You haven't explained to me how this house you're watching is even remotely related to this case you're not supposed to be working anymore!"

"Just pick him up," Bobby replied. "Ask him to come in and talk. Tell him we have some things from Roller's apartment we'd like him to look at. That will get his narcissistic reporter chops drooling. Whatever you do, get him before he runs. I think you'll have all the connections you need once we get in this house."

"All right, all right. I'm on my way. I'll have Stephanie start on the warrants. You'll have to tell her how you know so much so she can actually get you one."

"Fuck a warrant. If he's got missing girls in there, we don't need a warrant. I'm certainly not waiting around six hours."

"Don't do shit, Shep. Just sit tight and wait. We're on our way. And unless you have a good-faith reason to believe someone's in that house and that someone is in danger, we're gonna need a warrant."

Bobby hung up the phone, cut the engine, and stared up at the house. He tapped impatiently on the steering wheel, his mind racing. It made perfect sense now. Felding was sending himself the portraits—

any trace evidence that did come back to him would be expected, since he handled the paintings. Felding was the first reporter on the Boganes sisters' murder scene in Fort Lauderdale, arriving at either the same time or right after the cops did. Felding was waiting at the McDonald's for Janizz because he had set up the meet. He was The Captain. He was Picasso. It was Felding who had received as much national attention in the press as the killer himself, making a name for himself on the cable news shows as the shocked messenger boy for a madman. The faces of the missing runaways that filled the corkboard in Bobby's office flipped through his brain like a card catalog in a windstorm. Allegra Villenueva. Nikole Krupa. Adrianna Sweet. Eva Wackett. Lainey Emerson. So many missing girls. Too many who weren't even missed.

Was Katy in there?

Zo and the boys would be here in twenty minutes. All he had to do was sit tight for twenty more minutes. Much as he wanted to rush the door right that second, he knew that it would be foolish to go into the house alone. If the girls were being held in there, there could be booby traps set to prevent them from getting out, or to stop someone else from getting in. There was also a chance that Felding worked with a partner or partners, and even though he might be down at the station working off his fifteen minutes of fame, his buddy could be waiting somewhere in the dark house with a meat cleaver to greet any unwelcome visitors. Serial partnerships were rare, but they notoriously did happen. The Hillside Stranglers. The Chicago Rippers. Henry Lee Lucas and Ottis Toole.

He watched the sign creak in the strong breeze that had kicked up. Dark clouds were forming in the not-so-far distance over the unending fields of sugarcane. A storm was coming. If he couldn't go in the house yet, he could certainly look around the outside. Twenty minutes was a lifetime. While he had no intention of waiting for a warrant, he knew Zo was going to want more reasons to justify them knocking down the front door. At least for the report he was gonna have to file. Maybe he could see something through the windows or around the back.

Bobby stepped out of the car and started up the dirt and gravel driveway, pushing aside scattered brush and weeds that in some places had grown almost three feet tall. Tire tracks carved a swathe through the mangy growth, ending on the side of the house. Someone had been here recently. Then his eyes caught on something in an upstairs window. A quick flicker of orange.

The waiting was over. Bobby bolted as fast as he could for the front door.

84

By the time he'd called 911 and kicked in the front door, flames were licking at the top of the staircase on the second floor. Smoke had started to fill the old house.

Bobby drew his gun, cautiously stepping into the foyer, wincing at the sharp pain in his right hand. An accidental fire while he was sitting in the driveway waiting for the cavalry to arrive was no accident. Felding was here. Somewhere. Or his partner. And while Bobby didn't want to give away his position for his own safety, if girls were locked away or hidden in the house and they were still alive, the quickest way to find them would be to have them call back to him. That meant they had to know he was here.

"Police!" he shouted, almost tripping over the two- and three-foot stacks of old newspapers and cardboard boxes filled with what looked like junk that lined the dark hallway leading to the stairs. The sun was almost down, there were no streetlights, and a noxious gray haze was quickly filling the house. "This is the police! Call out if you can hear me! Police!" An old wood-frame Victorian was a tinderbox. Bobby knew it would not take long before the whole place went up. Maybe he could get the fire under control himself. Buy a little time till the fire department—which was God knows how many miles away—finally arrived. He raced up the stairs.

The fire had obviously started in a front bedroom on the second floor, which was now engulfed in flames. If there had been anyone in there, he or she was no more. The door had been left open, and the fire was quickly spreading into the hall. In fact, the pink flowered draperies that decorated the picture window were already lit on one side, the flames feeding on the wall. Once they ignited the hall ceiling, flames would roll over the heavy old plaster like the wave at a baseball game. There was no way to put it out. And once it entered the walls, it would shoot up into the attic, and it would be over in minutes. He didn't have much time.

"Police!" he yelled again. Three more rooms shot off the upstairs hallway, but those doors were all closed. The smoke was thick and it was almost impossible to see more than a few feet in front of him. He dropped to his knees and crawled to the first closed door. He heard the crack and pop of glass behind him in the front bedroom, followed by a whoosh as the fire welcomed in the oxygen from outside. Visibility on the floor below the rising smoke was better—at least he could see where he was going. He had to take his chances that either Felding or his possible partner weren't waiting for him behind one of the doors, sitting on a bed with an AK-47 and a twisted smile. He reached up and flung open door number one, rolling into the room quickly to dodge a bullet, if necessary.

There was no Felding. No deadly cohort lying in ambush. But the bedroom itself looked like a scene from out of a horror movie. Even through the heavy smoke he could make out the long chains, suspended from the ceiling like chandeliers. Iron shackles were secured to metal bedposts. It was either a torture chamber or a masochist's playroom. He checked everywhere—no bodies, alive or dead.

He crawled back out into the hallway and over to door number two, reaching up again and praying as he turned the knob that the wrong person wouldn't be there to greet him on the other side. Again he found the same macabre ceiling fixtures, plus a medieval-looking high-back chair with metal clamps fastened to a headrest and spiked shackles to lock in the arms. No bad guys. No bodies.

The third bedroom was completely empty.

"Police!" he shouted as he crawled out into the hall and back to the stairs. "Shout if you're here!"

And just like in a movie under the hand of a skilled director, right on cue, Bobby got his response—the deafening, unmistakable blast of a shotgun.

85

Where had the shot come from? Where the hell was the guy? Had it been aimed at him?

Bobby's head jerked in a hundred directions. In the thick smoke he lost his bearings and half stumbled, half fell down the stairs and back into the foyer. He recovered quickly, his Glock still clutched firmly in his hand, which was throbbing. He squinted into the smoke that was growing heavy on the first floor, and looked everywhere, all at once.

Where the hell was he?

There was no time to sit around and strategize. No time to worry about himself. Once the fire got into the attic, the roof would likely collapse. Floor by floor, the layers of the house would fail. He wiped the smoke from his stinging eyes.

Think, Bobby, think. Where would he have put them? Where the hell would they be?

He thought of Jane Doe's hands, the dirt pushed so far up her nail beds it was embedded in her skin. She had been clawing her way out of her own tomb . . .

WELCOME TO BELLE GLADE. HER SOIL IS HER FORTUNE.

Downstairs.

A basement.

But Florida didn't have basements, right? They had crawl spaces. Where the hell would the crawl space be?

He stood up and, hugging the wall, followed it into what looked like a round reception parlor. More cardboard boxes of junk and bundled newspaper stacks cluttered the floor. His head darted everywhere, searching for a madman through smoke that was growing increasingly thick. His eyes were tearing, his throat closing. Through the parlor he exited into what had at one time probably been the dining room for the B&B's guests. Several small tables had been pushed to the far wall. Chairs were stacked on top of them. A tremendous red-velvet Chippendale wing chair sat facing the room's dark oak fireplace, its worn back to Bobby and the room's entrance off the parlor. Flanking the fireplace on display easels were three paintings. Portraits. Macabre renderings of death, styled like Gale Sampson, Rosalie and Roseanne Boganes, and Jane Doe's final moments.

Bobby edged closer. He could see the milky white flesh of a hand on the armrest. The tip of a loafer on the carpet. With his gun aimed in front of him, he came upon the chair.

Sitting there, like some ghoulish greeter at the Haunted Mansion, was Mark Felding, dressed in a suit and tie, his WTVJ 6 press credentials around his neck, a Bible on his lap. Atop the Bible was a shotgun. Felding's gloved finger was still on the trigger. He was missing his face.

Fucking coward got off way too easy, Bobby thought in disgust, kicking the bastard's foot to make sure he was dead. The body slumped over.

He rushed past what was left of Felding and into an enormous kitchen. A bed and breakfast would have to have extra room for food storage, he thought. Perhaps a root cellar or a wine cellar. Or a canning room. He only had time for one guess, and this was it. The fire was probably already in the attic. He thought of his daughter.

Look, Daddy, you're famous! You're a hero!

But am I your hero, Kit-Kat?

Always, Daddy . . .

He hoped for her sake he was right.

There was a door next to the refrigerator. He ran over and pulled it open.

It was a pantry. Still filled with tons of canned goods and gross-looking glass jars filled with what he hoped was just old fruit that no one had thrown out after a few years. *Damn.* He desperately looked around the kitchen. *Where would the crawl-space door be?*

"Police! This is the police!" he shouted again, circling the room like a caged animal. They were almost out of time. "Is there anybody here? Elaine Emerson? Lainey? Katy? Katy, are you here? Can anybody hear me? Anybody? Damn it! Answer me, somebody!" he pleaded.

And to his surprise, someone did.

86

"Police! This is the police!"

It was very, very faint. The voice. But it grew just a little closer.

"Call out if you hear me!"

Almost simultaneous to hearing the voice, Lainey smelled the smoke. It, too, was very, very faint. But getting stronger.

Footsteps walked somewhere above her and Lainey started to shake. She was petrified. Literally paralyzed by this cold fear that gripped her body where she sat. She thought of that time with Katy when they were convinced they were being rescued, but it was really just the Devil back from a long holiday. He had taken Katy after that. And Lainey had vowed she would always be a good girl. She had promised him. She didn't want to be taken away. No matter how much she wanted to go home, she didn't want to go away screaming like Katy.

"Police!"

It was probably a trick. A test, was all. The Devil was testing her to see if she would be good. If she was true to her word. That was it.

But then there was the smoke. It was definitely smoke. And not cigarette smoke. Or burning-leaves smoke. It was heavy, noxious-smelling smoke, like the Easter when her brother had set an oven mitt on fire. It wasn't overpowering, but it was definitely there.

Her fingers went to her bandaged eyes. What should she do? What if it really was the police and she never spoke up?

She heard Katy's voice in her head. Her words sounded loud and clear, like the day she had excitedly uttered them, a few months or weeks or days back.

Maybe someone's here to save us! And if we don't make noise, they'll leave and we'll never be found. Yell! Yell with me, Lainey, so they can hear us! We're underground somewhere. They won't find us unless we yell!

Lainey fingered the thick tape. Her panic was growing. What if the smoke was bad? What if there was a fire? Worse than starving to death would be burning to death . . .

She moved over to the door, pressing her hand against it to see if it was hot, like the firefighter who visited her class in fifth grade had taught them. It wasn't. But the smoke smell was unmistakable. She put her head on the floor, near the doorjamb, and breathed in.

It was definitely coming under the door.

Yell! Yell with me, Lainey!

"I'm here . . ." Lainey yelled, but at half the level she could have. She held her breath to see if she could hear the Devil, breathing at the door. Snorting at the cleverness of his trickery. She braced herself, waiting for the door to open.

But it didn't. And she didn't hear any snorty chuckles, either.

Yell! Yell with me, Lainey, so they can hear us! They won't find us unless we yell!

The worst she could do would be to do something half-assed. Either she'd get caught and punished anyway, or she might not ever get found. "You can't go swimming and not get wet," her grandma used to say. "Dive in and do it right."

"I'm in here! Help me!" she yelled as loud as she possibly could. As loud as she ever had. "I'm underground. I'm down here!"

And if we don't make noise, they'll leave and we'll never be found!

"I'm in here! Help me!" she screamed again, this time banging on the door with two fists as hard as she could.

Then the door flung open and she tumbled out into the darkness.

87

She landed flat on her face on the dirt floor. She cringed, her hands protectively covering her head, waiting for the Devil to chuckle. Or whisper. Or do something terrible. But nothing happened. Nothing at all.

There was no Devil. But there was also no police officer. No rescue team. There was nobody. The door had just opened when she pounded on it. Either someone had unlocked it, or her banging had maybe jostled it open. Or Katy—wherever she was—had lent her a hand and sent her a message. The last thought made her smile.

The smell of smoke was really strong now. She had to get out of here. Instinctively, that much she knew. And she wasn't going to be able to do that without seeing where she was going. Her hands went to her face and with one quick tug she pulled at the bandages and plastic discs that he had, like Katy had warned, glued on to her face after she disobeyed him. She felt the soft, delicate skin around her eyes and eyelids peeling away with the bandages. It hurt, like the rip of a thousand Band-Aids off the worst boo-boo. But there was no time to cry. If she didn't get out of here, bloody eyelids would be the least of her problems.

She squinted and opened her eyes slowly, blinking a few times, like a newborn puppy. Her fingers gingerly explored her face—she was bleeding, but she did have her eyelids. That was a good thing. And although she could only see lumpy shadows, she still had her eyes. And that was a really good thing.

"Police! This is the police!"

The voice was back. And it sounded like it was right above her.

"Elaine Emerson? Lainey?"

"That's me! I'm Lainey!" The tears were already spilling. Her screams were now hoarse whispers.

"Katy? Katy, are you here?"

Katy! He was looking for Katy, too!

"Is there anybody here? Can anybody hear me? Anybody?"

She wiped her face and took a deep breath. *Don't screw this up now, Lainey.* "Me! I hear you! I'm down here!" she shouted. "I'm down here! Help!"

There was a slight pause that to Lainey felt like a lifetime.

"I hear you! This is the police! We're here! Let me follow your voice. Keep yelling!"

"Help me, please!" Lainey screamed, crawling on her hands and knees. She felt her way to a wall and followed it along with her hands. There was a faint, blurry light coming from somewhere. "Oh God! There's smoke down here!"

Then the voice stopped. It just stopped.

"Hello? Are you still there? Officer! Sir! Help me!"

No response.

She started to cry. "I'm down here!" The wall ended. She crawled through a doorway. It was no use. She couldn't see anything, and the smoke was burning her throat. Then her hands fell on a pair of shoes. She reached up, feeling legs. She grabbed them and held tight. "Help me!" she cried. Relief washed over her. It had never felt so good to hug another human being. "Please help me!" she whispered, both her voice and her fight gone.

"Of course," came the whisper back. "Of course I'm going to help you."

Then the Devil squatted down beside her and patted her head.

88

He tossed the jars of what he hoped were just preserves on the floor and felt his way along the back of the pantry. Bobby was never really a religious man, but he prayed now as his fingers felt for any opening, any crack, any mystery panel. He got down on his knees and felt along the floor. There was no more time. He could hear the faint voice, yelling below him somewhere. Yelling for help.

"Please, God, let me find her!" he screamed out loud. "Don't let it end this way! It can't end this way!"

Whether it was divine intervention or just plain luck that led his fingers to the dent in the floor, he couldn't say. But he wasn't taking anything for granted. "Thank you," he whispered, "Thank you, God. . . ." as he pulled up the floorboard. It was a trap door. He looked down into the pitch black. The stink of mildew and decay overwhelmed even the acrid smoke. It smelled like death.

"Are you still there? Officer? Sir?"

The voice was still a little far off, but it was definitely down there. He slid feet first into the opening, not knowing how deep the drop was or what might be waiting down there in the darkness for him. All he heard were the whimperings of a child and he knew he had to go.

He landed on his feet on hard dirt, rolling off to the side, his shoulder hitting against a wooden piling. He was underneath the house. He looked around. A pull-down staircase was mounted on the ceiling next to the trapdoor opening. Small orange lightbulbs were strung up on electric wires and tacked sporadically along Sheetrocked walls that wound like a maze off into the darkness. Tunnels. Someone had built tunnels down here. Jesus Christ . . .

Bobby felt his way along the wall, in the smoky, dimly lit haze, ducking as he moved forward because the ceiling height dropped. There were too many offshoots, too many turns. How many rooms were down here?

Then he heard the scream that made his heart stop and he raced forward into the black claustrophobic maze, praying once again for a miracle to guide him to the right place.

89

Lainey screamed.

"Can you see me now?" the Devil asked, his sweaty fingers crawling over her face, pulling it closer to his own. "Take a good look now. I am eyes to the blind and feet to the lame . . . "

Bobby raised the muzzle to the back of Mark Felding's head. "Move away from her," he commanded. The ceiling in the cramped, cavelike room was very low. In some places it sloped even lower than six feet, where the first floor above had sunk and settled.

"Or you'll do what?" came the controlled but excited response.

"I won't ask a second time."

"Sure you will. Because you want to know what I've done with your daughter."

Bobby moved the muzzle down and fired a single shot into Felding's shoulder at point-blank range. The reporter yelped in both pain and surprise as bone and muscle exploded. He fell back onto the floor, grabbing his spurting arm, rolling in pain on the dirt.

"No, I won't," Bobby replied. The small figure on the floor held her arms over her head and screamed. Felding tried to get back up, but Bobby pushed him against a cement wall, placing himself between the reporter and the girl. Metal chains rattled like wind chimes. Felding slammed his head into a low beam with a thud.

"Stay down," Bobby commanded Lainey. "And keep your head covered." Then he turned his attention back to the animal against the wall. "Where is she?"

Felding squealed.

Bobby raised his Glock again and fired a shot into Felding's other shoulder. "I told you, I won't ask twice."

The reporter flopped about like a fish out of water, howling in pain, bouncing on and off the wall and back and forth into the beam. "Fuck you! Fuck you! Fuck you!" he screamed.

The wail of sirens was fast approaching. The fire department was finally here.

"Where's my daughter?" Bobby demanded.

"You mean sweet baby Katy?" Felding cackled, finally collapsing against the wall, his body wrapped in chains. "The little girl you never did bring home, did you, Daddy?"

Bobby fired again. This time he took out a knee. "I'm running out of body parts. Where is she?"

"He took her!" cried Lainey in a small, trembling voice. "He took Katy!"

The wood walls above them suddenly creaked with a huge heaving sigh, followed by a thunderous crash. The attic had just collapsed. The single-bulb ceiling fixtures that had dimly lit the maze of tunnels in the crawl space flickered and went out. It was now pitch-black.

"Ask me another question," Felding croaked in the darkness. Bobby could hear him squirming and writhing on the floor. "Anything. Ask me anything. G'head! Ask me!"

"Come on, up! Let's go, honey!" Bobby holstered the Glock, reached down, and picked the small girl up in his arms. She wrapped her arms in a death grip around his neck and buried her face in his chest.

"I'm Lainey," she said softly.

"I know. I've been looking for you," Bobby replied.

"Looks like you're out of time, Super Special Agent Dees," Felding mumbled in the dark.

"Not yet," Bobby answered as he felt his way back along the wall. He remembered to duck when he went inside the four-foot-tall tunnel that led back to the trapdoor and pull-down staircase. "But you are. Welcome to hell," he called out behind him. "Hope it's hot enough for you."

90

He wanted to turn back. He wanted to check every inch of the sprawling, damp, mildewed crawl space that Felding had outfitted into a dungeon. He knew there were more rooms. More secrets. More victims.

But there was no more time.

Where the wall finally ended, he reached up, felt around for the rope, and pulled down the staircase. With Lainey still in his arms, he scrambled up the steps that led back to the pull-out pantry. He could see through the twelve-by-twelve square floor cut-out above that there was still a kitchen. The second floor had yet to fall on the first. He had only seconds.

He pushed Lainey up and out first. "Go to the window! Hurry!" he yelled. It was impossible to breathe.

"I can't see!" she screamed.

Neither could he. The smoke was black, the heat intense. It felt like his skin was melting. He climbed out behind her and grabbed her hand in his. He pushed her down. "Close to the floor! Follow me!" On his hands and knees, he worked his way like a soldier to the back of the house, dragging Lainey along behind him. In the breakfast nook area off the kitchen he had seen a bay window. He reached out in front of him into the blackness and felt glass.

"Jesus!" a fireman at the window yelled. "Back! Get back!" he commanded, breaking out the window with his ax. Glass rained down on Bobby's head, followed by a deafening whoosh as more oxygen rushed in and smoke poured out.

"Get them out!" yelled another firefighter from somewhere. Bobby saw a figure waving at him to come on. To hurry. The firefighter at the window reached through the shattered glass and plucked Lainey's limp body from Bobby's hands. It took everything to just get to his knees. Then hands reached in and pulled him out, too.

Two more firefighters rushed up. One grabbed Bobby, the other Lainey. Slinging their bodies over their shoulders like rag dolls, they carried them through the thick cane fields to the front of the house. Fire trucks were everywhere, it seemed. The evening sky was awash in red and blue lights.

And bright orange flames.

Bobby looked back one more time at the inferno that lit up the night. All around it, rustling rows of sugarcane whispered and gossiped excitedly in the gusty breeze. The storm that Bobby had thought was headed this way was finally here. Lightning bolts crackled, zigzagging haphazardly over the sugarcane fields.

He took her! He took Katy!

Bobby closed his eyes just as the House of Horrors collapsed in on itself.

91

"How you feeling there, Shep?"

Zo Dias stood over his hospital bed in a charcoal-gray suit and black silk tie, a bouquet of flowers in his oversize hands. It was such a surreal sight, Bobby thought for a second he must have died. He wanted to snap off a witty comeback, but talking would be way too painful—even with all the drugs they had him on. He'd just been taken off the ventilator last night and moved from the Burn Intensive Care Unit. All he could do was nod.

"Gotta love this, LuAnn!" Zo laughed. "He can't talk. Isn't that a wife's wish come true?"

LuAnn took the flowers and moved to the nightstand to put them in one of the extra plastic pitchers the nurses had brought over. The room was filled with flower baskets, plants, and balloons—more than one of which already had Zo's name on it. "I think that's a husband's fantasy, Zo," LuAnn returned with a slow, tired smile. "We want our men to talk more. Tell us what's on their mind. You need to watch *Oprah*."

"Hmmm . . . so yapping more will make Camilla happy? I always thought she meant it when she told me to shut up." He pulled up a chair next to the bed and his face grew serious. "You are one lucky son-of-a-bitch, let me tell you. You should be dead, pal."

LuAnn reached over and clutched his hand. Bobby squeezed it back. "Another minute in that place and he would have been," LuAnn said, her voice cracking.

"How long before you can start back jogging?"

"The doctor says his lungs were pretty bad," she answered. "He took in a lot of carbon monoxide, too. No marathons for a while, that's for sure."

"Speaking of should be dead but isn't, so is that little girl you saved. I think she's getting released from Joe DiMaggio tomorrow." Joe DiMaggio was the children's hospital in Broward County that Lainey had been airlifted to for severe smoke inhalation. "I had Larry and Ciro go talk to her yesterday. It'll take years to get over what she went through. When you're feeling up to it, she wants to see you again."

Bobby nodded.

"Thought you'd want to know her crazy mom says thanks. Don't get too excited, though. Before you can say 'You're welcome,' she'll probably follow that up with a loss of consortium lawsuit because her pedophile husband's going upstate for the next twenty years. LaManna's taking the plea on Friday, and that doesn't include any charges that are coming from messing with his stepdaughters."

"Bastard," LuAnn said.

Bobby nodded. "Felding?" he mouthed.

Zo paused. "We pulled two bodies out of the ashes. Felding's dentals matched the one found in the basement. The other was found in what the fire inspector tells us was once the dining or living room. It was a female. ME says the cause of death wasn't smoke inhalation— it was the buckshot that filled her head. We found the melted remains of a Winchester 12-gauge under her body."

"Who?" Bobby mouthed.

Zo didn't answer.

"Who is she?" Bobby mouthed again.

"We don't know yet," he said finally.

"Katy?" Bobby managed to whisper.

"Get me her dentals," Zo quietly replied.

LuAnn sucked in a sniffle and closed her eyes. "I'll have her ortho-dontist send them to the medical examiner," she said with a nod. "I'll do it."

Painful silence filled the room for too long.

"What else?" Bobby mouthed.

"What else? OK, while you were snoozing the past couple of days, the rest of us have been working. You were right. The house on Sugar-land was owned by Felding's grandmother, Mildred Bolger. She died twenty years ago in a farming accident. The house then went to his mom, Loretta Felding, who lived there before she went nuts and died in a nursing home in 2005. When she passed, it went to Felding, her only child. The last time it was used as a B&B, according to the locals, was in 1990, almost twenty years ago. Local gossip has it that for the seven years before Mama Felding went into the nursing home, no one actually stayed there, though. Not a single solitary soul. But the signs stayed up. Talk about creepy.

"Some of what Felding shared about his life was true. We talked to his ex out in LA. She was real. The daughter shit was a lie. They had no kids. Wife knew about the Belle Glade home. She said that years ago Felding's crazy mom had talked about restoring it to a B&B and host-ing murder-mystery parties there. She thought the old lady was nuts then, because she'd been to Belle Glade once and, like most visitors, never ever wanted to go back. Then her and psycho divorced and she didn't talk to him about the house again. In fact, she never talked to him about anything again because, lucky for her, he dropped out of her life and out of sight. Felding's life in a nutshell: Crazy, possessive mom. Social loner. Met wife working at a Friendly's in Fresno. Went to some BS broadcasting school in LA. Tried to be a success for a few years out west, both in LA and San Fran, flopping around from network to net-work mostly bringing coffee to the cameramen. Got a few gigs, but none lasted. Two years ago, he pulled up stakes and showed up here in Miami. We've found a string of teenage disappearances that look a lot like ours happening in and around San Fran about the time he was re-porting there for CBS 5. In fact, turns out he interviewed the moms of two of the missing girls, just like he interviewed Debbie LaManna and Gloria Leto. We're getting those tapes as we speak."

"That's sick," LuAnn said quietly. She clenched Bobby's hand tighter.

"Pretty warped, is right. Gets his jollies off on asking the mothers of the kids he's whacked how they feel. He's a psychopath—he *was* a psychopath—if ever I've seen one. And a narcissist, too. But that is maybe the one thing we have going for us. He did not attempt to contact you when Katy first went missing. Her disappearance made local headlines, even national ones, if you consider an update in *People* national news. Felding could have definitely exploited that, both to move forward in his career and to feed his sick fantasy, but he didn't. So if the body we found in the dining room isn't Katy's"—Zo shrugged before continuing—"well, maybe he never had her. We've got cadaver dogs out working on the Sugarland property. So far, nothing, and I think that's good, too."

"But what about Ray Coon? The picture he sent me?" LuAnn asked.

"Well, that's interesting because we matched the .44-caliber slug found in Ray's head to the Magnum used in a home invasion in Lake Worth last week. Suspect in that, a Trino Quintero, gave it up yesterday to PBSO robbery detectives. The meeting in the park in Belle Glade in November was a drug buy. Ray tried to stiff him on an ounce of heroin and Quintero wasn't having it. Quintero claims he never met Felding, didn't know him from Adam. Looks like Felding maybe spotted the blurb about Ray's murder in the *Palm Beach Post*, thought about you, Bobby, and decided to take the opportunity to freak you and LuAnn out. For some reason that we will never know, Mark Felding was obsessed with you. Maybe like that profiler said, he felt you were a challenge. But as far as we can tell, the fact that Ray was offed in Belle Glade was a matter of pure coincidence. Some of Ray's Mafia Boy homeys live up near Glades Correctional. He was probably crashing with them, running his drugs closer to his peeps."

"And Katy?" LuAnn asked bitterly. "If Ray was back in town, living with friends in Belle Glade, what happened to her?"

Zo shrugged. "No answer for ya, Lu. I wish I did."

The painful silence was back again.

"What about that sex offender who you thought was Picasso?" Lu-Ann asked finally.

"Roller? Yeah, he had me, all right," Zo replied with a laugh. "Perfect background for it, including the young victim and a stint as a teen working in an art store. But coincidences being what they are, it looks like Roller was just eyeing the undercover in the tight clothes 'cause he thought she was cute. He never actually called himself Captain or her Janizz or mentioned their online chat. What he was gonna do with Natalie once he got her in the car is anyone's guess—maybe he just thought he'd score easy, maybe, given his background, it was more sinister. But we're thinking that Roller was just in the wrong place doing the wrong thing and running from us at the wrong time. From what Ciro has learned, the guy was selling dope to get by. Might have had some samples in the car and knew that, if he was stopped, he'd be going back to prison on a parole violation. That's why he ran. We never found nothing else that would link him to either Felding or support the theory that he was The Captain. Felding was Picasso. Felding was The Captain. Felding was ElCapitan, and Felding was Zach Cusano."

"Could they have been acting together?" LuAnn asked.

Zo chuckled. "You should've been a cop, Lu. Maybe it's been you whispering how to work cases in Bobby's ear all these years, and he's just been taking all the credit. Listen, if Roller and Felding were in it together, then that's a secret the two of them just took to their graves. Lainey Emerson is saying that, as far as she could tell, there was only one captor, but she couldn't see who that captor was, so take that for what it's worth. Now, I'd better go. I still have to get through the third degree with Camilla about my visit with you today, and my throat is already hurting from talking too much."

Bobby nodded. "Thank you," he whispered.

"Please. Stop. It's painful. You're welcome." Zo rose to leave. "I'm leaving before this becomes a Hallmark and we all cry. Oh, and another thing. Veso still owes me for the group flowers, but he's headed back up to Pensacola. Your job's still yours whenever you get back. Even Foxx has had a change of heart—thanks, I'm sure, to the barrage of 'save Bobby Dees's ass from forced early retirement' phone calls his office has been flooded with. I personally called twice," he added with a wink as he kissed LuAnn and headed for the door. "So when the docs here say you're not full of hot air anymore, Shep, we'll all be waiting on you to come back."

92

Lainey sat up in bed shaking, her body drenched in sweat, her heart pounding in her chest. She anxiously looked around her brightly lit room for the clock. It was 12:10 a.m. She tried to calm herself like Dr. Kesslar had told her to: Check your surroundings, take deep breaths, realize you *have* been sleeping, realize you *are* safe, recognize it's just a nightmare. It's just a terrible nightmare. You're home now. He can't hurt you anymore.

She watched, her breath catching, as the red numbers on the clock changed to 12:11. She was up to forty-three minutes. That was an accomplishment, she supposed. Just last week, she was afraid to even close her eyes. Sleep, when it did come, was only in ten-minute catnaps.

Lainey looked around her newly decorated bubblegum-pink bedroom, with its pretty white sleigh bed, dresser and desk set, funky checkered beanbag, and cool Rob Pattinson and Taylor Lautner posters. It looked like a bedroom right out of a Pottery Barn furniture catalog, all the way down to the heart-shaped throw rug and cool crystal chandelier. The only thing missing, of course, was a computer. The makeover was courtesy of the generous donations of hundreds of strangers all over the world who were apparently moved by her "shocking" story. Channel 6 had made the biggest donation of all, but her mom said they weren't allowed to touch that unless and until she went to college.

Everything looked so picture perfect all around her, yet Lainey's life was anything but. Here she was in her pretty bedroom with every single light on, completely terrified of what was outside her windows or down the hall, her heart beating so hard she thought she would die—afraid to cry out, afraid to lie back down, afraid to so much as move. Every time she closed her eyes, she saw his face. Zach. The man in the car. The Devil. Laughing, smiling, yelling, cursing, preaching. It had been weeks and she was only up to forty-three minutes. At this rate she might get a full night's sleep when she was thirty.

"Lainey? You OK?" It was Liza, standing in the doorway of her room, a cell phone in her hand, a frown on her face.

Lainey shook her head.

"Just go back to sleep. You'll be fine. Nobody's here. OK?"

Lainey nodded, wiping the tears from her cheeks, clutching the pillow to her chest.

Liza walked back down the hall to her room. It had been a few weeks since all the drama had ended and her patience for her little sister's panic attacks was running thin. Lots of bad shit had happened in her life, too—you deal, that's what you do. She just couldn't understand why Lainey couldn't get over it already.

Of course, Liza hadn't been down in the crawl space.

Her mom was still at the answering service, pulling another shift until one a.m. "Doing what I have to do," as she explained with a sigh to Lainey, "to put food on the table." With Todd in prison, there was only one income now, she liked to remind everyone when she was around. Even though Lainey hated being alone—her biggest fear ever—it was better when her mom was working, when it was just her and Bradley and Liza. Because when her mom was home, she was constantly hovering—hanging around every corner, in every room, asking Lainey what "that man" had done to her, or asking her what she'd seen "down there in the dungeon." Questioning her if there was any way she could have escaped when she wasn't tied up—any way at all. And always silently blaming her, Lainey figured, for getting into the horrible mess in the first place, making all of their lives flip completely upside down forever.

She could never tell her mom what the Devil had done to her. Never. She could never tell anyone. All she wanted to do was forget, not remember. She hugged the pillow tight to her chest and tried hard not to see his face in the window—a face she had never really seen, a face her imagination had twisted into a terrifying red-eyed, SpaghettiO-breathed monster, with pale pockmarked skin and big coffee-stained teeth. She never wanted to see clippings of him on the news. She never wanted to see what Mark Felding really looked like because then she could never face anybody ever again. She could never go out. She could never trust anyone. It was better to see the Devil as the distorted monster he was in her head, better to believe that the next time she would be able to see evil coming, rather than fear it living and breathing beside her in every crowd, on every train, on every street corner, grinning at her through a normal-looking smile and perfect blue eyes.

Next time. She couldn't get her mind away from that thought. She rocked back and forth on the bed. *Normal.* What a word. When would it all be normal again? When would she feel right? The kids at Sawgrass had treated her like a freak when she went back, so she'd switched over to Ramblewood, but Melissa and Erica and Molly all treated her differently now. Nothing was the same anywhere. No one was the same. Especially Lainey. And she didn't know how to bring it back to normal. How to shift her worries to scoring tickets to a Jonas Brothers concert like everybody else her age, instead of being completely paralyzed by fear when she walked into the computer lab at school.

Give it time, Agent Dees—her hero—had told her. *It won't get better for a long time, but then one day it will. It will be a little bit better.*

She grabbed her cell phone and dialed the number. "Brad?" she asked while it rang, reaching for him at the foot of the bed. Her little brother stayed with her every night now, sleeping head-to-toe. She made him, but he didn't complain. Brad grunted. Lainey took his hand and held it fast in hers.

"Hey there, little Lainey," a sleepy-sounding Agent Dees answered on the second ring. "You doing OK, kiddo?" He was used to this; Lainey called every night.

One day it will be a little bit better.

Lainey shook her head and bit her lip. "Not tonight," she whispered. "Not tonight . . ."

93

The Picasso task force headquarters at FDLE was no more. The conference table was gone—moved back down the hall—as were the corkboards, dry-erase board, and growing montage of disturbing crime-scene photos. In their place was a small, fat silver Christmas tree, decorated to the nines with ornaments, flashing lights, and gold tinsel. Colorful wrapped presents and gift bags overflowed from under the tree. The Crimes Against Children Squad's Secret Santa gift exchange would take place later this morning, followed by the MROC office Christmas party on the first floor. The whole building already smelled like roasted pig and Cuban coffee.

At the Monday morning weekly SAS meeting led by Zo, everyone had joked at the impeccable timing of Bobby's return to the office on Christmas Eve. No one in government actually worked the week before Christmas, the week of Christmas, or the week after Christmas. In fact, pretty much from Thanksgiving to the New Year, nobody did much of anything. There were live bodies in the office, for sure, but since most judges cleared their calendars till January and prosecutors went AWOL scrambling to use up accrued leave time, nothing really went down at the courthouse. Crime still happened, but solving it and prosecuting it took a back burner for a couple of weeks while everyone visited family and drank eggnog at the almost constant happening of Christmas parties, holiday luncheons, and festive happy hours.

On the day before Christmas the halls of MROC were definitely thinned out, and that was why Bobby decided to come back today. He'd been out for four weeks—the longest he'd ever been away from the office—and he wanted a chance to catch up on things without being hammered with questions come January 2 from people who now suddenly needed answers two days before the statute of limitations on their cases ran out.

He set the box full of wrapped presents that LuAnn had picked out for everyone from the new regional director to the CAC squad analyst out under the tree and headed into his own office, ducking as he did under the low-hanging strands of green garland that decorated his doorway. Without supervision, someone had gone a little crazy with the holiday decorations this year. Like the halls of an elementary school, cardboard dreidels and Santas were scotch-taped everywhere.

But for the six or so bottles of wine on his desk—presents from agents and support staff personnel already set out on their mad holiday treks around the country to see family—the office looked the same as when he left it, five days before Thanksgiving.

"Hey there, Bobby," Larry said with a big smile, walking into his office. "Good to have you back, man. What a freaking story you got to tell! Holy shit! Glad to hear you're feeling OK."

"Good as new. Only I can't make February's Ironman Triathlon."

Larry laughed. "That sucks. Come work out with us at McGuire's. Ciro and I will get you back in shape." McGuire's Hill was an old Irish bar in Fort Lauderdale and a frequent haunt of Larry's.

"So that's what keeps you so trim, eh?" Bobby returned with a smile.

"Listen, I heard from Zo about the ID on the body found in the Sugarland house. You must be feeling relieved. That's great news it wasn't your kid."

Bobby nodded. Great news for him. Not so great news for the grandmother of sixteen-year-old Shelley Longo of Hollywood, Florida. Two days shy of her seventeenth birthday, dental records had matched her to the corpse found in the charred ruins of the house in Belle Glade.

And not so great news for the mom of seventeen-year-old Katy Lee Saltran of Anaheim, California.

Forensic facial reconstruction of Jane Doe #1 had finally led to an identification of the body found at the Broward dump site. Ironically, it had been a follow-up article on Bobby in *People* magazine where Sue Saltran—sitting in a beauty parlor in Long Beach, California— had seen the reconstructed, two-dimensional sketch of her daughter's face, Katy Lee. Katy, as she called herself. An aspiring singer, eight months earlier, Katy had told friends she was sneaking off to Orlando to meet up with a guy she'd met online who was going to introduce her to Jay-Z. Katy's new friend's name was T.J. Nusaro, but his stage name was El Capitan. A search of the airlines showed Katy Lee had made her American Airlines flight, but no one had heard from her since. Last Saturday, Sue Saltran had flown in to pick up her daughter's remains and fly her back to California. Bobby had paid for the ticket.

"You headed down?" Larry asked, moving back to the door.

"Yeah. In a little. I gotta look at some things first. I'll meet ya down there," Bobby answered as Larry walked off and disappeared down the hall.

Bobby turned and looked out the window. Even on Christmas Eve the traffic was still stopped up as far as the eye could see. The road crew was back out there, but it was down to only two or three guys, who were sitting in a City Works truck drinking coffee. Everything looked and sounded exactly the same as it did the last time he'd stared out this very window—down to the Christmas trees of some late shoppers strapped to the roofs of their cars—but once again, the whole world as Bobby knew it had completely changed.

That's great news it wasn't your kid.

But was it really great news? Bobby looked at the flyer of his daughter stuck prominently on the corkboard of the missing in his office. While it was true that he didn't have to bury a child, he already understood their intense pain. He had buried his own daughter twice in his mind over the past five weeks—only to discover it wasn't her. Only to discover that he had no idea where she was. Left to wonder again what terrible things might have happened to her. Was she drugged out? Was she dead? Was she a prostitute? There would be no healing for him. Ever. So while he was thankful that dental records had proved his daughter was not dead, his life existed once again in a terrifying emotional limbo, because those records couldn't prove that she was still alive. Or that she was healthy. Or happy. Or not scared. And he would forever remain in that state—putting off vacations and cross-country moves with LuAnn—wondering, waiting, hoping, fearing, until the day they put his own body into a casket.

His eyes trolled the rest of the corkboard. There were so many flyers. So many young, pretty faces. And in the month he'd been out, he knew there were even more to put up. More kids who had decided to run away from something horrible. Or run to someone horrible. Kids who didn't want to cope anymore. Or couldn't cope. He found the runaway flyer for Shelley Longo and pulled it off the wall with a snap.

And there were more to take down.

The cadaver dogs that had been brought in to look for bodies buried under the cane fields behind the Sugarland house had alerted. So far, three skeletonized human remains had been found. And they had acres and acres to go. The first to be identified was pretty Eva Wackett, who had wanted to be a ballerina when she was five. How many more parents would get the phone call that they had dreaded receiving from the moment their kid stopped answering her cell on the day she never came home? From the moment they first held their precious little baby in their arms and prayed to God to keep her safe forever?

Or worse, how many parents wouldn't even give a damn?

The phone at his desk rang, pulling him out of his thoughts.

"Dees."

"Got a call for you," said Kiki. "I'll put her through. You coming to the party? I made flan."

"Ooh. I can't miss that. Did you use rum?"

"Don't even ask me that. Of course. Lots."

"I'll be down in a second."

The line clicked over. "Dees."

"Daddy?"

Someone sucked the air out of the room.

"Daddy, are you there?" repeated the small, fragile voice that he knew in an instant.

"Katherine? Katy?" he managed to say. "Is that you? Oh my God, is that you?" He sat down. The world was spinning.

"It's me, Daddy. It's me." She was crying.

"Jesus Christ . . . Katy, where are you? Where have you been?"

"I'm at a bus station in New Orleans, but I don't have any money—"

"I can send you money. I can give you money. Tell me where you are. Are you OK? Are you hurt?"

"I . . . I . . . I saw you on the news, Daddy. I saw you on TV. And I've been really messed up, Daddy. I got myself real messed up."

He closed his eyes. "That's OK, Katherine. It's OK. We can fix that."

"I miss you and Mom . . . I miss you, but I've been so messed up. I've done some bad things . . . "

"We love you, Katherine. Mommy and I love you so much. Whatever you've done, we can, we can work it out . . . " It was hard to talk. Tears streamed down his face.

"I really want to come home now. Please, Daddy, can I come home?"

"Oh God, yes, you can come home. You can always come home, Katy. You can always come home."

Bobby closed his eyes again and whispered another thank-you to the sky above.

Christmas had come a little early this year.

ACKNOWLEDGMENTS

Writing a book, even one of fiction, involves the assistance and input of many people. I'd like to thank the following individuals I have called upon (some on numerous occasions and at varying times of the night) for their expertise and knowledge: Special Agent Supervisor Lee Condon of the Florida Department of Law Enforcement; special agents Larry Masterson, Chris Vastine, Bob Biondilillo, and Don Condon of the Florida Department of Law Enforcement; Marie Perikles, Esq., Office of the Inspector General; Julie Hogan, Chief of the Office of Statewide Prosecution, Broward County; Special Agent Jeff Luders of the Federal Bureau of Investigation; Detective Joe Villa, Broward Sheriff's Office; Nick Gaudiosi, director of life safety, Barclays Capitol, and former fire captain, Fire Department, City of New York; Floy Turner, security consultant at Fox Valley Technical College and former FDLE CAC special agent; and last, but most definitely not least, Assistant Medical Examiner Reinhard Motte of the Palm Beach County Medical Examiner's Office, who always cheerfully provides the answers to my most gruesome questions. As for Larry and Chris, thanks for continuing to pick up the phone, even on Saturday nights. I'm glad you're back!

As a former prosecutor who has handled her fair share of sex-crime and kidnapping cases, having two cell phone–equipped daughters—a tween and a teen—and a computer in the house provided the necessary inspiration to write about the terrifying dangers of the Internet. I naturally have to thank them as well.